CHILDREN OF LIBERTY

Also by Paullina Simons

FICTION
Tully
Red Leaves
Eleven Hours
The Girl in Times Square
Road to Paradise
A Song in the Daylight

The Bronze Horseman Trilogy
The Bronze Horseman
Tatiana and Alexander
The Summer Garden

PAULLINA SIMONS

Children of Liberty

wm

WILLIAM MORROW
An Imprint of HarperCollins*Publishers*

CHILDREN OF LIBERTY. Copyright © 2012 by Paullina Simons. All right reserved. Printed in the United States of America. No part of this book may be used or reproduced in any manner whatsoever without written permission except in the case of brief quotations embodied in critical articles and reviews. For information address HarperCollins Publishers, 10 East 53rd Street, New York, NY 10022.

HarperCollins books may be purchased for educational, business, or sales promotional use. For information please write: Special Markets Department, Harper-Collins Publishers, 10 East 53rd Street, New York, NY 10022.

This book was originally published in 2012 by HarperCollins*Publishers*, U.K.

FIRST WILLIAM MORROW PAPERBACK EDITION PUBLISHED 2013.

Library of Congress Cataloging-in-Publication Data has been applied for.

ISBN 978-0-06-210323-9

13 14 15 16 17 OV/RRD · 10 9 8 7 6 5 4 3 2 1

To my good friend Nick,
without whom this book, and many things,
might never have been

The world was all before them, where to choose
Their place of rest

John Milton

Each of us Inevitable;
Each of us Limitless—

Walt Whitman

Part One

THE BARBER'S DAUGHTER

Love—what is love? A great and aching heart;
Wrung hands; and silence; and a long despair

Robert Louis Stevenson

Chapter One
DAUGHTER OF THE REVOLUTION

THERE had been a fire at Ellis Island the year before Gina came to America with her mother and brother in 1899, and so instead of arriving at the Port of New York, they had set sail into the Port of Boston.

Salvo had been in a bad mood since the day they left Napoli. He had left his sweetheart behind—the girl wouldn't part with her family. This, among other things, soured him on his. He refused to stay with the girl he loved, but resented his family for his own choice. "As if Mimoo and Gina could go to America by themselves," he scoffed.

"We don't have to go, Salvo," his mother said, and meant it.

"Mimoo!" cried Gina. "What would Papa say?"

"Papa, Papa. Well, where is he, if he is so clever?"

It was summer and Gina wished for a cloudless day. She

stood at port on tiptoe and gaped at the sky, wishing for a view of what they had been sailing to for weeks: a city line across the wide open bay to show them the glimpse of a life that was just around the corner. Stretching up she squinted straight into the July fog, her palm in salute to focus her sights on what she had imagined was urban beauty: sprawling metropolis bustling, smokestacks billowing, ships to and fro, civilization. But she could see nothing beyond the thick slate mist and oppressive melancholy. "Ahoy, Salvo!" she called, despite the lack of sight. "Come see!"

Salvo did not come see. Like a sack he sat behind her on the main deck and smoked, his arm around his black-clad mother. They had just lost their father. Five of them had been planning to go to America for seven years, but Gina's oldest brother had been killed in a knife fight six months ago. A drunken mob had run amok, Antonio had got caught in the middle, there was a struggle with the police, people trampled by horses. It wasn't a military knife that had taken him, but a hunting knife. Like it mattered—Antonio was still dead.

And less than three months later Papa's heart stopped.

Papa had wanted to go when the children were still small, but Mimoo refused. She wouldn't go without money. Imagine! Going to America, starting a new life with nothing. *Assurdo!* She wasn't going to come to America a village pauper. But we *are* village paupers, Mimoo, the great Alessandro had said. He didn't argue further, there was no point. Gina's mother declared that when she came to America, she would walk in on her own two feet, not crawl in with her hand outstretched. Papa agreed with that, but then he died.

Some of the money the Attavianos had saved went for Alessandro's funeral. But Mimoo had promised her husband she would go to America no matter what, and so, a month after he was buried, they borrowed just enough for three steerage beds. When Gina said borrowed, she meant stole: her mother's older sister took the money from the kitchen lock box of their blind father, putting a note inside which he couldn't read, saying that the "debt" would be repaid when Mimoo and her children got on their feet in the new land.

Salvo, the middle child, had told Gina, the baby, that Massachusetts Bay, emptying into Boston Harbor, was almost as wide as the ocean that fed it. A vast expanse of water flowed in from three corners of the globe, peppered with flat, green, rocky islands. Lighthouses stretched up from the rocks. Gina was eager to see these lighthouses, these islands. "That's the problem, Gina," Salvo said. "You can't. Lighthouses are supposed to be beacons to guide your way? You can't see them either in this fog. That's how it always is. Can't see nothing until the rocks you're about to crash into are already upon you. Much like life."

Frowning, Gina stepped away from her brother and he looked self-satisfied, as if that was exactly what he wanted. She watched the water, wondering what instruments you needed to navigate waters you couldn't see ten feet in front of, if instruments like that even existed. Please don't let us crash against the rocks when we are so close. Was that likely?

"If you can't see where you're going? I'd say *more* than likely." Salvo smirked. He was a maestro smirker. He had an elastic face, ideal for grimaces and sneers. His condescension was so irksome.

She walked from the stern to the bridge to talk to the second in command who was standing like a monument at the bow, peering through a telescope. What impressive concentration. She told him what her brother had said, and asked him to deny it.

"He is right."

"So how does the ship not crash?"

The adjutant showed her. On the map in the blue, black oval marks were circled in red. "We try to avoid those."

"How?"

"By navigating away from danger. We have a map." He tapped on it impatiently.

She left. "What if you don't know where the danger is?" she called to him. "What if you don't have a map?"

"Well, you wouldn't set out on a voyage without knowing where you're going, would you?" he called back to her, young and smart-alecky.

The ship seemed to stay on course due straight, though it was hard to tell. The bay below looked the same as the sky above, like granite. There was a whipping wind, and the waters were choppy.

Gina's mother started throwing up again. The journey had been relatively uneventful except for the vomiting. Mimoo's stomach couldn't endure what Salvo and Gina bore with no problem. It's hard to be old, Gina thought, bringing her mother a fresh towel, a new paper bag. Yet Mimoo was so brave, at nearly forty-five heading west into the possibilities no one could see.

"It's unseemly for you to be this excited," Salvo said to Gina, watching her skip across the gun deck, inhaling the ocean air.

"It's unseemly for you *not* to be excited," she replied. "The sails are set and filled with wind, Salvo! Why did we even set off with your attitude?"

"Why indeed," Salvo muttered.

"It's what Papa wanted. You want to go against the will of your father?"

"It isn't what we planned," her brother said.

Gina didn't want to admit to grumpy Salvo that her own excitement waned when she couldn't see where she was going. She had imagined it differently—there was going to be abundant sun, twinkling lights, perhaps a sunset over the skyline, tall buildings to welcome her, a dramatic invitation into the new life, an arduous voyage that ended with a landscape full of color. She hadn't expected gray fog.

She remained on deck at the railing, looking for a sign, hoping for a sign.

Just like Papa had dreamed, his remaining children would build a different life in the awe-inspiring vast land. While Mimoo pinched pennies, Papa taught his children to read so they wouldn't be illiterates. And then he taught his children English. If only Papa hadn't gone and died. Never mind. Gina could read, and she could speak a little English. Her wavy hair was getting tangled standing on the windward side of the open waters. Mimoo had ordered her to tie it back up, but there was something undeniably appealing in the image of herself in a light blue dress, standing like a reed with her long, tanned arms like stalks on the rails, her espresso hair flying in the drizzle and mist, all against the backdrop of steel gray. If only someone could paint a picture of her searching for America while the wind was wild in her hair. It pleased her to draw this picture in her mind. Sure, we might crash against the rocks like Salvo predicted, but this is how I'm going to stand in my last minutes, proud and unafraid.

Gina didn't really believe they would crash. She believed she was immortal, like all the young.

Eventually she got cold and went back to sit with her family. Like three sacks they sat huddled, their hands folded on their knees, her mother holding the rosary beads, worrying them between her fingers, her mouth mutely

9

moving over the words of "Ave Maria" and the invocations of God. *Mary, pierced with the sword of sorrow . . . Maria, trafitto dalla spada del dolore.* Her mother said that loudly enough for Gina to hear, so she could respond with *pregate per noi.* But Gina was not in a praying mood. So she tutted under her breath, saying nothing, and her mother tutted, *not* under her breath, and moved closer to Salvo who took his mother's hand and echoed, *pray for us.*

"Do you think she is grieving, Salvo?" Mimoo asked about Gina, though Gina was sitting right there and could hear.

"Of course, Mimoo. She just hides it. She grieves where we can't see."

"Impossible!" exclaimed Mimoo. "When you mourn, everyone knows. You can't keep such secrets."

After a short glare across their mother at Gina, Salvo kept pointedly quiet. Gina knew that Salvo knew his sister could indeed keep secrets. She hid her first crush (no easy feat in a town where everyone knew everyone else). Hid her tasting too much wine at the Feast of the Holy Theotokos. Hid not going to confession every week. Made a big show of pretending to go, then didn't. Was that in itself a sin? Hid her terrible grades. Even hid not knowing English as well as her father believed she did. Pretended she knew it better!

All the things Gina *had* to keep to herself, she kept to herself. Like her anxiety now. She was worried about the stark contrast between the anticipation of their sun-filled arrival and the ocean of blindness the ship was actually navigating through. She went to find the co-captain again.

"How far do you think we are?" she asked.

He pointed. It was like pointing at the wheel he was holding. "The docks are less than a kilometer away. What, you can't see?"

When she ran to tell her brother and mother they were almost at land, they didn't believe her. They were right not to, for the ship took another two hours to reach the shore. She could have swum faster! She was going out of her mind with impatience and boredom.

"Where's the fire?" Salvo demanded. "Where are you planning to rush off to? What do you think will happen when you walk ashore? What, you think your whole life is going to change the minute you step off this boat?"

Gina had thought so a week earlier, somewhere near Iceland. But into his imperious expression, she said, "Don't be so negative, Salvo. No nice American girl is going to want you when you get like this."

"Who said I want an American girl?" He swore, then quickly apologized to Mimoo. He was usually such a good sport about things. Nothing could get Salvo down for long. His good looks and cheerful disposition assured him of finding comfort when he needed it. This late afternoon, they stood shoulder to shoulder at the masthead, watching the dockhands tie up the boat. Though she was four years younger and a girl, they were nearly the same height, Gina and Salvo. Gina was actually taller. No one could figure out where she got the height; her parents and brothers were not tall. Look, the villagers would say. Two *piccolo* brothers and a *di altezza* sister. Oh, that's because we have different fathers, Gina would reply dryly. Salvo would smack her upside the head when he heard her say this. Think what you're saying about our mother, he would scold, crossing himself *and* her at her impudence.

Chapter Two
SONS OF LIBERTY

Mimoo disembarked on Gina's arm. Salvo pushed their three trunks on a dolly, bobbing down the plank. Gina was wobbly herself from being so long at sea.

They passed through the health control tent before they were allowed to step foot onto solid ground. No leaky eyes, no unexplained rashes, no single women traveling alone, all papers in order. Slowly they dragged their steamer trunks behind them.

"I don't feel so good," Mimoo said. "Where are we?"

Gina looked around for a sign. "Some place called the Long Wharf. Or Freedom Docks," she said pointing. Her hair was hidden in a respectable bun as Mimoo had ordered.

"You're just excited, Mimoo," Salvo said. "Sit. Get your bearings."

"You are a fool, Salvatore," his mother said.

"I am not!"

Mimoo was a stout, solid woman dressed from her gray head to flat toe in widow's black. "I haven't kept anything down for six weeks. I am not remotely excited."

They all sat down for a rest on a low wall near the water. So many people had left the boat before them that all the benches by the waterside had been taken by other families. The mother prayed, the brother and sister wiped their brows, glanced at each other. Where to now? Where to get some water? It was loud and chaotic; a swarm of seagulls flapped overhead, anticipating food.

"Señora! Señor! Señorita!" A sturdy male voice sounded to the right of them. Turning toward the tenor they were confronted with two young men, beaming and American, the taller one carrying a jug of water and bread, the other one a wicker basket with shiny red apples and half-moon oddities with thick yellow skin.

"Señora!" the shorter, friendlier of the two exclaimed again. He took off his skimmer hat and bowed to them, turning to face Gina. When he straightened out, he smiled widely at her, his brown eyes locked in. He seemed like the most genial of young men. He was open of face, effusive, extroverted. "You look tired and thirsty, please, let us help you, we have water." Putting down his basket, he deftly grabbed the jug from his mate and poured water into a small metal cup, handing it to the sitting Mimoo. "Here, drink, señora. We have a little bread. Harry, offer them some. Would you like to try a banana?" He lifted his basket to show Gina. "They're an extraordinary delicacy from the southern Americas, soon to be available all over the world." Gina wanted the apple, but it would have been messy to eat. She didn't want juice running down her chin as she

13

was trying to look lady-like. Salvo, not caring about his chin juices, grabbed the apple. No one eyed the bananas with anything but rank distrust.

"I'm Ben Shaw," the amiable man said to her. "Absolutely delighted to make your acquaintance." He smiled.

The quiet taller boy stepped forward. "Would you like some bread? Or just the water?" He was rumple-haired and wiry, but wore a smart suit with a vest and tie, though the starched white shirt was coming loose from the trousers and the silk tie was askew. One of his gold cufflinks was about to fall off. Gina's father would've liked him—he wasn't boisterous. He had clever, serious eyes. Gina decided he was shy, which she found instantly appealing. He watched her calmly, not friendly, but not unfriendly either. She smiled at him—nothing timid about her—showing him her white Italian teeth, her gleaming unsubdued eyes, her flushed face. "I'll take some bread, please," she said in English. "Hello." She stuck out her hand. "I'm Gina."

"I'm Harold," he said, leaning forward, extending his. "Harry. Pleased to meet—"

But before he could finish, or touch her, Salvo stepped between them, his back to his sister. "I'm Salvatore Attaviano," he said, shaking Harry's hand. "Gina's older brother." She had no choice but to retreat, tutting with frustration, and pinching her *ridicolo* brother hard between his shoulder blades.

"I'd like some bread, Salvo," she said with irritation. "Would *that* be all right?"

Salvo broke off a piece from Harry's loaf and handed it to her. She grabbed it from him. "This is our mother, Maria," he told the two men. "But everyone calls her Mimoo."

"Even her children?" Ben smiled.

"Especially her children," Gina said, moving this way and that.

Ben brought some bread to Mimoo. "Where are you headed?" he asked. "Can Harry and I help you, take you somewhere? We have a carriage waiting."

Mimoo nodded vigorously from her sitting position on the wall. "I can't walk, my ankles are swollen. Salvo, tell him a ride would be most welcome."

"We need to get to a train station," Salvo said. "We are going to Lawrence."

"Lawrence!" Ben exclaimed. "Whatever for?"

Gina began to speak, to explain the significance of Lawrence, but Salvo cut her off. "That is where we are going. What is it to you?"

Ben shrugged, unprovoked. "It's nothing to me," he said. "*E niente*. Just trying to, um, *aiutare*." They bickered in two broken languages.

"Help me by pointing out the train station," retorted Salvo.

"All right. But you'll have to sleep at the station. Last train was at four." Harry nudged him in the back with his fist and rolled his eyes. Ben didn't glance back. Everyone looked up at the clock tower downtown. Four fifteen, the clock read. Salvo swore not so quietly under his breath.

"How about this," Ben said in an animated voice. "Go tomorrow. Tonight you stay at one of our apartments." He shook his head when he saw Salvo's face. "No charge. As our guests."

"Why would you do that?" Salvo asked with suspicion. "What do you get?"

Harry kept knocking into Ben's shoulder as if to stop him from talking. Ben stepped away. "Harry, it's fine. It's just

15

one night." He smiled at Gina, still half hidden behind Salvo. "My friend and I manage several apartment buildings near here in an up-and-coming area, full of Italians like yourselves. We rent apartments, and then help you find jobs, loan you a few dollars."

If Salvo's eyes had been any narrower, they'd be slit shut. "Why do you do it? You do it like . . . *caritá?*"

"A little bit, yes, indeed!"

"We don't need your *caritá*," Salvo said. "We are not *povera.*"

"Then it's not charity," Ben said, just as firmly. "No, sir. It's a loan is what it is. We lend you the money, and you pay us back when you find work."

"We don't borrow money," Salvo said. "And never from strangers."

Ben looked like he'd been outplayed. Gina shook Salvo's sleeve. It had become muggy, and everyone was wet with perspiration. The sun wasn't shining, yet it was stifling hot, and the air wasn't moving. At sea it had been cool, with a breeze. Now it felt like the coal kilns were on all at once. Gina would not acknowledge the oppressive standstill air, the drops of sweat trickling from her forehead. One drifted into her mouth. She licked it surreptitiously, trying to act cooler. She caught Harry's amused yet distant eye. Both men wore suits and the suits seemed to be of the same good quality. But for some reason, disheveled Harry looked like he was born in a suit, while tidy Ben looked like his had been given to him.

"Leave them alone, Benji," Harry said, motioning away his friend. "They'll be all right." He pointed to another nearby family of five or six resting with their belongings. "Let's try them."

"No!" Gina whirled to her mother beseechingly and to

her brother accusingly, yanking on him, stepping in front of him. "It's just for one night, Salvo," she whispered vehemently. "Don't be such a ninny." She wasn't above bullying him with her height if the situation called for it. And clearly the situation was screaming for it now. If Salvo had his way, these two nice well-dressed gentlemen would be helping some other family.

Salvo shook his head. "No, Gia. It's one night too long. We can't repay them."

"You don't have to repay us," Ben interjected, overhearing. "Really. The apartment is furnished and vacant. Use it like a hotel room. If you like, you can pay for dinner. That should cover the cost of the room. Dinner and wine. And tomorrow morning you can go to Lawrence." Ben's expression read, *though why you would want to is beyond me.* And Salvo's expression read, *I would rather sleep on the street like a drunk than take one of your empty rooms.*

It was Mimoo who ended the impasse. "Salvo, your mother is exhausted. Say thank you to these two men. We accept."

Gina nearly clapped. Thank God for her practical-minded mother. She knew Salvo would never relent; his pride was too great. She never understood that. Did that mean she had no pride? She didn't think so. It just meant she wouldn't let foolish pride stand in the way of what she really wanted. And what she really wanted was to see what the two young men were offering her family. "Pride is a *peccato capitale*, Salvo," she whispered into his ear as they hurried to help their mother.

"Lust and sloth also, sister," he retorted.

"Our carriage is waiting for you just there," Ben said to Mimoo, solicitously taking her elbow and pointing to the far end of Freedom Docks, toward the city, where a number

17

of other carriages stood arrayed, waiting for fares. "Will you be all right walking?"

Mimoo smiled at Ben. Salvo, who saw everything, muttered a bad word to the heavens. "Young man, I just traveled six thousand kilometers. Will I be all right walking a hundred meters? Let's go. Let me take your arm."

Gina walked behind Ben and Mimoo, pulling her own trunk, exorbitantly pleased. Salvo dragged the rest of the baggage. "Where did you learn to speak Italian, young man?" Mimoo asked Ben.

"Oh, just a word here and there to help us with our business. Most of the immigrants we greet are Italians."

She appraised him approvingly. "Are you a good son to your mother?" she asked.

"I am a son," Ben allowed.

"She must be proud of you." She glanced back at Gina, walking next to Harry, and frowned. "You two are brothers?"

"In spirit," Ben said, "In *spirito santo*."

Salvo managed not only to drag the two largest trunks, but also to walk ahead of everyone else, as if he knew where he was going.

"Your brother is leading the way?" Harry quietly asked Gina with a shrug. "In the kingdom of the blind, the one-eyed man is king."

Gina didn't quite understand, but she couldn't speak even teasingly against her brother to a stranger. Before she could think of something witty to say, Mimoo disengaged from Ben and motioned her to come. "Gia, come here. Walk with me. Let the men carry the heavy things."

Gina hurried ahead, taking Mimoo's elbow, freeing Ben to direct Salvo to the appropriate horse and carriage.

"Your mother is a wonderful woman," Ben said to Salvo, stopping at a sickly gray mare.

Salvo eyed him with disdain. In Italian he said, "What you're trying to get next to my mother too?"

Ben didn't understand the words, but got the gist. With a tip of his hat, he stopped making nice to Salvo and untied the straps of the open wagon. The mare didn't look like it would live through the ride with the trunks. It didn't look like it would live through the heat of the evening.

After the baggage was loaded, Mimoo and Gina climbed up and sat in the open carriage facing the road, while Ben and Salvo perched on the bench opposite and Harry climbed into the driver's seat, grabbing the reins. The pale horse lurched forward, its jerking motion nearly dislodging the carefully arranged and roped trunks on the rear rack. Ben admonished his friend to be more careful.

"I'll try," Harry said, "but you know it's my first time at the reins."

Ben calmed Mimoo down. "He is only joking. Harry, stop it, you are frightening our lovely passengers." Even Mimoo smiled benevolently at being called *bellissima*. Salvo looked ready to punch him.

"Will this take long?"

"Not too long. But it's dinner hour. The traffic will be heavy. We're about a mile away. We're headed to an area of Boston called the North End. Have you heard of it?"

"I haven't, no," Gina said. "Is it nice?"

"You'll see." Ben smiled at her. She smiled back. Salvo glared at her. She stopped smiling and stuck out her tongue at her brother.

"So what's in Lawrence?"

"Our cousin Angela lives in Lawrence," Salvo said, directing Ben's attention to himself. "She is waiting for us. She thinks we are arriving today. We are going to live with her."

"Is this Angela going to get you a job?" Ben asked.

"Are *you*?"

"Of course." Ben looked across at Gina. "What do *you* like to do, Miss Attaviano?"

"Please call me Gina." She smiled. "I like to swim."

"Hmm. I don't know if I can get you a job swimming," he said. "Harry, what do you think?"

Harry said nothing, and Mimoo sat with her hat down over her heavy-lidded eyes, as if seeing nothing, hearing nothing. Suddenly she said to Gina in Italian, "Gia, think how wonderful—soon we will celebrate your birthday in our new country."

"Yes, it's good," echoed Gina, puzzled at the sudden change of topic, and opened her mouth to continue talking to Ben about her other interests and hobbies, like running, planting flowers, making tomato paste, delicious crusty bread, occasionally singing.

Mimoo's eyes opened slightly, to take in Ben across from them, to make sure he was listening. "We should do something special for your *fifteenth* birthday, no?" she said to her daughter. "Salvo, what do you think?"

"Do I look at this moment like I care, Mimoo?" said an exhausted yet watchful Salvo.

But you know who did look at that moment like he cared? Ben. For all his declarations about barely speaking Italian, he managed to understand the only important thing in Mimoo's statement: the tender age of her only daughter. Gina was only *quattordici!*

His crestfallen face said everything. Above Ben's head, Harry's slim shoulders bobbed up and down as if he was laughing.

"Well, then, yes—um—excuse me for a moment," Ben said, getting up suddenly. "My friend doesn't know where he is headed. I must direct him." He climbed up to sit next to Harry, grabbing the reins out of his mirthful hands.

Gina pulled the bonnet over her own eyes, to hide from the disappointment on the American's downcast face. Mimoo was such a troublemaker. What was the harm anyway?

"I'll tell you what the harm is," Mimoo whispered semi-privately. "You're too young for their attention. Do you hear me? This isn't Belpasso, you running around barefoot in the dusty gulleys with children. These are American *men*. They're probably older than your only living brother. You think this is what your father wanted for you, to get yourself in the family way at fourteen with men in their twenties? *Troppo giovane!*"

"Mimoo! Family way? We were just *talking*."

"How do you think it all starts, o naive child? You think it goes straight to baby-making?"

"Mimoo!" hissed a mortified Gina. "I don't want to talk about this with you."

"Correct, this is not open for discussion. Stay far away."

Pulling away from her mother, Gina leaned forward, to hear better what Ben and Harry were whispering about. But the city was too loud, the hooves on the stones were too tap-tappy, and Mimoo pulled her back, keeping her daughter close.

"I *told* you," Harry was saying to Ben. "I *warned* you. As soon as I saw her from a distance, do you remember what I said to you?"

"Yes, yes. You said she was trouble. You were wrong then, and you're wrong now."

"Benjamin, I know about these things. She is *trouble*."

"You know nothing except the idiocy you glean from your insipid books that tell you nothing about life. You don't know how to live."

"And you do?"

"Yes, I do. She is not trouble. She is Life!"

Harry rolled his eyes to the heavens. "More fool you. How *else* do you define trouble?"

"Like a femme fatale," Ben said.

"Give her time, Benjamin. She is a *fille fatale*. *Quattordici* indeed!"

Ben moved away from a mocking Harry, his shoulders dropping.

Chapter Three
NORTH END

NORTH End was across a horsemeadow from Boston proper, rising out of the soot and the afternoon coal heat. It seemed slightly detached, as if separated from the rest of Boston by this natural boundary. You had to cross a manure-covered field before you entered Salem Street that stretched and wound past a tall church, past merchants on the streets hawking their wares, past the shops and the stalls. A trumpet band played loudly on another block; there was yelling from the children and shouting from the mothers. Men stood around in circles and smoked; the smell of the city was strong, the traffic—human, horse and tram—hectic, almost deranged. Everyone was moving one or another part of their bodies, their lips going a mile a minute, their legs carrying them who knew where, with their bags, their prams, their dreams and umbrellas.

It was love at first sight for Gina. Her mouth open, she gaped, forgetting the mother, the brother, even the sand-haired silent boy who eyed her at the Freedom Docks. She sat near Salvo, who for some unfathomable reason looked less enraptured. "*Santa Madre di Dio*," he said. "This is awful."

Gina blinked. "What? No—just the opposite, Salvo. Look at it!"

"Papa told me about Milan. He said it was like this."

"Well, if Papa wanted us to go to Milan, that's where we would've gone," snapped Gina. "He wanted us to come to America, so here we are. Oh, it's wonderful!"

"You're crazy." He got up to get away from her, to take his place by his mother's side. "Mimoo, she likes this!"

"Leave her be, Salvo," Mimoo said. "Your father would be happy to know she likes it."

Reproved by his mother, Salvo scowled at Gina even more resentfully.

Gina didn't care. Her gaze was turned to the city.

The hurdy-gurdy man with the barrel organ played "Santa Lucia" from Gina's native land. She was surprised she could hear it over the clomping and braying of the horses, the screeching from the electric trolleys she'd heard her father talk about, but never seen, the rush-hour swarms of people, the vendors yelling in Italian selling garlic and tobacco, the ringing of the church bells on the corner of Salem and Prince, perhaps announcing it was six o'clock and time for Mass. The trolleys didn't move, the horses barely—the congestion was intense, and Gina feared any moment a fight would break out because people stood so close to each other, while the horses did their business right on the cobbled street which businessmen in shined shoes crossed to get home. Italian signs over the shops were everywhere,

24

the boy on the corner proclaiming that he had the *Evening Post*, and the paper was Italian also. Everything smelled not just of manure and garlic but also of sour fermented wine.

It was the greatest place Gina had ever seen. She was smitten with it, bowled over. With her mouth open in happiness, she gulped the air as their dying steed moved forward a foot a minute. She had time to dream about the goat cheese and the sausages swinging from the hooks outside the storefronts. Another boy with a cart was selling raw clams with lemon juice, but shouted in English.

"What is this thing, *clams?*" she called to Ben and Harry.

Mimoo slapped her arm. "You are not having raw anything from a filthy street corner. Not even a carrot."

"I'm just asking, Mimoo. I'm not eating."

"Don't even ask. And stop speaking *first* to men you don't know. It's neither polite nor proper."

Tutting, Gina turned away and saw why the church bells had been ringing. It was a wedding. Six white doves were tied to two waiting horses and a white carriage.

"June is a very popular month to be married," said Ben from the driver's seat.

Harry scoffed. "Then how do you explain that it's July?"

"Why else would you get married on a Thursday evening in July? Churches are booked. They're fitting in the weddings when they can." Ben gazed benignly at the bride and groom coming out of the church doors. The man with the harmonica was playing and singing "My Wild Irish Rose." Gina and Ben had nearly the same expression on their faces as they watched the procession, the white doves being released, flying away. Mimoo and Harry carried entirely different expressions—hers sorrow, his stress. And Salvo wasn't even looking.

"Is this horse going to move?" Salvo asked Ben. "*Ever?*"

"We picked a bad time to travel."

"Maybe we should get out and walk."

"But Salvo," said Gina, "you don't know where you're going."

"Better to move than sit here."

"We're almost there," Ben said. "Just one more block, one right turn, and we'll be on Lime Alley."

"There's got to be a better way to ride across town," said Salvo.

"Across town?" Ben said. "Did you say *across town?*"

"Oh, no, *mon dieu!*" Harry exclaimed to the sooty heavens.

"*Listen my children and you shall hear,*" Ben recited loudly to no one in particular, "*Of the midnight ride of Paul Revere/ On the eighteenth of April, in Seventy-five/Hardly a man is now alive/Who remembers that famous day and year.*"

Gina listened intently. "What is this poem?"

"No, no," Harry said to her over his shoulder. "Don't interrupt him. Or he'll just start from the beginning."

Ben did start again from the beginning. It passed the time, though Gina faded in and out of listening. She kept hearing Italian being shouted down the streets, kept breathing in the smells of tomato sauce, watching women fishing with their hands for wet balls of fresh mozzarella, it was so familiar and reminiscent of the things she knew, and yet so strange. Though she was tired and hungry, she didn't want any of it to end. Papa would've liked it, she whispered to herself under the strains of Ben's, "*A cry of defiance, and not of fear/A voice in the darkness, a knock at the door,/And a word that shall echo for evermore!*"

Chapter Four
GREAT EXPECTATIONS

1

IN a narrow alley, away from the bustle of Salem Street, the main artery of North End, they pulled up to a three-story building and Ben and Harry jumped down. Ben tied up the horse, while Harry helped Mimoo down from the carriage. He was going to help Gina down too, and she wanted him to, extending her hand to him, but Salvo intervened before Harry even came close to touching her. Salvo helped her down, too roughly for her liking.

"Thank you, young man," Mimoo said in the meantime to Harry. "I hope we are on the first floor. I am very tired."

"Unfortunately we are on the third."

"Ah, but from the third floor," Ben said, "you can see Boston Harbor if you lean out the window and look to the left."

"Boston Harbor?" Salvo repeated contemptuously. "I lived a road away from the Adriatic sea. I was born and raised on the Mediterranean."

"I'm sure it's very nice," said Ben. "But we don't have the Mediterranean here. Just the harbor."

Mimoo turned to Harry. "Forgive Salvo for squabbling. It's been a long journey."

"Nothing to forgive. He is in better spirits than most people we meet."

Mimoo smiled. "You do this often?"

"Every week when the ships come in. If we have the space."

Mimoo looked inside the front doors. A dark wide staircase ran up the center of the building like a spine. "How are we going to get our heavy trunks up three flights of stairs? We are such a burden. You shouldn't have bothered with us."

"It's no bother," Harry said. "None at all. This is what we do. We'll get you upstairs, don't worry."

Mimoo appraised him, her face softening.

"Believe me, you won't mind being on the third floor," said Harry, helping her to the landing. "On the first floor you hear the sailors outside your windows all night in the summers. They tend to get rowdy by the docks."

"You are so well mannered. How did you get into this line of work?"

"I'm not in this line of work," Harry corrected her. "My father owns some apartment buildings. In the summers when we're on a lighter load at university, we help him manage them. Ben and I see to the three he has here on Lime Alley."

"He's got more?"

"A few more."

28

"Isn't that the understatement of the decade," Ben said, propping open the front door with a piece of driftwood. Harry glanced down the pavement at Gina, who in her blue dress and faded hat stood entranced by the little boys playing ball on the street. He watched her for a moment. Maybe two.

"She won't like Lawrence," Harry said to Mimoo, nodding to Gina. "It's too sleepy. You're sure you don't want to stay? We can help you. We'll find you work."

Mimoo shook her head. "Too sleepy for *her* maybe, but ideal for her mother, who worries too much. I don't need excitement in my life. I've had enough of it, thank you." She shrugged. "Gia will be fine. She'll be fine anywhere."

"Gia?"

"It's Gia when I love her," said Mimoo. "My husband never called her anything but that. Me, I love her, but she drives me crazy. *So* headstrong. To call her stubborn like a mule is an injustice to mules. The mules are St. Francis compared to her."

Harry laughed.

"It's my husband's fault, bless his soul," Mimoo went on. "Now he was a saint. Adored her. And she took every advantage. Wouldn't take no for an answer. You know what my husband used to say, may he rest in peace?" She crossed herself. "He said many wise things. Like your father, I imagine?"

"My father is mostly silent," said Harry. "But if he did speak, perhaps he would say wise things."

"Well, my dearest departed Alessandro, the second greatest man ever to walk this earth, and the greatest man to stand before the gates of St. Peter, said about his children, *they find a life everywhere they look.*"

Mimoo held on to Harry's arm. He nodded politely,

listening as if deep in thought. The day was waning and the shadows were long.

"But if that is true, señora," Harry said, as they began slowly to walk up the stairs, with Ben carrying one of the trunks behind them, "why did you leave your homeland? You must have thought you could find a better life here, no?"

"No," replied Mimoo. "That is not why we left."

"Why then?"

The weary Italian woman nodded at her children behind her. "Where we come from, everybody lives only one kind of life. Alessandro said he wanted his children to choose the life, not the life to choose the children. And also," she added, panting, slowing down and wiping her brow, "he said America is the only place in the world where even the poor can be smart."

"Well, Harry wouldn't know anything about that," Ben cheerfully chimed in, hurling one of the trunks onto the landing. "Because he, unfortunately, is neither."

2

Harry and Ben and a reluctant Salvo left to go get some dinner, while Gina and her mother nested in the two small rooms by putting fresh linen on the dining table. Mimoo ordered Gina not to take too many things out, since they would have to repack them before they left the following morning. Gina unpacked too much anyway. She was hoping her mother might change her mind and let them stay. "I'm not a child, Mimoo," she said quietly, while fixing her hair, hoping her mother wouldn't hear, but wanting her mother to hear.

"You are still a child," said Mimoo, who heard everything. "And I want to keep you that way—for your father—as long as possible."

"Papa would want me to be happy, no?"

"No, be a child first. Happy much, much later. If ever. Put on a cardigan this instant. Don't let the men see you at night with bare shoulders."

"But it's hot, Mimoo."

"What did I say?"

"It's stupid! I'm hot."

"Gina!"

How Gina wished her papa were here.

Ben was right: the third-floor rooms did allow Gina a glimpse of the waters just beyond Lime Alley. After Mimoo lay down, a perspiring Gina in an itchy cardigan went to sit by the window, waiting for the men to come back. She stuck her head out, to better inhale the scent of the sea, to see more clearly the sight of the water, to catch the breeze that might cool her. She didn't want to sleep, didn't want to even blink for fear she'd miss something. When she was sure Mimoo was asleep, she threw the cardigan off.

The two rooms were clean and comfortable. They had two beds and one sofa. While hauling trunks up the stairs and showing them the apartment, Ben had said proudly that Harry's father's renovated houses were the first residences in the North End to have standardized iron pipes for running water that was pumped in from the streets. The toilet and bathtub were just down the hall, Ben told them. "You don't have to go downstairs and outside to use the privy."

Gina realized she was hungry. It was after seven, and the smell of food permeated the stairwell. Lard grease, onions, the smells of fried tomatoes, garlic, basil, all of it was comforting to Gina, yet novel and desirable.

"Did you remember the wine?" was the first thing Mimoo asked from the sofa when the three men returned with dinner.

"I took care of it, Mimoo," said Salvo, showing her the two bottles of red he carried.

"Did you buy one for Pippa?" Pippa was Angela's aunt, and Mimoo's cousin. Pippa liked her wine.

"No, I forgot."

"He forgot."

"We'll buy another one tomorrow."

"Where are we going to get one tomorrow? Do they sell it at the train station? Now we will arrive empty-handed."

They brought back pasta, sauce and Italian bread. Harry wouldn't hear of Mimoo offering him money. He turned away from her purse. "It's not necessary," he said.

"Harry is right," Ben said, "it isn't, but perhaps next week we can come to Lawrence to visit and have dinner in your new home?"

"Oh yes, please!" Gina beamed.

Harry cleared his throat, Salvo glared and Mimoo pretended she had gone suddenly deaf.

"Take the money, Harry," Mimoo said. "Take it." He still refused.

It got stifling in the apartment with four adult bodies and young Gina (in her cardigan, which Mimoo glared her into putting back on) crowding around one old table. They lit just two candles, to make it no hotter, and fitted around as best they could in the parlor room. The men took off their hats and jackets, Gina opened all the windows, but it didn't matter; she rolled up her sleeves to the elbows, and her bare forearms glistened from perspiration; she fanned herself with a newspaper and *Atlantic Monthly* magazine as she ate, sitting flanked by her mother and brother.

Mimoo was too tired for conversation, Salvo too cranky for it, and Harry too reticent. Only Gina and Ben chatted agreeably, though he was more reserved than before. She spoke to him mostly in Italian, and he answered her mostly in English. Soon Mimoo left the table to go lie down in the next room, and Gina breathed out, relaxing a little. They spread out at the wooden table. Now that Mimoo had gone, Harry was next to her and Ben across from her. She wasn't afraid of Salvo. Annoyed by him, yes, but not frightened. She threw off her white cardigan and took a long drink of water, ignoring Salvo's malevolent glares.

"So what's wrong with Lawrence?" she asked Harry, turning to him, trying to get him to talk, to glance up. But he didn't raise his eyes from his plate, not when he was sitting so close to her. Salvo was eyeballing all three of them like a hawk. He was so exhausting, her brother.

Harry shrugged. "I said nothing about Lawrence."

"There is no work," Ben interjected.

"We will do something," Salvo said. "Don't worry about us."

"Who is worried? I'm just saying."

"Leave them be, Benji," Harry said. "Everybody finds something to do."

Ben poured everyone more wine. Salvo intervened. He said it was too late for Gina to have even a little bit of wine. Keenly Gina felt her age. Perhaps Ben could offer her a milk bottle and send her to bed, would Salvo prefer that?

"Do you live here in the North End?" Gina asked Harry.

It was Ben who answered. "No, we're from Barrington. Just a small town in the hills about ten miles northeast of here." He smiled. "Not too far from the ocean."

"Ah, Mr. Shaw," said Harry, turning to his friend, "so now *you're* from Barrington?"

Ben punctuated his blink with a swig of wine. "Oh, that's right. My friend forgot to tell you his full name. Gina, Salvo, he is Harry *Barrington*."

Gina and Salvo sat, taking this in.

"Barrington like the town?" Gina said finally.

"Exactly like it. Full relation."

Gina gaped at Harry, but stopped when she glimpsed from the periphery of her vision Salvo's sour face. "You have a whole town named after you?"

"Oh, not after *him*, miss," Ben said. "After his productive and illustrious family. They built that town, you see. All Harry does is use the town library."

"That is not true," Harry said. "I also eat at the restaurants."

Gina was impressed and slightly surprised. Harry in his dapper suit and fancy hat and slightly indolent air didn't look to be the kind of young man who worked with his hands. "You're from a family of *builders*?" she asked, trying not to sound incredulous.

"My father isn't there with a hammer and nails, if that's what you mean," Harry replied. "He's a merchant. He makes sure other people do the work."

Ben laughed. "I can't wait to hear you tell your father this. That seven generations of Barringtons, who built not only Boston but funded the expansion of the very university you get all your snooty notions from, got their solid reputation from nothing more than making sure other people did the work. I can't wait."

Harry waved him off. "Ben, you forgot to tell our new friends who *you* are."

"I told them. Ben Shaw."

"Yes, but who is Ben Shaw?"

"Humble engineering student?"

"Son of Ellen Shaw," said Harry. "Who just happens to be the youngest sister of Robert Gould Shaw, the man who commanded the only all-black regiment in the Union Army during the Civil War."

If Gina didn't know any better, she might have thought they were trying to impress her, or perhaps in a game of one-upmanship emerge victorious in their teasing of each other in front of her. Salvo did know better, and it was certainly what he thought, because all he said by way of comment was a gruff, "Your uncle is black?"

"No, quite white," said Harry. "*And* a colonel. He just happened to be the white colonel who took the job no one else wanted, or would take."

"I keep telling you," Ben said. "No one's heard of him."

"Well, someone must have heard of him, Benjamin," Harry said pleasantly. "Because an architect named Stanford White spent fourteen years sculpting your uncle's memorial." He leaned back with self-satisfaction. "Ben comes from a very illustrious family," Harry continued. "Aside from his martyred uncle, he is also the nephew of Josephine Shaw Lowell, who is a living legend in New York, advocating for peace, for women's rights, active in politics, and she happened to co-found an organization with Erving Winslow called the Anti-Imperialist League right here in Boston."

"In a tiny airless room in a walk-up on Kilby Street," Ben said. "Not exactly remodeling Harvard Hall."

Gina had never heard of the people they were talking about. She felt young and stupid. "Anti-Imperialist?" was what she echoed.

"I assume anti-American-imperialist," said Harry. "Right, Benji?"

"Since my mother will be running it, can there be any other kind?" Ben turned to Gina. "But this has nothing to do with me."

"What does my grandfather," Harry interrupted, "or my father for that matter, have to do with me?"

"Oh, come on! It's a direct relation." Ben rubbed his hands together.

"And your mother is not?"

"Am I a descendant of Robert Treat Paine?"

Harry groaned.

"Aha!" Ben was triumphant. "Robert Treat Paine was one of Harry's ancestors on his mother's side."

"Who is Robert Treat Paine?" It pained Gina to ask; she feared she should have just known.

Ben smiled benevolently. "He was one of the founding fathers of the United States."

She knew she shouldn't have asked.

"He had quite a reputation, didn't he, Harry?"

"I don't know what you mean. A reputation as a ladies man? As an intellectual?"

Ben leaned across to Gina. "Robert Treat Paine was known as the man who proposed nothing, but opposed everything proposed by others. He was called *the objection maker*."

"How is this relevant?" Harry demanded. "Why would this young lady and her brother care? Look how bored they are."

Ben laughed.

They continued to talk and joke and drink while Gina faded into the stiff wooden chair, trying to sit like a lady, to keep her elbows off the table, her bare damp arms straight. But her back hurt, her neck hurt, her legs hurt from being up so long—on the boat, on the docks, walking through

36

North End, and now sitting here with these smart men. Salvo was smoking, trying to stay vigilant and awake. Mimoo was soundly sleeping. Salvo needn't have worried. Gina policed herself. With a slight tremor she realized how infantile she was to think even for a moment that she could hold a conversation with actual men. That's how she knew she was infantile. Because she thought she could. To think that a curl of her brown hair or a sway of her long girlish skirt, or the sheen of her tanned Sicilian soft skin could make up for the fact that when she opened her mouth she was nothing more than a *contadina* from the rural outskirts of a Sicilian town, where they milked the cows and took the olives off the trees in season. They fished all summer and hoped the volcano wouldn't erupt, again. Oh, the fallacy of herself!

Reluctantly she withdrew from the conversation, hoping they would interpret her intimidation as exhaustion. One side of her hair bun had come loose and was dangling a long wavy strand down the side of her neck. Her brother kicked her chair. She ignored him. He kicked the chair again, harder. She looked over at him. *What*, she mouthed with irritation. He gestured to her hair with his eyes.

You want me to tie up my hair, she rhetorically mutely asked him. Fine, here you go. Raising her hands to her head, she pulled out all the pins and laid them on the table, in front of her plate. Her hair was now out of the bun and fell down her back and over her shoulders, chocolate, wavy, ungainly. Completely ignoring what she knew with delight was her brother's appalled expression, she lifted her hands to her head and section by section proceeded to pin the hair back in a high chignon. The three men watched her; no one moved; only her bare arms moved.

37

Salvo croaked, "It's getting late . . ."

Harry and Ben ignored him.

"What does your friend Angela do in Lawrence?" Ben asked, gaping at Gina in the near dark from across the table as the candlelight flickered out.

She wouldn't allow herself a glimpse at Harry. "She works in a textile factory."

"Is that where *you* want to work?" Ben smiled. "On the looms?"

"No," she replied. "Too hot on the looms. I want to work in the mending room. It's more refined."

"No," Salvo cut in. "Gina and I are going to open our own business like true Americans."

"Salvo, be quiet," Gina snapped. "Who has money to open their own business? We don't have money to pay these kind gentlemen for staying here. We have to find work first, save a little money. Then maybe we can boast about what we *plan* to do."

"That is what *I'm* going to do, sister. No use arguing me out of it."

Harry and Ben appraised the sister and brother.

"A business is a good idea," Ben said.

Harry said nothing.

Sticking his fingers in Harry's ribs, Ben tried to explain his friend's silence. "My friend is conflicted about business."

"Not at all," said Harry. "I know exactly how I feel about it."

"Yes—conflicted." Ben chuckled. "Harry is burdened by his father's expectations. Now some might argue it's better to have a father, even a demanding one, but Harry disagrees."

"It's better to have a father," Gina said quietly, "even a demanding one."

"Oh, I agree with you, Gina," said Ben. "But Harry struggles every day against unfulfillable projections, while I run scattershot from hobby to hobby, having no burdens placed on me whatsoever."

"Except by your radical mother," said Harry.

"Where is your father?" Gina asked Ben.

"I don't know. I've never met him."

Gina pondered that—not to know your father. It was inconceivable. In Sicily, every child knew who his father was.

"I, on the other hand," said Harry, "have met my father, but I know him even less than Ben knows his."

Gina wasn't sure how to respond. "Doesn't your mother want you to become someone, Ben?"

"I don't know," Ben said. "She doesn't say to me, son, you *must* follow in my footsteps."

"Yes, she does," said Harry. "And my father doesn't say this either. He says, whatever you do is *fine* with me. Which is even worse. Aside from being wholly untrue."

Gina *really* pondered that one. "*That's* worse?" she said at last. Was it the language barrier that made comprehension of this insurmountable? What were they actually saying?

"Yes, it's worse," Harry said. "Because action on my part is implied and required. Do what you like, he says, but do *something*."

"Ah." There was a significant pause—it was late at night, after a long day. "But you do want to do *something*, don't you?"

"I'm not sure." Harry half-smiled at her. "What if I don't?"

"Harry is joking," Ben said.

"A man has to do something," said Gina.

"What about a woman?" Harry's fog-colored eyes twinkled a little.

"A woman's role is clear. She must keep house, raise children."

"What if she wants to work?"

"She *is* working."

"Work outside the home."

"In Italy, there is no such thing," Gina said. "If she sells fruit at the market or sews for other people or cleans big homes, she must do it between hours. First her own house, her own children. Then everything else."

Ben gazed at her in appreciation.

Pensively Gina stared at Harry. "Are you an only child?"

"I am an only son," he replied, not looking directly at her. "I have a sister."

Ben made a dismissive sound. "Esther is invisible to your father."

"*Just* to my father?"

"What?" When Harry didn't elaborate, Ben shrugged with a dismissive chuckle. "It's like royalty at Harry's house. Only the male offspring can inherit the throne."

They were joking! Except that really *was* how it was. Gina's father was an anomaly among Sicilian men. He adored his sons, but believed his only daughter too could become anything. Gina wanted to tell these two boys about her remarkable father, but decided not to. She was losing the power to make sense in her new alien language. Silently she thanked her father for being a relentless taskmaster, for teaching her English for so many years even when she had seen no sense in it.

"Our father believed," she said cautiously, unsure of her English words, "that those who lived without expectations

40

were not blessed but cursed." She looked across the table. "Right, Salvo?"

"I know nothing," Salvo said in Italian, "except that it's late and I'm tired."

"Your father wasn't the only one who believed this," said Harry, in reply to Gina, not Salvo. "My father, too. And Alexander Pope."

"Who?"

"The poet."

"No, Harry," said Ben. "Pope thought a life lived without expectations was the ninth beatitude. Blessed are they who expect nothing, was what Pope wrote."

"You *completely* misunderstand Pope," Harry said, yanking up Ben by the arm, and glancing around for his jacket and hat. "As if you have any idea what a beatitude even is."

"As if you do."

"At least I'm not quoting him incorrectly! We must go."

"Actually you did quote him incorrectly," said Ben, as they bade their goodbyes to a battle-fatigued Gina.

"I didn't quote him," Harry said. "I was merely being polite in a conversation with our new friends. Goodnight. We will see you tomorrow. Please give our regards to your mother."

"Pope ended it with 'for they shall never be disappointed.'"

"Let's go!"

They tipped their hats before they put them on and bowed politely.

Gina could see Salvo would have loved to have refused their help, but he didn't know where the train station was and couldn't get the three trunks downstairs without them. To pay her back he stood between her and the young men so they couldn't take her hand, couldn't treat her like a lady when they wished her goodnight.

* * *

After Ben and Harry left, Gina and Salvo retreated to separate windows from which they both looked longingly at the sea beyond, but for different reasons: Salvo because he yearned to be back home; Gina because she wanted never to leave the big city. She hoped Lawrence would turn out to be a little bit like a big city, only smaller. But no matter what it turned out like, it wouldn't have Ben and Harry in it.

"A fine pair they are," Salvo said to her at last.

"Aren't they just," echoed Gina. Especially the sand-haired, laconic one.

He sighed with exasperated disdain. "Sometimes," he said, "I think you forget what Papa said to you."

She bristled. "I don't forget anything."

"Then why do you act like you do?"

Gina turned away. She didn't want to hear it. Leaving the room where her brother was making her defensive, Gina went into the room where Mimoo was snoring and sat in a wooden chair by the open window. She still heard horses clomping outside, a distant bell of a trolley car, noises from sailors, laughter, a city alive, pulsing and thumping into the night. *Never forget where you came from, Gina Attaviano,* Alessandro said to her before he died. *Then it will always be easy.*

I think it will be easy, Papa, she whispered, gulping the night air. In thrall to the new city, the old life for Gina had vanished with the tide.

Chapter Five
SUMMER STREET

THERE was Boston, and then there was Lawrence. The steam train connecting the heart of the revolution with the immigrant town thirty miles north was modern, and the stations from which it arrived and departed had electricity and stone walls and wood doors and a ticket-taker. But besides the station and the lonely trolley car running down Broadway across the Merrimack River, Lawrence might as well have been Belpasso under an active volcano, a town to which electricity and plumbing had yet to come—though magma came, lava came, every year a rumbling, every five a smoke eruption, every ten a pouring of liquid rock. At least that's how Lawrence felt to Gina, who had briefly breathed in the rarefied air of civilization and now once again was left with the cows. Yes, both sides of the burly river on which Lawrence was built were flanked by long, spread-out mills and tall smokestacks, one after another, but otherwise the town was unpaved dust and horse carriages. It wasn't even like Belpasso, Gina complained to Salvo as they waited on the bench for Angela. In Belpasso, the streets were paved!

"Yes, paved with the red blood of martyrs, as your father would say," said her mother, looking around. "Paved with the igneous lava remains of the sinners' post-apocalyptic bones. No volcanoes in Lawrence. So much the better."

"Are you sure?" Gina said sullenly. "How do you know?" Where Boston had manicured grasses and landscaped parks, where the North End steamed with noise and life, Lawrence on this Friday afternoon was like a drawing room—peaceful and singularly uneventful. Gina sauntered from the bench to Broadway, where she stood watching a few women carrying packages and pushing baby prams, just like in the old country. Salvo called her back. A carriage clomped by, without Angela.

Gina wanted to cry. This is where women retired to have children! Her life was over. She had had Boston at her fingertips, she had by a stroke of fate met two men, a warrior and a revolutionary, who could help her—help all of them. But no. Oh, dear merciful Jesus, what was she going to do?

"This isn't like Boston," said Mimoo.

"No, no it isn't," Gina grimly agreed.

"Look, Salvo, your sister is sulking." Mimoo found that amusing. Gina turned away.

Harry and Ben had used the wrong metaphor about this town. Lawrence was like Boston only in the way an infant was like an adult. They shared some fundamental characteristics, but not any of the important ones. Gina, flagrantly disappointed after the joy of yesterday, focused instead on

44

the brown plainness of her summer clogs while they waited for Angela.

They came from Sicily—where beauty was embodied in blue water and rolling hills, in vivid grasses and trees, in sailboats and dramatic coastlines, in sandy beaches, with Mount Etna in the background of every memory, hissing smoke all day long. Gina wasn't a painter. She wasn't disillusioned because she wanted to render Lawrence in oil on canvas. But she had promised her father she would make something of herself in America. How could she make anything of herself in Lawrence?

"Angela has done all right for herself here," Salvo said. "Why can't you? What, you're too good for it?"

"Too good for what?" Gina snapped back, but finally there appeared a horse and a wagon with a waving Angela in it.

"Gina! Salvo! Mimoo!"

Except for the ear-to-ear smile, Angela didn't look like the girl who had left Belpasso two years earlier. She had put on weight and makeup. At seventeen, she looked decades older than Gina. She hugged them profusely. "I'm so happy you're here! You must be exhausted! Where did you stay last night? I have been waiting for your telegram all week, your boat took so long to get here, mine too of course, nearly killed Aunt Pippa, but wait till you see her now, she's doing well. I'm so excited to see you! You will stay with us until you get work, there is plenty of room, and we'll find something for you. It would've been better if you'd come two months ago, because Everett just hired forty people, but Washington might be hiring. You must be starved! Salvo, do you need help loading? We made bread, fresh mozzarella, I made it myself last night, I'm so sorry about Papa Sandro, I can't believe he is not here, all he talked about since I was a baby was coming to America.

45

Oh, I'm not Angela Tartaro anymore, I'm Angie LoPizo."
She chuckled. "Annie LoPizo, actually. It's a long story, but
a good one. I'll tell you the *whole* thing in detail. But the
short version is, I couldn't get overtime work unless I lied
about being fourteen, so I lied about being fourteen, we got
a work card for me with another girl's name, and now I'm
Annie LoPizo, and eighteen! I'm on sixty hours a week as
a weaver, not a spinner in those horrible humid rooms, you
know, Gia?"

"I know."

"All the kids are there. You might have to start there
too, but it'll only be for a little while, Gia, my peach."

"I don't want to change my name," said Gina. "I—"

"She is going to go to school," Mimoo said. "It's what
her father wanted."

"She needs to work, Mimoo," said Salvo. "*I'm* not going
to school. I'm going to work."

"You are, yes."

"She is, too."

"Maybe I can get something part-time, Mimoo?" said
Gina.

"You're going to school full-time," said Mimoo. "It's what
your father—"

"Hold on, Mimoo," Salvo said. "Let's see if we can pay
our bills first."

"You stay with us," Angela said. "Not so expensive. My
English is so good now," she continued, "I can pass for
a native, almost. I say I'm second generation, and it's
my Aunt Pippa who came from Italy. Everyone believes
me."

"I want to work," Gina said, "but I don't want to start
my life with a—"

"And go to school," Mimoo said.

"—lie," Gina finished.

"Hey, Salvo," Angela called to him as he loaded their heavy trunks onto the wagon. "Want me to introduce you to Pamela, my friend at work? She's a real nice blonde." She giggled. "You like blonde girls?"

"I don't know," he said. "I never met one."

"Wait till you see this one. I'm sorry you and Viola split . . ."

"We didn't split. She refused to come."

". . . But it's better to begin your life anew. Right, Mimoo? How are you feeling? Good? Gina, my friend Verity is dying to meet you."

"This Verity is a girl?" Salvo asked.

Angela giggled. "You silly boy. A girl, of course. You don't need to worry about me, Salvo, I'll be Gina's permanent chaperone, I promise. And Verity is studying to become a nun."

It was all Gina could do to not scream.

"Are we loaded up?"

"Angie," said Mimoo, "it's nice to see you haven't changed a bit."

"But I have, Mimoo, I have."

"You might not look the same, but everything else . . ."

"No, I'm grown up now. I help with the rent, I go to the bank. I buy my own clothes. I'm a young lady."

"Yes . . ."

"You can work with Aunt Pippa, Mimoo, cleaning houses up in Prospect Hill. That's where the mill managers live. Pippa said she'll split some of her pay with you until you get your own customers."

"That's not going to help me meet expenses, splitting Pippa's pay. I can also sew," Mimoo said, "and cook."

The horse had taken off; Gina held on to the wooden

armrest. On top of everything, the dust from the road was blowing up into her face, making her choke.

The houses were simple Victorian, doors closed, no one sitting on stoops. They rode down cobblestoned Essex Street. Angie said it was the main shopping street in Lawrence. Gina rolled her eyes. One little Salem Street in North End was four times as busy.

"What do you think of Lawrence, Gia? Nice, isn't it? Mimoo, Aunt Pippa sews too. Many Americans can't sew. They rely on us to do it. But she takes in the work, because it's getting too hard for her to clean. You're going to help her a lot. She has her own sewing machine. Her legs have swollen up."

"Because of the sewing machine?" said Gina.

"Mine too," said Mimoo. "But why hers?"

"You'll see. But what will Salvo do?"

"Don't you worry about me, Ange. I'll take care of myself."

"Aunt Pippa is seeing a gentleman, who doesn't care about her swollen ankles. Maybe he can help you, Salvo. He is a glazier." Angela squeezed Gina. "There are lots of young men, *managers*, at the mill, and they looove Italian girls."

"Yes," said Salvo. "Girls other than my sister."

"Come on, Salvo. I didn't mean it like that."

"*Basta*, Ange."

"I'm saying to help her get a job."

"We are *not* asking any men to help my sister get a job."

"*Basta*, Salvo." That was from Gina.

At Canal Street, the horse made a right and stopped in front of a narrow row house amid four or five blocks of narrow row houses. Pippa was waiting for them in a chair right outside the door. Canal Street had no trees and the view across from the row houses was only of the long wall of the textile factory stretching half a mile in each direction. The mill workers got up at dawn, rolled out of bed, stepped outside their little homes, walked fifty feet and were inside the factory doors.

"You live here?" said Gina.

"For five years now!"

Gina pointed. "Is that where you work?"

"Yes," Angela said happily. "The Washington Mill. So convenient and close, right?"

Gina saw the reason Pippa had swollen ankles—she had gained a hundred pounds. It wasn't swelling that was on her ankles. Mimoo and Salvo failed to hide their shock.

"America has been good to you," Mimoo said, hugging her cousin.

"*She* has a gentleman caller?" Salvo whispered to Gina. "Aunt Pippa! So nice to see you! You haven't changed a bit!"

"Salvo, you've always had a silver tongue. But don't waste it on me, I already have a man." She swallowed him in her skirts.

"Aunt Pippa, how you kid. Please let go. I'm suffocating."

Pippa herself had no children, but had raised Angie as her own after Angie's mother died ten years earlier.

"Will there be room for us?" Mimoo asked. "We don't want to impose."

"Don't be silly. There's plenty."

But it was Pippa who was silly. There wasn't plenty. There was barely any. She and Angie lived in two small rooms on the second floor.

"It's really two and a half rooms," said Pippa, pointing to half a closet in which an oven stood.

Salvo looked around. "What is your plan?" he asked.

"I know it may not look like much," said Angela, "but it's cheap and it's close to work."

"So is that boat on the canal," said Salvo. "But we don't live in it."

"Salvo!" That was Mimoo. She sat down heavily in the chair in the living room and took Pippa's hands. "This is very good and kind of you, Pippa," she said. "We'll be fine."

"Of course we will be," Pippa said. "As soon as you find work, we will look for a bigger place, perhaps a proper house, like they have over by the Common."

"I like being close to work, Aunt Pippa," Angela said.

"You can stay here. Why do *you* have to come?"

They bickered but all squeezed in: the four women piled into the bedroom, with Gina and Angela on the floor, while Salvo took the couch in the living room.

"Salvo is not complaining, Pippa," Mimoo said. "He's just in a bad mood."

"He's been in a bad mood for a year," said Gina. "What's your excuse now, Salvo?"

"I need an excuse?" He spread out on the couch with the small window ten feet from him. "In Belpasso, I had my own room, my own space. Now I'm next to the dining-room table."

"Gina, if you want, you can stay with Verity," Angela said. "She lives a few blocks from here, across the river on Ashbury. Her parents have a little house. She said you could stay with her."

"How would Gina staying somewhere else help *me*?" Salvo snapped.

"It's not all about you, Salvo," Gina said.

"No, it's all about you, Gina."

"Stop it, you two," said Mimoo. "Maybe Gina *should* stay with Verity."

"No," he said. "The family stays together."

"Fighting every minute?"

"Together."

"Cheer up, Salvo," Angela said, pinching him. "You'll get work, we'll find a bigger place. In the meantime, upstairs there is a young lady I can introduce you to. She's nineteen but not blonde. She's not blonde *or* Italian." Angela tickled him, kissed him. "I'm just joking with you. Come on, it's not so bad. You can take her out for ice cream. Gina, you want some ice cream?"

"How often do the trains run?" Gina asked suddenly.

Angela was momentarily rendered speechless. "Trains run where?"

"Anywhere. Say, to Boston?"

"Gina!" That was Mimoo. "Don't even think about trains or Boston. You are not allowed to go to Boston."

"I'm just asking a question, Mimoo. I'm allowed to ask questions, no?"

"No!"

"I don't know about trains," Angela said. "I don't go to Boston."

"You don't go to Boston?" Now it was Gina's turn to be speechless.

"Not since the day we came. And Verity has never in her life been. Why do you need a train to Boston?"

"I don't. Just curious."

Salvo elbowed her. "No," he said. "Not even curious."

"*You* leave me alone." She moved away.

"Gina," said Mimoo, "stop your lollygagging and help me unpack the trunks. We need fresh clothes. Train to Boston— ignore her, Angela. It's dinnertime soon."

Dinnertime! Gina couldn't believe it. On top of all its other sins, Lawrence swallowed time.

They unpacked as best they could and helped with supper. They had spaghetti with tomato sauce and clams, "caught

51

fresh yesterday!" The bread was good, as was the homemade Buffalo mozzarella, though Salvo later, and privately, pointed out to Gina that his mozzarella was much better and Gina pointed out to Salvo that the two rooms they had stayed in yesterday were much bigger.

After three glasses of wine, Mimoo began to cry about Alessandro and Antonio, and Gina took that as a cue to leave the table, because she knew that once her mother started, her mother would not stop. She went into the bedroom and lay down on the blankets on the floor. She didn't even look out the window because there was nothing to see except the alley behind Canal Street.

But when she closed her eyes, she heard the bagpipes and the barrel organ and the wedding mandolins, saw the beautiful people in their urban haze, riding uphill in cable cars and trolley cars, and a busker with a harmonica on the jammed city street, who played and sang. On her first disillusioned night in her new home town, Gina fell asleep to the memory of the singing man, yearning that someone someday might want to win her heart like the pretty girl had won the heart of the lonely musician.

"Since we met I've known no repose, she's dearer to me than the world's brightest star, and my one wish has been that someday I may win the heart of my wild Irish Rose . . ."

Chapter Six
A SUNDAY IN A SMALL TOWN

"BARRINGTON is the heart of the American way of life," Ben Shaw would add after he had introduced his friend Harry as the son of the man who founded and built a town entire. It was the way he had introduced him to Alice, a few years back, whom they both wanted to impress and were even more impressed when she wasn't, and it was the way he had introduced him to Gina, whom they both wanted to impress and were even more impressed when she was.

And what a small town Barrington was. By train or stagecoach, close to Boston, the thriving hub of the Northeast, Barrington nested in sloping oaks and bushy maples on hilly roads. From the top of the town square on a clear night you could see Boston's downtown lights twinkling in the distance. This Sunday the deep green of the trees and the startling white of the houses and the church steeples were sleek with fog and rain. Herman Barrington could've built his homestead anywhere, on a thousand acres with a mile-long winding driveway, like his brother Henry, but he chose instead to live four blocks from Main Street, in a stately but traditional colonial estate right off the sidewalk, from which passersby could glance into his bay windows. And when the family and their friends gathered in the drawing room or the library, sipping their drinks, fire crackling, amiably chatting, they could also see all the way down the wet and winding street.

This Sunday afternoon, as every other, Esther Barrington waited with her brother in the library, adjacent to the drawing room. Harry only pretended to wait. He was reading. The fire was on, their drinks were at their sides. She sat in the wingback, staring out the window.

"Is that staring out the window *longingly*?" asked Harry from the Chesterfield without raising his head. "Waiting for Alice, are we?"

Esther primly folded her arms. "I will not be mocked by you."

"No?" He smiled.

"Oh, you're brave now."

"I'm not that brave."

"Harry, I need to speak with you."

"No."

"You *have* to stand up to him."

"No."

"Ben and I can't keep defending you."

"You call what you do defending?"

"Don't let him talk to you like that—and in front of Alice!"

"She finds him charming."

54

"She finds everyone charming. That's her gift. And soon she won't. He's planning to put you into quite a spot during dinner."

"Just during dinner?"

"I'm giving you fair warning, brother. He is growing impatient."

"Busy men are always impatient. What is it now?"

She took a breath. "Is Ben coming today?"

Harry glanced at her, amused. "Not just Ben but also his mother. Are you going to try to get on her good side?"

"Why would I need to? Stop being cheeky. Oh, Harry, you have to defend yourself."

Getting up, he took his books and walked over to where Esther was sitting by the window in the leather armchair. He sat on the low footstool by her side, and, looking up at her, said, "But it's so much more fun when you come to my Pyrrhic rescue, Esther. I wouldn't have it any other way."

Patting his head, Esther laughed. She had a good, hearty laugh, like a man's—though she herself was nothing like a man. She was subdued and proper, never flirtatious or coquettish, but what reduced her occasional severity and gave her an ephemeral air was her skin: it was the color of parchment because she never went in the sun without a parasol, even on Revere Beach. Her translucence made her seem fragile, but despite her narrow bone structure, her thin face and nose, her slender slits of eyes, Esther was tough and strong. Her voice was the genteel voice of a well-born woman who was aware of her position, and yet its alto pitch made it sound as if she could swear like the sailors on the Long Wharf. She didn't swear, of course. But Harry knew what she was capable of, should she so choose. "Let's have it, Esther. What will it be about today? My future?"

"Yes, and no. Your and Alice's future."

"Ugh."

Alice was the only child of Orville Porter who owned the Massachusetts East Timber Company, which supplied Herman Barrington with lumber for most of his construction projects. Alice was sporadically enrolled at the Society for the Collegiate Instruction of Women, which had a few years earlier begun offering university-level instruction to women, though without the attendant Bachelor of Arts degree. It had also renamed itself Radcliffe College, after Ann Radcliffe, a colonial philanthropist. When they first met, Ben had mentioned to Alice that Harry's family were also colonial philanthropists, to which Harry said, how philanthropic could they have been? They still have all of their money. This made Alice laugh. So though Alice wasn't swayed by Harry's position in life, she was swayed by Harry.

They started dating, cautiously. That was two years ago when he was a sophomore; now he was entering his fourth and final year, and it occurred to him that they were still dating, cautiously. They were both still young, he reasoned, Alice barely twenty-one. Also, he had a few poorly developed concerns about their mutual suitability. He was bookish, while she was very much her father's daughter, going on river drives up north to inspect lumber, walking in her thigh-high waterproof Wellingtons on the logs, wielding her branding axe and searching for imperfections. Did Harry really want Alice searching as assiduously for his? The fallen trees had no chance under her stern boots. She was known for limbing and debarking them herself. Mostly he felt he was not good enough for her, and it was only a matter of time before she discovered it.

"Don't worry," Harry said to his sister. "I have everything in hand." He looked down at the books on his lap, one of them a book he was thinking of doing his senior thesis on next year, a short story by Edward Everett Hale. Under it was volume four of the ten-volume *History of the United States* by George Bancroft, which he was supposed to be reading for his advanced seminar, but wasn't.

Harry didn't tell Esther how just last week he overheard from the open bedroom window his father and Orville and Irma Porter below on the lawn discussing the topic of their children. They talked of the proper way to do things in Boston: a family heirloom ring, a formal announcement, a modest but well-publicized engagement dinner, followed by a long, productive period during which Harry graduated and settled on a career, while Alice methodically planned their extravagant and very public nuptials. A high society ball, a fancy affair, *the* wedding of the new century. The way the three parents extolled the romance of it, Harry himself was drawn in.

Esther leaned into him. "He plans to ask you point blank when you intend to honor him with grandchildren."

Harry whistled. "Isn't that putting the cart before the horse?"

"He will ask you to put the horse before the cart."

"At Sunday dinner? Well, better perhaps than the usual."

"If by better you mean more mortifying, then yes. Why put poor Alice on the spot like that?"

Harry rubbed her hand. "Don't fret, Esther. Look forward to the plank walk. I do." They sat side by side for a few minutes. Esther seemed restless. "What's the matter with you today?"

She shrugged. "Do I look nice?"

"As always." And she did, with a bow in her ruffled peach blouse, a camel-colored skirt, subdued beige high-heeled pumps. Her fingernails were buffed and shiny, her makeup was light, she even wore lipstick. Esther always tried to look especially attractive on Sundays. She just seemed more anxious than usual today. "What? Tell me."

"Nothing." She sighed. "I think Father might be bringing someone for dinner. He told me to dress up a little." She waved Harry off. "I don't want to talk about it. How was your week? What are you reading? For school?"

"Yes, because you know me, school's the only time I crack a book."

"You know what I mean."

"It does happen to be for a seminar I'm taking. Colonial America. Visions and Dissertations."

She was distracted. "Did you and Ben work last week?"

"All week. The boats never stopped coming. Father is going to have to do something, convert one of his other buildings perhaps. We're out of room. We rented the last two apartments Friday."

"Talk to him about it at dinner. How is Ben?"

"Ben is, as always, fine. Soon you will see for yourself how he is."

She stared out the window.

Presently a carriage pulled up and a youngish man popped out, not Ben. Esther sat up straight, emitted a small sound of distress and got up. "Put away your book, Harry. Someone's here to see you."

He glanced outside. "To see *me*?"

"Well, who *is* that man?"

The young clean-shaven gentleman was nervous and portly as he lumbered through the gate and to the portico.

"He looks as if he hasn't started shaving yet," Harry remarked.

The doorbell rang. "Louis, the door!"

Louis Jones, their butler, the man who ran the house,

had been with the Barringtons since before the Civil War. They were supposed to call him Jones, but throughout their childhood they called him by his first name because that was what his mother had called him, and they couldn't alter this when they got older. Louis and Leola were escaped slaves who made it to Boston in the late 1850s. They were hired by Harry's grandfather and lived in the back of the house in the servants' quarters, working for three generations of Barringtons. Leola died at eighty-seven a few years ago. Seventy-two-year-old Louis was almost completely deaf but pretended he wasn't. "I hear the doorbell, you impertinent children. I'm right here." He moved slowly, hobbled by arthritis and cataracts, but still retained his sharp tongue, his sharper memory and his shock of white hair. Esther and Harry joked that if he weren't careful, the rest of Louis would soon turn white too. "I'll drop dead before that happens," Louis would retort.

"Who do you think that is?" Harry said to Esther with a glint in his eye as they stood in the doorway studying the young man at the front door.

"How should I know?" Under her breath she tutted.

At the back of the house, a heavy door creaked open and Herman Barrington's firm footsteps echoed down the hardwood, darkly paneled center hall. "Elmore!" they heard him say. "Come in! How are you? Thank you, Jones. Would you please fix the creak in my office door, it's getting worse. Do you not hear it? Come in, Elmore. Let me introduce you to my children." As Herman walked by, he appraised them—Esther briefly, Harry longer, his son's frockcoat, his pressed herringbone trousers, his starched white shirt and gray vest. Harry slowly took his hands out of his pockets. He knew his father found that habit obnoxious.

The sister and brother exchanged a mute look. *Elmore?* they mouthed.

Fumbling with his umbrella, the plump man awkwardly removed his coat and hat and then dropped them all, one by one. Louis helped him pick everything up, as the three Barringtons stood and watched. Herman was tall, gray, stately, impeccably groomed and crisply dressed in a chocolate sports coat and tan slacks. He looked like a male, more elegant version of Esther.

Elmore was dwarfed by Herman.

"Elmore Lassiter, I'd like you to meet my daughter, Esther, and my son, Harold."

Harry shook Elmore's soft hand. "Please call me Harry."

"Yes, thank you," the young man said. "Please call me Elmore."

With great amusement, Harry glanced at an exasperated Esther.

"When is everyone due to arrive?" Herman asked. "They're running late." His punctuality was legendary.

"Not for another thirty minutes," Harry replied. But he didn't carry a watch on Sundays.

"Shall we take our drinks in the drawing room? No, let's go outside. It's a beautiful day. Jones!"

"I'm right here, sir."

"Ah," Herman said. "There you are. Please tell Bernard to hold dinner so it doesn't burn."

"Dinner won't be ready for another ninety minutes, sir."

"Well, let's hope the tardy guests get here before then. Otherwise, Elmore, we'll just have to eat the entire feast. Bernard is a wonderful cook. Would you like a refreshing mint julep? Esther, come, please. Would you like a tour of the house? Esther will be glad to show you around. Perhaps there's time for a walk. Have you been to our little town before? No?

Well, it's a fine place." Herman's hand went soothingly around Elmore's tense shoulder as he led him down the enormous high-ceilinged hall to the French doors that opened into the yard. "Esther, Elmore is a resident at Mass General . . . surgical unit, is that right?"

"That's correct. I've got another two years of residency."

"It's a good thing you're at Mass General and not City Hospital," Herman said to Elmore as they exited the house onto the rolling and manicured lawn. "I hear they've closed five or six wards there, including the men's surgical unit."

"Oh, yes," said Elmore. "You're quite right. The men's, the women's, the medical beds, even the gynecological ward."

Harry and Esther were following close behind. Speechlessly they turned to each other. "Did he just say what I think he said?" Esther whispered.

Harry shook his head. "Get your mind out of the sailor's gutter, Esther," he said. "Honestly. What kind of gentleman would he be, saying something like that in the presence of a lady the first time he meets her?"

"Or even the fiftieth. Father," Esther called, pulling Harry to a stop. "I'm going to run back and get my shawl."

"I'm going to help her," said Harry, and turning, they hightailed it back inside through the open doors. He put his arm around his sister. "That's what you get for galli-vanting with medical students. I don't know how you'll be able to resist."

"Who said I'm going to resist, Harry?" countered Esther as they ambled through the center hall, both having no intention of going back outside. Lightly she shoved her brother. "Father continues to make the vulgar error," she said, "that to a woman, *love* is her whole existence."

"Isn't it?" said Harry, at the very moment Ben opened

61

the front door and walked in unannounced, followed by his mother and the three chattering Porters.

"Mrs. Shaw, hello, how good of you to come today," said Harry to Ben's mother. Ellen Shaw was the epitome of deceptive appearances. She was tiny and round, had a pleasant nondescript face, an unfashionably short, austere hairstyle, was friendly to strangers and carried a benevolent smile. Yet she was Harry's brother-in-arms when it came to unpopular political notions and a lot less silent about them at the dinner table.

Carrying a bunch of yellow bananas like flowers, Ben headed straight for Esther. "Est! Look what I have."

"Oh, no. Not bananas again."

"Esther, you simply *must* develop a taste for them." Ben pulled off one of the bananas like a rose and handed it to a reluctant but smiling Esther.

"You mean a *dis*taste," said Esther, taking one from his hands. Her entire demeanor changed. She became soft like chiffon, almost girlish.

A pristine Alice approached Harry.

"Hello, darling," she said, raising her face for a kiss.

"Hello, dear." He kissed her cheek. "What have you been up to today?"

"I played tennis after church, and then went riding, as always."

"You look so fresh, you don't look as if you've been playing tennis and riding." His hand went to her back.

"I cleaned up, darling, before I arrived at your father's house."

"And you clean up *quite* nicely," purred Harry. "Oh, hello, Mrs. Porter, Mr. Porter, sir. How are you this afternoon?"

Alice didn't look like anyone's idea of a girl who managed lumberyards and sawmills, and this is what appealed to

Harry. She was petite, blonde and a debutante. A few years before she met Harry, she had been one of the most sought-after young ladies in Boston, bejeweled, dazzlingly dressed, spending the entire of her eighteenth year dancing and glad-handing at coming-out balls and social functions. By the time Harry had met her, she had already been courted by all the Lowells and the Cabots, and he wasn't forced to compete. As if he would have. He deemed her out of his league, and it took several slight breaches of etiquette by Alice herself to show Harry she was interested before he invited her and her best friend Belinda for a stroll along the Charles with him and Ben. Belinda wasn't what Ben was looking for, but Alice was what Harry had been looking for. Alice, whose clothes were crisp, her blonde hair ironed, her makeup flawless —and yet who rode horses and canoes, played tennis and golf, was a senior member of four different charities, arranging fundraisers, cookie bakes, plant sales, old book swaps to raise money for hospitals for the poor. She read history and loved poetry. She was bright and indefatigable, and it was she who chose Harry over the swarm of other eligible Boston men and now stood confidently and silently by his side, while Ben fraternized with Esther.

"Are you going to eat one, or aren't you?" Ben said to her. "They are the future."

"If I eat one, will you promise to stop bringing them?" Esther said, peeling down the skin. "*Bananas* are the future?"

"Your brother's friend is not entirely wrong, Esther," said Elmore in the banquet-hall dining room that afternoon. "Tropical fruits *are* the future." He was seated to the right of Herman, the most honored place at the table. Even Ellen Shaw, usually Herman's most welcome guest, today sat one demoted place over. Herman's two children did not sit by their father. Ever. Ben sat there once, after he had been accepted at Harvard ("On a scholarship, no less!" pointed out a delighted Herman. "Didn't cost his sainted mother a penny.") Alice sat there half a handful of times, because Herman was quite fond of her. Often Alice's father sat there, because they were friends and business partners. But not today. Alice sat between her mother and father. Ben sat between Harry and Esther, who was seated mutely next to the verbose Elmore.

"I know I'm not wrong," Ben said, casting a sideways look at Esther, as if to say, I need this person to approve of my bananas?

"Benjamin is soon starting his last year at Harvard," Herman explained to Elmore. "He has just changed his concentration to engineering. He is thinking about his future."

"Giving bananas to my sister is engineering his future?" asked Harry. "See," he said, "while Ben is concentrating on tropical fruit, I, who am also, *inter alia*, starting my last year at Harvard, am writing my senior thesis on the Civil War. I thought you'd be impressed, Father. I'm writing it about Ben's relatives."

"Why would that impress me?" Herman wanted to know. "You're always writing about one war or another. You're consumed with other people's conflicts."

"Be *that* as it may," Harry said, "my main topic is a juxtaposition between Robert Gould Shaw and Philip Nolan."

"Not again!" Herman exclaimed. "Didn't you do an essay on Nolan in secondary school? Philip Nolan, the man without a country?"

"I wrote a five-page paper on him in Andover," said Harry. "Hardly the same as a university dissertation."

"But, son, Nolan's story is only about five pages."

Everyone laughed.

"Thirty-nine, sir."

"I beg your pardon. You can read it in its entirety while waiting for Jones to serve the second course." Herman steadied his gaze on Harry. "You know this story by heart. Why are you taking the easy way out?"

"It's never easy, sir," Harry said.

"Be that as it may," Herman said, "what I'm interested in is whether you've heard from the Porcellians."

"Not yet." Harry looked into his bowl. "But fall semester doesn't begin for almost two months. There is time."

Porcellian was *the* final club at Harvard, the club of all clubs, members of which included the governor of New York, Teddy Roosevelt, chief justice of the Massachusetts Supreme Court, Oliver Wendell Holmes, oh, and Herman Barrington. But not yet Harold Barrington. This was Harry's last chance, and everybody knew it.

"The potato soup is delicious, Herman," Ellen said, intruding to change the subject. "Bernard has outdone himself."

"I'd like my butler to bring the second course. We're having cod today. And then pork chops with roast potatoes."

"The scallops wrapped in bacon were also wonderful," Ellen continued, giving Harry a sharp look as if to say, stop talking.

"I'm working to graduate first in my class, Father," Harry continued unheeding. "That counts for something, no?"

"Can't make a living from books, son," Herman said, ringing for Louis.

"Can't make a living from the Porcellian either," Harry countered quietly.

"Oh, but I heard," said jolly Orville, "that the legend

goes that if a member of the Porcellian doesn't make his first million by the time he is forty, the club gives it to him. Is that true, Herman?"

"I wouldn't know, Orville. Perhaps Harry will be given a chance to find out."

In front of Alice's parents! Harry looked across the table at Orville who, as if on cue, without even bothering to clear his throat, opened his mouth and, buttering another piece of crusty bread, said what he said nearly every week at Sunday dinner: "You know, I'm grooming Alice to take over the family business upon my retirement."

And then there would be an awkward silence while the guests scraped the last of their salads and soup bowls. Just like today.

Harry ate all of his cod before he filled the silence with his stock reply to Orville, steady and ready as the hour chime.

"Fortunately," Harry said, "my father is not even close to retiring. Are you, Father?" In his precise syntax, Harry inserted the same two sentences into the same pause after the same Porter preamble Sunday after Sunday.

Herman, who often said nothing, today was clearly feeling objectionable himself.

"No, I'm not close to retiring," he agreed, but didn't stop there. "How can I retire? I've got no one to take over the family business."

"Oh!" exclaimed Alice. "Could you pass the biscuits, please?"

Esther refused to keep her mouth shut. "Alice, darling," she said, passing the bread basket across the table. "Perhaps you can also take over *our* father's business? Father has such high regard for you."

Harry laughed. Alice chuckled uncomfortably into her

napkin. Before anyone else could take a breath, Esther calmly continued. "He loves you, Alice, like a daughter he never had."

Everyone got feverishly busy cutting up their meat—everyone except Ben.

"Mr. Barrington, sir," Ben said, putting down his knife and fork, "I don't know if Harry mentioned it, but our Lime Alley buildings are full."

"Harry didn't mention it," said Herman. "Harry was busy telling me we were charging too much rent to the immigrants."

"We are," Harry said.

"Why don't we just let them stay there for free then?"

"I don't know. Why don't we?"

Herman put down his own fork. "Because of the Sherman Act of 1890, son. Also, do you really feel that able-bodied human beings should not have to pay rent on their dwellings or are you just being contrary? Residences that someone's money renovated, upgraded, painted, put water and plumbing in, ran electricity into?"

"Not just someone's money, Herman," said a rotund and robust Orville Porter. "Yours."

"Harold, answer me, do you feel all that should be received *gratis*?"

Ben kicked Harry under the table and hastily continued. "Harry is just joking with you, sir—"

"Actually, I—"

Ben kicked him again, harder. "The next liner is due in on Tuesday, and we're out of room. Three full ships are coming in week after next. What do we do? We have nowhere to put anyone."

Herman went back to buttering his bread and pouring himself a drink. "Benjamin, I'm taking care of it. We have

67

four more buildings nearly ready on Charter and Unity; almost two hundred apartments."

"Will they be ready by Monday?"

Looking Ben over with admiration, Herman smiled. "Probably not by Monday, but very soon. You boys have done a fine job managing the buildings for me. Too good a job. I don't know what I'm going to do when you go back to school."

"Well, next year your son will graduate," Ben said. "He can manage Lime Alley for you full time."

Now it was Harry's turn to kick Ben under the table.

"I'm not holding my breath," said Herman. "In the meantime, Unity and Charter just need painting and some furniture."

"By Monday?"

"Ben, have them move in, give them a discount on the rent, and tell them we'll paint and furnish in the next week or so and as a bonus keep their rent the same."

"Good idea. Perhaps we can also convert the back of Old Wells House, sir? I know there are at least eleven apartments we could put back there."

Herman nodded his approval. "Good thinking. I'll talk to my man first thing Monday morning."

"We have one apartment available on Lime Alley," Harry interjected. "The family decided not to stay. Left after one night."

"Ah, *yes.*" Ben said that so dramatically that everyone's ears perked up. "I'm being facetious," he assured them, seeing their curious expressions. "Really, Mother."

"Not entirely, um, facetious," said Harry.

"Harry's right," Ben said, hand on his heart. "Truth is, I *have* been hit by a raven-haired thunderbolt."

Everyone smiled in delight, except Harry, and Esther, who

68

became paler if that were possible, lost another shade of herself, and squeezed her suddenly tense white fingers around the tines of the fork, as if trying to stab herself with them.

Herman followed his delight with advice. "Benjamin, I hope it's just an infatuation."

"No, sir," said Ben. "It's more than that, I'm afraid."

"Ben, stop it," said Harry.

"Yes, Ben, stop it," echoed Esther, wilting noticeably by dessert, rum cake with coffee, shoulders sunk with maidenhood.

"Where is the family from?"

"Sicily. They got tired of living under a mountain that kept vomiting fire."

Herman shook his head. "Do yourself a favor, Ben, stay away from unsuitable Sicilian females. They're trouble."

"For more reasons, Father, than you can possibly imagine," Harry muttered under his breath, but loud enough for everyone to hear.

"I know them all," said Herman.

"Not this one."

"Son, why do you think you're the only one who knows everything?" Herman's attention turned back to Ben. "You should stay away from things in which there is no future," he went on.

"Oh, I agree, sir. The bananas are the future. I'm sticking with them."

"There's no future in them either. They're a funny little fruit that will never catch on. But I'm pleased they amuse you."

"Mark my words, sir," said Ben. "They will absolutely catch on. We've got a businessman here in Boston, Andrew Preston, who started the United Fruit Company. He is one of the reasons I switched to engineering."

"A man who runs a banana company," Elmore asked, "is the reason you're studying engineering?"

"Ben," asked Harry, "isn't Andrew Preston your mother's friend?"

"Oh?" said Herman with a sly smile at Ellen. *"That's disappointing."*

While Ellen blushed, a nodding Ben was all infectious smiles. Even Esther didn't look quite so pale anymore: they had stopped talking about Italian girls in the North End.

"He's a brilliant man," Ben said, "this Preston fellow. A true visionary."

"Ellen, do you agree with your son?"

"I reserve all comment."

"Is he a handsome man?" Herman pressed on.

"I *really* reserve all comment," said Ellen.

"Well, that is *truly* disappointing."

Everyone laughed and the tension lifted. Louis served raspberry sherbet to cleanse the palate. Raspberries were in season and Bernard had made the sherbet from scratch earlier that afternoon. Harry smiled to himself as he asked Louis for second helpings. How did Ben do it? Make all situations lighter, better?

But for Ben, the bananas were not just a conversational play at the dinner table to help his friend. Later, by the fire in the library, sipping some brandy, he continued to extol the virtues of the export business to a relaxed Herman, an attentive Esther, and a delightfully disagreeable Elmore. "I really am thinking of going into exports, sir," Ben said to Herman. "The bananas are not going to walk to Boston by themselves."

"Perhaps it's best they don't," said Esther.

Ben bowed to her comically. "They need to be grown. That requires development of not only the most efficient

70

farming techniques, but also construction of housing for the workers. The bananas need to be collected, appraised, counted, packaged and crated. Someone has to do all this."

"And someone has to make the crates," Herman said, seeing the nails because all he carried was a hammer.

"First they have to procure the lumber to make the crates," Orville cut in, seeing the nails because all he carried was a hammer.

"Absolutely," Ben agreed, who carried a number of tools with him. "Even lumber has to be delivered and processed into an end-product for the crate-making. The crates should be made locally, in Costa Rica. Which means someone there has to be taught to make them."

"How difficult could that be?" asked Harry.

"Well, and someone has to be sent there to teach them," said Irma Porter, who had once been a teacher.

"Right, Mrs. Porter," Ben agreed. "And then the bananas have to travel eight thousand miles by ship or by land to Boston where I can offer them to an underwhelmed Esther."

"No, no," Esther said, straight-faced. "I enjoy them very much. Have you got any more?"

Ben gave her an exaggerated glare, but the Porters didn't stay and partake of the conversation further. It was getting late and their carriage had to travel quite a way south across the Charles, to Brookline.

After they left and Herman came back inside the library, he resumed the conversation as if no time had passed. "I still don't see how this is an engineering problem, Benjamin," he said.

"It's nothing but," said Ben, happy to keep talking about it. "From beginning to end. What complicates matters is that bananas do not stay fresh for long. Mercilessly they continue to ripen until they rot. Refrigeration has been shown to stave off spoilage. So now there is one more thing to think of, to build, to generate. The fruit needs to be picked while still green and transported from Costa Rica to California, then across our entire country. Railroad tracks must be built through Central America, an unwelcoming terrain if ever there was one. And now, to answer your question, sir, this is the part where the engineering comes in." Ben grinned. "This is also the part my sainted mother, as you call her, is least happy about."

"Oh, no," Ellen said from the couch when she overheard. "Don't start that again. And why are you all standing there like giraffes?"

They finally got off their feet, and made themselves comfortable on the sofas and chairs. Louis poured more brandy and relit Herman's cigar.

Ben continued excitedly. "I'm writing several detailed proposals to the Isthmian Exploration Commission to reopen the research into the efficacy question of building a canal that cuts straight across Central America, either in Nicaragua, which is close to Costa Rica and my bananas, or Panama, which happens to be geologically better suited for a canal."

"Lunacy!" Ellen exclaimed. "He wants to build a canal in Panama." For a moment there was silence in the library, even the crackling fire quiet.

Elmore spoke. "Mr. Shaw, how can you say a canal would be geographically better in Panama?"

"I didn't say geographically."

"Perhaps like your friend Harry, you ought to study history instead of engineering."

"I *have* studied history," Ben said. "Also geology. Which is why I know for a fact Panama is the best place."

"Have you read what happened to the French ten years

ago?" asked Elmore with polite disdain. "During *their* botched national attempt to build a canal in Panama?"

"Elmore is right, Ben," said Esther. "I don't know what you're thinking. Panama is too far away."

"It's close to the bananas, Est."

"This isn't about distance," Elmore said. "It's about the French losing over 20,000 men chasing this supreme folly."

"Not to the canal," said Ben. "To influenza."

"It wasn't influenza," Elmore returned. "It was malaria. And the reasons for the malaria are not going to go away by the time you send Americans to Panama."

"Ben isn't going there himself," Esther said quickly. "He's just writing a report."

Ben frowned. "I thought a virus killed the French?"

Elmore nodded. "Yes, but spread by what means?"

"How should I know?" Ben was irritated to veer so off topic. "Sneezing?"

"Mosquitoes," Elmore replied. "Perhaps if you get rid of those, you can build your canal."

"More to the point," Herman interrupted, "you don't need a canal to sail a boat on the Caribbean. Ben, I wonder if your mother is right about this one."

"I am always right," said Ellen.

"With all respect, my mother is wrong on this one most of all," said Ben. "Tell them the real reason you're against it, Mother. Despite your budding friendship with Mr. Preston—"

"I am set against the looming war with Spain," Ellen declared. "Spain has deep colonial interests in Cuba and the Philippines."

"And most important to me, Colombia," Ben added, "which is about to go to war with Panama. America has no choice but to defend Panama with whom they have a treaty. Naturally, Mother is on the side against America."

"America must stay out of it!"

"They can't."

Ellen threw up her hands.

"Now, now. Many people are against the war, Benjamin," Herman said diplomatically. Everyone knew he wasn't one of them. "Mark Twain for one. Why give your poor mother a hard time?"

"He lives and breathes for nothing else, Herman," said Ellen.

"I know what you mean, Ellen," said Herman without so much as a glance at Harry.

"But it doesn't matter," Ellen continued. "Because Ben knows his Aunt Josephine and I, along with the esteemed Erving Winslow, are heading the newly chartered Anti-Imperialist League to protest U.S. involvement precisely in places like Panama."

"I wish impatiently for the opportunity to hear your side of things," said Ben. "When and where will your little society meet? I'll bring Harry. Maybe Esther too."

"Thursday evenings. Old South Meeting House," she added nobly. "A perfect place for dissent and open debate for people like us. Seven o'clock."

"You're quite the revolutionary, Mother," Ben said. "I'll be sure to make my appearance."

"Ben," said Ellen, "you may come, but you're absolutely forbidden to collect even one of the five thousand signatures you need for the canal exploratory commission to reopen their research."

Harry was utterly delighted. "Benji, you're joining your mother's newly minted league *against* the development of the canal to collect signatures to help *build* the canal?"

Ben looked tremendously pleased with himself.

"Not even one signature, Benjamin," Ellen repeated. "Not even your own."

It was Elmore who burst Ben's balloon. "You'll never get enough signatures," he said in his high-horse voice. "Because the canal is a terrible idea. It's a waste of our resources."

Ben tilted his head in fake deference. "Yes, I am well aware that many people hold this opinion."

"It's the Henry Ford fiasco," Ellen said. "Did you *hear* that the man just formed an automobile company in Detroit?"

"I heard, Mother, yes. Everybody's heard."

"Well, Ford thinks his horseless carriages are going to catch on with the general public," Ellen went on, her shoulders squaring with derision. "There's been *no* evidence of that. It will never be as popular as the modern bicycle."

"I completely agree with you, Mrs. Shaw," concurred the medical student.

"It's another folly, if you ask me," Ellen said. "Pure vain folly."

"Just like the canal," Elmore underscored.

Ben would not be provoked into being insulting. "From an engineering perspective alone, a successfully built canal will be a man-made wonder of the modern world," he said. "Perhaps like Henry Ford's horseless carriage?"

"And if it's not successful?"

Ben shrugged. "If we don't build it, it will definitely not be successful."

Elmore shook his head. "You'll all die—like the French. You won't be able to get rid of the mosquitoes."

"Elmore is right, Ben," said Esther.

"No, he isn't. We'll put up nets to keep them out."

"You'll have to put the nets up all around Panama," Elmore said.

"If that's what it takes," said Ben.

Herman shook his head in amazement at Ben and got up. "Ellen, your son is astounding," he said. "But I must bid you all a good night. My day starts early tomorrow." He kissed Ellen's hand before he left.

The long evening ended shortly thereafter. Harry, with Ben at the open door of the horse carriage, said to his friend, "There are no superlatives left for you. How did you do it?" Ellen was already inside and waiting for her son.

Ben smiled. "Anything to entertain your father." He patted Harry on the shoulder. "Don't forget to remind him about Old Wells House." He held on to Harry's arm for a moment. "However, old friend, since I've just helped you out . . ."

"Name it."

Ben lowered his voice so his mother wouldn't hear. "Come with me to Lawrence next Saturday."

"Except that."

"Harry!"

"I'm serious. Anything else. You know how much I hate to agree with my father . . ."

"Yes, Mr. Objection Maker, we all know this, including your father."

"Yes, because you and your mother see eye to eye on everything. But in this one narrow circumstance, my father happens to be right about the girl. And you didn't even tell him the main reason why. But *I* know. Ben, it's ruinous."

"Don't be so melodramatic," Ben said, dragging Harry away from the coach. "You're not writing a book. We're going to hop on a train and take a little ride north into the country. We're going to explore and research Lawrence for your father. To see if there are any real estate investment opportunities there." Ben adopted a businesslike tone. "Also, and this is critical, I absolutely must get five thousand signatures in order to bring this Panama Canal study before the Commission."

"Now you're going to *Lawrence* to get canal signatures?"

"*We.* Come on, you can't spend the entire summer reading in your chair."

"I also work, remember? And Saturdays I have a seminar on the economic history of the United States. At the pleasure of Dr. Callender. I can't miss it."

Ben waved him away. "Seminar ends at eleven. And you have many a time missed it. No excuses." He hopped inside the carriage, closed the door and stuck his head out. "Also, you have it all wrong," he said quietly to his friend. "We have business to conduct. Afterward, if there is time, we *may* pay a brief visit to the Attaviano family."

"We don't know where they live."

"Oh yes, we do." Ear to ear was Ben's smile. "We helped them send the telegram to announce their arrival, remember?"

"Why don't we just drive this carriage off a cliff instead?" said Harry, slamming shut the door as the horse clopped away, and faint in the night he heard Ben's tenor voice singing, "*My wild Italian rose, the sweetest flower that grows . . .*"

When Harry turned around, Esther was standing rigidly behind him on the portico, waving goodbye.

Chapter Seven
IMMIGRANTS, DEBUTANTES, STUDENTS

1

"WHERE in the world did you get this?" Salvo asked. "You must have stolen it."

They were looking at the suit Gina was holding out for her brother. "What are you complaining about?" she said. "You think God would help you find work in a stolen suit? You'd be trampled by a horse before you got to the end of Canal Street."

Salvo examined the wool trousers, the finely made jacket, the waistcoat. She had even got him a worn white shirt, a gray tie and some used shoes. He dressed while she watched and then they both stood in front of the mirror and appraised him.

"You should trim your hair," she said. "It's too wild."

"You're a fine one to speak."

"I'm not a man in a suit."

"Where did you get it?"

"Society of St. Vincent de Paul," she replied.

"I don't know what that is."

"A mission to help the poor. Yesterday I was asking around . . ."

"I thought you were looking for a job."

"I was. For you."

"*Sciocca ragazza.* I can look for my own work, thank you."

"You were out yesterday in the clothes you sailed in on. How did that go?"

"I don't see you having a job either," he muttered.

"Yes, but today you have a suit."

Salvo smiled. "I look quite dashing, don't I?"

"Yes. If you cut your hair you'd look almost American."

"I didn't see that vagabond you were so keen on with a haircut."

Stepping away, Gina busied herself with a sudden need to rid the sewing machine of loose thread. "I don't know what you're talking about," she said. "But listen, don't waste your time applying to be a machinist at the Pacific Mill."

"Okay. Why would I? And why not?"

"Their 'jobs offered' signs are everywhere," she said. "But they only hire skilled union men."

"And I'm neither."

"Right. But perhaps at the glaziers? Or the shoemakers?"

"I don't know how to cobble shoes, Gia," Salvo said. "Why do you keep mentioning all the things I can't do? Why don't *you* get work as a plumber? No, I'm going to apply at the restaurants. They must need cooks."

Gina said nothing.

"What?"

"They pay poorly."

"How do you know this?"

"I asked."

"Who could you possibly ask? We got here five minutes ago."

"We got here four days ago, and what do you think I was doing yesterday?"

"Looking for work—or did you also sin not only by your indolence but by lying to our mother?"

"I asked at St. Vincent's."

"It's like the Boston Public Library, this St. Vincent's," said Salvo. "Maybe they have work too as well as information?"

"Oh, they do." She sighed. "Not paid work, though."

Salvo laughed. "That's not work. That's a hobby."

"Okay, Mr. Clever. But in the meantime I found out what jobs you shouldn't bother with."

He put his palm over her mouth. "You think *you're* the only clever one? I know what I'm doing. I'll find some day work."

"Day labor is neither stable, nor well-paying. Don't you want to move out of this boarding house? I saw such nice houses near the Common. They have porches and big windows, and the streets are lovely and lined with trees."

"*Prima le cose,*" he said. "First work, then a house. And don't get all fancy on me. You know we can't live in the nice areas."

"It's not that nice. It's for people like us."

"Mimoo asked you to find us a different church," Salvo said, trying in vain to slick back his unruly hair. "Did you? She didn't like the priest on Sunday."

"Mimoo is full of opinions. It's the only Italian church in town."

"She said Italian is not a must. Proper Catholic is a must."

Gina whistled in surprise. "St. Mary's of the Assumption that runs St. Vincent's is some church. Father O'Reilly is the priest there. He's famous around these parts."

"Where could you possibly hear that? No, don't tell me . . ."

"St. Vincent's," she confirmed, pausing. "I hope to hear from the mill today," she said.

"About what?"

"A job as a wool sorter."

"So you did look for a job!" Salvo scoffed. "I thought we agreed you wouldn't work at the mills?"

"It's skilled labor, Salvo," she said. "Many people crave those jobs."

"What in the world could *you* possibly know about wool?"

"Clearly something." She shrugged. "The manager at Washington told me I apparently have a gift of hand sensitivity." She smiled. "I can tell the difference in the quality of the fleece just from touching it. I'm fast too. He gave me a pound of fleece to separate, based on curl, length, softness. He said he'd never seen anyone do it so quickly. So he wants me to interview with his boss."

"What are you going to wear?"

She flared her dress with her hands.

"Should've gotten *yourself* a dress instead of me a suit, sister," Salvo said, looking over her drab rags. "It's okay. You don't want to be a fleece sorter anyway."

"Oh, really? Angela gets paid three dollars a week for over fifty hours of work. You want to know how much they will pay me if I get this job?"

"How much?"

"Twelve dollars."

Now it was Salvo's turn to whistle. "Oh, how badly you need to be a sorter," he said, hugging her.

"That's what I thought. Go kill 'em, Salvo. And stay away from carpenters."

Don't count me out, Salvo whispered into the mirror as he adjusted his tie and hid the frayed collar under the jacket before leaving.

He came back late that night, his suit dusty and soiled. They had already eaten and Mimoo and Pippa—who had cleaned three large houses together, working over sixteen hours—were exhausted and asleep. Angela was upstairs visiting with a girlfriend. Gina dutifully waited for Salvo on his couch, nodding off with an English book on her lap.

"How did it go?" she said as soon as she heard him open the door. "Are you hungry?"

"Starved," he said, sitting at the table, crossing himself, and gulping down the bread with salt and olive oil before he could speak. "I did all right. I have work for tomorrow. I found work for a week as a grinder." He almost smiled but was too tired. "Don't need a suit for that."

"No," she said sitting with him, putting her head on the table.

"How did you do? Why do you smell of sheep?"

"I washed in the river. What, didn't help?" She shrugged. "I must get a new dress at the mission."

"Did you get the job?"

"Sort of." She said it without enthusiasm. "They hired me, Salvo, but they didn't want to pay me the going rate. They said other women would get extremely upset to see a young kid like me taking away the job they spend years trying to get promoted into. It's union work. So they said they could hire me but pay me only five dollars as non-union."

"I hope you told them in perfect Italian what they could do with their sheep sorting."

"Except I really want to move to a different house," Gina said. "What I told them was I'd work part-time for five dollars. If they wanted to give me half the pay, I'd only work half the time. Then no one could complain."

"Did they agree to this?"

"Reluctantly. The manager liked me. He thought I was productive." She was too tired for inflection. She showed Salvo her hands, dried and abraded from the thorns and burrs, from rough wet and dry work. Hives were forming on her fingers from the sheep grease.

"Gia!"

"Well, I know. It's not great. It's better than being a skirter and wool washer, don't you think? Tagging off manure-filled fleece. Yuk. And Washington has the nicest mending room in Lawrence, Salvo. That's where I want to get promoted to. Ladies work there, and they sit behind a table and the room is sunny with big windows. I would get to dress up. So I took *this*, hoping in time for *that*." She pulled out a large shopping bag from under the table, stuffed to the brim with clean pale fleece. "I got four more just like this. Almost a pound total."

"You *stole* from your new employer?" Salvo couldn't believe it.

"Why do you attribute the worst motives to me? I didn't steal it, I took it."

"Oh! Fine difference."

"They told me I could take it. It's the discard pile. Downrights and abbs and breech." She shrugged. "Don't worry, it's been thoroughly washed."

Salvo inhaled the bean soup, the half block of mozzarella and fell away from the table, wiping his mouth. "What are we going to do with your sheep hiding under the table?"

"First thing I have to do is pay St. Vincent's back for your suit," she said. "Then buy me a dress. After that I have a plan. You'll see."

"You and your plans."

They fell asleep on Salvo's couch, sitting up, leaning against each other.

2

Alice stood in front of her closet and waited for Trieste, her lady's maid. Trieste was late and Alice was already running behind a carefully constructed schedule, though it was barely eight in the morning. She decided on a dark blue wool skirt and a white lace blouse. She kept her jewelry simple and was already putting on light makeup—by herself. She thought her face looked swollen from having slept too long on one side, having been in bed since nine the night before. She made a mental note not to sleep on her side, because it creased her cheeks, made her look puffy. But she needed her beauty sleep. She worked hard during the day and she needed to get proper rest at night. Mother said so, and it made perfect sense. Ever since she had been a little girl she loved to sleep, though the opportunities for unabashed rest were lessening with the years. Once she turned eighteen, and had gone to forty balls and functions, she just got busier and busier.

After a short knock on the door, Trieste came in with a tray of tea and soft biscuits with jam. She apologized for running late, but they couldn't get the stove to turn on, to heat up the water for the tea. Trieste thought an engineer needed to be called in. Alice said she didn't care about the silly old tea, "but what I do care about, Trieste," she continued, "is that a shipment of six thousand logs is waiting for me at Roxbury, and do you know where I am? Not at Roxbury. That is my problem. I'm going to be late for all my appointments."

"I apologize, Miss Alice. I know you like your hot tea in the morning."

"Not more than I enjoy being on time, Trieste."

Trieste apologized again, while quickly spreading jam and clotted cream on the scones.

"Where is your day journal, Miss Alice? Would you like to go over your schedule?"

Irritated, Alice pointed to her bedside. She had looked at the schedule the night before, but she couldn't remember anything past the sawmill. She continued applying her makeup while Trieste read aloud the day's events.

"At 8:30 you're supposed to be in Roxbury . . ."

"Where I am not. What's next?"

"At ten you have a late breakfast meeting at the Mayflower Club to go over the final menu for the annual fall bazaar in September."

"How long will that take? I have lunch with Daddy at noon."

"Lunch with Mr. Porter is at 12:45 at the Bavarian Club back here in Brookline. Your carriage will be waiting for you on Commonwealth."

"How long from there to the Club?"

"Probably forty-five minutes."

Alice sighed. She had a bite of scone and a sip of tea. She only liked apricot jam, and today Trieste had given her blackcurrant. Nothing was going right. She made no comment. She never forgot her manners no matter what she was feeling like inside.

"Lunch until two o'clock, at which time your father and you will ride out to Timber Mills for a board meeting on next year's fiscal projections."

Alice set her jaw. That was her least favorite part of her father's business: sitting in a stuffy room with closed windows going over numbers on paper. She liked the inspection of the lumber, dealing with actual product despite the many problems that arose with shipments—the quality of woods, dampness, rot. All of it was better than board meetings, and best of all were the quarterly river drives, when she traveled to Maine for weeks at a time and oversaw the forestry operations from felling to bucking. Walking atop the huge tied-together trunks floating in shallow rivers was a joy akin to riding horses—dangerous and thrilling. She would do that every day if she could. Board meetings were another matter entirely.

"How long is that meeting?"

"Until 4:30."

She groaned. She could do that in front of Trieste, make noises of dissatisfaction she could not make in the outside world. "Am I going to have any fun at all today?" she asked plaintively.

"At 5:15 you have tea at the Boston Public Library. Your father has made a generous donation to BPL, and they want you to approve their catalogue purchases."

Alice brushed out her hair before she pinned it up, appraising her fine features in the mirror. She was delicate and dainty, she had a small nose, a perfectly formed mouth, big blue eyes, high cheekbones, and thin silky blonde hair.

"Please tell me the rest of my week is not as full, Trieste."

86

"It is quite busy, Miss Alice," Trieste said, leafing through the subsequent pages. "Ah, but I see here, on Saturday you have some free time. Harry has begged off Saturday's activities. He said he was helping Ben with some engineering problems."

Alice sighed. "Can you schedule a longer trail ride for me on Saturday then?"

"Will do, Miss Alice. But tonight you have an appointment at 6:30 at the Back Bay salon for a manicure before your evening."

Alice glanced at her polished nails. "I don't need it," she said. "They were done just two days ago."

"Yes, but after the lumberyard, they will be a mess."

"I'll be careful."

"If they become rough and cracked before your dinner, then what?"

Alice sighed. "What time is dinner?"

"Harry is meeting you at the Hasty Pudding Theatricals promptly at 8:45 in the evening. The show starts at 9:15. You'll have just enough time, if you rush, to return home to change. I want to lay out your dress now, so we can be quicker later. Your mother is coming with you."

Alice pointed to her closet. "On the right-hand side is my mauve velvet and organza dress. I received it as a present from Mother last Christmas and have not had a chance to wear it."

Trieste retrieved it from the closet. "Beautiful," she said. "But we will have to redo your makeup."

"Will you be here for that, or will the stove be broken again?"

"I will be here. Shall I arrange for some hot canapés and wine while you get ready?"

"Cheese and crackers only. And a glass of sherry. I don't

want to get too full. Hasty Pudding feeds us till midnight."

"Quite right. The show is over at one a.m. Can I release the driver? Harry is staying at the university and indicated that his driver will be more than happy to take you and Mrs. Porter home."

"That'll be fine." She was glad to have rested last night. It was going to be a full week. She turned to Trieste, her hair up, her face flawless, her dress perfectly pressed. "What do you think?"

"As usual, exquisite, Miss Alice," said Trieste, straightening out one of the pleats on the skirt. "I will get your boots and coat and umbrella ready."

Alice glanced outside her floor-to-ceiling windows. The morning sun was blazing.

"It will rain," said Trieste. "As soon as you get to the sawmill, it will pour. You know Boston."

3

"How do you not see what a giant mistake this is?" Harry said to Ben after they boarded the train.

"I don't see even what a little mistake it is." Ben had come prepared. He had brought pamphlets about Panama, information about the canal, brochures about geographical advantages and advertisements for railroad jobs in Central America. He also came dressed in his best suit and hat. Harry looked as if he had forgotten to shave. He had been up late reading, so he was late getting up, having forgotten what train they were catching. He barely made it to North Union Station to find Ben pacing the platform.

"You are impossible," Ben said. "Please tell me it was

Alice that kept you up so late on Friday night you nearly missed our train."

"Paine's *The American Crisis*," replied Harry, disheveled but smiling. "'The cunning of the fox is as murderous as the violence of the wolf.'"

"*That* kept you up? Why didn't you try some *Common Sense* instead? 'Our calamity is heightened by reflecting that we furnish the means by which we suffer.'"

"Who is suffering?" Harry said. "I was never more happy than to stay in and read." Once the 9:05 got moving, he examined the papers Ben carried. "Ben, you've gone insane."

Ben took his research away. "I don't recall asking your opinion."

"I offer it freely."

"Shut up."

"You think your profits and bananas are going to sway an Italian girl?"

"Two separate issues."

"Why don't I think so?"

"Because you understand nothing."

Harry pulled the hat over his face and settled into his seat, thinking he might have a quick nap. "I hope she never discovers," he said, "your fickle and changeable nature. That last year it wasn't bananas that kept you up late but boric acid. You don't want her to draw any conclusions."

Ben knocked the hat off Harry's head. "Sit up straight," he said. "We have an hour to learn what we can about Lawrence."

"And how, pray tell, do we do this?" The train had been moving for five minutes.

From his bag Ben produced two books and a dozen pamphlets. Harry groaned and grabbed for his hat. "Start

89

reading," Ben said. "I'm counting on you. We have to fake knowledge."

"Now there's a way to win a girl's heart," said Harry. "Deceive her."

"All right, paragon of virtue, let's begin." Ben opened the book on the history of Lawrence and stuck it under Harry's face. "And I suppose you've been straight with Alice and told her you have no intention of doing anything, ever, but reading books."

"She hasn't asked." Harry busied himself with the introductory chapter. "We are going to impress a fifteen-year-old—sorry, a fourteen-year-old with arcane minutiae about a town she's been in for five minutes? Well thought out, sir."

Ben ignored him. "Look—are you studying? Lawrence was incorporated in 1853. Not even half a century ago."

"If that doesn't get her to fall in love with you, what will?"

Ben continued reading. "Smart businessmen saw that the Merrimack River was a plentiful source of electric power, so they dammed it with the Great Stone Dam above the city, past Andover, and then built textile mills on both north and south banks."

"I know for a fact that the damming of rivers is enticing to young girls."

"Ah! Did you know that in 1860 one of the mills collapsed and burned, killing over a hundred workers and injuring thousands? The Pemberton Mill."

"You are deranged."

"No, this is useful. We can wisely counsel her not to get a job there."

"I thought you just said it burned down?"

"They rebuilt it, numbskull. Did you know that Lawrence

has more immigrants per square mile, of which there are only six, than any other city in the world?"

"Six immigrants?"

"Six square miles."

"Useful as evidence for committing you," said Harry. "Are there any sanatoriums in Lawrence?"

"Immigrant girls from Ireland, France, Germany, Belgium, Poland"—Ben smiled—"and of course, Italy . . ."

Harry slunk down on his seat. "I will not come visit you in the pokey," he muttered. "Not even at Christmas."

"That's the difference between you and me, old boy," Ben said. "Because I will come and visit you in the pokey."

"Why would I be up the river? Do you see me being threatened with certain prison or risking death at the hands of an irate Italian male? I don't think so."

"Harry!" Ben stopped with the books for a moment, looking wistful, softened, dream-like. "Did you see her?"

"I could hardly avoid it."

"You have to admit . . . her mother trying to hide her under those awful clothes . . ."

"Not hide her, save her."

"Nothing could hide that girl. That hair, that mouth." Harry leaned back, his hat over his inscrutable face.

"Well?" Ben nudged him. "Thomas Paine, or a nubile beauty from Sicily?"

"Clearly Thomas Paine. I'd be asleep now in my bed."

"Do you remember the name of the street they live on?"

"Let's see . . . Crazy Street? Cuckoo Street? Commitment Street? Cranial Injury Inflicted by Enraged Sibling Street?"

"Canal Street! Thank you."

"I'm going to stop speaking."

"Harry, admit it, if you weren't so utterly uninterested in all women save Alice, you would be sitting on this train yourself."

"Ben Shaw, I hate to point out the startlingly obvious, but I *am* sitting on this train myself."

"Exactly!"

"Ugh."

"I'm surprised to learn that Lawrence is the world leader in the production of cotton and woven textiles. Are you?"

"Stunned."

They spent the rest of the ride bickering like this and alighted in Lawrence nearly an hour and a half later. After buying a quick bun at a local mart on Broadway, they walked to Essex Street, found an acceptably busy corner on Essex and Appleton, took out their clipboards and pamphlets, and began approaching anyone who was willing to stop and talk to them for a minute or two. After forty-five minutes of being cut off on, "Please can we have your signature to reopen the study on the advantages of building the Panama Canal to help American trade and the American economy—", after being ignored, insulted, pushed past, shouted at and misunderstood, they had collected six signatures.

"How many more?" Harry asked.

"Four thousand nine hundred and ninety-four. If you sign, then four thousand nine hundred and ninety-three."

Harry put down his clipboard. "I'll sign right now. Can we go home?"

"Yes—when we get a thousand signatures."

"Ben!"

"You're not even trying!"

"Can you do math? Are there even a thousand people in Lawrence?"

"A *hundred* thousand."

"How many?"

"I thought you'd read the pamphlet I gave you."

"I completely ignored it. Ben, you do understand, don't you, that these people don't speak English? They don't understand when you say, 'Study, advantages, Panama, canal, American, trade.' You say the word 'economy,' they hear gibberish, gibberish, gibberish."

"You're giving up already?"

"Aren't engineers required to do rudimentary math? If it took us nearly an hour to get five signatures . . ."

"Six with you."

"How long will it take us to walk back and catch the 3:20 back to Boston?"

"Harry? Ben?"

The female voice came from behind them. When they turned around, Gina stood before them smiling broadly. To say she looked unreservedly pleased would be to under-define her expression. Ben smiled broadly back. She was dressed in a green skirt and a white high-necked lace blouse, and she carried a basket on her forearm. Her hair was properly tied up. Next to her stood a skinny homely girl.

"Hello, Miss Attaviano." Ben was beaming. "And is this your cousin Angela?"

"No, this is Angela's friend Verity. Verity, Ben, Harry. Harry, Ben, Verity. I'm sorry, but I can't remember your family names." Gina smiled apologetically. "What are you two gentlemen doing here?"

"We are collecting signatures to open research on the construction of the Panama Canal," Ben said. "What about you?"

Gina pointed. "I live just down the street on Canal," she said.

"Oh, is *that* where you live?" said Ben. "So close. We had no idea."

"We are doing a bit of shopping. Negotiating for some

cheap fruit. Verity runs the mission bazaar table on Sundays and I'm helping her collect some things to sell to raise money for the poor." She smiled. "Like me." She cleared her throat. "I mean, poor like me, not sell like me."

Ben laughed. Harry took a step back. Ben took a step forward. "How is your family?"

"Very good. Thank you."

"Are you working?"

"More or less." She nodded. "We're doing okay. I'd invite you to the house, but it's so small, you wouldn't fit in our living room. We're hoping to get a bigger place soon."

"Are you going to go to school?" That was Harry. It was the first time he had spoken.

Verity nodded her head. "I tell her she should. They are trying to encourage more children to attend school and improve reading and writing."

"I'm literal," said Gina. "I can read. Even in English."

For some reason this amused Harry, who smiled from behind Ben, looked at his fine black shoes, fiddled with the hat in his hands, and said, "Going to school is good."

"Yes, but it doesn't pay me money," Gina said, squinting at him in the sun. Her shoulders were covered with a shawl, but her teeth sparkled, particularly white against her dark skin, her vivid lips. "I need to work," she said. "Make money, be independent."

"Education is so important," said Harry.

"So is paying your rent," said Gina. "And buying gloves."

"Let your mother and brother worry about that," Harry said.

"That's what I keep trying to tell her," Verity said. "Come to school with me." She was offputtingly skinny. She looked like a boy.

Ben just stood smiling. He paid attention to nothing but

94

the Sicilian girl. "So what *are* you selling at the bazaar, Gina?"

"A little bit of this, a little bit of that." She smiled back.

They moved to the side of the street to let rushing pedestrians pass and stood under an awning of a cigar shop. Verity eyed the two men curiously but suspiciously, especially Harry.

Foolish girl, Harry wanted to say to her, it's not me you need to watch out for. Meanwhile Ben and Gina stood next to each other, chatting.

"Gina, we should go," Verity said. "We promised the sisters we'd be back soon with the fruit."

"Soon is so vague, Ver," Gina returned.

"Yes, but we don't have any fruit yet."

Gina turned away from her friend. "How long are you gentlemen in town for?"

"For the afternoon," said Ben. "We need to get a thousand signatures, but unfortunately we're not having much luck. I'm afraid we'll have to return to Boston soon if we don't do better."

"A thousand signatures is a lot," Gina said. "How many do you have?"

"Six," Ben replied.

"Eight if you two girls sign," Harry said. "Oh, wait. You have to be over sixteen to sign."

"I *am* over sixteen!" Verity exclaimed. "I'm eighteen."

Ben cast Harry a look that said, you're just pure evil, aren't you? You had to go and bring up age.

"Though I can't sign, Ben," Gina said quickly, "perhaps I can help you? What do you say, Verity?"

"We said we'd be back."

"Look what a lovely afternoon it is. We're just out and about."

95

"Gina . . ."

"It's fine."

"Let's just go, G."

"Well, you go ahead, then. I'll stay and help."

Harry and Ben exchanged stunned looks. It was rare indeed in the circles in which they were born and raised to have a young girl remain even on a public street alone with two men. By rare, Harry meant unheard of. And Verity was obviously torn. Though she was really too young to be entrusted with such a responsibility, she was nonetheless entrusted with looking after her young charge, and yet couldn't budge her from the street.

Verity stayed. Harry watched her timidly trying by turns to rein in and to mimic Gina, telling her not to stand so close, watching her every move, trying to fling her own hair about, adjusting her tiny bun, fixing the bows on her dowdy blouse.

Gina had no imitators though. She turned out to be uncannily good at getting people to stop, much better than Ben and Harry. The green peasant skirt made her look untailored, yet fresh and young. She was tanned, looked happy, and walked up and down Essex Street, shouting at the passersby both in Italian and English. In three hours she collected seven hundred signatures. The boys and Verity collected eighty-four—combined.

"You clearly have skills we can't ever hope to attain," Ben said with an impressed glitter, as if he needed one more thing to impress him.

"Not at all," Gina said graciously. "You could be successful. You just give them too much information." She smiled. "It's the education university. Shoppers don't want to hear about swamps and mosquitoes and ships. Please sign the petition to bring exotic tropical fruit to Lawrence. That's all you have to say. And next time you come, bring your bananas, Ben," she added. "We'll give away a banana with every signature."

"I don't think I can get four thousand bananas," said Ben.

"Do you want the canal or not?"

What could Ben say?

"If you come next Saturday," Gina said, "Verity and I will make a barrel of lemonade . . ."

"We will?" muttered Verity.

"Yes, and we will set up a little table, where on a hot August afternoon, for every signature, we'll offer a free cup of lemonade. A banana would be good too. That's almost a full lunch."

The boys stood and gaped as she beamed with satisfied pleasure.

"But, Gina, we have no money to buy lemons and sugar," whispered Verity.

"Don't worry, I'll get some," Gina whispered back.

4

Four steaming August Saturdays blew by in a whirlwind, and by the end of the month, after trolley cars of bananas and barrels of lemonade, with four clipboards and some much-needed help from the humid weather, Ben had his 5,000 signatures and his heart in a mangled twist. He had already begun feebly insisting that what he needed was not 5,000 but 10,000, so he could keep on coming indefinitely to Lawrence. But on the last Saturday, Pippa, who usually didn't venture out, was unfortunately one of the people into whose hands Ben thrust a glass of lemonade and a pen. She signed first, then she saw her cousin's daughter, in a borrowed dress too short for her, her hair up only by the loosest of definitions, and her sleeves inexplicably three-quarter length, though no acceptable dresses were made with three-quarter sleeves anymore. Moreover, Pippa saw Gina as she really was—relaxed, laughing, the way no fifteen-year-old girl was supposed to act on the street with men many years her senior.

"I'm in trouble, you two," Gina whispered, as Pippa's plump, moist hand went around her forearm. "Goodbye!"

All of these conclusions about Gina's impropriety in dress and demeanor Pippa revealed not only to Gina when they got home but to Mimoo and Salvo later that evening. She saved it, actually saved it, for when Salvo returned from the quarry.

"So *this* is how Verity has been looking after you?" Salvo bellowed.

"Don't blame Verity for this! It's nothing!"

"This is not nothing, Gina!" shouted Mimoo. "But this isn't Verity's fault, Salvo, it's your sister's! Verity is not her keeper."

"She actually *is* her keeper, Mimoo! We let Gina out on Saturday afternoons because we thought she was organizing donations at the mission—with Verity!"

"We did that first," Gina defended herself. "We did it quick. There haven't been that many. Mostly toys. It's not so hard, Salvo."

"This is despicable and inappropriate."

"What was *most* inappropriate," said Pippa, fanning herself, sitting down, sweating, "was their banter, as if they were old friends!"

"Do Verity's parents know this is what their devout Catholic daughter has been up to?" asked Mimoo.

"No one was up to anything, Mimoo!" Gina desperately didn't want her new friend to get into trouble.

They went around like this, with Gina sticking up for Verity and pretending they were simply on a busy street in the middle of an afternoon in plain view of the whole town. No one in the house believed her, except for her mother—but only because Mimoo finally became too exhausted to fight. When Angela came home late from being out with friends, she defended Gina like a trooper, calling them all ridiculous, old-fashioned, stuck in the last century, and blowing all manner of things out of proportion.

"All right, Salvo, stop the puffery," Gina said. "You see? I wasn't doing anything wrong. Like Angela said. I was standing on a street corner—"

"Exactly!" yelled Salvo.

"Asking for signatures for a canal in Central America."

"For what?"

"A canal!"

"Is that what they call it nowadays?"

"Mimoo!"

"It's a ploy," Salvo said. "It's a ruse."

"Salvo, you are crazy. Ben is going to be an engineer. He is going to build the greatest man-made wonder of the world. It's incredible, Salvo . . ."

"You're swallowing his lies hook, line and sinker, sister."

"They're not lies, Salvo. He's going to build banana plantations in Costa Rica."

"Banana plantations in Costa Rica? You said a canal in Panama?"

"How are the bananas going to get here, Mimoo?"

"Salvo is right, child," Mimoo said. "I don't like bananas and will not eat them."

Gina wanted to yell in frustration at the unfairness of it all. They were pacing around the tiny living room. "Will you eat sugar?" she said, not hiding her impatience. "Coconuts? Chocolate? Ben will grow that too. And ship it here."

"Gia, those two men are laughing at you right now," said Salvo. "Have you looked at a map? They don't need a canal to ship it *here*."

"Now who's the one being laughed at, Salvo?" said Gina. "They need one to ship it to Italy. To China. To France. In other words, to the rest of the world."

"I'm not going to stand and argue with you about this," said Salvo.

"Then why are you?"

"They're going to have to build this canal without you, Gina Attaviano. Because no sister of mine is going to stroll the streets with two drooling men in their twenties. Do you understand?"

"*You* don't understand, Salvo! They're not drooling!" She ran to her room. What she wanted to say was they were not the ones who were drooling.

She overheard her family from the next room. The whole block overheard them. Salvo told Mimoo that Gina wasn't allowed to see Verity anymore, but Mimoo stopped him. She pointed out to her son that Verity was studying to become a nun, that she had two devout parents who attended Mass daily, that her volunteer day job after school was collecting donations for the poor. "Is that really the kind of person your sister shouldn't be around?"

Salvo still said yes.

"Come on, son," said Mimoo. "It's all right to be friendly with this Verity girl. Maybe some of her piety and love for the Lord will rub off on your sister. Maybe Verity will be a good influence."

"Maybe," Salvo said. How Gina regretted letting him in

on her secrets in Belpasso! "But did you ever consider, Mimoo, that *your* daughter may not be the best influence on Verity?"

To help her learn the correct behavior, Pippa gave Gina *The Young Lady's Friend* to read. Gina glanced at the first page in the slim volume of manners, checked the date of publication, and when she saw it was 1838, she promptly slapped the book shut in a huff and complained to Angela about the uselessness of learning manners from sixty years ago.

Angela tried to play mediator. "Okay. But Pippa is right. There is a proper attitude to be maintained at all times toward gentlemen."

"Bah," said Gina. "Actually, the real test of good manners is the proper attitude that gentlemen maintain at all times toward ladies. It's their responsibility."

"And yours?"

"I pretend I don't quite know what good manners are," Gina said with a smile. "That makes me seem impetuous and brave. I'd say I seem rather adventurous to my two new friends," she added.

"Don't let your brother catch you talking like that," said Angela. "You should develop some natural modesty that will guard you against any intimation of familiarity with young men."

"Of course, Angie. I'm going to hop to it."

"Since breeding is something you don't possess, then let your good taste help you in this regard."

Gina fell quiet. She wasn't sure she had any of the latter either.

"You must remain at all times delicate and refined."

"Of course, Angie."

"I can see you don't think much of what I'm telling you,"

Angela said, "but understand that manners is the only thing that separates the plebeian from the upper classes."

Gina frowned. "Ange," she said, "I don't mean to be improper, but I'm not from the upper classes. I never was. And no matter how hoity-toity I act, not sneezing in public or touching a strand of my hair, I'll never be mistaken for an upper-class lady. Won't my airs just seem fake and put-on?"

"Better than no airs at all," declared Angela.

After Salvo's unwelcome intercession, September came, though the two had nothing to do with one another. But in September, life stopped being measured by mystical Saturday afternoons of lemonade and bananas, by two boys in dapper suits and bowler hats standing with a girl on Essex Street, her serving the drinks, them collecting signatures, having fun and making jokes, being young.

Chapter Eight
THE REWARDS OF MISSION WORK

Ellen Shaw came from too illustrious a family. She was the youngest by far of four daughters and one son, born to Francis and Sarah Shaw. Her grandfather had been a hard-working merchant who made enough money so his family didn't have to. They lived off his labor on the family estate in Roxbury, Massachusetts, then sold it, divided the money and moved to New York to pursue their separate whimsies—all except Ellen's brother Robert, who, as soon as the war broke out, joined the Union Army. When he was getting slaughtered at Fort Wagner, Ellen was barely out of diapers.

Ellen was the runt of the family in every way including the physical. She was an afterthought, was raised like an afterthought, and behaved like an afterthought. After her brother was martyred fighting the Confederates in the 54th Regiment and Josephine founded the New York Consumers' League and campaigned for raising wages and working conditions of women in New York, Ellen decided that maybe if she was outrageous, her family might notice her. So she was most outrageous—and no one batted an eye. She rebelled against tradition the only way she knew how, by pretending she held it in contempt.

When she was barely eighteen, she became pregnant by a man in a dance club who was out on furlough and had to return to prison after the long weekend. Finally, a much-desired scandal. Ellen was left with an impossible choice. She could quickly get involved with another man and pretend the child was his, or give the baby up for adoption. She opted for neither. She left New York to spare her family the continued humiliation, moved back to Boston, rented an apartment in Back Bay and became a single mother.

After a few months she realized that single motherhood was not as romantic as she had envisioned. The baby demanded all her time without any division of labor. She wanted to go out but there was no one to leave the child with. After six months, she came home to Staten Island to drop off her son for a visit with widowed Josephine while she went up to Canada, to the Niagara Falls. It was eleven years before Ben Shaw saw his mother again.

For over a decade he was passed like a parcel among the sisters, and finally Josephine, with whom he stayed the most, had had enough and traveled up to Boston to find Ellen.

They found her living happily in a lush Back Bay house that belonged to the family of her second husband who was now deceased. It turned out he was more of a common-law husband, and she and his family had been in court for years in their attempt to force her out of their home.

Josephine may have been judgmental of her younger sister's vagabond ways, but Ben, who had been living under strict scrutiny of his busybody aunts, took one glimpse of his mother's free life and decided he wanted it too. Ellen tried to explain to her son that freedom came only with lack of responsibility, and the relationship between freedom and responsibility was, tragically, inversely proportional. He begged to stay with her anyway, and she finally gave in on the condition that he call her Ellen and not let any of her potential suitors know that he was her child and not her nephew.

Josephine offered to pay the rent on a new residence so that Ben wouldn't have to pack up and move every time Ellen found herself a new beau. Ben couldn't explain to his aunt that that was the part he found most appealing. He had been a content and smiling boy, having been raised by three loving aunts and grown up with a gaggle of cousins. Suddenly he was thrust into only-child loneliness of living among adults. But Ellen had discovered some latent maternal talents, and while hardly formidable, they were nonetheless sufficient to learn how to cook and to be home at a reasonable hour on some evenings.

Young Ben was too often left to his own devices, however, and he started to engage in behavior that bordered on and then crossed over into the illegal—which made it all the more difficult for Ellen to pretend that parenting involved little more than cooking a plate of food for a twelve-year-old three times a week.

With the situation between them spiraling out of control, one fine Saturday afternoon on State Street Ben tried to deprive a certain Herman Barrington of his wallet in full view of a constable and an astonished Harry Barrington out for a stroll with his father. Ben was promptly seized and arrested. Had it not been for Harry's intervention, Ben Shaw surely would've been held in juvenile detention until he was eighteen. As it was, Harry recognized a boy shouting for help when he saw one. He was one of those boys himself.

After the unexpected death of his mother, Harry had chafed and bucked against his older sister's control and his father's sudden preoccupation with his business. His misgivings and abundant loneliness turned him inward to himself, and outward to books. He managed to find something to do that consumed him, but had turned him even more away from other people.

The urchin boy stealing twenty dollars from his father's leather wallet was a revelation to Harry. He persuaded his father to drop the charges and then invited the boy over for dinner. Ben stayed overnight and returned the following weekend. And the following.

It worked out well for everyone. Ellen and the Barringtons divided custody of Ben. Ellen had him during the week so he could go to school, and on the weekends he stayed in Barrington. He had Louis set him a sleeping cot in the corner of Harry's bedroom, refusing a room of his own. When it came time to apply to the prestigious and expensive Andover preparatory academy, Herman Barrington didn't even need to be convinced to offer to pay. Two years later, he delighted in telling everyone that Ben was admitted to Harvard on his own merits and received a full scholarship.

"Could it be, Father," Harry would say, "that the Harvard Admissions Board by rules of simple deduction knows my name is Barrington and you're one of the largest contributing endowment members, while Ben's name is Shaw, nephew of a man who just happened to be a martyr and a war hero, not to mention an honored Porcellian? Perhaps if we told them my last name was Shaw instead, I could get a scholarship also."

For the first few years at Harvard, Ben flitted from one ephemeral passion to the next, getting excited about chemistry, economics, business, mathematics, only last year settling on engineering—while Harry, straight and narrow, was interested in nothing but philosophy and history.

"Are you majoring in philosophy to upset me, son?" Herman would sometimes ask. "Because it doesn't."

"Believe it or not, it has nothing to do with you, Father."

"I don't believe it."

Ellen, a frequent guest at the Barrington home, upon hearing this said to Herman, "No, Herman, yours is a very good boy, but how do you explain that my son wants to build a fruit farm in Central America as a stepping stone for taking over the world, while his mother advocates demilitarized isolation?"

"Believe it or not," Ben said, "it has nothing to do with you, Mother."

"I also don't believe it."

2

"Are you coming on Thursday?" Ben asked Harry.

"Coming where?" They were walking briskly across the Yard to Memorial Hall for lunch, Ben from Applied Mechanics, Harry from Ethics of Social Questions.

"To my mother's League meeting."

"I wasn't planning on it, why?"

"Do you remember Verity?"

"No. But why do you answer a question with a question?" Semester had started a week ago and Harry wasn't crazy about one of his courses with Professor Royce: Fundamental Problems of Theoretical Philosophy. He was thinking of dropping it, but Royce was good friends with his father, and Harry didn't want it to seem as if he was dropping the class because he didn't want Royce to make weekly reports to Herman about Harry's progress.

"Come on. You remember."

"All right, so what?"

"Verity is quite interested in my mother's Anti-Imperialism."

"Is she?"

"Why the surprise? Yes, she is. So much so that she came to Old South last week."

Harry stopped walking. "Verity came to a League meeting?"

"In this you are precisely correct."

Harry contemplated a moment. "Who was the guest speaker?"

"Is that important? W.E.B. Du Bois."

"Ah." They resumed their steady pace down the winding path. "She must be fond of him."

"I don't know. He's against miscegenation laws. The League women will not invite him back. He called all the women racists." Ben cleared his throat. "But do you know what's more important than how Verity feels about Du Bois?"

"I can't imagine that anything could be. Don't dawdle at the gate, Ben, it's not considerate. Come on, push on through." He prodded his friend through the narrow iron opening.

"Who Verity came with." Ben's whole face was alight.

Harry shook his head. His hat fell off; he had to catch it. "I thought we were over this."

"You also thought my canal obsession was a passing fancy."

"One of those things must be true."

"That's a logical fallacy. They're both false."

They walked inside the mobbed and noisy Memorial Hall, ordered chicken soup and pork with potatoes, paid and sat down. It took them a while to find two seats together.

"I forgot to ask—weren't you waiting on the Porcellian decision this week?"

"I was, but don't change the subject."

"I'm not. You don't change the subject. What did they say?"

"Ben," Harry said in between hungry bites. "All other too-obvious-and-not-worth-pointing-out—*again*—dangers aside, your mother wants you to stop coming to her anti-canal meetings. Have you not noticed? She fears you will disrupt things."

"What did they say?"

"They said no," said Harry. "They said I'd be a better fit at one of the other final clubs." He paused. "What? It's fine. I don't much care. Don't look at me like that."

"Like what?"

"You know I don't care," Harry said. "I just don't want him to lord another thing over my head. That's really the only reason I wanted in. So I'd stop hearing it from him. But now it's done."

Ben gave Harry a long blink of regret and sympathy and swallowed his food. "How do you know this about my mother?"

"Know what? Oh. Two weeks ago at afternoon tea she told my father, who told my sister, who told me."

Ben shrugged. "Ignorance of facts heavily influences my mother's position. The canal is an economic enterprise. It can and will square with her pacifist organization. She just doesn't know it."

"Yes, because you're the only smart one in the room."

"I thought *you* were the only smart one in the room?" Ben grinned.

"This is indeed so." Harry tried not to smile. "But what about Panama fighting Colombia for its independence even as we speak?"

"So? Let them fight."

"Why are we siding with the Panamanians?"

"Is that a real question? We've been through *this*. Because we're at war with Spain over its untrammeled colonization policy in places precisely like Colombia. And second, because we can't build a canal through Colombia. Perhaps a geography course is in order before you graduate from the most prestigious university in the United States."

Now Harry laughed. "Perhaps a common sense course for you! The women, led by your own mother, are going to hang you from the rafters."

"My mother has never been particularly fond of me. Her conformist bastion needs a dissenting voice. They can't just have a group of yah-sayers at Old South. The Tea Party began there for God's sake! It's a rebel debate hall. I'm going to find an opportunity to inform them that their pacifism and my canal are not mutually exclusive."

"I want to be there for that one."

"You will be."

"Metaphorically speaking," said Harry.

"However you meant it."

Harry adamantly shook his head and wiped his mouth with a napkin. "No. I really can't," he said, standing up. "I'm carrying a full load this semester. I've got a Metaphysical seminar, Labor Questions in Light of Ethical Theory, Socialism and Communism with Cummins and he is very tough. He told me I'm not reading enough every night. Can you imagine?" They cleaned up their trays, shouted greeting and parting words to their classmates, and started out.

"And Alice has roped me into another charity extravaganza besides. You and gangly Verity are going to have to draw in the tanned Italian fly by yourselves."

Ben took Harry's arm. They had been walking through Harvard Yard, and now stopped so Ben could be more persuasive. "Harry, listen to me . . ."

"I will not, and grabbing my arm is not going to persuade me."

"*We cross the prairie as of old, the Pilgrims crossed the sea, to make the west, as they the east, the Homestead of the Free!*"

"Poetry also won't work."

"Harry, not five minutes ago cows grazed in the Boston Common! Now look at our city. How do you think it got this way? Counting houses, markets, factories, your father helped build this town . . ."

"Please don't bring my father into this."

"Hide, leather, merchant fleet, textbooks, smell your city, Harry!"

"Manure, trash, you're right."

"No! Molasses and bananas. Coffee, newspaper print, books on the streets. All hallmarks of civilization."

"All somehow without a canal."

"But the rest of the world isn't so lucky. With the canal, civilization will come to all."

"Because of the canal?"

"Yes! They will bring us bananas; we will bring them lobsters and shoes."

"And this is why I have to come with you on Thursday?"

"You have to come with me because you're my friend."

"Benjamin, I am your friend, but I'm not supposed to be marrying you. Alice, bless her, demands I attend some charity ball this Thursday. I wasn't joking about that."

111

"Charity ball or the world's greatest fruit industry created and expanded right here in Boston?"

Harry tried a different tack. "What about Gail from Grays? Just two months ago, she was on your arm and you were dreaming about Truro together."

"You're imagining things. I walked her from Grays to Gore Hall once. She mentioned her family used to go clamming in Truro. From this you draw lifelong commitment?"

Harry sighed. "Is that what we're talking about here? Lifelong commitment?"

"First things first." Ben smiled widely.

"Honest to all that is holy, this is the most insane I've seen you. Tell me," Harry said as they quickened their step on the way to University Hall, "is it Panama or the girl?"

Ben didn't reply. Harry wondered if Ben himself knew the answer.

3

Verity Dunne had never been to Boston before she became friends with Gina. She and her two younger sisters had been born and raised by two Irish parents in Lawrence. Her father was a day laborer and her mother a textile mill worker, among other things, and they had once taken their children north to Hampton, and east to Salem, but not south. Last week had been her first train ride, her first outing. Though she was three years older than Gina and ostensibly Gina's chaperone, she seemed substantially younger, and lacked Gina's passion for the big city. Her excited curiosity was slightly tempered by her anxiety.

Gina got Mimoo to agree to let her occasionally stay overnight at Verity's because they worked late at

St. Vincent's and started their day early. Verity went to St. Mary's School for Girls while Gina walked to Pacific Mill.

After a few exemplary overnights, Gina and Verity gained parental trust, and Gina decided the time was right to take the 5:15 train to Boston. Gina knew what Mimoo and Salvo and Pippa didn't know and Angela had long forgotten, which was that Verity's mother worked two night jobs besides her day job at the mill—as an undertaker's assistant four days a week and as a caretaker to a blind gentleman the other three. The reason she worked two more jobs was because her husband was sporadically employed at best. The reason her husband was sporadically employed was that he tended to come in late to work and get fired. And the reason he tended to come in late to work was that he was a drunk, and spent most of his nights passed out on the couch. Naturally the family kept this grubby fact of their daily life in strict confidence. Verity's two younger sisters stayed with their grandmother in Methuen during the week, while Verity was responsible, diligent, hard-working, and largely on her own. As long as Verity came home before her mother walked in the door at 11:10 p.m., she could do as she liked. Gina knew this, and had learned to exploit it. As a result Gina was the first person to gain Verity's trust. Verity could barely stop spilling out the details of her sad life to a sympathetic and receptive Gina. Everyone got what they wanted: Verity a sorely needed friend, and Gina a narrow passage out of the trapped existence of a fifteen-year-old Catholic Italian immigrant.

Latching gladly onto Gina and allowing herself to be swayed without much persuasion, only fear sometimes spoke to Verity's timid heart, fear of getting caught, of getting into trouble, of facing the righteous wrath of the adults—but the excitement of getting a little dolled up and going to Boston by train—by themselves—was so exhilarating that fear became nothing more than fuel on the fire of her freshly minted independence.

The girls, of course, had no proper clothes to wear to Boston; for most of her adolescence Verity wore lumpy dresses, slightly let out, patched up with fabric as she grew, and Gina fared even worse. She had come with a trunk full of peasant clothes that she now wouldn't be caught in a nunnery wearing. The few dollars she made working all went to the new house fund. The Attavianos, with Pippa and Angela, had just weeks earlier moved out of the crummy row house to Summer Street, right off the Common, where they had found a simple but charming folk Victorian for rent. They rented almost the entire house, upstairs and downstairs. A walkway through a small front garden, eight steps up to the deep porch, a living room and dining room combination, with a kitchen stove off to the side, three bedrooms upstairs and a coal room and washing facilities down in the basement. It was a mansion! It even had a small overgrown backyard. In the attic lived Rita, a widow. Mimoo liked her.

So the family had more room, but also greater expenses. Every cent they earned went into the kitty to pay the rent, utilities and food. There was nothing left for Gina's shoes, or a new hat, nothing even for material for a dress. But back in Belpasso, Gina had learned how to spin from Rafaela, the old blind herder down the road whose goats she milked and whose sheep she sheared, and she became so swift that each year she won awards as the fastest hand-spinner in town under the age of twenty. She considered it a wasted talent, until she got to Lawrence.

She could have instantly got work on the mechanical lightning-fast spinning machines at the mills, but to sit long hours in a stifling, humid room year round for slave pay held surprisingly little appeal for Gina. Instead she offered St.

Vincent's sisters her services to card and spin the scraps of poor quality wool she brought home. The nuns found her a medium-sized, beat-up wooden spindle and distaff and a pair of carding paddles with half their teeth missing and put her in the small backroom they used for storage. In poor light, racing to keep the wool from drying out and matting, Gina teased, combed and disentangled the raw fleece, twisting it into rovings that could be drafted and spun. Compared to carding, spinning the wool into yarn took almost no time at all. Carding would've taken even less time had she not had to wash the fleece so thoroughly. Leaving a little of the natural sheep lanolin in the wool made it more elastic, easier to work with and had the extra benefit of keeping her hands soft. Rafaela's hands had been like a baby's bottom. Alas, Gina's hands were still like sandpaper.

After she had sold a hundred and fifty skeins of undyed yarn for a 100% profit at Saturday's bazaar and made five dollars, the nuns took up a collection in church on Sunday and bought Gina a used, large one-thread hand- spinner that rested on the floor. She wanted a two-thread spinning wheel but that cost a hundred dollars. It would take them two years to collect that kind of money. Some of the sisters volunteered to help her card the wool, and though they weren't very thorough, afterward Gina's cones of yarn appeared much faster. What began as a volunteer side job developed into hours of backbreaking work. She couldn't bring home enough free wool to spin.

Eventually she took three of the nuns with her to Washington and met with Percy Clark, her floor manager, asking him, with full intercession from the divine sisters, if he would like to donate some of the more unusable scraps for the mission at St. Vincent's to help the poor of Lawrence. "Everything can be used," Percy said. "There is no such thing as unusable. Except for the breech pile, but you don't want that." Gina didn't want to admit that that indeed was what they had been using. He offered Gina—but only if she sorted and washed it herself on her own time, not the company's—ten pounds a week of head fleece, or grade four out of eight. The nuns were delighted. Gina, too. Now she could leave a little lanolin in the wool—grade four was softer, and the spun yarn was better and sold for a penny more. The money they raised went for doctor's bills or to women with children whose husbands were infirm or unemployed or dead, or whose houses burned down—a frequent occurrence with all the open flames from candles and kerosene lamps and fireplaces.

Gina was no fool. True, she offered her services to St. Vincent's for free, but the one thing she asked for in return was the proceeds from one hank for every five she sold. The sisters readily agreed. Now Gina had virtually unlimited supplies of wool to work with. She became blazingly fast. As she spun the wool ever thinner—parsing a pound into sixteen skeins, then twenty-two, then, if she was supremely careful, thirty—she dreamed about the spinning machine, and how much yarn she could draft and sell once the nuns acquired one for her, and how much more money she could earn. She had plans to set up her own industry. The more delicate her yarn, the more she charged for it. She started dreaming of ways to dye it cheaply, so she could charge four pennies, six, even eight, instead of two or three like now. In the meantime, with the few dollars she eked out, Gina bought a couple of yards of moss green cotton, and some white and black lace and sewed herself a pretty day dress. One more week of non-stop work purchased her a hat to go with it and a taffeta ribbon to tie up her hair. *Dio vi benedica, Rafaela.* You learn something every place you look.

* * *

When her mother saw her in the new dress, there was a scandal and she was forbidden to wear it. "Your skirt is too fitted," said Mimoo.

"No, Mimoo, you're mistaken. I've gained weight. And there is no let in the silk. Lend me money to buy some more fabric, I'll sew myself a looser skirt."

"You haven't gained weight," said Mimoo, who had.

What was clearly white, Gina shook her head and called it black. "I have, I have."

"Aside from being too slim, it's shamelessly short," said Mimoo. The hem barely covered the middle part of her two-inch heel.

"My skirt is exactly one inch off the ground," said Gina.

Mimoo and Angela flung open *Harper's Bazaar* magazine to prove to Gina beyond any argument that all respectable women's skirts dragged on the ground half a foot at least.

Gina refused. She made a cogent, articulate, rational argument that fell entirely on deaf ears. First she said she was not a woman. Second, that she never wore skirts that long in Italy. Her mother pointed out, correctly, that they were no longer in Italy.

Gina then applied the inconvenience argument. Long skirts made it impossible to go up and down stairs, to go down the street without tripping, to carry anything—to be independent. Mimoo and Angela, with Pippa joining in, pointed out that all other young girls and young women, all women in fact in Lawrence, Boston, Andover, Lowell and everywhere else in the New World somehow managed.

She followed with the ignorance argument. "Mimoo, you and Pippa don't know what you're talking about. Mine is called a walking dress. Or a rainy day dress. All the ladies in Boston wear them, and they are by definition more comfortable to walk in."

In desperation Gina pulled out the life and death argument. Long skirts, whose hems constantly swept across the filthy ground, picked up disease from the dirt, the garbage, from the horse manure left on the streets. It was a health hazard—it could cause infections, skin conditions, blood poisoning, tuberculosis, pneumonia, typhus, diphtheria, death!

"Oh, isn't she just an amphitheater of tragedy!"

"Yes, she's a regular La Bohème!"

"Mimoo!" yelled Gina. "They let horses decompose on the streets! You want my skirt to roll across horse remains?"

"Don't go where the horses decompose. And don't yell at your mother."

"You want me to drag my skirts across the carcass that has been left there for days, sometimes weeks?" Gina asked, just as loudly. "You think that's better than keeping my hem one inch above ground?"

"All I know," Mimoo said loftily, "and Pippa and Angela agree with me, is no one is supposed to see your shoes when you're a young lady. That's how it's done in *this* country. That's how *you're* going to do it. You do know, don't you, what kind of women keep their skirts that short?"

Gina didn't ask and wasn't offered more information. Railing privately against the insanity, she sewed a five-inch velvet panel into the waist of her dress with the too slim skirt now covering her shoes by three inches, and carried the heft of the dress in her hands so she could rush to the train without falling.

4

They got to North Station at twenty minutes to seven and had to hurry to miss the first introductions at seven o'clock. They were going to take the subway ("The first subway built in the United States was built right here in Boston"), but even Gina was uncertain as to how the subway that she kept reading about worked. You went down below ground, and there was a train there, and it took you several stops to your destination? But what if you got on a train going the wrong way? What if you had to pull a lever to stop and forgot to pull it in time, how could you get back? And there was something about riding an underground trolley that was terrifying. The girls were curious, but not that curious. The above-ground trolley cars also confounded them. Which one stopped near Old South? In the end they walked to Washington Street; they knew how to do that.

It was still light out and warm. The color of the leaves had barely started deepening. Gina slowed down her stride, to breathe the air fragrant with life, with molasses, sausages, olives, cigarette smoke, horses, the hot metal from the trolley car rails, the leather from the briefcases men carried, rotting fruit, all of it in one breathtaking, breathless inhale of the heart. If she could live in Boston and never leave, and be carried feet first out of this magnificent sprawl, with all its congestion and chaos, she would be carried out happy. She would live even then, when she was dead!

"Isn't it glorious, Verity?" she exclaimed, dragging her friend down Nashua Street, holding an open map in front of them. "Isn't it simply glorious?"

Verity's squeezed-together expression made her look as if she had swallowed vinegared cabbage. "We're going to get into so much trouble."

"We'll be fine."

"Gina, truth will out. You know this."

"We're learning about life."

119

"A little less learning might do us good."

"Did you know," Gina said, "that when King James was asked by the Pilgrims for permission to sail to the New World, he said to them, 'What profit might arise by this?' and they told him there was fishing on the shores of this new and blooming England, to which he let them go free, replying, 'So God save my soul! 'Tis an honest trade. 'Twas the Apostles' own calling.'"

Verity's eyes were round as plates. "How do you *know* this?"

"Because while you were staring out the window on the train, I was busy brushing up on my Boston history." Gina tapped a book she brought with her: *A Short History of New England.*

"Why?"

"What if we're required to converse with smart people? I don't want to appear stupid." What if I have a chance to converse with Harry? He wasn't there last week, but perhaps tonight . . .

"Isn't it better *not* to be stupid?"

"Verity, Verity." Gina pulled her friend by the arm. "Don't you know anything? *Forma segue la funzione.*"

"I have no idea what you just said. And why would anyone at an anti-colonialism meeting ask you about King James?"

"Just in case, I also brought and read the pamphlet Ben gave me about the League. Come on, don't dawdle."

"How do you even know a word like dawdle," Verity muttered, speeding up slightly. Gina was almost running. "You've been in this country five minutes."

"I've been reading English aloud. And Papa started teaching me English when I was four years old," Gina replied. "He taught me well, no?"

"Hmm," the gawky girl grumbled. "Too well."

The Old South Meeting House was crammed to the rafters with people, just like the week before. There wasn't enough seating by half—not even in the organ loft and the choir galleries. The girls entered through Milk Street and squeezed in under the pillars of the balcony toward the back, standing against the wall, peering over the shoulders of the men and women in front of them. Gina searched for Ben. Verity whispered, pointing to the pulpit, "Hey, isn't that the gentleman from last week?"

Gina looked across the pews to the wineglass-shaped rostrum. A handsome Negro man dandily dressed in a beautiful black hat stood inside it speaking, his voice passionately rising and falling. "I have no idea," she said. "Who *is* that?"

"Girls!" a voice next to them whispered excitedly. It was Ben—with Harry. Eureka! They had just walked in themselves. Now Gina didn't feel so self-conscious. But before they could say a word of greeting, they were promptly shushed by a row of disapproving women. Gina surreptitiously glanced at Harry. He looked as distracted as she, and carried a heavy school bag. Had he just come from university? Perhaps he had been at the library, studying. His suit was less pressed around the knees and elbows, as if he'd been sitting at a table, learning smart things about the world. She imagined him reading, a lamp on the table lighting the pages, sitting by himself in a quiet wood-paneled library, writing things down with his quill pen, looking off into the distance, thinking about the things he had just read.

Leaning over to Ben, Harry said a cryptic, "I thought they weren't going to invite him back?"

"He's packing the hall, isn't he?" Ben whispered back and was promptly shushed again by a stern backbencher.

Acutely aware of the passing of time, Gina fidgeted, was restless. She kept adjusting her hat, the ribbons in her blouse, flattening the front of her already flat skirt, twisting the silver bracelets she had "borrowed" a month ago from Angela and not returned. The carbon microphone kept cutting in and out; the acoustics of the new technology were still terrible, the sound of the man's voice bouncing in fragments off the ivory walls.

As he spoke, people clapped, hollered, even whistled. Women stood up and cheered. Some booed. They behaved as if they could hear the man with the shiny black cane, could understand what he was saying. Gina glanced over at Verity. The girl was entranced.

The train back was 8:45. Gina didn't know why the meeting had to drag on so long. She suspected that the dapper man on the podium, talking in front of an ample crowd, loved the sound of his own voice.

She thought it would never *ever* be over, but finally it was. Now the four of them could turn to each other. Ben moved to stand next to Gina. "How was your train ride?"

"It was good, thank you. The walk was even more pleasant."

"Walk? Why didn't you take the subway?"

"You think we should?"

"No," said Harry, who had appeared not to be listening. "Young women should not take the subway unaccompanied."

Her heart skipped, raced, swirled in exclamation points. He was listening! He heard! And he was being protective! He didn't want them to go into the dungeons by themselves! Was he offering to accompany them, perhaps? Oh!

Once again Gina's reverie was interrupted by real life. Ellen Shaw sought out her son, though she went straight to Harry, kissing him on both cheeks. "Harry, dear, it's so nice of you to join us." She turned to Ben. "You see? Your friend is on our side."

"You know it, Mrs. Shaw."

"Stop sucking up to my mother, Harry," Ben said, giving Ellen a kiss. "It won't do you any good."

"Oh, so now he's speaking up," said Ellen. "Did you notice, Harry, how quiet my son remained when I had asked if anyone had anything else to add?"

"I didn't think your lively crowd was receptive enough to listen to me," Ben said, in mock-defense.

"Yes, this crowd of meek women. Yet they were perfectly comfortable with a man who called us all, again, backward racists for refusing to support his fight against racial injustice."

Ben stepped forward. "Mother, you remember Verity and Gina."

Ellen waved a curt hello. "Yes, of course. How are you, young ladies? What did *you* think of our esteemed speaker? How did he compare to last week?"

"Oh, I thought he was marvelous again!" Verity exclaimed. "So passionate and eloquent!"

"What about you, Gina?"

"Yes. Absolutely. Me too. I thought he was. Marvelous. *And* eloquent."

Ellen waited. Verity was not coming to the rescue. Gina had no idea what the man had said, what position he staked, what country he was protesting American involvement in. She didn't even know who the man was and had forgotten to look at the program for a profile on this evening's speaker.

Not wanting to embarrass herself in front of Harry, who must have thought her already foolish and young, after chewing her lip for a few seconds the best she could do was recite a quote she had almost memorized on the train ride in. "Well, it's like your Thomas Jefferson said," Gina began, after repeatedly clearing her dry throat. "America does not go a-*bread* in search of sea monsters to destroy. If America kept getting herself involved in continued wars of interest and greed, they would, um, they would . . . *burp* her color and take her standard of freedom. Her fundamental, um . . . *princes* would *defensively charge* from liberty to force. She might well become the, uh, *doctor* of the world. Certainly she couldn't be the ruler of her own spirits."

She said this solemnly, righteously, exactingly, correcting herself as she spoke, scouring her visual memory for the words she remembered seeing on the page. And now, she kept her gaze solely on Ellen, afraid to see the expression in Harry's eyes.

Verity stared at her with incredulity. Gina couldn't miss Ben's delighted grin. Was Harry also delighted? She couldn't check, not even for a second. "Well said, Gina," Ben complimented her. "Perfect. I think you may have meant John Quincy Adams, though."

She saw Harry elbow him.

"You may be right," Gina allowed. "Though Thomas Jefferson also said some smart things." She hoped getting the name mixed up was the only infelicity she had made.

"Nothing as smart as *that*, child," Ellen said to Gina, taking her son's arm. "Though what that has to do with tonight's speaker, William Du Bois, I'll be damned if I know. Ben, can I steal you away for just a moment? I'd like you to meet Jane Adams, no relation, I think. She is one of our newest members. Do you know we have almost twenty-five thousand members?"

"Yes, and they all seem to be here tonight, Mother. Maybe

next week you can bring some extra chairs. Excuse me, Gina, excuse me, Verity."

"No, no, Verity, come with us. I want you to meet Mrs. Adams also. She is quite a prominent lady in today's circles. She didn't care much for Mr. Du Bois. You'll enjoy meeting her."

"Oh, but I liked him and what he said enormously," Verity clucked, flattered, hurrying off with them.

Gina and Harry were left alone.

She squeezed her hands together. He squeezed his hat and his book. She smiled politely. He smiled politely back. He was crumpled again, his hair swept every which way without benefit of a brush. His face had light stubble shadow, his suit was less than fresh, less than pressed. She didn't know what to say. "So what are you reading these days?" she asked, pointing. She tried not to look directly at him; she didn't want to be perceived as staring and was afraid he would see the confusion in her eyes, the slow blink when she laid her eyes on him. Could she help it that she found him so tremulously appealing, despite his laconic nature, his aloof demeanor, his lack of interest in her? Or perhaps because of all those things? It didn't matter. She wanted to believe his lack of interest was fake, and so she did.

He showed her the book he was holding.

"*The Man without a Country*? Still? Weren't you carrying it two months ago when you came to the docks?"

Harry frowned slightly. "How do you remember that?"

"You left it on our table after dinner."

"*That's* where I left it!"

"Well, yes. But I gave it back to you the next morning."

"Oh. Must've misplaced it again." He clucked at himself. "Sometimes I can't keep track of my things."

She filed that away. "You like this book very much?"

"I'm doing my senior thesis on it."

What was a thesis? "I read it the same evening you left it," she told him. "I read it the best I could."

"Well, that's very good. Did you like it?"

"I think so. I tried to understand it."

"It's not hard. It's not Shakespeare."

Gina had heard of Shakespeare. "No, of course not," she said wisely. "But then, what is?"

"Well, quite right. Milton perhaps?"

Gina had never heard of Milton. "Yes, yes," she agreed, looking very solemn. "Close, but not quite. But back to Philip Nolan," she continued. "To me he was a sad man to turn his back on his country."

"But look how he paid for it."

She nodded. "He paid for it with a terrible price. Yes, a terrible price. It is a good story."

"One of the best," said Harry, putting his hand on his heart and raising his voice a little. "'*I wish I may never hear of the United States again!*'"

"He was granted his wish."

"Yes, he was. He never set foot on American soil again."

"That's what I mean. That is very sad," Gina said. "I love my Italy. I hope to see it again someday."

"And why not?" said Harry. "You can go back any time you want."

"I have to work a long time, and get my citizenship first. Then we'll see."

They both looked down, Gina at her hands—they were scabbed and hurting from working with the wool. Slowly she put them behind her back and made an intense mental note to spend her money on *nothing* else until she bought herself a pair of lady's gloves.

"So have you started school?"

"I can't work and go to school at the same time."

"I thought work was only part-time?"

If he knew how much time she spent carding and drafting and selling the yarn, he would understand.

"Why not go to school *and* work?" said Verity, who had returned with Ben. "I do."

Verity always intervened at the wrong time. "But also, I help my mother clean houses on weekends," Gina continued, citing family obligations. "And I sew for Aunt Pippa. We are very busy. But you are writing your book report just on this Philip Nolan?" She continued to speak to him as if Verity and Ben were not there.

"No. I compare him to Ben's uncle Robert, the honorable colonel. One man dies for his country; the other man renounces it."

"But then he learns."

"By that time it's too late," said Harry. "He says at the end, '*Behind all these men, behind officers and governments, there is the country herself, your Country. You belong to her as you belong to your own mother.*'"

Ben groaned. "Oh no! You found a poor innocent child to listen to your caterwauling on Nolan?" He pointed out the exit door to Gina. "Go. Please. Save yourself. Trust me, if he thinks he's found a sympathetic ear, he'll never stop talking. Believe me, I know. I've been hearing about this Nolan character for nine years. I'm no longer sympathetic. Listen," Ben continued as he led her away, Verity and Harry following close behind. "My mother is arranging some light refreshments, some bread and wine," he said. "Would you and Verity care to join us?"

Gina glanced pleadingly at Verity, who, temptation written all over her face, shook her head. They could not get home after eleven, they simply couldn't.

"You know we can't, Gina," Verity said, just as pleadingly. "In fact, we need to get going if we're to catch the 8:45. We have a twenty-five minute walk."

"No, no," said Ben, clearly disappointed. "We won't hear of it. It's dark and late. We'll get you a carriage. Right, Harry?"

"Verity, please?" Gina said. "Please? We'll only stay for fifteen minutes."

"No." Verity glared at her. "We. Have. To. Catch. The. Train."

Gina frantically chewed her lip. Bread and wine with Harry! In this historic place. The only thing that stopped her from sending Verity home on her own was fear for the future. If Verity balked next Thursday and refused to come or to cover for her, then Gina's secret trips to Boston would end. To save her Thursday nights, she reluctantly agreed to leave with Verity.

Gina was lucky that Verity was such a willing participant in this blatant deception. Angela would have been a harder convert. Verity, on the other hand, lapped up the talk on the Philippines, Spain, Central America, China and Japan, while Gina drummed her fingers, chewed her nails, waiting for the interminable meetings to be over so she could have a minute at the end of one evening a week with Harry.

5

Alice and her mother were walking down Commonwealth Avenue, parasols over their heads and their skirts hitched up so as not to drag along the ground. What Alice was trying to do was escape from her mother, who was *deeply* irritating her this morning, but who wouldn't relent and wouldn't slow down, feisty both in gait and provocation.

"Mother, I don't know what to tell you," Alice said, out of breath. Of all the days for her carriage to break one of its wheel spokes. They had been so close to her destination, nearly at Massachusetts and Commonwealth. "I'm very late for my ten o'clock piano lesson because of our unfortunate mishap, and then I have a charity recital at noon at which I'm playing Lizst and you know how much trouble I have with his *Consolations 3*. And you heard Daddy yesterday, didn't you? You *were* listening to your own husband? There was a walkout at one of our mills in Andover two days ago. Fifteen men demanded twice their salary and then just up and quit. So now we have lumber being delivered and dumped outside the gates and no one to operate the forklifts or the saws. I have to write up a 'Help Wanted' advertisement immediately and telegraph it to the *Andover Gazette*, so we can get it in the paper by tomorrow and have some men show up to be interviewed on Wednesday. Am I going to my riding lesson this afternoon? No. Am I seeing Belinda for afternoon tea? No. Am I cutting the ribbon on the new infectious ward for small children at City Hospital? No." Now Alice was really out of breath. "These are the important matters, Mummy. Not what you're . . ."

"All I'm saying," said Irma calmly, not out of breath and keeping up with her daughter while twirling her own parasol to keep out the cold bright sunshine, "is I don't understand why you've asked him four times to come with you to the charity dance and he has refused to."

"Mother, he hasn't refused!"

"He promised a month ago he would come, and then the day of the dance he bowed out. And he hasn't come since."

"He can't come to a dance every week, Mummy."

"He hasn't come to any."

"Okay. Thursdays he is busy. At night he goes with Ben to Mrs. Shaw's League meetings."

"One Thursday he can't come with you?"

Alice was almost running. "We went to the theater last Saturday night. We had a wonderful evening."

"It wasn't to raise money for a children's library."

"No. It was just to have fun—which we did." Alice wouldn't even glance sideways at her mother. "Why do you constantly make mountains out of—"

"I'm going to say something this Sunday, I really am."

Alice stopped walking. She put down her parasol and turned to Irma. "Mother, I'm talking to you like an adult to an adult. You have your life, you have Daddy, you have your friends, your clubs, all your hobbies. Please don't ruin my life. Don't do anything, *anything*, to scare him away. You know how skittish he can be. I can't believe I have to explain it to you. Why do you care so much?"

"Because it's not proper, that's why! All the other ladies know he is your steady. And you're dancing with strangers. It's just not done."

"I don't dance with just him even when he does come!"

"Yes, but at least he is present. He is there. There was a dressage competition last week. Why didn't he come to cheer you on?"

"I didn't need him to be there, Mother." They resumed walking, though a little slower. Alice was spent from fighting. "I won without him. And he is in his last year at Harvard. You know how hard he works."

"He has time to go with Ben on Thursday nights, doesn't he?"

"He is allowed to have friends, or would you like to

inform him that he must spend every second of his spare time with me?"

"I have a good mind to say a few things to him this Sunday."

"Mother, I will forbid you to come to his father's house," said Alice. "All his father does is embarrass him. You want to be that person too? We are trying to get him to be your son-in-law one day. You think humiliating him in front of his father is the way to go about that?"

"Clearly for one reason or another," Irma declared, "he won't make up his mind."

"All right, but . . . let's give him until graduation. Let him concentrate on his studies; I know we don't think much of them, but you know how important they are to him. I don't want to be a shrew before he even asks Daddy for my hand. I'd like to wait until just after. Would that be okay with you? And maybe you can wait to be a shrew until just after also? All right, Mother? A plan?"

"You're being impolite to your mother," Irma said.

"I do apologize," Alice said. "But please, Mummy, stop talking."

They got to the corner of Commonwealth and Dartmouth. "*Consolations* are waiting for me," Alice said. "My recital is at noon at Copley Hall. I'll see you there."

Without waiting for a reply, she kissed her mother on both cheeks, gave her a little squeeze and walked up the stairs and inside, taking care at all costs not to slam the front door behind her.

6

Salvo had been having a hard time finding steady work and it grated on him. Every morning he got up at six not knowing if he would find work that day or make money—and all the while his mother cleaned the Prospect Hill houses and his sister somehow did a load of nothing yet always brought home money. Money, bags of uncombed wool, paper cones. Cotton thread, linen. She sewed skirts and sold skeins and made money! Even her English was progressing.

It's not that Salvo didn't try. He got hired for a shoveling project for two weeks, but he and a dozen men worked so hard that they were done in eight days and were released without so much as a bonus or a handshake for a job well done.

He spent a few days painting, another day or two pretending he could pass as a cabinet maker—just like Gina pretended she could be a wool sorter. He fooled the glaziers into keeping him for nearly a month, but this morning he was taking a train to nearby Andover because he had read in the local paper that a sawmill was hiring twenty men and paid well. If it didn't pan out, he would have to find restaurant work. It was all he wanted to do anyway. Having a steady trickle of cash was better than this hardscrabble subsistence. He wasn't able to save anything for his dream, and to make matters worse, his baby sister was giving Mimoo money every week, sewing skirts for herself to wear and even putting a few dimes into the glass jar on which she had painted the words SALVO'S DREAM. She was infuriating.

At the sawmill gates, Salvo found himself standing with forty other men, all stronger than him, bigger than him—and clearly more experienced, the way he overheard them talking about board feet and mitred edges, running measurements, lathe lumber and panels. Hundreds of logs were piled two stories high and a block wide on the ground near the gates. They clearly needed help.

"How many spots are there?" he asked a relatively friendly-looking man standing to his right. The man instantly became less friendly. "Just eighteen," he grumbled, stepping away. "Eighteen *experienced* men."

They're going to need more than eighteen men to move all that lumber, Salvo thought, anxiously hoping that would be true.

It was a woman who unlocked and opened the gates and came out to inspect them as if they were bat blanks or carving stock. They all tried to hide their shock, including Salvo. It was a drizzling misty Wednesday, and she was dressed for the weather, in high rain boots, a long dark overcoat, a wide brim hat. But her hair under the black hat was nearly white, her face pale, and her eyes very blue. She covered herself but Salvo could tell she was *donna molto attraente*, there was no hiding it. He pushed himself to the front of the crowd, moved his cap jauntily off his face, and stood still, hoping she'd notice him.

He shouldn't have pushed. He just angered the other men, and the *bella donna* asked them all to stand in one line anyway, walking up and down, appraising them. In a refined, high-class voice she informed them that she wasn't looking for boomers, or short-termers who worked and then quit. She was looking for good, hard-working men who wished to be compensated well for loyalty and long hours. She asked those who thought that sawmill work was nothing more than snoose and mulligans to turn and walk away. No one moved, even though Salvo knew for a fact some of the men were definitely in it for the short term: the sawmill was hard work in bad weather. He wasn't going to snitch on them—unless she didn't pick him.

The woman was all business and unsmiling, and he heard some of the men muttering uncomplimentary things when

133

she walked by without selecting them. When she came to Salvo, he cocked his head, looked at her a half-second too long and smiled politely. She frowned at first, stood quietly, then crooked her finger at him. Now he really heard some choice words from the men she had not picked. He flipped them the bird as he sauntered through the gates, following her inside the yard.

On the job he learned quickly. That had always been his number one skill. Maybe not as quick as his sister, but enough to blend in and not look too green. Mainly he had to listen to someone else and then follow along like a semi-trained monkey. At first he was put on a job that required barely any skill at all: cutting off the branches. Salvo limbed with aplomb. But once he was moved to decking, or sorting the tremendous logs by species, size, and end use, his day got harder and he made mistakes. It all looked like wood to him, he couldn't tell the difference between the bark of a pine and a fir, or between a maple and an oak. How his sister could fake knowing the difference between soft wool and extra soft wool, he would never know. His boss saw he was struggling and moved him over to debarking, which was tedious but simple. At the end of the long day they lined him up as the off-bearer for the head sawyer. Establishing a jovial rapport with the man, Salvo asked casually about the blonde woman who had hired him.

"She is no one," said Don McKay. "Absolutely no one. No one for you to ever think about, ask about, no one for you to even glance at."

"I'm just asking a polite question," said Salvo. "Can't I get a polite answer?"

"Mind your own fucking business, that's my polite answer," McKay said. "You want me to get less polite?

Because I can, and I will." McKay paused. "Just keep your head down and work and don't think and don't ask. *Capito?*"

It was his friend Bario who told him as it neared closing time that the woman was the owner's daughter, and the one unspoken rule at her father's mills was that no worker was allowed to even acknowledge her presence. "It's a sackable offense," said Bario, as if it weren't clear.

Salvo had worked like a brute and by the time the train brought him back to Lawrence, it was so late that his dinner had gone cold. He ate it anyway. Gina was not home. She had been staying with Verity a few nights a week.

Salvo slept like a thick piece of lumber, and the next morning was back at the yard early. He wanted to make a good impression on the fine-looking owner's daughter. But he saw her only briefly that day, and from a distance. She had overseen another large shipment that had come into the yard, hired ten more men, and disappeared. It didn't matter. His charm with the fair sex was legendary around Belpasso, or as Gina called it, "*famigerato.*" Salvo would keep his head down, work hard, and wait for an opportunity to present itself.

7

"You know my name means truth?" Verity said to Gina, watching her change into new garments at St. Vincent's before they boarded the train on Thursday.

"Really?" said Gina, putting on a flared skirt and a white cotton lace blouse. "I thought your name meant friendship."

Usually the boys got there early and saved them a seat. But on this Thursday in early November when the temperature had dropped and the leaves had all gone, Gina and Verity not only had to sneak in the side door but had to stand the entire meeting because Harry and Ben did *not* save them a seat. The girls stood for over an hour, listening to the evils of going to war with Spain and the massive protest demonstration the League was organizing just before Thanksgiving right in front of Old South, on the site of the Boston Massacre. Gina listened with only half an ear, because she was too busy wondering about the prim woman sitting between Harry and Ben, with her elaborate hat and proper purse. Gina watched her in profile, her straight nose, her refined demeanor. At first she found the woman's extravagant hat amusing; it was so dramatic and perched so high on one side that it blocked the view of people for three rows behind her. But then Gina's mood darkened. The woman seemed too familiar with both Harry and Ben. Gina touched her own hat, which had cost her twenty skeins, a wide brim hat with a short crown, neither silk nor fancy. She wished she could take it off.

At last the torture was over and the meeting adjourned. Gina waited anxiously for the two men to make their way to them, but they didn't. Instead they walked forward to the podium to speak to Ellen and a group of women. The high-hatted woman went with them, and was obviously quite familiar with Ellen also. Gina stood silently at the back, observing it all with a darkened gaze.

"Let's go say hello," said Verity, who had no ulterior motives. "The meeting ran so long, we're going to have to get going. The train is in less than forty-five minutes."

"How are you *always* so mindful of the time?" Gina muttered. Clearly she didn't think this was a virtue.

"Someone has to be. Or we'd never get anywhere." Verity pulled on Gina's reluctant white sleeve. "Come on, let's go, say hello, goodbye, and be on our way."

"We can't leave yet," whispered Gina. "We just got here." Verity had to nearly drag her to the front of the hall.

"Oh, hello," Ben said formally, as if it were completely normal that he didn't come to say hello, or save them a seat. It seemed fake, put on. The woman in the billowing hat decorously but instantly swirled around to see who Ben was speaking to. Gina thought that was quite impressive of easygoing Ben to engineer such a swift response in someone who a second earlier seemed to be paying no attention whatsoever to him. The woman had been talking to Ellen and a group of other women and couldn't immediately disengage herself. The only thing she did was to focus her eyes unblinkingly on Gina. Suddenly Gina felt keenly the poverty of the third-grade cotton fabric which comprised her lacy smock. The woman was dressed in finest gabardine.

Harry was more reserved than usual, barely even nodding in greeting.

"Sorry we couldn't save you a seat," Ben said. "You must be exhausted. We were late ourselves. Esther, Harry's sister, is here with us."

Gina's face broke into a relieved smile. "Oh," she said, trying not to sound high-pitched and thrilled. "It's your sister."

Harry nodded. "It's my sister."

Presently the sister came over. Harry calmly introduced them. But he was always calm, and this time Gina couldn't interpret it. "You're Harry's sister," she said smiling, sticking out her gloved hand. "So nice to finally meet you." She was proud of her black silk gloves. They cost her seventeen cents and had only two previous owners. And they hid her hideous hands from Esther who Gina was certain had never in her life touched unclean raw wool with plant matter in it.

Esther nodded to her, glancing disdainfully, but did not shake Gina's proffered hand. It must be a breach of etiquette. Young girls didn't offer their hands to adults. Esther wore a dark navy pintucked suit, plain with a bit of lace, but custom tailored and exquisitely pressed. Though she had been sitting down, she didn't have a wrinkle on her clothes. Stepping between Ben and Gina, Esther spoke to the girls as if from a great height. "You two are interested in imperialism?" Her voice was skeptical. Gina didn't want to wear her clothes like Esther, stiff and severe. She wanted to dress for elegance, for flair. But oh, did she love the expensive fabric.

"Anti-imperialism," Gina corrected her. "But yes, very much so."

Esther said nothing in reply; not a hair on her eyebrow moved. From behind Esther, Ben grinned at Gina. Esther, her manners impeccable, remained supercilious, eyeing Verity, intensely eyeing Gina and the impassive Harry. "You have an accent," she said.

"Not me," Verity said. "I was born here."

But Esther was not speaking to Verity.

"Yes. I am from Italy," said Gina.

"Where in Italy?"

"Sicily. It's down south—"

"I know where Sicily is," said Esther. "Do you live in one of my father's apartments?"

"No," Gina said. "We stayed for one night only."

"And now?"

"We live in Lawrence."

"Lawrence," Esther said. "I don't know where that is. And who is *we*?"

"My mother, my brother."

Verity pulled on her. "We need to go, Gina. The train."

"Oh yes," echoed Esther. "You don't want to miss your train."

Ellen came over. "Hello girls. Where were you two hiding tonight? I was looking for you. I'm having a small reception. Nothing fancy. Ben's Aunt Josephine is here. Will you join us for a few minutes?"

"We'd love to, Mrs. Shaw," said Verity. "But you know we have to catch the 8:45."

"Oh, for shame. Not even for a few minutes? We have fresh lobster as a treat."

"Ellen, they probably need to hurry," said Esther. "Do they even have trains to Lawrence this late at night?" She shrugged. "I have never traveled by train. I wouldn't know."

"I hadn't either," exclaimed Verity. "Until Gina started bringing me to Boston. They do have trains—and even a subway that runs late."

"A *subway*. You don't say."

"Harry," Ben said. "Why don't you stay here with your sister. Eat some lobster. Placate my mother."

"Nothing will placate her," said Harry. "Not after you just told her you're continuing to work for Mr. Preston, also known as the devil incarnate."

"I know. But do your best. She likes you. Est, I'll see you later. Girls, shall we go?"

Moving away, Esther took Harry's arm.

"It was nice to meet you, Esther," Gina called after her. Esther did not reply.

"Goodbye, Harry."

"Yes, good evening," said Harry.

Esther turned around—to watch Ben walk out of the meeting hall between the two girls.

* * *

"Who does that impertinent child think she is, calling me Esther," Esther fumed to Harry. "Like we're old friends. These immigrants have no manners, none whatsoever. Why didn't you tell her to call me Miss Barrington?"

Harry shrugged. "I was using my manners, Esther. I didn't want to embarrass her by correcting her. Also, they call us Harry and Ben. I didn't want to age you."

Pivoting slightly away, Esther continued to complain. "It's simply scandalous. Why, I don't think that girl was wearing a corset."

"Perhaps," offered Harry after a considered pause, "she wasn't wearing one because she doesn't need one."

They made their way to the food tables. As they took their plates, Esther spoke. "That's the girl, isn't it?"

"What girl?"

"The girl Ben keeps talking about."

"When does Ben talk about a girl? In between bananas?"

"Yes, every Sunday since August. The immigrant girl from Lawrence."

"I don't remember," Harry said. "And I thought you'd never heard of Lawrence?"

"Don't be obtuse."

"Not me. I honestly don't pay attention, you know I don't."

"Oh, you pay plenty of attention—just to the wrong things." Esther critically cleared her throat. "She seems worryingly young."

"Worryingly? I have no opinion."

"Is she in school?"

"I know nothing." In the vast and spacious great hall, the crowds thinned out. Harry wanted to get himself a drink. He asked Esther what she wanted.

She waved him off. "I wonder if they go to school."

"Esther, a drink?"

"I don't know. A glass of sherry. Is she pretty?"

He left without replying and in a few minutes brought his sister some white wine. "They didn't have sherry. Who is pretty?"

"Harry, why are you being so unpleasantly dense?"

"Not deliberately. I'm hungry, cranky, and thirsty, not necessarily in that order." He drank down a glass of beer. "Less thirsty now. But the lobster is all gone. I had an eight o'clock class this morning in Faustian Philosophy, or Kantian Cryptology, or Darwinian Dialectics, I don't remember anymore. Last night I was studying for my Socialism and Communism exam until three in the morning . . ."

"Oh, you're not actually taking such a ghastly course, are you?"

"That's amusing. And this was after going to a charity function with Alice and only narrowly escaping joining her in a ten-mile-long trail ride. What was your question?"

"Is she pretty?"

"She is barely out of grammar school. I couldn't tell you."

"Has she even had any schooling at all? And are you protesting?"

"Yes, Esther, she is the most beautiful elementary school girl I've ever seen. I don't know why she is interested in politics and not beauty pageants."

"Don't make fun. Tell me what you think."

"I told you, I have no opinion."

"Don't sound so intellectual about it. Like you're looking at a painting."

"Not even something as emotional as a painting."

"Do you ever bring Alice here?"

"Oh, dear heavens. She'd leave me for good if I did. All this talk about rights of man and exploitation of the natural

141

resources. Why in the world would I bring Alice here? She sells lumber. I don't even know why *you* came. That was *not* a question." Harry grimaced impatiently. They were near the remains of the food, his mind already wandering to the cheese and bread before him. He handed Esther a buffet plate, taking one himself.

"I came," Esther said, "because I was curious about your and Ben's intellectual pursuits."

"Oh, for sure."

"How was I to know they weren't intellectual?"

"Because you came to this shindy, that's how. Look, there's Ellen and Josephine. Wait, let's refill our plates. You know once we start listening, they won't stop talking."

"Where's Ben?" Ellen asked, coming up to them. Josephine had lagged behind. "Did he already leave to take the girls home?"

"No, not home," Esther corrected Ellen. "To the train station."

Ellen began to speak but suddenly ran off to say goodbye to someone. Harry and Esther turned to each other, his mouth full of cheese and the finest Boston lager.

"Why aren't you eating?" he asked.

"Not very hungry for some reason," said Esther. "Ben's mother hasn't changed in all the time we've known her."

"People don't change, Esther," said Harry. "Leaves change."

Ellen returned just in time for Esther to glance at her pocket watch and say, "Ben should be coming back any minute. It's been well over an hour."

Ellen shook her head. "He isn't coming back soon. I told you, he's on the train with them."

Harry continued to chew.

"He's *what*?" Esther said in a stunned voice.

"Ben is a gentleman," said Ellen, and Harry wasn't sure

if she meant it proudly or snidely. "He is hardly going to put two young girls on an evening train by themselves."

Esther slowly turned to her brother. "Harry, is that true? He is taking the train all the way to Lawrence? But why?"

"I suppose to make sure they get home safely."

"And then he takes the train all the way back?"

"He doesn't stay overnight in Lawrence if that's what you're insinuating."

"I wouldn't presume. How often does he do this?"

"Every time they come."

"Which is how often?"

"Every week, I guess, wouldn't you say, Ellen?"

"Yes. Verity is dedicated to our cause."

Esther made a sound of inflamed derision. "Why anyone would want to ride back at midnight on a train by himself is beyond me."

"What do you mean by himself?" said Ellen. "Harry goes with him."

There was a long silence. Harry said nothing. Esther said nothing.

On the way home, they didn't speak a single word.

8

The train was monstrously delayed. A tree had fallen across the tracks, and the train didn't move for over an hour while the workmen removed the trunk and branches from the rails. By midnight, a very concerned Mrs. Dunne left her intoxicated husband on the couch and paid money she couldn't spare to take a carriage to Summer Street, where she woke a deeply sleeping Mimoo and Pippa and a half-asleep Salvo, to ask if they had seen her daughter.

Salvo was most unsettled by this. He thought the girls were at Verity's house. Mrs. Dunne explained that she worked until eleven.

"Well, where is your husband? Isn't he watching over them?"

That Mrs. Dunne could not explain. He is home, she said, but he is asleep.

Tensely the adults waited out the minutes. No one dared give voice to the preposterous proposition that the mission work may have been a ruse.

"There is a very good explanation," said Mrs. Dunne in a weakening voice. "After all, my Verity wants to become a nun."

The Attavianos didn't speak. No one wanted to point out to Mrs. Dunne that Gina did not want to become a nun, not even a bad one.

After half an hour, Salvo realized they were waiting at the wrong house. If Verity and Gina came back, they'd be at the Dunnes'. Piling in, they took a carriage to Ashbury Street, where they discovered Verity and Gina asleep in Verity's bed. Not wanting to cause a scandal late at night and wake the neighbors, they waited impatiently until the next day, when Verity, confronted by the wrath of her mother and the Reverend Mother, remorsefully admitted the duplicity of their arranged Thursday nights.

The girl confessed to everything except Ben and Harry. She had the good sense to talk about the League of Anti-Imperialists and economic conditions in Colombia and Costa Rica, and the Americans fighting the Filipinos at Luzon, and growing coffee and other tropical beans, and John Quincy Adams and Gina's mangled efforts at profundity, but not about the two young men they met up with every Thursday.

Stupefied by the depths of Gina's calculated deception

and drawing a simple mathematical line between tropical winds and Ben Shaw, Salvo and Mimoo were at a loss as to what to do. Their baby was in the gravest danger, yet they both worked too long a day to give Gina the kind of chaperoning she required, which was constant. Sensing trouble by the breathfuls and needing divine intervention, they dragged a bucking Gina to Reverend Mother Grace at Notre Dame Catholic high school. Notre Dame was run by the nuns at St. Mary's who were generally well disposed toward Gina for her work at the mission—except for Reverend Mother.

Mother Grace was a tiny woman with a penetrating black-eyed gaze and a booming voice that resounded through the stone walls of the abbey. It was a voice that made you stand at attention even when you weren't asked. The Attavianos stood at attention. The throaty timber reflected the indelicacy of her questions.

"You think she needs a chaperone?" When they didn't answer, the nun tutted disapprovingly. "Let me explain something to you, Mrs. Attaviano, and I hope your daughter is listening, though I cannot be sure. Morally speaking, the only chaperone a young girl of good character requires is her own sense of decency and pride. She who possesses these qualities doesn't need a chaperone—ever. She who lacks them . . ." The nun laughed lightly. "Argus himself couldn't chaperone her."

Salvo and Mimoo had now been reduced to silence. Gina thought this was a terrible start. Nothing could go well from such a grim beginning. And who was Argus?

"Your daughter doesn't need a chaperone," Mother Grace flatly stated. "Do you know what she needs? An education."

Mimoo opened her mouth. Weakly Salvo nodded his head. Fervently Gina shook hers. Mother Grace ignored them all. "Why isn't she in school?" the nun demanded. "You want to know what's wrong, how she can be put on the right road? With an education, that's how. A girl of fourteen—"

"Fifteen," Gina interjected.

Mother Grace stared her down. "Excuse me. I was addressing your mother. A girl of *fifteen* should not be working."

"Many girls *do* work," Mimoo limply defended. "And we need the money."

Mother Grace opened her hands in front of her. "Well then, what more is there to discuss, Mrs. Attaviano? It sounds as if you've already made your decision."

Mimoo hurried with an explanation. "What I meant to say is . . . she is barely working."

"That is also a problem. She is barely working *and* not going to school? The devil dances in an empty pocket. Only a full-time education will save her."

"From what?" asked Gina.

Salvo stabbed her with his finger. Mimoo crossed herself. Mother Grace sat silently and watched the three of them. "Can you quit your job, Mrs. Attaviano, and devote all your time to watching your daughter? Making sure she is at the factory when she says she is, walking her from the mill to the mission? Collecting her when she has done her work with us? Can your son?" They did not answer the nun. "I didn't think so. That is not the normal order of things. You must work, your son must work, and your daughter must receive academic instruction—in writing, in arithmetic, in reading English, in history, in theology. And clearly also in rules of acceptable behavior."

Gina glared at her mother accusingly. After a loud "Hail Mary," Mother Grace asked to speak to Gina alone. Despite Gina's vehemently shaking head, Mimoo and Salvo speedily departed—ran was a more accurate description.

Gina hung her head as the door closed and the nun in

front of her sat and counted her rosaries. After she had finished praying, the nun sat quietly. "Well?" she finally said. "Your mother and brother have left. There is no need to be coy. Tell me your plan."

Gina was now required to speak. But her plan was to circumnavigate every question about to be asked of her. She would make like the vessels that sailed all the way around the South American continent. She said nothing.

"By your silence, I take it to mean you haven't got one?"

It was best in all circumstances not to speak.

"I know you would prefer to avoid the responsibilities that come from being a charge under adult care," Mother Grace said. "But you can't. You can't make your own decisions. You know how I know? Because you thought it would be a good idea to take the train by yourself to Boston in the middle of the night."

"It wasn't the middle of the night, Reverend Mother. There was a problem with—"

"Please stop. The only problem was with your behavior, your actions. I don't know what you have been taught in Italy; I hazard not much, but here in your adopted country the rules of propriety that all modest young ladies are required to exhibit dictate without exception that you cannot be on the train by yourself at midnight."

"I wasn't by myself."

"Verity Dunne doesn't count. She is also a young lady."

Gina clamped her teeth together. She suspected that one of the other rules of behavior in this unfathomable country dictated also, without exception, that she could not be on the train at midnight with a young unattached gentleman. Or two.

"I'm sorry, Reverend Mother," she repeated. "The train was delayed."

"The train was not delayed, my child. The train exposed your flagrant impropriety so that it could be corrected. The train did its job. Now your guardians have to do theirs."

Gina's lip was twisted as she hopped from reply to reply inside her head.

"You lied to the woman who gave you life and to your brother," said Mother Grace. "How does it feel, Gina, to lie to the ones who love you most? Does that make you feel more holy—or less? What about tempting your new and impressionable friend into lying to *her* parents to cover up for your behavior? Taking advantage of your friend's affection for you, and of her weaknesses, does that make you feel more dignified? Or less?"

What *was* the proper response to this? Absolutely no response at all. Somewhere inside, shame tickled the back of Gina's throat. But her tongue was dried up with fear. What if she couldn't go back to Boston again!

Mother Grace squinted, staring at Gina more closely. "You're quite an enterprising little soul, aren't you? You've got mysteries inside that motivate you. My words are barely registering. Well, never mind. I'm not going to waste my breath further."

"Verity is against the impending war with Spain," Gina suddenly blurted out. "She didn't accompany *me* to the Anti-Imperialist League. I accompanied her."

Mother Grace calmly studied a red-in-the-face Gina. "Tell me," she asked, "in *your* opinion, is it or is it not a sin to lie to an ordained servant of God in an abbey of our Lord?"

Gina swallowed down the fear and the remorse and looked away from Mother Grace's black-eyed gaze.

"The war will or won't happen with or without Verity's participation in an anti-war organization," said Mother

148

Grace. "But you know what definitely won't happen without *your* participation? The rest of your life."

"I understand, Reverend Mother. I'm trying to participate."

"Your father, God rest his soul, wanted you to come to America. For what purpose, do you think?"

"He wanted me to make my own choices."

"Are you making them now?"

"Yes, Reverend Mother."

"Are you making the right choices?"

Gina kept quiet. She thought she was.

"Are you interested in life in the church?"

"Yes. I mean, no. I mean, yes, most ardently, but not as . . . I don't think I'm cut out to commit myself fully to the Church, Reverend Mother," she admitted. "I don't have the requisite traits."

"What traits are those? Honesty? Humility? Modesty?" She stared down at Gina's shoes and ankles, which were both clearly visible below the satin hem of her gray linen dress. "Do you love God?"

"Most fervently. But . . ."

"There is a but after that?"

Why was the Reverend Mother pressing so hard?

"What is it? Do you want to be married? Do you want a family?"

"Something like that," Gina said vaguely. She didn't want a family in the least. Marriage was not on her mind—children even less. But she couldn't explain her actual plans to a *nun*. She couldn't speak aloud about the other Love that was not the Agape love her mother had taught her about, the selfless love meant for your family and for God. She wished this conversation were over.

"I will work harder, Reverend Mother. It will be as you wish."

"It's not work you need."

"I won't be deceitful anymore. I won't use my friends. I'll do as you wish."

"Not as *I* wish. As the path of your own life necessitates. What kind of person do you want to be?"

"An American woman," Gina whispered. "An American young lady."

Mother Grace nodded almost approvingly. "Very good. Do you think American women, urban Boston ladies, scrape the skin off their fingers disentangling wool? Do you think their hands look like your hands, abraded, roughened by hard work, calloused, bruised? Could anyone kiss the hand of a working wool-sorter like you, Gina, a gentleman inviting you to your first dance? Or, do you think the young ladies, such as you hope to be, read books, adhere to firm manners, learn the piano?"

"I can only do now what I can do," Gina said grimly, squeezing her hands into fists and hiding them behind her back. "I'm hoping the rest of it might follow."

"That depends on you, Gina Attaviano. You are on a journey. You started in Italy. Now you are here. Where will you end up? That part is up to you."

Gina knew where she wanted to end up.

She desperately didn't want to be trapped in a school. The Catholics would never let her go. Service in the Church was for life. She would never help Salvo save money to make his dream happen, even if he himself seemed to be so far from it. She'd never buy herself silk or velvet. She'd never dress like a lady, dance with Harry, maybe . . . somehow . . .

The agonizing conflict played out in her soul and on her face. Mother Grace sat and waited. Her fingers counted out the rosaries, her lips moved in the silence.

"Reverend Mother," Gina said in one last beseeching attempt, "may I speak freely?"

"You mean you haven't been?"

"Please don't take this the wrong way, but on the one hand you tell me it's *my* journey and *I* must decide, yet on the other inform me I really don't have a choice at all. I want to work, Reverend Mother. I don't want to go to school." She wasn't going to remain a wool-sorter for life. She would get promoted to the mending room.

"Do you feel it's the right choice?"

"I need to work, yes. I need to help the mission, help my mother . . ."

"You didn't answer me. You do this quite often."

"Education has to be chosen freely," Gina said. "Like faith. I'll answer you—it's not what I want. Education, I mean," she clarified. "I want to make my own money, I want to help my brother open his restaurant. I want to live on my own."

"Women do not live on their own," said Mother Grace with finality. "Or you will remain in a textile mill the rest of your life, working sixty hours a week. Nothing will raise your income level. Without education there can and will be no advancement. You will be like your cousin Angela."

"But she is happy!" Gina exclaimed.

"You don't want more for yourself?"

This was so hard for Gina. Her father *had* wanted more for her. But her father didn't care if she wore rags. *She* cared. "Angela has money, she can buy herself things," Gina explained. "She helps her aunt, donates clothes, buys toys for the children at the orphanage."

"Can you buy yourself what *you* want most in the world, child?" Mother Grace asked.

In a stone silent room, Gina had to admit that she could not.

The nun persisted. "If you had the best job in the world, if you were a successful businesswoman, wealthy like Andrew Carnegie, could you buy what you want most in the world?"

Gina was silent. "Am I supposed to answer that question?"

"You are if there is an answer."

"Yes, Reverend Mother," said Gina. "I do believe that money can buy freedom."

"Is freedom what you want most?"

"Freedom to do what I want, yes," Gina averred.

"Choice is not a virtue," said Mother Grace. "You're misunderstanding what I'm telling you. You're misunderstanding freedom. There is absolutely no virtue in making *a* choice. Only in making the right one."

"But it must be one freely taken!"

"Yes, a freely taken *right* choice!"

"The right one for me."

"Oh, so it's a personal opinion now, virtue." Mother Grace sighed. "Gina, you are fifteen years old. You are not old enough to make these decisions for yourself. You're not old enough to protect yourself; you're not old enough to support yourself. And without an education you will never achieve the latter. So right now, I'm afraid it's time for Compline for me and time to *comply* for you. You've taken up my entire prayer hour. And I sense that you're still very far from understanding. No matter. We will give you the tools, and you can later decide if you will use them. Your mother has made her wishes clear. She wants you protected and educated. You will go to Notre Dame six days a week. You may still volunteer a few hours at the mission after school if it doesn't interfere with your studies and your chapel work. It can be part of your overall curriculum. But your studies must and will come first."

"Please, Reverend Mother," Gina said, trembling. It was a nightmare. "I have a part-time job at Washington . . . that's where I get the wool to help the church."

Mother Grace bowed her head. "Somehow," she said gently, "this church and this town's poor managed to survive for fifty years without your wool, and we're going to try to do so again. I'm not saying we won't miss it."

"Reverend Mother, please, I will work hard . . ."

"Yes, at school," said Mother Grace. "Who is your manager at Washington? Is it Percy Clark? He is a parishioner at this church and I can intercede with him personally, ask if he would continue to make his generous donation to the mission. After all, he is not making it for *you*, is he, Gina?"

Gina protested bitterly to her mother, shouted and cried, all to no avail. Her wool-sorting job over, her Thursday trips to Boston over, her budding friendship with Verity nearly over, resentment for her mother rampant, the vagaries of fate that caused that awful tree to fall across the rail tracks and ruin all her plans, all of it threatening to burst out of her with every breath, Gina gritted her teeth and started attending classes at the Notre Dame school for girls. She bided her time, pretended to listen, sang at church services, cleaned the nave and the narthex, carried candles and rosaries. Twice a week after school, she still walked over to Washington and with tears in her eyes received Percy's gifts of fourth-grade wool. While she was praying by rote and spinning in her spare time, in her rich and pulsing inner life, Gina feverishly twisted a gossamer thread of a new plan, audacious in its scope, brazen and fearless, but one that might, just might, allow her to spend time with Harry—without Ben and without Verity.

Part Two

THE OBJECTION MAKER

Il y a une femme dans toutes les affaires;
aussitôt qu'on me fait un rapport, je dis:
'Cherchez la femme.'

(There is a woman in every case;
as soon as they bring me a report, I say,
'Look for the woman.')

Alexander Dumas

Chapter Nine
THE NATIVES AND THE PILGRIMS

1

Harry noticed that recently things had been un-characteristically tense. Thanksgiving was his favorite holiday and Esther was helping Bernard cook a comforting meal, using their mother's precious recipes passed down the centuries from Stephen Hopkins who was the great-great-grandfather of Robert Treat Paine, who was the great-great-grandfather of Frances Paine Barrington. Hopkins wasn't just an early settler. He was *the* early settler. Esther and Bernard brined the turkey, made leek and bacon stuffing, jellied cranberry sauce, sweet potatoes, corn and cabbage. They made three different varieties of pie, all Frances Barrington perfections: pumpkin, apple, and cherry, Harry's personal favorite. The whole day was usually relaxed and pleasant, even if by the end of the evening, Alice's parents had had a little too much brandy, but this didn't upset Harry, because they were not mean, just tearfully sentimental, telling him how he was "already" part of their family, and how fond their beloved Alice was of him.

His Uncle Henry would come with his three strapping sons and dutiful and church-mouse-quiet Aunt Ruth. Harry liked his cousins, but had more in common with the mahogany umbrella stand. Until they left, usually blessedly early (because Aunt Ruth was prone to awful migraines, and was it any wonder?), the conversation around the dinner table revolved around nothing but the recounting, in tortuous detail, of the ignominy of losing the annual Regatta race to Yale eleven out of the last thirteen years. Last June was the first time Harvard had won in seven years, and judging from the celebration around Boston you'd think they'd won the Hundred Years War. All the Barringtons had gone down to New Haven for the sacred twenty-minute event and then talked about it non-stop for the next four months—all except Harry who afterward wished only to puncture his eardrums with rusty nails.

Ben and Esther usually played Parcheesi or got Herman and Ellen to make up a foursome for bridge. Ellen drank happily and socially with Herman, engaging him on all manner of lively topics, from the price of paper to the reasons for the decline of civilization, on which they heartily yet agreeably disagreed.

But this Thanksgiving, there didn't seem to be much of any of that—no maudlin protestations of love from the Porters, no Parcheesi between Ben and Esther, and no relaxed banter between Ellen and Herman. And no Uncle Henry. Aunt Ruth had had a minor stroke and could not venture out in public.

This Thanksgiving, Elmore came instead of Uncle Henry, bringing his own parents and grandparents. Harry would've liked to blame the tension on Elmore and his lack of compatibility with his sister, but he suspected the awkwardness of the celebration had little to do with the medical student. Two weeks before Thanksgiving, over Sunday lunch in front of everyone, Esther for some odd reason pressed Harry and Ben on extending a Thanksgiving invitation to their new friends in Lawrence.

"What new friends in Lawrence?" Alice instantly piped in.

"Harry, you haven't told Alice about your friends from Lawrence?"

"I don't have any friends from Lawrence." He stared into his roast potatoes.

"It is custom," Esther proceeded mildly, "in our country, to welcome newcomers by sharing our holiday table with them. Remember the story of Grandpa Stephen? The Pilgrims and the Indians? He walked off the *Mayflower*, the first immigrant, if you will, and the Indians didn't scalp him, no, they gave him corn. *That's* the true Thanksgiving tradition. We are the original immigrants, Harry. We feel an affinity with the newcomers. Now we've become the natives. But if not the immigrants at the table of the natives, then who?"

"Good question," said Herman. "Well said, daughter. Who *are* these people? And will we have the room? Jones? How many are you thinking of inviting, Harry? My brother is not coming, but Elmore is bringing his parents and grandparents."

"We have a banquet-sized dining room, Father," said Esther. She seemed to be pressing the point rather humorlessly. "Besides, Elmore is not an immigrant. Thanksgiving doesn't quite apply to him."

161

"Perhaps," Herman suggested, "you're taking the Indian-native thing too literally. We don't actually *have* to invite the immigrants."

"I think Ben and Harry might like to."

Harry saw doomsday up ahead. But Ben, deaf to nuance, lit up. "Why, what a fabulous idea!"

"Ben," said Harry. "Your mother is coming. She said she might bring your Aunt Josephine."

"Really?" Herman exclaimed. "Jones, did you hear that? Are you counting?"

"No, sir." Louis was standing by the door, not paying any attention.

"I'm thrilled your aunt can join us, Ben," said Herman. "I like her enormously. She's got so much sense. But now we really won't have room." He shrugged, his mouth curling upward in an ironic smile. "We'll have to set out the immigrant table in our breakfast room. I'm not sure that will be in keeping with the spirit of the holiday though. What do you think, Esther?"

"I'll invite them regardless," said Ben, barely able to contain his excitement. "We'll figure it out."

The girls had stopped coming on Thursday evenings, so Ben dragged Harry all the way to Summer Street, and called on the Attavianos on a Wednesday evening a week before Thanksgiving. Harry thought it was a terrible idea and said so to an utterly undeterred Ben. "I haven't seen her in weeks," Ben said. "I just want to say hello. What if she got in trouble after her train was late?"

"What *if*?"

Gina was there, but was not allowed to speak, or even permitted to leave her room, though she did come down the stairs and stood, surreptitiously pressed against the landing wall, watching the two young men, with their hats

162

in their hands and their coats still on—not being asked to sit down, not offered a cup of tea. This noticeably deflated Ben. Gina couldn't tell them what was wrong, though her eyes tried to speak all the things she could not say.

After Ben's awkward invitation, Mimoo and Salvo stared at him with such hatred and disbelief, as if they had misunderstood and he had come to invite them not to Harry's house for a feast but to spend eternity in hell.

"Oh, that would be *so* wonderf—" Gina began from the stairs. At the frontline, Salvo whipped around to shut her up with a glare and then turned to Ben and Harry. "Thank you," he finally managed to utter. "But unfortunately we won't be able to make it. We have plans to start our own traditions with our family and friends here in our new home." Salvo said nothing after that, and even Mimoo, who was usually polite to guests, didn't invite them to stay for a drink, or have a morsel of the delectable cheesecake that had recently come out of the oven and was cooling on the stove.

Gina was prevented from speaking a word to them, ushered upstairs before she could.

On the train back, Harry was unapologetically caustic. "So I couldn't tell, would they rather sit down for turkey with you and me, or . . . eat week-old fish? Mulled cider in Barrington or drink a gallon of salt water?"

"Why were they being like that? It's foolish. It's not reasonable."

"Benjamin, you're smitten with their fifteen-year-old daughter! Who is the one with no sense?"

"I have been nothing but respectful and proper."

"And foolish."

"They don't know how I feel."

"Oh yes, because you've kept it well hidden. Did you see

163

Salvo's expression? He wanted to strike you dead with the power of his hatred alone. He seemed shocked it wasn't working."

Ben tutted, tapping on the darkened window as the hiss and release of steam from the caboose car drowned out his irritated words for a few moments.

"Did you hear what I said?" Ben repeated. "Would *you* be so unreasonable if I were to inquire after Esther?"

Harry turned to Ben, his gray eyes unblinkingly focused on his friend. "Try me," he said. "Inquire."

Ben nodded. "Exactly! Why can't Salvo be like you?"

"For one I'm not Sicilian. They disembowel you in Italy for dishonoring their females."

"I'm not dishonoring, I'm honoring!"

"Please. You don't fool Salvo. You don't fool me." Harry wanted to add, you don't even fool my sister.

"They're not in Italy now." Ben took his hat and placed it over his chest, as if he were putting his heart into it. A minute went by in silence. Suddenly Ben said, "You could've helped me a little." His tone was accusing.

"Helped you how? I came with you, didn't I?"

"You just stood like a pillar and didn't say a word. You let me drown out there and you didn't come to my rescue."

"Did you see the look on their faces? On her face?" Harry said. "She must have gotten into such trouble after the train was late. I was reacting to that. I didn't know what to say."

"What have I done?" said Ben. "What do I do?" He looked crestfallen.

"Benjamin, what do you *do*? Ashley, from Apley Court. She has had her eye on you since Hydrostatics and Integral Calculus. Why do you think she's taking Dynamics of a Rigid Body?"

"Stop joking. This isn't funny."

"Forget the fifteen-year-old. Trust me, there is no future there."

"I'm not even sure I want a future," Ben said, turning to stare out the dark window at his mirrored reflection. "Perhaps I would like ten minutes now."

"And you wonder why Salvo wants you dead."

2

So here it was, Thanksgiving, and no one was happy. Only Elmore was oblivious to the undercurrents. He spent most of the reception hour regaling Esther with his knowledge of the advances in modern radiology treatments. Harry thought that men who courted women sure had some peculiar ideas about what women found enticing. Esther, while remaining silent, looked like she wanted to poke out her eyes (or his?) with knitting needles. Herman spent the time in the drawing room with Ellen and Josephine Shaw Lowell and the Porters. Josephine looked nothing like Ellen: she was tall, commanding, wore matronly clothes appropriate for a widow, and had her hair parted in the middle and wrapped into a severe bun that pulled the skin of her face back and made her expressionless. She didn't smile or frown, her skin so taut. She just loomed above her animated petite and round sister, pleasantly dressed and perfumed, nodding at Josephine in reverential agreement. Ben, clearly sick of Harry's company, endeavored to make Harry sick of his by talking non-stop about Panama. "I will sign any petition," said Harry, "I will give any amount of money, I will go to any demonstration, if only you will stop."

"Would you prefer to be over there?" Ben pointed to his mother, on the other side of the room, who was loudly accusing

Herman of approving the war with Spain only because he was a man. That paid diminishing returns with Herman who in return demanded of Ellen how she would like her pacifist namby-pamby ideas dismissed solely because she was a woman.

"I want to be like Louis," said Harry to Ben, pointing to his butler who had walked into the drawing room and now stood like a statue with his hands by his sides. "Blessedly deaf."

"If only," Louis said, announcing that dinner was served.

Before they took their first bite of turkey, Herman, who couldn't let it go, who couldn't let anything go, asked Harry to give his opinion on the war. And give it Harry did, agreeing with Ellen and Josephine that indeed it was a terrible idea.

There was vocal reprobation around the table. Even Orville came down on Harry, and he usually stayed away from politics. "That's unbecoming, Harry," Orville said. "A man has to be *for* war."

"That just proves our point!" Ellen exclaimed. "Right, Josephine?"

"I don't know how I feel about your long-term prospects with my daughter," Orville continued, "knowing you side with *women* about matters of war."

That stopped the conversation like a derailed train. Stopped the clinking of forks, the pouring of drinks. It was as if everything was still for a moment. Aside from the challenging insult, it was a moment in which nearly everyone at the table—Herman, Harry, Esther, a mortified Alice, Orville, Irma, Louis with a serving dish of mashed potatoes, Ellen, Ben and even Josephine—remembered a small detail: Harry had yet to ask for Alice's hand.

"Um, can you pass the salt, Father," Harry asked, reaching over. "And the gravy, too, please."

"Here, darling," said Alice, handing him the gravy ladle, her hand slightly trembling. "I have one here." Harry saw it, and gently patted her laced-up forearm, giving her a calming smile, as if to say, don't worry about a thing, my skin is too thick to care. She visibly relaxed.

Elmore was oblivious to all undercurrents. "Did you know Walter Reed is performing medical experiments in Cuba?" he said, ever the doctor in training. "Inducing yellow fever in dozens of unwilling subjects to prove that mosquitoes carry the plague that's decimating the tropics. Fortunately none of them have died."

"The mosquitoes?" said Harry.

"The unwilling subjects," appended Elmore.

"So *far*," said Ellen. "But do you know what thousands *have* died from? Imperialism."

"Mother, *please*," said Ben. "It's Thanksgiving dinner."

"What, people don't die on Thanksgiving? It's not a holiday in Puerto Rico, son."

"Your mother is quite right, Benjamin," said Josephine. "Eat your turnips." Josephine still thought of Ben as eleven years old, because that's how old he was when he stopped living with her.

"Yellow fever and malaria are the scourges of the tropics," Elmore went on, ignoring the songs of war, beating the disease drum.

"You know what the scourge of the tropics is?" said Ellen. "Imperialism."

Ben emitted a gurgling sound of throaty frustration.

Leaning to him, Harry lowered his voice. "See, now you know how I feel when you go on ceaselessly about your stupid canal."

"Mother, stop," Ben repeated. "Goodness, you'd think it was a Thursday night!"

"Actually it is, son. It's Thanksgiving." Everyone laughed and the tension lifted for a moment. "The U.S. forces are down in China," Ellen said to Ben, "allied against the Chinese who hate foreign intervention."

"China is not the tropics, Mother."

"In Cuba we are promising them intervention," Ellen pressed on, banging the plate with her fork, "to preserve what we call 'independence.' That's just another word for colonialism."

"No, it isn't." That was Herman. "What about our protection of individual liberty?"

"Another name for colonialism."

"Oh, Ellen, no. Come on." That was Josephine, the politically active feminist and philanthropist, the purveyor of all things anti-imperialist and even she was saying that Ben's mother was stepping over the line. Ben glared at his mother from across the table with gleeful satisfaction.

Ellen cheerfully ignored him. "Is there anywhere in the world we won't go to protect our interests?" she asked, undeterred. "Cuba, Puerto Rico, China, Panama . . ."

"Mother, leave my Panama out of this."

"Costa Rica . . ."

"Her too."

"Son, please."

"Mother, no matter what you think, we are going to sign a treaty with Britain to allow us to build a canal in Panama."

"That treaty will never happen," said Ellen and Elmore in unison. Ellen had found a lone supporter in the mosquito expert! It was a devil's alliance. Harry stayed out of it.

"Oh, I assure you," Herman intervened. "That treaty *will* happen. Your son is entirely correct, Ellen. I know this for a fact, because a fine man and a very good friend of mine,

Secretary of State John Hay, has been negotiating that treaty."

"Imperialism—naked and unabashed!"

"Mother, but the language of the treaty is explicit," Ben said. "The canal will be neutral and free to all nations. Just like the Suez."

Ellen showed supreme indifference to Ben's "facts." "So we build it, we use our money and then you think we will just allow anyone to pass through it? It will never happen."

"Your mother is right," said Elmore. "Sorry, Mr. Barrington. Congress will never ratify that treaty."

Ben chafed most when forced to reply to Esther's unsuitable suitor. "They *will* ratify," said Ben, "because the whole world will benefit."

"But none more so than America, right?" Ellen said.

"Does that make you unhappy, Ellen, my friend?" Herman asked. "Is there something wrong with our country benefiting from its honest labor?"

"We don't need it," Ellen said adamantly. "We don't need bananas. We don't need tea from China. We don't need sugar from Cuba. We don't need any of these things."

The table was quiet as they digested their pies and breads and swallowed their tea.

"Tell me again, Mother, why our business interests in Costa Rica must be cut off," said Ben. "But do have another bite of fried plantain first."

"Ellen, have you been in contact with Eugene Debs?" Herman asked. "He thinks like you."

"Oh, yes," she said. "He is coming to speak at our next week's meeting. Will you be joining us, Herman?"

Herman smiled benevolently. "I'm having lunch at the Porcellian Club with Mr. Wendell Holmes," he said. "But

169

thank you. Perhaps Harry will attend. Seems right up his alley."

"No, no, Harry is coming to a charity ball with me next Thursday," said Alice, with a fiery gaze at her mother.

Harry touched her hand as he reached for a white napkin.

"You know, Herman, it would behoove you to come," said Ellen. "So many women come to our meetings. Even young girls who are quite interested in progressive ideas." Ellen smiled. "They might not grow up to be bankers and merchants like you, but then they also won't go to war . . ."

"Like Uncle Robert, Mother?" Ben asked sharply.

Herman laughed. "Your son has a point, Ellen. To rail against war when your own brother was martyred in one seems unsuitable somehow."

"No," she said staunchly. "I rail against unjust war."

"There was a lot of protest against our Civil War also," Herman reminded her. "A president lost his life because of it."

The table became a little quieter.

"I don't know what *that* war has to do with what we're talking about here," Ellen said. "The right to keep within our own borders." She turned her gaze back to her son. "Have you asked your young friends what they think of your Panama Canal? Perhaps they can go to Panama with you."

"Perhaps they might."

"The tall one especially. Variety, is that her name?"

"Verity," Ben corrected.

"Right. She is *enormously* talented. Grasps concepts quickly, is fascinated by every speaker we have—and has her heart in the right place. The other one . . ." Ellen shrugged, kept going. "Frankly I don't have much hope for her. She has a vacant look about her, as if she understands nothing."

"She doesn't speak English well, Ellen," said Harry.

"Oh, she speaks just fine. Why does she come then?"

"Who are we talking about?" asked Alice.

Ben looked down into his sweet potatoes and corn.

"Just some ladies who come to the meetings on Thursdays. Though I haven't seen them in a while. Perhaps they lost interest?"

"Perhaps." Ben didn't look at his mother.

"They're funny birds, those two," Ellen went on. "Even the indifferent one. Do you remember her trying to quote from John Quincy Adams?" She laughed in mockery. "I never heard anyone mangle Adams quite so. She was trying to reproduce his anti-imperialism quote. Oh, how she butchered it. '*Doctor*' instead of '*dictator*' indeed!"

Harry and Ben exchanged a darkening quizzical look, as if both were surprised that a seemingly innocent conversation could suddenly get so churlish.

"Give the girl a break, Ellen," said Harry who saw that Ben couldn't say the things he was thinking of saying to his mother. "You should be pleased that at least it was an *anti*-imperialism quote."

"I can't understand why she comes, that's all."

"Well, she's not coming anymore, is she, Mother?" Ben said, throwing down his napkin onto his half-empty plate and standing up. "Thank you for dinner, Mr. Barrington. Happy Thanksgiving, sir. But we're late. Aunt Effie has been invited to the Cabots in Beacon Hill for seven-thirty, and it's well past."

They left soon thereafter, and Elmore left too, with his family. No one stayed for after-supper brandy in the library, not even the Porters, who feigned exhaustion before hastily departing. Herman thanked Louis for a lovely meal and went to bed. Only Harry and Esther remained in the library, nursing their drinks and their small sharp wounds.

*　　*　　*

"Alice is so fond of you, Harry."

"And I of her."

"So why don't you ask the girl to marry you? Make an honest woman out of her."

"Where's the fire? I haven't graduated. I don't know what I'm doing. Alice's father should never have said that. It just made poor Alice uncomfortable."

"Why do parents never fail to embarrass their children?"

"I don't know."

"He had too much to drink."

"An hour into the evening?"

"He didn't mean it. But what do you mean, you don't know what *you're* doing? What do you see as your options? Going to Costa Rica with Ben to grow bananas?" Esther gave a small scornful chuckle.

They sipped their cordials. The fire was lit. It was quiet.

"Do you *want* to marry Alice?"

"The question is, dear sister, does Alice want to marry *me*?"

"Who wouldn't?" she said, taking her brother's hand for a moment.

"Don't be a silly goose. *Who* wouldn't? Most of the respectable girls in Boston, that's who. All I do is read and think. And drink. You think that's appealing to beautiful society girls like Alice?"

"Yes," she said quietly. And then, even more quietly, "But what about the non-respectable girls?"

He glanced at her, frowning. "I don't know any of those, do I?"

"No?"

"What are you talking about, Esther?"

She said nothing. "Why are you so oblivious?" she whispered.

"To what?"

"Nothing, nothing."

"Tell me."

"Nothing, I said."

He let his drink go, but not the subject matter. "Everybody's oblivious, Esther. Have you noticed? No one sees what's under his very nose."

She assented with the deepest of sighs. Usually they stopped speaking here, stopping just short of confessions, of intimacies. But tonight was quiet and the fire was still going, gradually burning out, the evening didn't seem as long as the years in between, and so Esther poured her and Harry another brandy cordial and sat back down by his side. She eyed him, appraised him, delighted in him for a moment, touching his tousled head with affection. Then she spoke after the liquor had warmed her throat and made it easier for her to say what she had never said. "He doesn't see me," she said so quietly as if almost to herself, "because he doesn't love me."

Harry chewed his lip. "He is just oblivious, Esther. All he thinks about is bananas."

"Are you saying it because you want to ease my heartache or because you're defending your friend?"

Harry thought about it. "I don't know."

She nodded. "Of course you don't. I'll tell you. He's oblivious because I'm invisible to him. I know this to be true."

"He doesn't know how you feel. You're three years older. You've known him since we were kids. He thinks you're his sister too."

"But I'm not."

"So hint to him how you feel."

"If he knew I'd never see him again. He would stop coming."

"He grew up with you, Esther. He can't look at you any other way. You're *my* sister. It's wrong."

She shook her head. "It's wrong only because he doesn't feel it."

Harry said nothing.

Esther lowered her voice a notch further. "But one of these days, Harry, you might want to tell your closest friend the truth. Let him down gently, the way you've let me down gently, and Father, and Mother, and everyone else who's known you, tell him in your inimitable delicate detached way, Harry, that *she* doesn't see him either, that *she* is oblivious to him for the same reason *he* doesn't see *me*."

"Who?" said Harry, but even as he spoke, cold color came to his face. He looked away. "I don't know what you're talking about."

"No?"

"No."

They sat. She spoke again. "You know who that girl is *not* oblivious to, though?"

Harry jumped up. He spilled his drink.

"Eventually, do you think *you*, Harold Barrington, could let Ben know if you're oblivious to her?"

"I really have no earthly idea what you're talking about. But it's getting late, Esther. I'm quite tired. Good night. Happy Thanksgiving."

He was about to leave the library. "Are you coming up?"

"I'll sit here for a little while and finish my drink. Good night." She turned away.

Soon 1899 became 1900.

Chapter Ten
IN THE BOSTON WINTER

1

At the start of the new century, Gina wrote Harry a letter. She didn't ask Salvo about it, she didn't ask her mother, and she didn't ask Angela. She didn't even ask Verity about it, who was busy with church and school. Gina tried to leave the letter mysterious, yet impersonal enough that if it were intercepted, she could defend sending it by the sheer professional dullness of its content. She remembered glancing at only one or two worthwhile tidbits in that 1838 tome of nonsense she had tossed aside. One said, never, *ever*, write to a man. But if you absolutely must write to a man, never ever commit to paper anything you would not want published in the evening tabloid with your name above it.

Dear Harry,

I hope this letter finds you well. I have a proposal of a business nature I would like to discuss with you on behalf of my family. Is there an opportunity for us to meet sometime in the near future so I can present to you my idea of a business venture?

I look forward to hearing from you.

Yours sincerely,

Gina Attaviano

She kept it as formal as she could, hoping he would respond in kind.

"Harry, who in the world is sending you letters?" Esther wanted to know after he finished reading it.

"A man about a horse," replied Harry, stuffing the missive into his breast pocket.

She waved him off. "Seriously, who is it from?"

"Do you feel strongly that this concerns you?"

"I feel strongly that it does, yes."

"Well, do you want to know what concerns me?"

"Not until you answer my question."

"What concerns me," Harry continued, "is Elmore, whom I find all too frequently at the front door of this house, pretending to make house calls."

Esther flushed. "He is not pretending to make house calls."

"Oh? Is someone actually sick then?"

"He is just visiting. Who is the letter from?"

"It's from a man who wants to sell me a horse, Esther," Harry replied, going on without pause, "because you're aware, aren't you, that residency students who are not yet certified by the board are not allowed by law to make house calls?"

176

"He is not making house calls! This conversation is over," Esther said, bustling out, even the crinoline in her smart skirt starchly prickling.

Harry laughed. But he was aware that he didn't tell her who the letter was from. He didn't want to unpack the reasons why. Harry suspected Esther would think it was untoward to meet Gina to discuss anything, and Harry didn't feel like defending himself or explaining. He spent enough time explaining himself to his father in ways big and small; he didn't want to be flanked by his sister as well, who tended for all her propriety to blow things out of *all* proportion, perhaps because her outward life was so still and calm.

But also—and it was a small but significant also—Harry was afraid that Esther might mention it to Ben, as a mere aside, the way she casually mentioned the worst of things at Sunday dinners—it was a genetic family flaw—and what if Ben didn't think it was quite so insignificant? Harry didn't want to explain himself to Ben either, nor to hurt his friend's feelings for a silly trifle. If it was important, he would of course tell him, but because it was superficial but potentially hurtful, he kept the letter to himself, first in his breast pocket and then locked in his personal cabinet in his room.

Dear Gina,

I don't know if I can help you with your business proposal, I am tied up in personal and professional projects that take up the bulk of my time. However, not wanting to thwart a successful idea, would it be possible for you to come to Boston in the next two weeks? I have some time on Tuesdays between two and four, and Wednesdays between four and seven. I can meet your train at the North Street station if you can let me know what time you will be arriving.

Yours sincerely,
Harry Barrington

Dear Harry,
Can we meet next Wednesday? I will take the 4:15 and be at North Station by 6:00 in the evening.
Gina

2

She sat at her lessons on Wednesday paying even less attention than usual, if that were possible. She faked not feeling well, and at the end of her classes, stepped into St. Vincent's, and immediately informed the nuns that she was feeling faint and would not be able to spin tonight. She was going to go home and lie down. She changed out of her school uniform in the closet in the vestibule, stuffed the uniform into her ragtag bag, and ran down Haverhill and across Broadway to the train station.

The thirty-mile journey to Boston took eighty minutes— the longest eighty minutes of her life. The oceanic crossing from Naples to Boston felt like a summer night compared to the endless clang of the crawling caboose. She was jittery, mostly because she knew she had to stay calm to get Harry to take her seriously and, being Italian and always gesticulating with her hands and being overly expressive with her face, she didn't know if she could do that, stay calm enough for him to take her seriously. She was dressed deliberately dowdy: she wore her hair up in a severe bun, like Ben's widowed aunt, whom she had met a few times at Old South.

She had on a dark, puritanical skirt that covered a foot of ground around her shoes, and a long-sleeved, high-necked, no-frills dark blouse—a monastic uniform. From the nuns she learned, at least outwardly, how to keep the mask of decorum. She wanted to appear businesslike, not too lively. Her shoes were sensible and low-heeled and in any case invisible. She didn't borrow anything shiny from Angela, not like last summer when she served lemonade and procured signatures for clearing tropical swampland while jangling silvery bracelets from her tanned slender wrists in front of Harry's perspiring face. She scrubbed her skin and nails. If someone were to see them on the street, she wanted to remain without reproach. Not a smidgen of impropriety must pass between them. She tried to comport herself like his sister Esther, like Mother Grace. She debated whether to bring a rosary, but decided against it. Harry, being of a nebulous religion, wouldn't understand the significance of prayer beads, might think them peculiar. What if he was some kind of Protestant?

She was walking down the length of the platform, being careful not to trip over her skirt, when she spotted Harry standing under the massive clock. When he saw her, he took off his hat and held it in his hands. She walked up to him, all practical and solemn, allowing herself the smallest of all polite smiles. "Hello, Harry."

"Hello, Gina. How was your ride in?"

"It was fine. Thank you for asking."

"You're welcome." He was bundled up in a coat, a gray wool scarf and a smart bowler hat. He carried an umbrella like a walking stick.

She tried not to admire his freshly pressed double-breasted long overcoat, tailored, thick, beautifully made and draped. His shoes were black and shined despite the weather. Only his hair was rumpled and slightly too long, and his face looked as if he had not shaved very recently, perhaps late last evening, if then. She tried so hard not to look at him, and at the same time she needed to look at him, to maintain the businesslike aspect of the purpose of her visit.

She didn't know where to go from there. Were they going to stand and chat in the middle of the station? She hadn't thought out that part.

"Have you been waiting long?" she asked. "The train was a few minutes late."

"No, I'm always early. Unfortunately I've picked up my father's worst habits. Are you comfortable? It's miserable outside."

So they *were* going to go somewhere else. She was also dressed in a coat and hat, but drab not elegant like his. "This is my first cold winter. I'm not used to this weather," she said, suddenly flushed from their scandalous inequality. "It was never like this in Belpasso."

"No, I don't imagine it was."

"Should we . . . go sit somewhere?" she carefully suggested. "Verity and I used to pass a tea house when we walked to Old South, on Valenti Way . . . why are you smiling?" She was trying to be so proper. What now?

"We could go sit in the tea house," Harry said, "but you and I will be sitting in separate rooms."

"Oh." She was morbidly embarrassed.

"In this country men and women don't sit down together in public places. Do they in Italy?"

"Oh, absolutely, yes, of course," Gina stammered, trying to fake being progressive. "My mother and father went out to Luigi's twice a year . . ."

He said nothing. She said nothing. Before he forgot his manners and pointed out the brutal difference between them and a married couple, Gina, her humiliation flush on her face, busied herself with fastidiously buttoning her coat. "We can walk," Harry said, "if you like. I have an umbrella."

"No. I mean, yes. It—it will be fine."

He opened the station doors for her that led onto Causeway.

Outside snow fell from the inky sky. "It's perfectly wretched," Harry said, taking her elbow before she tripped. "Get used to this. It's going to be like this in New England until the thaw."

Personally she thought the thaw was already happening, since his palm was cupping her elbow. Perhaps if they had been on the South Pole, he would have taken her whole arm.

The sidewalk was treacherous; she soon slipped on the freezing sleet. How in the world were they going to discuss anything when their lives were imperiled?

"Here," he said. "Please take my arm. It'll be easier. I'll never forgive myself if you fall and break something."

She tried not to catch her breath as she took his arm. He held the open umbrella over their heads. She walked gingerly next to him, holding up her skirt with her right hand and every once in a while slipping in the icy rain so she could tighten her hold on his forearm. It was dark and the streetlights were on, dancing gold in the white flakes.

"Are you cold?"

"No."

They walked slowly down Causeway in the direction of North End. She pretended she was being careful. Mill Creek was to the left of them, and many bundled-up men sat on milk crates ice fishing. The park around Mill Creek had benches, appealing in the summer perhaps but now covered with slush. She couldn't believe her blessed good fortune to have these five minutes with him completely alone on a public street. She would have liked to talk about nothing at all, but simply after a silent meandering be escorted back to her platform, assisted onto the train, and then spend the eighty-minute ride reliving their walk in the snow.

"So tell me what this is about."

Reverie broken. She swallowed. "Harry, if you could hear me out first please, and *then* let me know what you think. My English can't sustain your questions."

"*Withstand.* Of course. I will say nothing."

"You know that my brother has dreams of opening his own restaurant."

"Do I know this?"

"I thought you said you would say nothing."

"Excuse me."

"You *do* know this. We told you and Ben when we had dinner with you our first evening in America."

"You told us so many things that evening, and such a fine detail must have slipped my mind, especially since your brother was disinclined to speak to us directly."

"Harry."

"Excuse me."

"My brother works two jobs now, at a local tavern at night and in a sawmill during the day. My mother cleans houses and sews."

"What about you?"

She didn't want to tell him she had been forced by nuns and meddling mothers to attend school, because she thought that an association with *high school* would make her more child-like in his eyes. Adults worked. Children went to school. "I'm very busy with St. Vincent's," she said, rushing through her reply. "We are saving our money so we can get a mortgage from a bank to open a restaurant."

Harry cocked his head in approving assent under the umbrella. "But what is it that *I* can help you with?"

"Ben mentioned that your family is in the property business."

"My father is a property developer, that is correct. But not me. I'm still at university."

"Yes, of course." Children went to school. To kindergarten. Men went to university. "But soon you will be working with your father, yes? This is your last year of studies?"

"Even *you* ask me this." Harry took a breath deeper than he meant to. "I don't know what my plans are yet."

"Right. But you *are* going to work with your father?"

"I don't know yet."

Gina frowned, keeping a steady eye on the slick pavement. The snow was coming down heavier. She didn't know what to make of this.

"What can I do for your brother today?" asked Harry.

"Ah. You probably don't know this, since you don't have the opportunity to analyze the Lawrence property market, but there are two wonderful places that are available for renovation."

"Right. I wouldn't know this. I don't even analyze the Barrington property market."

"One place is on Essex Street, in the middle of other restaurants, a wonderful location, very good for business, close to the mills. You remember how busy it was Saturdays?"

"It was quite congested, yes."

"Exactly. The other is on Broadway across from the train station. That location would do big business for travelers. So I was thinking . . . if we acquire these two places and make them new, because one is now a florist and the other a knitting shop that just closed, but a knitting shop near a train station is not very useful, don't you agree?"

"Perhaps that explains its difficulties."

Gina shrugged. "I suppose. But how do you explain the closing of a florist in the middle of a busy shopping street?"

"Too many florists? This one charges too much for flowers? The quality of the flowers is not good?"

"I don't think that's it," Gina said. "I think it is unlucky. But an Italian restaurant that serves inexpensive, well-prepared food . . ."

"Will be more lucky?" finished Harry.

"Yes!"

"Well, what is it you want *me* to do, Gina?"

"Here it is . . ." She was glad they were walking and she could keep her eyes on the road, not his face. "Harry—if you could somehow help my brother get a loan from a bank to acquire these two places, and then help us by making them into restaurants, the way your father makes those apartments in North End into, you know . . ."

"Apartments?"

"Yes. Just to get my brother started . . ." She didn't finish.

"You want me to provide the capital?"

Now she looked up at him. "I promise you, we will not let you down. We will be successful and we'll pay you back, with interest, and you will make money. Also," she quickly went on before he interrupted her again and she lost the gist of what she needed to lay out before him, "you might be interested in becoming part owner of our establishment? Minority owner, of course. But then our success would become your success, and you would make money from us, which would help your business elsewhere. You told me your father liked to help local business . . ."

"I didn't say this to you," Harry said gently.

She felt him looking at her. She studied where she was stepping. "It must have been to Ben."

"You call Lawrence *local* business?"

"It is a good business idea. And it would help my brother. Because no bank is going to give him money right now. He hasn't been in this country long enough. He doesn't have savings. He asked at First National Bank of Lawrence what it would take to get credit. They gave him a list of things so long, it depressed him for a week. He almost gave up."

He watched her thoughtfully. She tried not to blush or avert her gaze. "How do you know anything at all about business, Gina?"

"From my father." She smiled with open pride. "He had a barbershop in a very good part of Belpasso, right where all the bankers went to have their lunch and siesta in the afternoons. He advertised himself to be the quickest barber in town. In and out in under ten minutes or your haircut was free. In no time at all, he had to hire six helpers because he had more business than he could handle. Every day but one he closed by five o'clock so he could go home to his family. He was a good family man, my father."

"And a good barber," said Harry.

"Yes." Gina was happy that Harry remembered. "He became known all over our town and even in nearby Catania as the Barber of Belpasso—all because he took over a news-agent that was one of four in the same area."

"Your father was wise." Harry said. "And his daughter's plan is not bad. I have to think about it. I have no money of my own, so if this is to work, I will have to go and discuss it with my father. And he may be stretched thin in other areas, and may have objections to this I can't see because he is very good at business, while I'm just good at reading."

"I understand. Thank you for listening to me."

They were past Copp's Hill Burying Ground when Harry gradually stopped walking. "Shall we go back? Any further and we'll be in the harbor."

Regretfully she turned back. This time she walked even more slowly. She told him it was because she was tired.

"Should I get us a carriage?"

"No, no." She sped up just enough so he wouldn't offer to get them a carriage again.

"I have one question, Gina."

She waited.

"Your brother Salvo," Harry asked, "he knows you're here, of course?"

"Oh, he thinks this is a very good idea."

"Not what I asked, but all right. I mention this," Harry went on, "because I've met your brother. The most recent time was almost two months ago when Ben and I came to Lawrence to invite you to my house for Thanksgiving. He was too proud to accept our invitation for dinner. I'm just saying that a young man like that seems an unlikely candidate to accept help in procuring a loan."

"This is business," said Gina quickly. "The other thing, maybe he thought it wasn't business."

"The other thing wasn't business. It was hospitality. Much easier to accept than money."

"Not for my brother."

"Really. Well, he must be quite a special young man."

"He is."

The weather had gotten worse, the snow was heavy. Under his umbrella they walked down Causeway. Even the ice fishermen had fled. He tightened his grip on her arm. She didn't think this was the time to tell him she used to run barefoot up the jagged volcanic rock of Mount Etna. She was not born to fall on a flat paved street. It was

186

constitutionally impossible. Instead she squeezed his arm, without words.

He waited with her until the train came, helped her up to the landing, tipped his hat. "I'll talk to my father, and I'll be in touch," he said, as the train started moving.

Gina's wish had come true. Having forgotten all the words they had spoken, she had eighty minutes on the trip back to Lawrence to recall nothing but the feel of his wool coat under her ungloved hand as she walked beside him in the falling snow, as if he were a gentleman and she were a lady.

3

The opportunity took months, but finally presented itself. It had been sleeting and in the lumberyards, sleet coupled with dirt made all surfaces hazardous for young women in their oilskin coats and boots. And this young woman was walking too quickly to get out of the weather, and she slipped and fell. Salvo happened to see it from the warehouse, and in an instant he was by her side helping her up. She seemed dazed and slightly embarrassed.

"Are you all right?" he asked.

"I'm fine, thank you." She waited for him to let go of her, which, when he got the message, he did with alacrity.

"You could have really hurt yourself," Salvo said.

"I've fallen off horses," she said. "This is nothing." She glanced down at her mud-covered coat and boots and shook her head. "I am quite a mess, however. I will have to go clean myself up. Will you excuse me, please?"

He offered her his arm. "Please, let me help you inside," he said. His Italian accent sounded so heavy on him all of a sudden, and his third-hand and battered jacket so beggarly when in such proximity to her fine wool threads.

"That won't be necessary." She scrutinized him. "What is your name?"

"Salvatore Attaviano," he said, lifting his hat. "All my friends call me Salvo." He smiled, showing her the full set of his superb Sicilian teeth.

She didn't return his smile. "I'm Miss Porter, Mr. Attaviano. My father owns this lumberyard. And I'm fine. But thank you for your quick reflexes." And without saying another word, Miss Porter walked off, just as quickly and incautiously as before, slipping and nearly falling twice more in the viscous wet mud before she made her way across the yard and inside the managers' house.

4

Alice and Harry were having their customary Wednesday dinner at Alice's home in Brookline. Usually her parents surrounded her, but tonight Harry had gotten to Brookline later than usual and Orville and Irma, after sitting with them for a half-hour, retired upstairs. Only Sheffield, the Porter's butler, and Trieste, Alice's personal maid, sat in the dining room with them. They were almost alone.

"Why were you so late tonight, dear?" she asked after they had been served their soup and salad simultaneously to speed things up.

"I got caught up in things," he said. "And have you seen the weather? I saw three fallen horses on the way."

"I know, it's ghastly." She lightly tapped his arm before she took her knife. "I love it when you get caught up in things.

It's one more thing about you, darling, I find completely irresistible."

"How can I be that lucky?"

"Because you're adorable," she said, leaning in slightly and kissing the air above his nose. "That's why you're that lucky. Even when you're unpardonably late."

"Why is everyone being so accommodating to me recently?" he asked. "You, your parents?"

She smiled. "Perhaps they're being hopeful?" Before Harry got discomfited, she changed the subject to the first foolish thing that sprung to her lips. "Darling, did you hear about the two men who drowned not far from Barrington? Simply awful, isn't it? Their poor families. In icy water, too."

"I think it probably doesn't matter if the water is freezing or boiling," Harry said, staring blankly into his roast mustard chicken. "How did it happen?"

"No one knows. They were found in shallow, nearly frozen waters."

"Even more suspicious then. Sounds like murder."

"No, no. Nothing as exciting as that." She sighed. "Didn't you read the paper?"

"I did. But I don't read the gossip pages."

"This wasn't in the gossip pages."

"I don't read the obituaries either."

Alice suddenly stopped speaking and put down her utensils.

"God—I'm terribly sorry," she said, placing her hand over Harry's. "That was so thoughtless of me."

Harry blinked, once, twice. "Don't be silly. Tell me about some other horrible thing that's happened. Though, you know, Esther and I get plenty of that from Elmore." Harry forced a laugh, squeezing Alice's fingers. "I think it's one of the reasons Esther won't reject him outright. She is titillated by his stories of hideous infections."

Alice tittered in surprise. "Your sister doesn't seem to me the kind of woman who would be."

"Esther is surprising in many ways," Harry said. "Are you ready for dessert?"

Alice clapped. "Oh yes. I'm so glad you don't have to rush off. Sheffield said the crème brûlée tonight is heavenly."

"How appropriate," said Harry. "Because you're heavenly."

They smiled at each other, sipped their wine, nuzzled the air in front of them.

"The weather's been horrid, hasn't it?"

"Demonic."

"I actually fell today. On flat ground." She shook her head.

"Are you all right?"

"Fine. Nothing injured but my pride. It's unheard of. Just proves how terrible the weather has been. I love our city," Alice said, "but I do wish sometimes I lived in a place where it was a wee bit warmer. Don't you?"

Harry shrugged. "Never really thought about it," he replied. "Like where? Greece or the South of France?" He paused. "Italy?"

Alice became animated. "I meant more like out west. But you know I've always dreamed of traveling to Italy. The whole country sounds so delightful and romantic. And warm."

"Does it?"

"Harry!" Alice laughed. "Why do you sound so far away, as if you've never even heard of Italy?"

He smiled. "Unlike you, I'm so rarely outside, I barely notice the weather. Italy, Boston, all about the same."

"Do you see what I mean?" She gazed at him affectionately. "Completely irresistible. You don't go outside because you're always reading and writing, bent over a desk."

"I go outside sometimes," Harry said. "I walk out of my

front door and get into a carriage. But it brings me only so close to Gore Hall."

"Yes, that's true, you do have to walk a little bit." She stirred his tea. "I'm surprised you're in as good a condition as you are, considering how little you move your body."

He rapped on his temple. "I'm moving in here," he said. "Never stopping."

Crème-brûlée was indeed exquisite, the tea from India very aromatic. The after-dinner cognac warmed their throats, made Alice flushed and giggly and Harry less reticent than usual. They sat in the library while Sheffield stoked the fire every five minutes.

Alice was slightly intoxicated and giggling.

"What is he doing?" she whispered theatrically to Harry. "How much attention can a fire need?"

They broke out into a fit of laughter which they tried to suppress.

"We don't want him to be titillated," whispered Alice.

"Of course not. Or do we?"

Alice gasped in mock-horror. "Harry, what's gotten into you, darling?"

"I don't know," he muttered, moving closer to her on the couch, nuzzling her cheek. "Perhaps I'm getting tired of waiting."

Alice embraced him tightly. "Me too, darling," she whispered. "Me too."

He pulled away to stare at her. Blushing, Alice shook her head. "Dear heart," she said, kissing his temple. "Please don't misunderstand. I'm not the girl who gives away the milk for free."

Lightly he kissed her. "Of course you're not, darling. Forgive me for giving you the utterly false impression that I thought you were."

"You're always an impeccable gentleman, Harry," Alice said. "Sometimes I wish you would give me that impression."

"Now who's getting amorous?" He pulled himself up off the couch. "It's a good thing I'm not at the reins," he said. "Or I'd be in Mill Creek for sure."

"In *where?*"

"Oh, this little pond where men ice fish in the winter. Never mind." He gave her his hand to help her up. "It's late, Alice dear, and I bid you good night."

"I'll see you Sunday," she said at the open door, wrapping her shawl tighter around herself in the chill wind. "Will you promise me to think about things?"

"That's all I do," said Harry, bowing before he put on his hat. "I think about things."

When, a few days later at lunch, Belinda asked Alice why she so studiously insisted that Harry have dinner every week at her house, like it was church, Alice, batting her eyelashes, replied, "Because everybody knows, silly Belinda, that there is only one place for a gentleman to propose to a lady and that is under her father's roof."

"Ah. Of course, you little mannered sneak." Belinda laughed. "You think eventually he'll get the hint?"

"I hope so," said Alice. "And soon. I'm already twenty-two. How many child-bearing years can I possibly have left?"

5

"I don't think it's a good investment, son," Herman said to Harry when they spoke about the restaurants some weeks later. It had taken Harry until February to bring up the matter.

He was vaguely intrigued by the idea of investing in a business, separate from his father's developments, and all other hefty considerations aside—and hefty they were—thought on the surface of it, it was not an unwise plan, nor financially unsound. It chafed him not to be able to make a decision like this on his own; it made him feel small. Here was this immigrant girl coming to see him because he was a building manager, a superintendent of an entire block of houses in a teeming neighborhood. Ben had been feeding her stories about Harry's ancestors coming down the plank from the *Mayflower*, fighting for independence, signing the Articles of Confederation, and founding towns, yet here he was, unable to write his own check when he needed to pay for things. It had always been this way. He wanted nothing, but he also wanted for nothing. Whatever small things he desired, he received. He had his personal carriage and plenty of money. College was paid for, all his suits, his every comfort. When he wanted to buy Alice a silk scarf, he asked Louis to go pick one up for him, and that evening the scarf would be bought and wrapped and waiting in his room to give to her. Harry didn't know what it was like to be without, to go without. Yet suddenly at twenty-two, nearly graduated from Harvard, here he was, interested in investing in a simple business deal, and he had to go to his father, hand outstretched.

But worse, there was his father, shaking his head, saying he didn't think it was a good investment. It was what nightmares were made of. Finally Harry approaches his father with a small request and has it promptly rejected. Harry waited. It was always better to let Herman have his say. The man was not very good at rebuttal, but very good in firing the first long salvo.

"However, I'm pleased you're showing an interest in something, Harry," Herman went on.

"What do you mean, Father? I'm interested in so many things."

"I mean something real." He continued before Harry could interrupt. "I know something about Lawrence. It's not where you want to invest. The town has serious labor problems, and it won't be long before they'll be in trouble. You've seen what's been happening in Pennsylvania, in West Virginia. Lawrence is next."

"You're worried about the unions?" said Harry. His father was always worried about the unions. "The restaurants will be non-unionized. I'll make sure of it."

"It's not about the restaurants," Herman said. "It's about the demography. Lawrence is an immigrant town, and for some reason rife with the kind of influence that absolutely kills business. Apparently Eugene Debs is close to consolidating and forming the American Socialist Party."

"Who?"

"Oh, Harry. Honestly."

"Father, they have so many names, the socialists, I can't keep up."

"I mentioned him at Thanksgiving. Debs is a critical figure. You might want to keep up with him. Any business you go into, you'll have to contend with him, and the trouble he's stirring up." There was his father, subtly and fraudulently acknowledging that Harry might actually have a *choice* in the matter of what business to go into! "Just look at Burke, Idaho, or the Lattimer business in Hazleton, or the strikes over silver mining in Leadville, Colorado. What business can survive that kind of climate? Union violence, rioting, shooting, assaults, fires, deliberate arson, bombings and homicides. To get mixed up in it is to throw away good money. We will never see a penny return on it."

"Father," said Harry, "everything you say I hear. I'm not

disagreeing. Though Pulitzer and Hearst did settle the news-boys' strike last year and are still in business. But that's neither here nor there. What is here is this family came from Italy, and they live in Lawrence. They're not going to relocate to North End, or to Barrington, no matter how much we would like them to. They're going to try to improve the place they live by opening up two restaurants. That's admirable. You told me so yourself. You invested with your former partner in Florida . . ."

"Yes," said Herman blackly. "And we paid dearly for my hubris, for my mistakes."

Harry frowned. "That's not what I meant. You had said then, and I remember this, why go all the way south to throw away your hard-earned money, when you can throw it away on your own cobbled streets?"

"I should have listened to myself. And I didn't say that precisely, but all right." Herman gazed soberly at his son. "What's your interest in this family?"

Harry shrugged.

"Suddenly business interests you?"

He shrugged again. "The remaking of something old into something new interests me."

"This isn't reading, son. This is hard work. Are you aware that labor struggles in a small city make business property values fall off a cliff?" His father was softening.

"Reading is also hard work, Father. After all, I'm gradu-ating summa cum laude."

"So I've heard. Thanks to your exemplary grades, I get a standing invitation to the Harvard Club every Friday. Is Ben also doing well? I haven't seen him since Christmas."

"Me neither. He's thrown himself into his seminar work. He's become consumed with this Panama business, his work-study internship, his engineering field work. He is always out. I rarely see him around college anymore. I'll leave a note at his dorm. Perhaps he can come this Sunday and you can talk some sense into him."

"I'm still trying to talk some sense into you. But good for him. It's important for young men to find a passion, something they like to do, and are good at."

"So you keep telling me, Father."

Herman blinked from across his massive mahogany desk at his son. "Harry, you can find something you love to do, and you can find something you are good at doing. Rare and blessed is the man who happens to combine both these gifts into one vocation."

"I don't know that engineering is Ben's passion, but we'll see. He does seem to be quite good at it."

"Not engineering. Building a civilization as he puts it."

"Well, all right. I'm also trying to build a civilization. Right here on our own cobbled streets."

"On Lawrence streets."

"Twenty miles away." Harry got up. "Should I talk to Billingsworth about the business loan?"

"Yes." Herman sighed. "If that's what you want."

"I do, Father. And thank you."

"Is this an emotional decision? For reasons I can't fathom at the moment?"

"Not at all. It's a business decision, and a good one. In any case, I'd like to get my nose out of the books and into the real world. You keep telling me it's time. I prefer not to make a mistake, obviously, but if I do, and you turn out to be right, I'd still like it to be *my* mistake."

Herman studied Harry approvingly.

Harry was almost out of his father's office before he turned around. "Oh, and Father," he said, "seeing that this is my first effort, I'd like to participate in this quietly at the start, without much ado. I would appreciate it if we can keep this between us, at least for the time being. If the enterprise is a success, then let's blare it from the rooftops. I'll be the first to boast. But I would prefer not to be mocked at the dinner table just yet, while I'm getting my feet wet getting the whole thing off the ground, pardon the mixed metaphors."

"Understood," said Herman. "And pardoned. Your secret involvement in your family's multi-generational, traditional, New England building business is safe within these office walls."

6

When the weather was drier, Miss Porter reappeared in the lumberyard one morning, waiting for a shipment that had been delayed. She seemed irritated, frequently gazing at her gold pocket-watch as she paced up and down the yard. Salvo was walking from panel wood to scrap wood when he passed her. Taking off his cap, he bowed to her slightly and, smiling, said, "Good morning, Miss Porter. How are you today?"

She seemed surprised that he was speaking to her. She turned to him, recognized him, and then glanced away to the gates, through which nothing was arriving. "I'm fine, thank you," she said. And nothing more.

He bowed to her again. "Have a good day," he said, walking on.

"I may be wrong, Frederick," Alice said to her yard manager later that morning. "But I suspect Mr. Attaviano may be a masher."

"He is a very good worker, Miss Porter," said Frederick, "a quick learner."

"I'm glad to have him on board," said Alice. "But be that as it may, there is something improper about the way he looks at me. Please ask him not to speak to me first." She looked out the window to see if she could catch a glimpse of him. "He doesn't understand how things are. Who knows how they do things in his country, so don't be too harsh with him, but do explain to him firmly that in our country it's just not *done*."

"I will do, Miss Porter," said Frederick. "But what if I can't make him understand?"

"Well then, be as harsh as you need to be to make him understand, Frederick."

"Yes, Miss Porter."

Alice looked for the impertinent young man the next day in the yard but he had disappeared. A few days later, Frederick informed her that the Italian gentleman had taken great offense at being upbraided. He had denied any wrong-doing, said that rules of etiquette between all people demanded no less and no more than common courtesy, and quit on the spot. "Didn't even wait for his pay from the week before."

Flushed, Alice nodded. "So impertinent. He was right to resign, Frederick. It's a shame you didn't get to fire him first. I was right in suspecting he was on the make. No decent man would quit a good job just because of pride. That's cracked." She shrugged. "Oh, well. Perhaps he can be taught in his next position. I hold out little hope for him and others of his ilk. I try to help them, and look what happens. To even think . . ."

Chapter Eleven
THE QUARRY

1

Dear Gina,

I'd like to come to Lawrence to speak to you and your brother further about your business proposal. I would also like to bring my loan officer, the aptly named Mr. Billingsworth, to see the properties in question and give us a full appraisal before we proceed.

When would be a good time to meet with the two of you?

Yours sincerely,

Harry Barrington

IT was the most frightening letter Gina had ever read. What had she done?

She had expected it would take several more meetings with

Harry, perhaps with a stroll on the Common when it got warm, a promenade and an ice cream down by the Charles River to discuss the matter much more fully before it got *half* this far.

Harry was clearly a man of action; how terrifying. Maybe this was how things happened in the real world, not the world of dream-like make-believe that Gina inhabited. She hadn't told Salvo—she hadn't even *thought* of telling him. That her brother might, just might, have to get involved in her harebrained plan had not entered her head prior to receiving Harry's latest letter. The reason there was never even the *beginning* of a thought about Salvo was because Salvo lived to put paid to her girlish cotton-candy reveries, and it was no fun dreaming about Harry with Salvo's harsh disapproving face ruining the lemony delights for her. She didn't know what to do or how to answer the letter. So Gina did the only thing she could think to do.

Sleeplessly, anxiously, she ignored it.

> Dear Gina,
> I haven't heard from you and I have to assume that my earlier missive got lost in the post. I am writing again to let you know I am interested in your business proposal and would like to arrange a time to meet with you and your brother, along with my business manager, to go over the fine print details and to see the properties. Please let me know by return post when would be a convenient time to do that. Work on my final dissertation at Harvard begins shortly, and very soon I won't be able to take the time away from my studies.
> Yours truly,
> Harry Barrington

Now Gina knew all she had to do was wait. Just a little longer, and Harry would be too busy to help her, and then she could come to Boston and they could talk again about it. After another two weeks passed tensely and it was almost March, Gina finally wrote back.

Dear Harry,

I'm sorry to have been out of touch for a few weeks, my mother had caught a cold, and my brother lost his day job and came down with bronchitis. They're both better now, and so I have a few minutes to reply. I know you said you would be busy with your dissertation. Perhaps after your studies are completed, successfully I am certain, you can let me know when would be a convenient time for you to come to Lawrence. My brother, having been out of work mainly because of his illness, is now working two jobs again, and I don't know if he'll be able to join us for our next meeting. But I'll make sure he will join us for the subsequent one.

Sincerely,
Gina

Dear Gina,

I have a few weeks before my senior thesis. How does next Friday at 5 o'clock sound to meet with you and Salvo? Please let me know by return post.

Yours truly,
Harry

2

Salvo reacted like any proud Italian man might react if his baby sister had arranged a loan for him from someone he wished harm to. "*Tu sei un pazzo!* You have lost your feeble mind," he said after five minutes of gesticulating wildly and swearing in Italian. "I will never accept. *Mai!* I would rather beg on the streets for money than accept a loan from him. I would rather wash clothes, sit behind a loom. I would rather throw myself into the erupting Etna. Have I made myself clear?"

"Salvo, hear me out."

"I've heard everything I need to and want to. The answer is never."

"Salvo . . ."

"*Mai!*"

"Will you . . ."

"*Never!*"

"We are not the Hatfields and the McCoys, Salvo," Harry told Salvo the following Friday evening, sitting across from him at his table in Lawrence. "This is a business deal. I'm just helping you get money from the bank. It's a two-part loan. One, we will instruct the bank to provide the cash to buy the businesses. And then you will need capital to renovate them. That part we are lending you. But we're charging you interest, and we expect you to pay every month. So you will have your regular mortgage, and also this construction loan. Both will be entirely your responsibility. Billingsworth is going to arrange everything. After the restaurants open, Salvo, you'll be responsible for the day-to-day operations, for hiring, firing, for running the business. Are you up to it?"

"*Assolutamente.*"

"I will help you with the contractors who will do the construction work on the two properties. The building crew we use is very good. Billingsworth likes the location of the restaurants. He thinks you picked well. And the work shouldn't take too long. We plan to open by the beginning of summer. After that, you're on your own—though if you need help, of course we'll be here. You'll need a bookkeeper. Unless you think your aunt or your mother can do it?"

Harry sat back and waited. Billingsworth didn't speak. Gina didn't speak. Salvo didn't speak at first. Then all he said was, "Who in the name of the Mother of God are the Hatfields and McCoys?"

They continued talking, with the help of olive oil, salt, bread and red wine. This was new to Harry, Gina could see, and with enjoyment watched him dip a tiny piece of bread into the olive oil, sprinkle a few beads of salt on it, and gingerly put it into his mouth. Billingsworth refused to partake entirely, surveying the Attavianos and even Harry with considerable distaste.

Harry took another piece, this one bigger, put a little more salt on it. Mimoo had just baked the bread that morning, because she knew guests were coming, and the bread, her specialty, was crusty and warm. Gina could see the transformation on Harry's face, as he ate the bread and drank the wine. It was good. He liked it. "You will need a bookkeeper," he repeated.

"My mother can do it," said Salvo. "I want my family to work with me. This is a family business."

"You should get your mother to make this bread in your restaurant instead," said Harry.

"You're not running a charity," Billingsworth chimed in. "Competent bookkeeping is non-negotiable. You need someone sharp to keep records for accounts payable—"

"Are you insulting my mother?"

"—Accounts receivable," Billingsworth continued without pausing, "to keep payroll, to authorize repair work, and also to keep track of how much your daily operations are costing you and whether you can gain some efficiencies here and there. You need a real accountant for two restaurants."

"Angela has a friend."

"Does her friend have a qualification in accounting?" Billingsworth demanded.

They stared at Angela, who was sitting on the couch, pretending to mind her own business.

"He has a bank account," she said.

"Well, that's all you need," said Harry. Gina tried not to laugh. Billingsworth was utterly without humor when it came to matters of money, and perhaps with all other things too. He shot Harry a glare of deprecation.

Warily Salvo and Mimoo watched Harry sit and drink the wine and eat the bread in big chunky bites.

"Don't worry," Harry said. "Billingsworth will find you someone good. He knows lots of good men. These are just details. What do you say, Salvo? Are we going to shake on it?"

Salvo was proud but not stupid. He extended his hand, even stood up. Harry shook hands with his Italian immigrant partner. They poured more wine, raised their glasses in a toast. Even Pippa heaved herself breathlessly downstairs from her bedroom to drink a glass.

"What will you name the restaurants?" Harry asked.

"One will be called Alessandro's, for our father. The other Antonio's, for our brother."

"I didn't know you had another brother."

Mimoo became tearful; Pippa too. Salvo said, "He died a year before we came here."

Harry glanced at Gina apologetically and reached for his hat. She walked him and Billingsworth out. She could barely breathe the whole time the meeting was going on, and despite Salvo's intransigence, and Billingsworth's concern for their business abilities, she thought it went rather well. Harry agreed. "But your Salvo is one tough customer," he said to her on the porch with the broken swing. "I wish you'd said something about your other brother. I didn't mean to put my foot in it."

"I try to put the past behind me."

"Well, this isn't going to make him like me more, is it? He's already not so fond of me."

Gina squinted. Harry bowed to her lightly with an approving nod, and nudged Billingsworth. "Come on, Billingsworth," he said. "Don't just stand there. We have a train to catch." To Gina he said by way of goodbye, "Billingsworth will have the papers drawn up this week. Let's plan to meet next Saturday with a general contractor, to go over the construction details. If we want to open before the rush of summer, we don't have a lot of time. Soon I hope to have a car, so I won't have to take the damn train to Lawrence every week."

"A car or a carriage?"

He smiled. "An Olds Curved Dash. Though I hear the Benz engine from Germany is astonishing. If only you could get a German car here."

"Maybe Ben can arrange that through his Panama Canal."

Even Billingsworth almost reacted to that with a half-smile. Almost.

She glanced back at the screen door, through which, in the cold March light, she could see her brother and mother watching her. She sighed.

"Billingsworth," Harry said to his banker as they walked down the steps. "Did you hear they found more oil in Texas? Apparently it's seeping out of the ground! They don't even have to drill for it."

"I don't know why you're telling me this, Harry,"

Billingsworth said. "Your father has been quite clear. We are never investing in oil."

"A mistake, Billingsworth. Flagler and Rockefeller are two of the richest men in America."

"Your father is no longer partnered with Mr. Flagler." He paused. "Money is not everything."

"Only spiritual wealth for bankers and merchants, eh? Well, let's go. Get in and pray for rain." Before hopping into the carriage, Harry turned around and tipped his hat to Gina, who was still on the porch looking after him with girlish longing. "Have a good evening, Miss Attaviano."

"You too, Mr. Barrington."

When she came back inside, her family was around the table having a spirited discussion about Harry.

"Salvo, come on, put away your pride."

"It's not pride, Mimoo. It's something else. I don't trust him."

"Your horse sense is failing you," Mimoo said. "He's not like the other one. Now if that one came here, I'd be worried. But this one is a nice boy. What's his mother like, Gina?"

"Dead."

"Ah," Mimoo nodded, "that explains a lot."

"What?" Gina instantly wanted to know. "What does it explain?"

Salvo shook his head. "Mimoo, if it was the other one, I'd have fewer qualms."

"The one who won't heed your warnings to stay away from your sister?"

"Yes, that one. And he has heeded them. He hasn't been around, has he?"

"So far as you know," Angela contributed cheerily, which

prompted everyone to glare at her, but Gina turned back to Mimoo.

"What does it explain about Harry, Mimoo?"

"You don't see what I see," Salvo was saying to his mother. "You don't know what I know. Trust me on this, *cara Mamma*. I'm a man. I know these things better than you. The one who wears his heart on his sleeve is the one you as a mother should be least worried about. It's the silent one who does nothing but fake indifference that's dangerous."

"You are being so Italian, Salvo!" exclaimed Gina.

Salvo ignored her, forcefully tapping the table with his finger. "And worse, Mimoo, what *you* don't see is that your only daughter knows this with her whole heart, sees this clearest of all. Even better than me."

"*Tu sei pazzo*, Salvo."

"*Non vedo niente*," disagreed Gina with no sincerity, her lips moving, her heart pounding. Please, please, Salvo, please don't be wrong.

"I don't want to do it, Mimoo," said Salvo.

"You must do it. Listen to me, he doesn't even notice your sister."

Salvo simply shook his head.

3

Life was full of miracles in all shapes and sizes. As the spring thaw melted away the snows and frozen mud of New England, and renewal filled the April air, Harry came to Lawrence two or three times a week to oversee the renovation on Alessandro's and Antonio's. "It's my father's hard-earned money," he said to Gina the first time she beamed at seeing him at the work site. "I want to make sure it's being well spent." He brought his books with him, he told her, and studied on the train.

Her life reordered, Gina now flew to Washington mill after school to pick up the wool and with the large sacks made her way, not to Haverhill and the mission, but to Essex Street and Alessandro's. Or she ran across Broadway to Antonio's. She spent whatever remaining minutes or hours at the site with Harry until his train home, and then walked slowly to St. Vincent's, where she made an assorted number of springtime excuses, took her books and wool to the backroom, and studied not at all, but spun constantly, dreaming of silk and muslin, and ivory hats with chiffon bows and lace blouses, thinking of some clever questions to ask Harry the next afternoon about phases of plumbing codes and electrical wires and putty, all the while practicing contorting her face into businesslike seriousness.

She looked into her books just enough not to fail her exams as she twisted hundreds of skeins and paper cones and collected bark and blueberries.

"Why the inky fingers?" Harry asked her one afternoon. She tried to hide her pleasure at his noticing as she answered.

"I'm dyeing the wool rovings in blueberries and vinegar," she replied, and then hid her hands behind her back, swiftly recalling what her hands looked like. "Also beets and bark. The colors are so rich if I do it right after I card but before I spin. I now sell eight different colors at the market." She must remember to save up for some thin silk gloves.

He studied her carefully. "I don't even understand what you just said."

She laughed, not with too much delight, trying to control herself. "A little bit like I feel when you talk of moral hazards of adverse selection on costs and probabilities."

He laughed unabashedly. "You strung those phrases together randomly. Because I never talk of costs and probabilities."

"You did that one time when you were trying to explain one of your economics courses to me. Investing in Human Capital, was it called?"

He shook his head at her in surprise, his mouth still in a reluctant smile. "I can't believe I was so excruciatingly tedious. How ill-mannered and deadly dull of me. Please forgive me for my rudeness."

"No apologies necessary," she said trying to sound formal and less Italian. It was because of her immigrant immaturity that all she wanted to do was skip! She sold her fancy mulberry, maroon and scarlet yarn at a premium and saved enough for a paper pattern and material for a barely pink, combed-lawn dress for spring: soft, lightly lustrous, untextured. It had a slight flounce and sky-blue satin trimming around the waist. She sewed four rows of lace and ribbon ruching into the bodice over the smallest capped sleeves. She would need a shawl to go with it because her arms were bare, and it was just enough off the ground to see not just her shoes, but also her ankles. When could she possibly wear it? Every time he saw her, she by necessity and lack of choice was in her awful brown and white school uniform. And she spent every penny she had on the fabric, so there was no money for silk gloves . . . She despaired of her ugly hands!

Harry hardly noticed. Never anything but polite and pleasant, he carried himself unfailingly with an air of amused detachment—but Gina didn't care. With all pretense on her part gone, she lay on her bed stomach-down, legs kicking up, whispering confidences into the bedspread to Verity and Angela about the latest thing he said about running steam pipes, and having a wider access to the back, anticipating crowds at the restaurants, planning for success. Verity and Angela taunted her, but the fantasy was strong, and real life wasn't going to interfere.

Even Salvo became less hostile at the sight of his dream coming together under Harry's watchful eye. While Mimoo was cleaning houses with Pippa and learning a new language by playing Le Lotto in the basement of St. Mary's Church with all her new rowdy Irish friends, including Rita from upstairs, Verity studied hard for her final exams before graduating high school. Meanwhile Angela whispered to Gina about unions and women's rights, dreaming of finding her own young man, who cared about both.

"Harry is not Gina's steady," Verity corrected Angela.

"Oh, Verity, the sucker of joy. Not yet. But can't a girl dream?"

"He talks to you about plumbing and electricity. How do you get heady romance from this?"

"Angela talks to her young men friends about labor grievances and property rights. That's better?"

"All of it just seems pointless and confusing," Verity said. "Let's see what the Gospel says about Love, shall we?"

Gina and Angela groaned, burying their heads under pillows. Verity, sitting up cross-legged on the bed, opened the Bible with closed eyes and stuck a finger into a red-letter passage.

Gina didn't let her continue. *"If I have the gift of prophecy,"* she said, interrupting Verity, snatching the Bible from her hands, *"and fathom all mysteries and all knowledge, and if I have a faith that can move mountains, but have not Love, I am nothing.* How is that for Gospel? That's what Paul said. *Non sono nulla."*

"Too little knowledge is a dangerous thing," said Verity in exasperation, reaching for the Book.

"Too little Love also."

Gina lay on her bed as spring deepened and dreamed. She lived so much inside the balloon of her desires that she didn't want the needles of reality puncturing her carefully crafted, multicolored fragile daydream *palloncino*.

4

"He has fine manners," said Angela. "You can't fault him for his good breeding."

"Oh, please," said Salvo. "It's just a ruse to get what he wants."

"Which is . . . ?"

Salvo raised high his full-of-meaning eyebrows.

"Salvo, please. I disagree," Angela said, coming to Gina's rescue, and to Harry's. "I've seen him, and I've talked to Verity about him. She has talked to him, and both of us agree—he is exceptionally well brought up."

"You are so naïve."

"Salvo, judge him for yourself. He is not coarse or overly familiar with anyone. He doesn't presume friendship, or familiarity. He is unfailingly polite."

"I can vouch for that," Verity said. "He talks to everyone as he might have other men talk to his sister."

Gina smiled at that most of all. Other men like Ben? She must remember to ask Harry about Ben. They hadn't mentioned him in weeks.

"He doesn't call attention to himself," said Angela. "He doesn't criticize other people."

Salvo argued back. "That may be, but he is hardly kind."

"Yes, but he also doesn't promote himself. He is not glum or morose. He is polite and detached, that's different."

"He doesn't seem vain," Gina piped in. "He never talks about himself."

"He hardly talks at all," verified Verity. "It's hard to get him to say anything."

"In my opinion," said Mimoo, "he seems ashamed of where he came from. He seems ashamed of his mother and father. He is embarrassed by his family."

"No, not at all," Gina defended. "He just doesn't like to talk about their success."

"A well-bred man is not embarrassed by his family."

"He is not," Gina said, defending him. "He is just quiet. He is shy."

Heartily, throatily, Salvo laughed.

Gina had no words to describe Harry's impassive silence. She couldn't comprehend his neutral comportment—was it to keep in line with his noble heritage? She didn't think so. There was something about his expression, the utter indifference to certain things like his wealthy background or his well-established social status that suggested a more serious approach to life. He couldn't help being born a Barrington and enjoying the comforts of one, but his walk, his stare, the tilt of his pensive head, his bored manner suggested a laid-back drifter from the wrong side of the tracks—a man looking perhaps for trouble. He was not a man of many words; he acted like someone who took himself both too seriously and not seriously enough. He shared another quality with his famous ancestor Robert Treat Paine: while he was always the first advocate against a position held by someone else, he was not one to promote a particular position of his own. He just said no, as if the no by itself was sufficient.

After thinking about him obsessively for many weeks, Gina concluded that perhaps Salvo was right, that Harry wasn't shy—although it was that very quality that so appealed to her in the first place—something else stifled him. He remained silent not because he was afraid to speak, but because speaking would reveal who he was to the world: someone who was not going to follow Billingsworth into a life in banking, or Barrington to the life of a merchant, or even Ben to a career in engineering. Silent—because speaking would reveal who he really was to her.

Gina knew she was not sophisticated enough for him. How could she be? She had no money to buy a camel coat, she was too young to wear heels, or so her mother said. Papa would've understood. Gina said this to Angela in bitterness, but her cousin would have none of it. "Did your mother wear heels to make your sainted father fall in love with her? There you have it, then. There's your answer. She didn't have a camel coat. She didn't have high-heeled shoes, or a fancy bag." Angela laughed. "What, do you suppose if you have these things, a man will fall in love with you? How little you think of him. How little you think of yourself."

"If only we could all meet our lovers at the textile mill," replied an irritated Gina. "Perhaps we'd find just the right kind of romance."

"You'd certainly be happier." Angela laughed.

But to see him was everything. Her self-consciousness, her shame at her poverty took second place to running down Broadway in flat shoes and dowdy frocks that covered her from her chin to the ground with long cardigans over them, unlike the coats that real ladies wore. Holding herself upright, shoulders squared, she slowed down just in time,

213

and in calm, accented English, she milled around Harry, arms locked behind her back, asking him sober professional questions about mortar and spackle and plaster, questions about wiring, painting, wood floors, lacquer, the glass-fronted windows. At length they discussed signs over the restaurants, which color and how bright a blue. They discussed the shape and size of tables, the comfort of chairs, the quality of dishes, the drape of the curtains and the size of the trash cans out back. How big an oven should we get and do we need two?

But as she spoke to him about these things, she would offer him little bits of food that she brought from home. "Here, Harry, try this, you must be hungry, it's bread with tomato and mozzarella over it. It's called *bruschetta*." "Harry, this is smoked Parma ham with a little bit of red pepper and mozzarella." "Oh, this is very good, I hope you like it, it's called *tiramisu*. It's a liqueur and ladyfinger dessert."

And Salvo too, while he was working out the menus, would make something more elaborate than the antipasti his sister carried on a plate and invite Harry back to Summer Street for a sampling of his famous *gnocchi*, potato dumplings with pesto, or *pappardelle* fra diavolo. And some-times Harry came. He didn't cry off, citing dissertations and seminars and charity functions. Instead he sat at her mother's table, starved after a day's work, and ate Salvo's food with them. It was the one time when he said compli-mentary things to Salvo about his cooking. In private Salvo would say to Gina, "Why is he buttering me up? I'm not toast." But even more privately, Salvo was pleased enough to devise every week some newfangled dishes from the south of Italy to further impress his silent partner. Harry was especially partial to the homemade crusty bread. Salvo toasted it lightly with garlic and mozzarella and a little Parmesan and salt and pushed it in front of him. Harry called it a complete meal, with red wine over candle-light, and he sat like this with Mimoo and Pippa and Angela and Salvo watching him cautiously but eagerly, to gauge the sincerity of his reactions to their immigrant cuisine, to their immigrant home. Only Gina milled around elsewhere in the room, so that no one could see her hand clamped in a fist over her heart.

One time Salvo put some tomatoes on the toasted bread. Harry liked it. Another day Salvo cooked the tomatoes, made them softer, added more garlic, a little olive oil, some basil leaves. He spread it on the bread, put mozzarella and Parmesan on top and grilled it in a hot oven. Harry said it was the best thing he had ever tasted, and ate half a loaf to show he meant it. "Honestly, Salvo," said Harry, "I don't think you should have anything else on your menu. This crispy, doughy Sicilian tomato and mozzarella bread is your ticket to untold riches. Serve only this with red wine."

From behind Harry, Gina stared at her brother whose face was stretched in a satisfied grin from ear to ear. Even Salvo melted a little bit after that.

"But what should we call it?" Harry mused. "We could advertise it: 'Come to Antonio's, home of the original . . .' original what?"

Salvo shrugged. "In Sicily, a simpler version of this was known as the dish of the poor people."

"Oh, incorrect—this is the food of kings, Salvo," said Harry. "What did they call it?"

"*Pizza Margherita.*"

"Fantastic. *Pizza Margherita.* Sublime. You are going to be a millionaire, Salvo. Welcome to America."

After Harry left that evening, the Attavianos took back

every single thing they said about him. They praised him at the table, calling him their saving angel, while Gina lay on her bed upstairs with the door open, hearing their voices from below, basking in the stinging bliss that was her present life.

5

They couldn't find a carriage to take them back from the Riverview Stone Quarry. The one that brought them there left an hour ago, and it was at least two miles down the Merrimack River road to town. They had gone to the quarry late Saturday afternoon after she was done with the market to pick out granite for their cooking surfaces. Salvo insisted. To make the best dough, he said, the kneading surface had to remain cool at all times. There was nothing cooler than igneous rock, Salvo and Gina said, knowing something about this, having lived in the penumbra of hissing magma. Billingsworth needed two Saturdays to be convinced to spend the money on granite. Even Harry joined the chorus of the persuaders.

Salvo was supposed to come with them, but he must have gotten delayed. Either that or there was a God who performed miracles big and small all day long. Salvo worked as a day laborer on Saturdays, and had been digging and planting in the Lawrence Common. It must have been divine intervention, Gina thought, as they chose a suitable stone, the color of light tea with black specks and Harry signed off on it, because her brother would never otherwise have left her alone with Harry, even in a quarry.

They waited for him outside the gates for twenty minutes.

216

"The restaurants are opening next week," Harry said. "I think your brother is going to have to stop working his other jobs. Or he surely won't keep this one."

"He knows," Gina said, looking around the dusty quarry. "We just need a little bit to tide us over until the business starts earning. It's been tough since he lost his job at the lumber mill."

Harry turned to her, but slowly. "I didn't know there was a lumber mill in Lawrence," he said.

"Oh, there isn't. And I meant a sawmill, I think. I don't really know the difference. He went by train to Andover to work in one."

"Andover, really." Harry studied his feet while Gina put her hand over her eyes to squint down the sunny road for signs of her brother. There weren't any. *Grazie a Dio.* "So what happened? Why did he get sacked?"

"Oh, he didn't," said Gina. "He quit. He said they were insufferably rude to him."

"He left because they were rude?"

"I didn't say it was a good decision," Gina said. "But that's why he's been working so much lately, making up for those lost wages."

"I'll be sure not to be rude to him," said Harry.

As if you could be, Gina thought. "It was a woman who insulted him. Salvo will take almost anything, but he hates it when women disrespect him. Gets his blood right up."

Harry pulled his hat lower over his face, as if to keep the dust out of his eyes. "I'm sure it doesn't happen very often," he muttered.

"Almost never. He is so charming and courteous to women, my brother."

They waited another five or ten minutes. She didn't know what Harry was thinking, but she was praying so loud it

217

might as well have been *out* loud. Please don't show up, Salvo, please don't show up.

"How are we going to get back?" Harry finally asked when he got tired of standing in one place.

"I don't mind walking," said Gina.

"Really?" He looked over her diaphanous sunny pink dress, the heels on the Mary Janes he wasn't supposed to see. "It's quite a way."

"I don't mind." Her hair was up in a bun, the chestnut curls covered by a narrow-brimmed hat she had found donated at the mission, and "borrowed" until later that evening. She felt like a vision and hoped she looked it.

So they walked, in silence. She tried to make chit-chat, but her throat was too dry. On their right the peaceful wide Merrimack River flowed languidly to Newburyport. The sun was shining; the leaves had come in; it was late afternoon—cool and crisp, a beautiful day. She was happy to walk saying nothing, so happy just to keep in step, not too fast, but not too slow either; the pace made small talk unnecessary, *and* she didn't know the etiquette for it. Should she begin it, or should he? Should he defer to her? But if she is very young—as she is—should he *still* defer to her? She walked on, wishing for uneven road, a boulder here, perhaps a tree trunk there, fallen across their way. He walked a good respectable foot away from her; they weren't strolling together, they walked side by side down a path.

"I'm sorry, what?"

He had been asking her something, but she was so absorbed in her own thoughts, she forgot to listen to him. "I beg your pardon?"

He smiled. "A penny for your thoughts," he said.

"I don't know this expression," she said. "Are you offering me money?"

"Only in a figurative sense. To ask what you were thinking."

"I don't really know," she lied. "How is your friend Ben? I haven't asked after him in a while."

"Is that what you were thinking about? Ben?" He paused. "Or that you haven't asked after him in a while?"

Gina didn't know whether to blush or giggle. Desperately she tried not to do both.

"He's fine," Harry went on, not noticing or pretending not to notice her discomfort. "I hardly see him. He lives in a different dorm from me this year, and he is taking the most difficult courses. Methods in Mathematical Physics, Railroad Engineering, Field Seminar in Bridges and Buildings. He is either out or immersed in the books."

Gina wanted to ask Harry to say hello to Ben, but what if Harry hadn't told Ben he had been helping her and Salvo with the restaurants? She didn't want to put him in an awkward spot.

"What does he want to do after he graduates?"

Harry opened his hands. "Do you even need to ask? He inhales bananas and exhales Panama. He has no other life."

Gina felt better. She had once half thought Ben might have been sweet on her, and was happy to know it wasn't the case, that his excitements lay elsewhere. She smiled into her shoes. Of course she had sewn the lawn dress just a little *too* short ("I ran out of fabric, Mimoo!") and her cream shoes (that she also "borrowed" for the afternoon from a donation box at St. Vincent's) peeked out from under the hem. Harry was right, it was too dusty and dirty on the road for this dress. But when else could she wear it, except to church on Sundays and now? She felt like a princess on palace grounds.

"The granite you picked is very fine," Harry said. "Salvo will be sorry he missed choosing it."

"Excuse me again. What were you saying?" Very slightly she pulled the shawl down from her shoulders to expose her arms. She was hot under the wool covering, breathless while walking.

"Whatever you're thinking about must be very good," said Harry.

"No really, almost nothing." She had been searching the road up ahead for a crevice, a large rock, a pothole, something she could "accidentally" trip on, so maybe he could grab her bare elbow to steady her. Her heart was beating so fast, she couldn't possibly pay attention to the conversation and search for a boulder at the same time!

"So are you almost—?"

"So what was Belpasso—?"

"I'm sorry, you were saying?"

"No, excuse me. Ladies first."

He called her a lady! How could she talk after that? Pothole, pothole, where are you? "I just wanted to know if you're excited to be graduating? Must be exciting!"

"Excited or not," he said, taking off his bowler hat and wiping his brow, "the cap and gown have been ordered. It's warm, isn't it?"

"So warm." The shawl slipped down a little lower, almost at her wrists now. "Aren't you happy?"

"Happy, yes. Why? Oh, you mean to graduate?" He shrugged. "We don't get too excited about things in my family."

"Not even about Philip Nolan?"

Harry rolled his eyes. "He's behind me, thank goodness. I've spent too long with him. Relieved to be done." He turned to her. "How are the nuns treating you? Are you giving them trouble?"

"Me? No. Why do you say that?"

He smiled lightly. "Your mother told me last week they keep complaining to her about you."

Gina, not a blusher, felt herself turning red. Last thing she wanted was to be portrayed as a troublemaker. "It's their job to complain."

"I bet they don't complain about Verity."

"She's going to be a nun!" Gina exclaimed. "What's there to complain about?"

And then suddenly the air was not crisp anymore but thick with his unasked but low-hanging, follow-up question: *Are you going to be a nun, too, Gina?* His manners prevented him from asking it, and yet the fact that he didn't ask made the silence between them all the more stark. He didn't dare ask, because her answer—*of course I'm not*—might prompt another response from him, or perhaps a comment, both of which were flagrantly inappropriate. *I don't think you would make a very good nun, Gina,* he might say. Or she might tell him she wouldn't make a very good nun. To which he would agree, or disagree. It was an impossible conversation! Even inside her thirsty head, it was ablaze with indecency. That is why Salvo was suddenly needed with a horse and cart. Because sometimes simple questions resulted in this kind of screaming muteness. Gina focused hard on the small stones under her feet.

Casually he cleared his throat, moving a little closer to her. "Gina?"

She shook off her anxious musings. "Excuse me, what did you say?"

A smirk returned to his face. "So what's Belpasso like? Like this?"

She nodded, relieved and grateful. "The outskirts yes, a bit like this. Rural. But the little town itself is stone and stucco. A mercantile town. It has to be stone because it has to withstand Etna's eruptions. Otherwise wood huts would burn to the ground every few years. Stone is sturdier." She chuckled. "There is a very tall stone wall, built on one side of the volcano between the mountain and the town. It's kind of funny. It was built to keep the lava away. As if it could."

"Like the Great Wall of China?"

"The what of China?"

"The Great *Wall* of China."

"Oh. Did they build it against volcanoes too?"

Now it was Harry who chuckled. "I don't think China has volcanoes. I think they built it to keep out the Mongolian hordes."

In horror Gina thought Harry said to keep out the Mongolian *whores*. That seemed very much out of character for him, and she was at a loss as to how to respond. How frayed with disaster this whole small talk was! Every syllable something wrong came out. Once again she entered into an obsessive loop of teenage uncertainty that kept her not only from replying to him, but this time also from paying attention to the road in front of her. Quite inadvertently she tripped over a rock and lurched forward. Harry, his reflexes rising to the occasion, caught her in mid-fall, grabbing her by her bare arm, around the front of her waist, around the shoulder. The shawl had fallen to the ground, but he kept Gina from falling, though not from twisting her ankle. She hobbled forward, swooned slightly, became light-headed.

"I'm all right," she said. "I'm so silly. Very sorry."

He was still holding her, looking around for a place to sit her down. "Nothing to be sorry about. Are you all right? How is your limb?"

That reminded Gina that men were not supposed to refer to women's parts by their actual names. Arms, legs. They weren't supposed to know women had those. They called them limbs.

"Yes," she said faintly, "my, um, limb is fine." He was still holding on to her.

He sat her down on a pile of broken stones. She leaned against the short wall that separated the dirt road from the river. He squatted down on the ground next to her, afternoon suit and all. Her ankle was throbbing.

"It hurts?"

"Not too bad," she said, twinging.

His gray eyes became bluer, clearer, more amused. "Okay, you can't tell me again you don't know what you were thinking. That would be the third time. I simply won't believe you. So cough it up. What were you thinking?"

What could she do? She told him the almost truth. "I didn't know that word you said. So I was trying to figure it out from the meaning and tripped."

"What word?"

Gina couldn't very well repeat it! What if he did say *whores*? How mortifying that would be if she actually heard him correctly. "When you said, um, the Chinese built the wall to keep the Mongolian, um, something out."

"The *hordes*?"

"Oh!" She was so relieved. "I didn't hear the *d* the first time. What does hor*des* mean?"

Harry laughed. He flung his head back, closed his eyes, and laughed as if he had been with his best friend Ben, and they had just shared the most remarkable of jokes.

Gina sat on the rocks next to him, looking down at him, slightly below her, smiling uncertainly, not knowing what she had said that was so amusing, or what to do, but when he finally stopped laughing and straightened up, gazing at her, still with a smile on his lips, she became even more discomfited. Because she could almost read *that* expression on the normally dispassionate Harry's face. It was the enchanted face of her father when she did or said something that made him sweep her up and cover her with kisses. Before the sweeping and the kissing, there was *that* expression of—there was no other good way to describe it—tenderness. Affection. Love. *Tenerezza. Affetto. Amore.* Gia, Papa would say, you funny funny girl.

That was the look somber, impenetrable Harry had on his face at that moment.

Bewildered, throbbing ankle forgotten, heart pumping wildly, Gina tottered sideways, nearly falling off the rock. He reached out to steady her, taking her arm, looking up, leaning in. "Gia," he said. "Why are you *so* funny?"

She babbled incoherently; she didn't think he really wanted a reply. In the silent milliseconds of him taking hold of her upper arm and leaning in, if someone had seen them just then, from the outside, an observer perhaps, passing by, or Salvo on his way to chaperone his sister, or the Almighty Himself, he would have seen a young man besotted and an eager young girl terrified. The moment Gina most desperately yearned for came, and she wasn't ready for it. Came and went, and she could do nothing but act her age and retreat without rejoicing. Her assured bravado left her. It was so sudden, so unexpected. He laughed, and just like that his manner changed. I've been funny before, so why now? She didn't see herself from the outside in, and so forgot about the sheer young dress in the joyous summer color, forgot about her petite ladylike hat with the flowers and feathers, forgot about the strands of her unruly hair that escaped the chignon and curled downward, draping her face, forgot about her blossoming Italian lips that Rinaldo in Belpasso followed her around town for, pining and wailing like a lovestruck Romeo until she acquiesced out of smoky curiosity and kissed him. She forgot about all that now because Harry wasn't a weak Italian boy, he was a young American man, he didn't pine and he didn't wail; yet he fixated on her for those lightning eternal seconds as if the very next thing he was going to do was lean forward another three inches and kiss her madly. His head was already tilted. Her lips were already parted.

Instead he blinked, and came out of the trance. Springing to his feet, he gave her his hand to pull her up. His hand was warm, and hers was too. She struggled longer than necessary to allow him to hold it for a little longer.

"What do you think? Can you walk?" His palm cupped her elbow.

She took a step and wobbled—but not because of the pain.

"Not good?" he said cautiously. "Want me to take a look? If you've really hurt yourself, it'll swell up right away. We'll know."

"What good will that do us?" she asked. "It's a mile to town."

"I'll have to leave you, go get us a carriage," he said, pausing. He was still holding on to her. "Or I could carry you."

There was the briefest still-life of intense gray eye meeting baffled brown without another syllable uttered or a motion made because they both heard the unmistakable clomp of a horse, and Salvo's voice, calling for them from a not far enough distance.

"Gia! Harry!" He was standing at the reins waving from the open carriage. "*Mi dispiace!* I'm sorry I'm so late."

After a minute or two of Gina's stifled awkwardness and dusting off the hem of her dress, Salvo pulled up, stopping the horse near them. "I got my friend Alanzo to lend me his carriage for an hour. I gave him money for the *taverna*." Harry by that time had moved a whole person away. As they climbed in, they told Salvo almost everything that happened: they had ordered the stone, waited for him, started walking, then Gina twisted her ankle.

"My sister? Impossible! The girl skipped barefoot into the crater of Mount Etna. You don't trip on pebbles, Gia."

"A little sprain, not too bad." They were already sitting in the carriage, Salvo between them with the reins, chatting excitedly about the granite and the restaurants, and the complimentary glass of wine he was going to serve his first patrons.

The joy had been so fleeting. Did they talk in the carriage? Perhaps, so as not to alarm Salvo, she continued to tell Harry about her home town, that the volcanic eruptions had changed the course of the Belpasso River, drying it up, and it had disappeared. Most of the people moved out of town to nearby Catania, which was by the sea and safer. Perhaps she told Harry that her father made violins in his spare time. Even though he didn't play, he built them and sold them to the rich Sicilians, and got quite a reputation for his quality work, being paid handsomely for his labor. The barbershop paid their bills, but the violins were supposed to get them to America. But no quantity of violins or his reputation as the best barber could diminish living under the ash cloud, the constant rumbling, steam, smoke, pumice flying through the air. Alessandro hated the pine trees, the columns of gas, of volcanic ash. All he dreamed about was one day living in a safe place, free from acts of random terror like the death of his first-born son. Perhaps

Gina told Harry this. What is more likely is that he and Salvo talked about Belpasso and violins and Catania, while Gina sat nursing her ankle, her lungs too full to exhale. There will be another time like this, she repeated in a prayer, in a dream to herself. We will get another chance, more dazzling than this one. Somehow there will be time for a kiss for me to fall from your lips, with time left over to spare.

Chapter Twelve
TULIPS

1

IN late June Harry graduated from Harvard. Herman threw him a lavish party at which impeccably dressed and well-behaved people drank and congratulated each other on the fine results of an expensive education, while Harry— as usual slightly unshaven, but elegant in his light gray frockcoat, its broad lapels faced with black silk, a starched white shirt, a white waistcoat and lacquer-shined black patent shoes—ambled from circle to circle on the lawn, shaking hands and nimbly deflecting questions about his future. It was an unseasonably balmy Saturday, and the tables were set out on the Barrington lawn under the white entertainment tent.

Herman complained to Louis that they should have

rented a bigger tent. At first Louis pretended he hadn't heard. "We didn't realize so many people would be coming, sir," he eventually said.

"Oh, so you did hear, Jones," said Herman. "Then why are so many here? Did we *not* invite them?"

"Not all of them. Harry has many friends, and they all brought their families."

"Harry was required to give you a guest list three weeks ago."

"Yes, sir."

"He didn't give you a guest list?"

"No, sir."

Herman sighed and scanned around the unfamiliar laughing faces. "Well, what am I going to do? Yell at our boy on his graduation day?"

"That would not be fitting or proper," said Louis.

Herman took a drink from his hands. "Indeed, Jones, indeed. No trouble today. Just festivities."

"I think that's wise."

Under the violin strains of Baroque fugues and partitas from a live string quartet, the hundred and fifty invited guests and the hundred uninvited crowded around the white linen tables, crammed together under the refreshment canopy, eating chilled lobster salad and grilled cod straight from the sea that morning. Herman watched Ben and Harry happily natter a short distance away. Harry was spread out in a chair looking up at Ben, who was standing in front of him gesticulating. Harry was drinking and grinning. Herman overheard the separate notes of a singular topic of their conversation. Ellen came over to him with a drink in hand and together they watched their sons for a few minutes.

"We did well, Ellen, don't you think?" Herman said. "All things considered."

She shrugged but the pride was clear on her face. "Your Harry is a wonderful boy. He believes in all the right things."

"Your Ben is a wonderful boy," said Herman. "He *does* all the right things."

"Do you sometimes think, Herman," Ellen said, "that God, with his perverse sense of irony, switched our children on us?"

Herman put his arm around the much shorter Ellen. "I think he gave us exactly the children we deserve."

Alice, sitting by Harry's side, was trying to tease Ben out of speaking. It wasn't working. Ben, having graduated himself, though without the attendant extravagant fanfare, continued to regale the bored and the uninitiated with stories of Costa Rican bananas and mosquitoes that would be kept away with nets and sprays.

"Alice is a lovely girl, isn't she?" Ellen said to Herman. "You must be quite pleased she chose your son."

Herman shrugged. "It's not for me to be pleased, is it?" he said, ambling away with Ellen to a table full of grown-ups discussing the successful end of the Spanish-American War.

"Bananas kept away with nets and sprays?" Harry was asking Ben. Over a plate of cod and celery salad, they again became engaged in a cheerful "discussion" about digging a fifty-mile-long ditch through the continent instead of sailing 2,700 miles around Cape Horn. After the war, the treaty with Panama and the looming possibility of building the canal was *the* topic of fascination for polite Bostonians on this Saturday afternoon.

Harry, dressed in finery but his crimson Harvard tie already loosened, was in a good mood and game to pass the time. "Ben," he said, pretending to be serious, "better to go around Cape Horn? The expense of the new ships you'd need to build will more than offset the expense of traveling around Cape Horn while continuing to use the vessels already on hand, and with sailors who've made the trip, know their ship, live on the boat."

"Harry is right, Ben," said Orville, not realizing Harry was teasing. "Every country in the world will have to update its fleet. Do you have any idea how much that would cost?" But he rubbed his hands together, as if already anticipating the increase in lumber sales for the new ocean liners.

"It's a temporary expense, Mr. Porter," Ben explained patiently to Orville, glaring at a silently amused Harry. "After the new ships are built, what do you think will be cheaper, quicker and better—for the world economy and international trade—to continue to lose men to disease borne out of spending too long at sea, or to travel a few miles through a canal?"

"But the expense, Benjamin," said Alice, "the expense alone! Wouldn't it be prohibitive?" She was a vision today, dressed especially nicely for the party and for Harry, from neck to foot in thin, delicate cream-colored lace, in a sweeping skirt over a white silk drop-skirt with an ecru silk fringe. She sat by his elbow and every few minutes spooned some more lobster onto his plate.

"Alice, what about losing the men at sea?" Ben pressed on, sitting down. "What about the economic boon to a small fishing country named Panama? They've been fighting for their independence from the Colombians for ten years now. Are you saying it's all for naught?"

"Why does my son," Ellen wanted to know, coming over and placing a maternal arm around Ben's suited shoulders, "so love the idea of exerting American imperial power to intervene in another country's affairs?"

"Mother, how is it imperial power when we side with the

rebels?" Ben was in good humor and kissed his mother's hand.

Leaning down, she kissed his cheek. "You're siding with them on their soil, aren't you?"

"They've asked us to!" He pulled up a chair next to him so she could sit.

Slightly intoxicated, she spilled the champagne on her hands. "Did the Filipinos also ask you to fight a war in which they are the prize?"

"Um, Mother, keep to the subject, please," Ben said. "We are talking about Panama."

"Oh, Benjamin, *please*, can we talk about something else?" That was Alice, squeezing Harry's hand.

"Hear, hear," seconded Orville. "Let's talk about Harry."

Harry groaned dramatically, and everyone laughed.

"Harry, tell us—"

Esther interrupted. "No, no, enough about Harry. This day isn't *all* about him." Her gray eyes twinkled. "I'd like to find out more about Panama," she said, pulling her chair closer to Ben. She was elegant and attractive in her embroidered, lace-covered robin blue party dress. "Please continue, Ben. You were saying?"

Ben smiled at Esther, but his mother, flanking him on the other side, was the one who spoke first. "Yes, Ben, explain to Esther why America is so intent on extending its tentacles wherever and whenever it sees fit." She spoke so sharply for someone who was round and merry.

"Mother, while you allow Louis to refill your glass, will you please allow me the possibility that the canal could be an unmitigated good?"

Elmore instantly disagreed—on medical grounds. Standing behind Esther's chair, he said he was still concerned about the mosquitoes. "It's the small children that suffer most,

Benjamin. In South America, in Africa, they're the ones that die first from malaria."

"Oh, can we *please* not talk about death at a party," said Irma. "Orville, come with me." She pulled on her husband's arm. "Let the young ones talk. We belong at another table. Herman was looking for us. Ellen, come with us?"

No one moved, not even Orville at the behest of his wife.

"Elmore, with all due respect," said Ben, "the children are not going to be building the canal. The Chinese are."

"Are they worth sacrificing?"

"Well, there are an awful *lot* of them, Elmore," Ellen said agreeably.

"And it's the Americans that will bring the nets and the spray," said Ben with a smile. "So because of our work on the canal, the South American children will live longer." Ben smiled at his mother. "Mother, darling, you might not care about the Chinese, but you do care about the children?"

"What about the Chinese children?" That was Harry. "Would they cancel each other out?"

"Oh, Harry, don't tease!" exclaimed Alice, teasing. "I know you don't care about the Chinese *or* children!" Louis had brought an extra chair and they finally all managed to squeeze around one inadequate table, as the servers refilled their plates with lobster and their goblets with champagne.

"Yes, Harry, Alice is right. But tell us what you *do* care about," said Orville.

"Your daughter for one," answered Harry, lifting Alice's hand to kiss it.

Alice seemed to like that much better.

"What is the test of your devotion?"

"Father, don't start!"

Orville wouldn't let up. "Come on, you've been ducking the question like a politician for three years, today especially."

"I'm not ducking. I'm ignoring." Harry grinned.

"Now that you're a graduate, you must answer straight."

"Why?"

Orville rolled on. "We all know, indubitably, what Ben is going to be doing. But what are *you* going to be doing?" He smiled rotundly, patting his daughter's back. She blushed and tittered, and so did Irma. "Orville," the mother whispered. "Come on, all in due course."

"Daddy! Ignore him, Harry darling, please."

"I'm doing that ably, dear."

But everyone could tell, Alice didn't want Harry to ignore him. She wanted Harry to talk about nothing else.

"Ladies, gentlemen, please," Harry said, with a slight sitting bow toward Alice and her parents. "Could we agree, just for today—one party at a time?" Everyone remembered it was his graduation day, and the subject was almost changed. The servers came around again, pouring wine, serving shrimp and potato salad. There was clinking, another toast, loud laughter, another political conversation from an adjacent table wafting in on the wings of the breeze. But Alice's father, having had too much champagne, would not be so easily denied. "You know, son, you can always come and work for me," Orville said.

"Why yes, Harry, what a splendid idea." Ben grinned mischievously. "You can wash your own hands, so to speak, by producing the paper you need to print all the books you read."

"Exactly!" Orville carried on. "Though mine is not quite that end-product business. But we can always expand in the future. Look, I understand you not wanting to work for your old man. So come and work for me. Alice can teach

234

you the business. I run the largest lumber supply company in New England."

"Sir," said Harry. "I have known you and your daughter for a long time. I'm well aware what a fine company you've built." Yet he *still* did not answer the question! They all sat joyfully under the canopy and waited.

"Don't worry, Alice dear," Harry finally said. "I'm not going to go to Panama with Ben, if that's what you're afraid of."

"Who said anything about Ben going to Panama?" exclaimed Esther.

Elmore glanced at Esther peculiarly. "He's been talking about nothing else," he said slowly. "Have you *not* been paying attention?"

"I'd rather you go to Panama, Harry, than do nothing," Alice's father shot back amiably.

Alice gasped. "Daddy! Don't listen to him, Harry."

"Who said I will do nothing?" Harry became five degrees less cheerful.

Herman must have been listening from the nearby table where they had been discussing electoral politics. Clearly Orville had got Herman's short hairs up because he pushed back his chair, slid his wineglass to the side, stood up, sauntered over and leaned in between Harry and Ben. "Oh, you don't need to worry about Harry anymore, Orville, old boy," Herman said. "Harry is *plenty* busy. He is expanding into real estate. Right in his old man's footsteps. Isn't that right, son?" He patted Harry's shoulder.

Harry muttered something unintelligible in reply, leaned away and raised his hand to his father to quiet him, to remind him of something very important, a promise he had made. It was like crystal falling on the marble floor in slow motion. You reached out to catch it, just a moment behind it, a moment too late.

Harry saw the cliff edge the conversation was hurtling toward. But maybe it was a mistake to hold his father, who had had a little too much liquor, to promises made when he was sober. For once Herman was relaxed because it was a good day, and it wasn't every day your only son graduated from Harvard second in his class; it wasn't every day your son gave a salutary speech in front of six hundred Harvard graduates. On this day, Herman allowed himself a moment to be proud. And in that moment of punctured pride, he had plumb forgot that he had promised his son to say nothing. So he continued, "Harry started small, but from what my business manager Gray Billingsworth tells me, he is going to be very successful. When Billingsworth gets excited about a venture, you know it's going to be the next Standard Oil."

"Billingsworth told me we weren't investing in oil, Father," said Harry, belatedly attempting to derail him.

"I'm being metaphorical, son," an undeterred Herman said.

"What venture?" asked Orville.

"Yes, what venture is this?" echoed Ben, still grinning in his innocence. "Harry hasn't said a word to me about it."

The reminder of Ben's white ignorance was too subtle to stop Herman. "My Harry has invested in not one but two restaurants in Lawrence!"

It was as if Harry's hand flew out to catch the precious gem falling into the abyss. For him the silence lasted long enough for all the crystalline ions, molecules, atoms, lovingly arranged, divinely ordered, to plummet into the rock quarry, shattering and spinning into chaos in front of Harry's helpless eyes.

"I know, I *know*," Herman said when he chanced upon Ben's glassy stare. "Ben, I thought the same thing. Lawrence! Loony, right?"

"Yes," Ben said dully. "Crackers."

"But the textile union contracts were signed in relative peace, the town is prospering, and apparently the Italian man we've helped has conjured up some kind of a Neapolitan bread and cheese product that's setting the profits on fire. They call it pizza or something, right Harry?"

"Right, Father." Harry was palming his cut-glass flute. All the bubbles had fizzled out of the celebration potion.

"They have lines out the door on the weekends." Herman laughed with satisfaction. "Billingsworth thinks if they keep it up, they'll pay us our ten-year note five years early. And he is the most pessimistic man I know."

"Darling!" said Alice, grabbing Harry's cold hand. "That is *so* exciting! I had *no* idea you were doing something so wonderful. Why did you keep that a secret from me?" She didn't let him answer. "But what made you go all the way to Lawrence? You could have opened four restaurants in North End."

Harry couldn't miss a beat, not a single one, and so he didn't. "I didn't open them, Alice," he said slowly. "I just loaned them money."

"But how do you know anyone in Lawrence?"

"Ben and I told you about that Italian family we met last year."

"I don't remember at all. What Italian family?" She scrunched up her little nose. "I don't trust the Italians. The few I've met have not been nice."

"Well, these ones seemed like a nice enough bunch, right Ben?"

Pointed silence greeted Harry instead of Ben's easy reply.

Harry continued. "They were keen to open a place. There were two great locations. They presented this investment idea to me and Billingsworth. You know I know nothing about business, Alice. Not a thing." Harry sped up, like the

237

steady rattle of a jackhammer. "So he and I went out there and made an assessment. Billingsworth was the one who decided to take a chance. I couldn't have done it without him. He forecast it could be profitable. And my father is correct—so far so good. The restaurants have only been open a few weeks. Ben, now that you have a little free time, we should ride out there and take a look together."

Ben said nothing at first. Then he spoke, into his china plate, into his empty tumbler. "I don't have much free time. My plate is full. No time to ride trains." He wiped his mouth with a napkin and stood up. He didn't know where to look.

"Harry," said Esther, frowning, puzzling, "is *that* where you've vanished to the last three months? We've hardly seen you!"

Ben's hands started to tremble. Harry nearly snapped at his sister in full view of the guests. "I haven't disappeared, Esther. I live at Beck, remember, not at home. I've been working hard on my course. Salutatorian of my graduating class, lest you forgot. Not a lot of free time. Billingsworth helped me out a lot. He's the one who mostly supervised the renovations." Billingsworth wasn't present to confirm or deny the frequent supervisions. It was all Harry could do not to glare at his father. But Harry wouldn't dare lift his eyes to see the lowered confounded head of his friend. The table got an odd hush over it.

"I'm sorry, Harry," Herman said, suddenly catching the drift of the chill in the sunny air. "I hope you're not upset with me for speaking out of turn. I know we wanted to keep it quiet, but you said yourself it was only until the business got off the ground. And it seems to have gotten off the ground splendidly. I wanted to share your great success at this table. I didn't want my friend Orville besmirching your fine efforts."

"I didn't know he was making such a commendable effort, did I, Herman?" Orville bellowed.

"You don't have to worry about my boy," Herman said to Alice's father with a delighted smile. "Harry is easing himself into the life he chooses, though, as always, temperately. That's one of his strongest qualities, his lack of impulsiveness." He smiled fondly at Alice. "He is like a compass, my Harry. Says little but always points in the right direction."

"Oh, I agree with you, Mr. Barrington," cooed Alice. "I agree with you wholeheartedly!"

Neither Harry, nor Ben, nor Esther looked at each other or anyone else at the table when Herman Barrington proclaimed so unequivocally his son's steady navigation of the uncharted course.

With barely a bow, Ben excused himself, saying he would be right back, and fled. Getting up himself, Harry leaned over his sister to whisper to her. "Nicely done. Well played."

"I don't know what you're talking about," she whispered, smile glued to her lips like a ventriloquist, who speaks but doesn't move his mouth. "You've got no one to blame but yourself."

"Blame myself for what? I did nothing wrong." Harry was not a ventriloquist.

"R-r-really?" She rolled her r's without moving her grimacing mouth. "Then why didn't you tell him?"

"Why did you tell him? I didn't tell him because I was doing nothing wrong and didn't want to upset him. But you told him I was never home, which isn't true in any case, because you thought I was doing something wrong. Why did you want to upset Ben, Esther?"

She almost threw down her gloves onto the manicured

lawn. "My intentions are pure," Esther said through suddenly closed teeth.

"Oh and mine?" Harry retorted. "I didn't tell him because his feelings are more important than the silly truth. I thought they might be more important to you too, of all people. Clearly I was mistaken."

Esther blinked away tears, looking at the grass and her cream court shoes, her fingers tense like claws. "I didn't realize he'd be that upset," she said to Harry. "Why don't you ask him," she said quietly, "why a year later he keeps pining for someone who feels nothing for him?"

"Of all people, Esther, surely *you* must know the answer to that question," Harry said coldly, storming away to find Ben.

He caught up with him down the street when Ben was already some distance away.

"Sorry, I'm in a rush," Ben said, not slowing down and not looking at Harry. "I'm doing a presentation on engineering structures for the Army Corps tomorrow as part of my interview portfolio, and I just realized I'm woefully unprepared."

"Ben, come on," Harry said. "You left your mother just sitting there, you didn't thank my father, didn't say goodbye to me, to Esther."

"Please sincerely apologize to your father and to your sister. I'm not myself."

"Ben."

The dark-haired young man kept walking and said nothing. He loosened the tie around his neck, as though it was choking him, then ripped it off.

"Dear friend, please, don't be upset with me."

"I'm not upset."

Harry reached out to get hold of Ben's arm. Reluctantly

Ben slowed down and stopped. The two men stood in front of each other on the sidewalk, dressed as if for a wedding.

"Benji, I'm sorry I didn't tell you."

"Why didn't you?"

Harry willed himself not to look away. "Because I didn't want to upset you. That's the honest truth."

"You didn't tell me because you didn't want to upset me?" Ben repeated slowly and incredulously.

"Why do you sound so surprised?"

"Um, I don't know. Maybe because . . . that's the stupidest thing I ever heard?"

"Ben, don't be upset . . ."

"I'm not upset. But you should've told me, Harry. Told me what you were up to. I know we've both been busy, but it's not like we haven't seen each other. We just had lunch at Hasty Pudding two weeks ago."

"Yes, with eleven other men."

"What, hardly the time for confidences?" asked Ben.

"I have nothing to confide. It's all tediously above board."

"Why would it upset me if it's above board?"

"Not *if*. It is. But *you* tell me. Why are you cross with me?"

"Cross? Not me."

"Ben." He reached out to his friend. "You know I'm going to ask for Alice's hand."

"Do I know this?" Ben said, unmollified.

"What you're thinking, it's not proper. Or possible. More important, it's not real."

"What I feel for her is real."

Harry lowered his head briefly. He didn't know what to say. "You haven't seen her since November," he said quietly. "You're this close to shipping off to Panama."

"So? What is your point? And not at all close—just like you are to marrying Alice."

"Then very close. Look, it was just to help her brother . . ."

"Why do you care about helping him?"

"That's what my father's business is. We help the immigrants in North End. This time they're a little further north. It's the same principle. It's just business, Benji."

"If it was just business, why didn't you tell me?"

"I didn't want to upset you for nothing."

Ben remained silent. Harry took that as an opening. "Ben, I'm seven years older than her. Can't you see that what is impossible for you, is doubly impossible for me? Honestly, it doesn't bear speaking about."

"Soon she will be sixteen," Ben said.

"But you and I will be twenty-three!"

Ben rubbed his eyes, his face. "Jiminy Cricket. Sixteen is so damn young."

"Yes." Harry took one shallow breath with shattered crystal in it.

"Oh, Harry!" Ben exclaimed, almost like his old self, but with injury in his eyes and voice. "Why didn't you just tell me?"

Why didn't Harry have a quick enough reply? He feared that his friend, while diligently working on bringing the canal to life, dreamed every day of someday having the belle of Belpasso be old enough to no longer withstand his full-hearted, half-hearted advances. "I was afraid of confrontation," Harry finally said. "You know how much I don't like a contretemps. I didn't want to have one with you, of all people. We've never had any trouble between us."

"No. We never have."

They shook hands, giving each other a quick hard hug.

"Will you come next Sunday for afternoon tea? Tomorrow we're not entertaining. And all next week I'm moving my things back home. But then it'll be just you and us. My father misses you. Esther, too."

"And Elmore too." Ben rolled his eyes. "Did you see how famished he was for a fight with me? He is so deliciously hostile. Will he be there?"

"I'll make sure he isn't so we can avoid all that hostility, delicious or not." Harry shook Ben's hand again. "Benj, are we square?"

Ben almost smiled. "We're square," he said.

2

Next Sunday arrived, and Ben came. He greeted everyone, almost like normal, even teased Esther. "Where is Elmore, Esther? Oh no, he's working! What a shame. And on a Sunday too. No rest for the wicked, I suppose. Harry, did you rest today?"

They had drinks outside, because the weather was again splendid and sat for their finger sandwiches and scones under the covered gazebo. There was a slight breeze, no flies, and the gin and tonics were refreshing. Herman, delighted to see Ben at his house once more, peppered the young graduate with questions.

"Ben," he asked, "is it true what Harry tells me?"

"I don't know. What true thing does Harry tell you?"

"That United Fruit offered you a full-time position, and meanwhile the U.S. Army Corps of Engineers presented you with a spot on the Panama Commission. Are you trying to decide between United Fruit and the Army Corps of Engineers?"

"Yes," Ben replied. "Unlike Harry, I'm actually trying to choose a career."

"Quite wise of you," agreed Herman, glancing slightly perplexed at Harry. "Which way are you leaning?"

"I'm vacillating. Afraid to make the wrong choice."

Herman laughed. "Well, *that* sounds very much like Harry."

Ben shook his head. "No, sir. I know for a fact it isn't. Your son is enjoying an entirely different kind of problem."

Harry put down his gin and tonic, which suddenly didn't seem quite as refreshing, sensing veiled hostility.

"Oh, really?" Esther asked, curious. "And what do you think is my brother's problem?"

"A deep and abiding aversion to toil."

Ah, so not even veiled. Frowning, Harry said nothing to defend himself, averting his eyes from his discomfited sister.

"What did you say, Ben?" That was Herman. "I didn't quite hear. I'm beginning to sympathize with Louis . . ."

"Nothing."

"I've been hitting the books for four years," Harry said slowly. "Eight if you count Andover."

"And it isn't all Harry's been hitting," returned Ben.

No one knew how to respond to that comment, so no one did. It was all so unlike Ben. Esther studied her blackberry jam and clotted cream. Herman studied both his son and his son's friend.

"I'd say most of Harry's efforts have been largely chimerical," Ben continued. "Except of course for the extravagance of his labor in Lawrence—but what's *that* all about? I hardly know." He paused. "Perhaps it's a labor of love?"

"Oh, it's definitely that," agreed Herman, looking around for Louis. "But also, perhaps Harry is finally finding his way." He gave up and rose to pour his own cocktail.

"Yes, perhaps," Ben said casually coldly. "Or . . . perhaps it's like Joseph Conrad says, there are some men to whom the whole of life is nothing more than an after-dinner hour with a cigar."

"Don't knock after-dinner cigars, dear boy," said Herman jovially. "They're a delightful and well-deserved treat."

"Easy, pleasant," Ben said. "Empty."

Herman returned to the table with his drink. They sat without speaking. Harry wondered if it would go away, if they could all pretend for just a few weeks, and then all would be forgotten and things would go back to normal.

It had started out a fine Sunday. Where had it gone wrong? The briefest thought flickered in Harry: are we trying to put back together something that's irreparably broken? Harry refused to believe it. Nothing in life was like that.

Almost nothing.

But he had tried very hard to arrange his own days so that nothing in them would be like that again.

Chewing his lip, and concluding yet again that even the smallest of truths led only to vast unpleasantness, conflict to nothing but ugly scenes, extreme emotions only to hurt, Harry swallowed Ben's bitter words and tried to leaven the table with self-deprecation. "I'm trying to attain perfection through little more than thought and reflection, Benjamin. Is that so wrong?"

"Ah, is that what you're trying to do? Attain perfection?"

"Why not?"

"Because that's not a project worthy of us Christians," said Ben. "That's a project for ideologues and dictators."

"Ideologues, you don't say."

"Ideologues like Marx," said Ben.

"Marx was an ideologue? Well, count me in." Harry raised his crystal tumbler filled with untouched gin and tonic.

"*Is* there perfection and freedom in being a Marxist?"

"Why not?" Harry said. "We're not bringing you Marx by the sword, are we? Congregations of people get together and through a democratic process decide how they want to shape their own destinies." He paused. "Which is what *I'd* like to do." He stood up. "Now if you'll excuse me, I think the sun has gone to my head. Thank you so much for an enjoyable afternoon. Ben, Esther. Excuse me, Father."

Ben caught up with him in the galley between the family eating room and Herman's study. "So now *you're* walking away?" he said.

"I'm not feeling quick enough on my feet," Harry said. "Or with my tongue. I feel dull. I feel like . . ." He broke off. "What's wrong with you?" he said to Ben coldly. "I thought we were square."

"Oh, we were, we were," Ben said, just as coldly. "Until a minute after I left you and was on my way home last week, when it occurred to me that I forgot to ask you a small but all-important question."

Harry didn't want to be asked anything.

"Are you *still* cantering off to Lawrence every day of the week and twice on Sunday?"

His face falling, Harry said nothing.

Ben stepped away, opened his hands. "And you wonder why we're not square."

3

Motionlessly Harry sat in the drawing room. He asked Louis to build up the fire, though it was blistering hot in the late evening. For some reason he was cold, like the moon had

246

gone out. He felt blackly depressed. It was decided: he knew what he had to do, what he must do. He had no choice. He didn't have even the illusion of freedom. To save the only life he knew how to live, he knew what had to be done. Why then did it make him feel like a seaborne vessel from which all men had fled, leaving her to sink alone?

He didn't have long to sit and commiserate with himself. His father called him into his study. Reluctantly Harry followed Louis down the hall. He wished he had gone upstairs so he wouldn't have been bothered tonight. Perhaps a good night's rest would rid him of his malaise.

"Harry, sit down."

Reluctantly Harry sat down. "Elmore suggested a nurse he works with at Mass General," he began, launching into a campaign of distraction. "According to Esther, Elmore said she is quite capable. Rosa something or other. Would you like Esther and me to interview her this week now that I'm home? She wouldn't be a replacement for poor deaf Louis, merely an additional pair of hands."

Herman ignored him. "Later about Louis. Tell me about Ben."

"What about him?"

"Don't be obtuse. What's got into him?"

"I don't know. A bad mood, I reckon."

"Why?"

Harry shrugged.

Herman folded his hands. "He seemed uncharacteristically hard on you."

"Perhaps I deserve it."

"Ah. Now we're getting somewhere. What have you done?"

"I said perhaps, Father. I don't know."

Herman wiped a speck of dust off his wood desk, straightened out some papers in the corner, fiddled with the inkwell next to his quill pen. "I overheard some of your conversation with him in the hall earlier."

Harry folded his own hands. If he had been standing, he would've put them in his pockets, the way his father hated. "So if you know, why ask me?"

"But I don't know anything."

"It was hardly a conversation. Two sentences."

"That's why I'm still ignorant," said Herman. "I was hoping you could enlighten me."

"I'm trying to enlighten myself." Though opening his eyes was not such a wonderful thing.

"I also had a chance to speak to your sister."

"I'm glad, Father. Will there be anything else?"

"What do you mean, we just sat down."

"Surely you don't need me to hear that you talked to Esther. You do that quite frequently," Harry said. "After all, you *are* related. Also, you live in the same house."

"Son, don't be upset with your sister. She only wants the best for you. As I do."

"Do you?"

Herman frowned. "Of course. I would have liked this Lawrence situation to be something foundational, not built on the ever-shifting sands of your mercurial nature or another passing whimsy. I had been so excited to help set you on your way. Esther, however, seemed to indicate . . . but no. I have to ask you directly, and be straight with me, don't give me your runaround. Is it real?"

Harry didn't answer for a few minutes.

Not long ago she had brought him a dyed carded roving to open his eyes to wonders he didn't understand. She had combed the wool and braided it and then steeped the plump spool in vinegar water colored with the deep juice of blueberries. The wool had dried by the time she showed it to him, and he touched it like he was touching a purple pupa—with the barest tips of his fingers. How does *this* become anything one can possibly use, he asked. With a breathless laugh she said—by magic. Like electricity. A week later she gave him a gift of a violet scarf, soft and scarlet like bloodied down. But in that untouched week she and the roving went into the chrysalis together. She emerged on the other side of Tuesday floating in a pink sunshine dress, and the sheep fur in her hands became a faint millstone around his neck that he took with him to Beck Hall. Near the scarf fringe an ivory letter "H" was knitted. He asked: for Harvard? For Harry, she replied.

"No," said Harry to his father. "It's not real." And the stallion of joy just up and galloped away, leaving his heart balled up like his fists.

Herman heaved a disapproving sigh. "That *is* disappointing."

Harry tried to divert the frontline assault by using rules of combat he wasn't used to. "I don't know who I am yet," he said, apathetic now. "I'm still looking. I'm not ready to make a number of difficult decisions that are being thrust upon me." *Forced* upon me. "I'm exploring my options." He shook his head. "I'm not ready."

"That's fine," Herman said. "But until you make a career decision, you cannot ask for Alice's hand in marriage."

"Really? But okay. *Am* I asking for it?"

"Don't you soon intend to?"

"I don't know," Harry said evenly. "No point in continuing to put me on the spot as sport, though, wouldn't you agree? It's hardly going to make me rise to the occasion."

Herman sat back. "You don't think it might shame you into it?"

"Shamed into marriage? Not very likely."

"I meant shamed into a career."

Harry tightened his mouth. "Father, you've told me my whole life I've come into privilege accidentally and with it came freedom that other people didn't have."

"With it also comes responsibility that other people don't have."

"I know. But freedom first?"

"You've had twenty-three years of nothing but."

"I've had twenty-three years of schooling and studying and reading, and learning and thinking. I haven't had freedom."

"Not enough time?"

"Not nearly."

"Okay, but can we agree on a time limit for vacillation? Say six months?"

"No," said Harry. "We can't agree to it. I will not put arbitrary parameters on the most important decision of my life—my role in it."

Herman sat patiently. His brow looked weary. "Alice is not going to wait forever, son."

Harry studied his hands. "Okay."

"What are you going to do about Ben?"

"Ben is under a lot of pressure, Father," Harry said. "His allegiance has shifted, as allegiance sometimes does, and he is realizing, somewhat belatedly, that he cannot serve two masters—the canal builders and the banana growers. Time has come for him to decide. And he doesn't want to. Andrew Preston has been Ben's most loyal benefactor. Aside from you. But the choice between two opposing things of equal weight are tough. So he struggles. Some of this you saw at dinner. Please accept my apologies on his behalf."

"Nonsense," said Herman. "That is not what I saw at

250

dinner at all. And you know how I enjoy feisty discussion. We don't have enough of it. Most of it is so chaste. That's why I adore it when Ellen comes to visit, she makes our dinners so lively. Clearly her son has inherited some of his mother's spark. Our tea today was entertainment of the first order. Much like the running of the bulls I keep reading about." Herman paused. "That's not what concerns me."

In a minute the concerns were going to be unloosed on Harry's indifferent head.

"What concerns me," Herman went on, "is that your sister seems to think that behind Ben's antagonism and your adventure in Lawrence is something of a rather more personal nature. From the snippet of your conversation with Ben, I fear Esther may be correct."

"She is wrong." Harry sighed. "Don't mind her."

"Why *didn't* you tell Ben about your business venture in Lawrence?"

"I didn't tell anyone."

"But why not him?"

"For the same reason why not anyone."

Herman raised his hand to stop Harry. "I'm not delving into your affairs, son. But I *am* going to suggest that you delve into your motives and figure out what's important to you. Do you have ulterior motives, as Esther alludes?"

Harry opened his mouth to tell Herman of Esther's ulterior motives and then closed it. He didn't want Ben's presence in his father's house to be anything but what it had always been, easygoing and familiar. Was it too late for that? He refused to believe it. He had already made up his mind by the fire; he was going to set things right. If only his father wouldn't interfere, as always, and make Harry's every decision more tortured. "Esther doesn't want Ben to go to Panama," he said. "She is worried about him. She would prefer he stay in Boston and work with Preston at United Fruit."

"Why?"

What to say to that? There was once something about tulips Esther had said to Harry. It was a few years ago in the spring and Ben had his wandering eye briefly set on the flower shop owner's daughter on Main Street. Esther said, *sometimes I truly believe that even tulips are agonized.*

Only today did Harry *feel* what she had meant.

They sat without speaking.

"The affairs of the heart are complicated, Harry," Herman said quietly.

"I don't need you to tell me that, Father."

"I don't claim to be an expert. I will not presume to offer either of my grown children advice."

"And I for one can't tell you," Harry said, "how much I appreciate that."

"Please think carefully about your place in your own life."

Harry stood up before he was dismissed. "Father, it's as if you don't know me. That's *all* I do."

Herman got up in a measured manner. "Unfortunately I'm beginning to realize I know you too well."

Harry bowed before he left. "I hope one day to either surprise you or to fulfill the expectations you have of me."

"Son," said Herman, "I would much rather you shocked the hell out of me."

4

Gina crossed Broadway and was rushing to Antonio's restaurant by the station when she saw the carriage draw up. This made her so happy that she lifted her dragging skirt and started to run. She hadn't seen Harry in over three weeks and was nearly at the point of going to his house in Barrington to call on him. Breathless and flushed, she forced herself to slow down as she neared the black covered carriage.

Billingsworth came around, barely nodding to a smiling Gina, and opened the door. A woman stepped out, wearing sensible shoes as if she were dressing for the country, a smart oversized hat and a tweed suit. Esther took her bag and calmly turned to the restaurant, acknowledging Gina by pursing her already tense mouth. Gina stopped smiling.

"Hello." She didn't know what to say next.

"Oh, hello," Esther said coolly, as if uncertain she'd even met Gina before.

"I'm Gina Attaviano. We met last fall . . ."

"Did we? I do apologize, I'm terrible with faces. Are you Salvatore's sister?" Esther pointed to Antonio's.

Gina nodded. She stood awkwardly, not knowing what to do next. Billingsworth scurried by like a mouse, from the carriage to the front door.

"Hello, Mr. Billingsworth," she called after him. He barely acknowledged her, deliberately not catching her eye.

Gina turned to Esther. "We met at Ben's mother's Anti—"

"Of course, of course. How are you? And your friend? Valerie, was it?"

"Verity."

"That's right. My apologies. I'm also terrible with names. How do you do?" Esther asked an inert Gina. "Have you finished your studies?"

"Uh, no. I've got two more years left." Why was Esther asking her this?

"I meant for this year."

"Oh, yes. Thank you. We are on summer recess."

"Very good. If you will excuse me, Mr. Billingsworth and I are here for our monthly meeting with your brother. I hope this is not a bad time. The place looks crowded."

"It is," Gina said. "But he's not here."

"Oh. We thought he was here for lunch? Harry told us Antonio's at lunchtime, Alessandro's at dinner."

Gina frowned, her heart missing a beat. "Harry's right. But Dotty quit. She was our manager. Until we hire someone new, Salvo is at Alessandro's all day. It's on Essex Street, not far from here . . ."

"Who's covering Antonio's then?"

"Me."

Esther inspected her. "As a *manager?*"

"I just make sure other people are doing their jobs. It's not hard."

"But you have to tell people what to do, young lady. *Men.*"

"I do that."

"Do they listen?"

"Usually."

"I see." Esther started to write officiously in her large notebook. She looked smart and serious, like a business-woman. Gina became aware how comical she must look in her threadbare summer frock. Surreptitiously, so Esther wouldn't see, she pulled out the blue lotus wildflowers from her hair and let them drop to the ground, stepping on the blooms, tamping them into the dusty sidewalk for good measure.

"Is everything okay?" she asked Esther. "Is Harry all right?"

"Of course. Why wouldn't he be?"

As nonchalantly as she could, Gina shrugged. "Usually he comes with Mr. Billingsworth."

"Not anymore. These two restaurants are a Barrington

family investment. Harry asked me to take over their management . . ."

"*Asked* you to?"

"Quite right. After his graduation, he decided to spearhead the renovation of a commercial block on Charter Street in North End. It's a major and complex undertaking for our father's company. Harry is staying focused on his biggest priorities."

"Yes, Lawrence is quite far," echoed Gina.

"Oh," Esther exclaimed, as if just remembering, "did you get a chance to have a gander at last week's *Boston Register* by the way?"

Gina didn't even know what that was. "I missed it last week," she said. "Is there any news?"

"Indeed. Harry and Alice Porter are engaged to be married. He asked her father for her hand, and she graciously accepted. There was a full-page story about it in the paper. I'm surprised you missed it. The engagement dinner is in July. Would you like us to send Salvo and you an invitation? And Variety too, of course. It's going to be *the* engagement event of the summer. Alice is one of the most sought-after young ladies . . ."

"I should hope not anymore."

Esther laughed.

"If you'll excuse *me*," Gina said, standing straight and tall, her face a blank, her body motionless. "It's lunch hour, and I must attend to my own priorities."

"Business does seem to be very good." The front door never stopped swinging open and shut.

"It's my brother's pizza. You must try some if you get the chance."

"Maybe another time," said Esther. "Harry said your brother is a hard-working young man. And Billingsworth

255

told me the restaurants are outperforming their projections by 86%. Which means—"

"They're making nearly twice what we planned." Gina smiled. "Goodbye, Esther." Etiquette be damned. Without waiting for a reply, Gina disappeared inside the noisy maul of Antonio's.

5

She lay on the bed face-down all day Sunday. It was a gorgeous day and both Angela and Verity sat on the bed tugging at her to go boating on the Merrimack. "Come on, don't be sad, you silly girl."

They consoled her that day and the next and the one after that. But all Gina could do was work and lie motionlessly on her bed. "You're fifteen, for goodness sake!" Angela finally exclaimed. "This is only the beginning. You've got a lifetime of boys to look forward to. Why are you so upset? Gina, you're barely off the boat and out of diapers. He is a graduate from Harvard. His father owns an entire town, and a whole section of another. He is not your man."

"Doesn't own it. Helped build it."

"Don't quibble. Ah, so you *are* listening."

"On his mother's side, one of his ancestors walked off a boat called *The Mayflower*, I think. In his heart, he is an immigrant, just like me, searching for a new world."

"He is done searching. You have it wrong. He is born and raised and will die in the very world for which *you're* searching. But for what it's worth," Angela added, "you are much prettier than he is handsome."

"That's not true. Have you seen his eyes? He is lovely."

"Only you think so."

"Clearly not." Gina flew up off the bed like an incensed wounded bird, hobbled over to her dresser, grabbed the damn *Register*, flung it open and pointed at the Announcements page. "Look at her! Alice Porter of Timber blah blah, one of the five largest blah blah in New England, oh, and *she* is a Radcliffe attendee."

"She is wasting her time," Angela said wisely. "No man wants a smart woman."

"Harry does!"

Verity glanced at the newspaper. "She is so blonde and pretty."

Flinging the paper onto the floor, Gina fell back on the bed.

"You'll see, Gina, this will be your lucky day."

"I will never see that."

"Verity is right," said Angela. "Even if he was remotely interested, Salvo and Mimoo would not let you out with him."

"Look how they were with Ben," said Verity, "and he had a real yen for you." She said this with slight regret. "That's the part I don't understand. If you're going to go for the unattainable, why not go for the one who is already swooning over you?"

"Verity," said Gina. "I may be fifteen, but *you* know nothing about love."

The girls laughed at her. She stood her ground, so to speak, as she lay prostrate. "You think you *choose* who to love? How easy that would be. *It* chooses you, Verity. Love comes from the heavens, pierces your heart, and claims it for itself. Don't you know *anything*?"

"Am I the one moping on the bed during a hot summer?"

"Verity's got a point," said Angela. "Gia, what about Tommy who comes to St. Vincent's every day you're there to donate his sister's toys and clothes? She's got nothing

257

left! His parents are going to have to buy her one new set of everything. He only comes because you're there. He plays this newfangled thing called baseball, he is athletic and handsome. The other day he saw you walking across O'Leary Bridge and nearly fell off his horse. He offered to carry your wool for you. Am I right, Verity? All the pious girls at St. Mary's would sacrifice their rosary-kneading fingers to have him fall off his horse for them. Why are you pining over some old guy?"

Gina shook her head. "He's not old. He is wise and smart."

"He's not an owl. He's an old man. And it's nothing but a crush."

Gina shook her head. Angela was wrong. It *was* extravagant, but it was not short-lived.

"You don't even know what you want to do yet."

"I do."

"You don't know who you are."

"I do."

"You don't know what you're going to become."

"I do."

"Soon you will be a young lady," said Angela, caressing Gina's back. "You'll be a beauty queen, and he'll be a silly old lumber merchant in a tweed jacket."

"That's not who he is."

"Gina's right, Ange, that's not who he is," said Verity. "Have you heard him talk? It's book this and book that. Idea this and idea that. It's boring even to me."

"It's not boring," said Gina. "It's fascinating."

"I never liked him," said Angela, "for what it's worth."

"It's not worth much."

"Me neither," said Verity. "I liked Ben more."

"You did, did you? You'd better not tell Mother Grace that. She'll expel you from the nunnery."

258

Verity turned bright red. "I meant for you."

"Sure that's what you meant."

"It's summertime!"

"I'm aware what time of year it is, Verity."

"So stop fretting and come to the Merrimack. The boys and girls are having a race. Tommy will let you get in his boat. He'll row the skull for you." Angela and Verity giggled.

Gina turned her back to them, curling up. "You've never been inside a boat yourselves. You don't know what you're talking about."

"For your information, gloomy girl," Angela said knowingly, poking her in the shoulder blades, "I've been on boats every summer, not lying in bed all droopy-eyed after some boy who doesn't know my name."

"Harry knows my name!"

Angela lowered her voice. "If you don't come outside and play with me and Verity right now, I'll tell Salvo what you're doing."

"Go on then. Run along. Tell him I'm lying on the bed."

"Pining."

"He'll ignore you."

"Will Mimoo?"

"Doubly so."

On Monday Gina was up. She was not dressed for the river or work or schoolgirl summer adventures. She was dressed in church clothes and church shoes. She wore a gray skirt and a prim white blouse buttoned to her chin. Her hair was wound so tightly into a high bun that she looked almost hairless. She worked the lunch shift at Antonio's, and then, after the crowd dissipated, and when no one was looking, she crossed the street, proudly clutching a little brown purse she had "borrowed" from Angela and caught the 2:45 to Boston.

It was one paragraph in the *Register* that had done it. She just couldn't get it out of her mind. She couldn't rest until she saw him, one last time. There was no point in being maudlin, she saw that. Obviously the Cupid's arrow that had passed between them in the dust outside the quarry was pointing one way only; in her own exuberance she had badly misconstrued his intentions. But she thought it was cowardly of him to hide behind Esther, to send her, to delegate the dirty, roll-up-your-sleeves work to a woman, his sister of all people. She wanted to catch him in it. She wanted to confront him face to face.

It is with great pleasure that Orville and Irma Porter announce the welcome engagement of their only daughter Alice Mary, 22, of Brookline, to Harold Barrington, 23, of Barrington. Miss Porter is a worthy and exemplary young lady and is popular with her friends. She is one of the city's best-known society ladies. Mr. Barrington, an upright and enterprising young businessman, is a summa cum laude graduate of Harvard University, where he read economics and philosophy. Miss Porter, a Radcliffe attendee, is the heiress of East Timber, the largest lumber company in New England and one of the largest in the United States. The date for the wedding has not yet been set, but the engagement dinner will take place by invitation only at the home of Mr. Porter in Brookline on July 18 at two o'clock in the afternoon. May their future happiness be well seasoned with all the spices of life.

6

Gina found him on Charter Street overseeing the placement of new window frames into an old building. Ben was on the second floor, guiding the crane's jaws into proper position in the opening, while Harry was down below on the street. He didn't see Gina come up to him. It was a late June afternoon. They both stood shielding their eyes from the sun, looking up at Ben.

Ben waved. That's when Harry turned and saw her.

"Oh, hello," he said, taking off his hat, leaving it dangling in his left hand. His gray eyes deepened slightly, and then became blank. "How do you do?"

"I'm fine, thank you. How are you?"

He mumbled something in reply. "What are you doing in North End?"

"I've come to ask you a question," she said, wasting no time. It was to her great satisfaction that she saw Harry become as uncomfortable as she'd ever seen him. He shifted from foot to foot, paid phenomenal attention to the slightly loose laces in his shoes, nearly dropping his hat, and searching in vain through his five pockets for a non-existent pair of glasses. Gina watched him calmly as he twitched through the maneuvers.

What saved him was Ben, who had come downstairs and outside. "Hello, Gina." He was cool at first, but couldn't help but smile at seeing her. "It's been such a long time," he added mildly, with a bow to her, something Harry had not done. "My mother has been asking after you. So many wonderful guest speakers are attending Thursday nights. Last week Frederic Heath came."

"I'm sorry I missed that," said Gina. She had no idea who Frederic Heath was. "Verity and I wanted to come to the city for the annual Charles River Festival."

"Oh, yes, you should. That's lots of fun."

"I'm sure. But it starts too late. Eight in the evening is too late for us to be in Boston."

"It's also on Saturdays during the day," Ben said quickly. "At two, I think."

"I know. But I work Saturdays. I have the market early and then it's our busiest afternoon at the restaurants."

"Yes, Harry told me about the restaurants."

"I'm glad to hear that."

The three of them stood. Harry said nothing.

"Congratulations on graduating," Gina said.

"Thank you."

"How is the banana business?"

"Exploding."

"Exploding bananas!"

And they chuckled.

"What about the canal?" she asked.

"Still ongoing—in the research phase." Ben paused. "I'm sorry if that delayed train back in November caused you trouble," he said at last.

"Oh, it did," Gina said dismissively. "But that was a long time ago. It's forgotten now." She paused. "Of course we can't go to the meetings anymore, which is unfortunate. But otherwise, all's forgotten. Verity is turning nineteen next week. She has graduated herself." Ruefully Gina smiled. "*She* may be able to come to the meetings. If she can get one of her other friends to accompany her."

"Not you?" said Ben.

"Not me." She struggled against letting her shoulders slump under the great weight of her regrettable youth. Managing a smile, despite the prickles of pain, she stood stiff like the stalk of a flower. "I actually have to run, Ben. I can't stay. I just came to ask Harry a quick business question regarding some items we need at the restaurant. But it's nice to see you again," she finished. "I hope I see you again someday."

The smile left Ben's face. "Of course," he said. "Nice to

see you too, Gina. Excuse me." He walked away before they could stop him.

Charter Street was stale and heavy with the reek of their awkward silence.

"Why is Ben upset with me?" asked Gina.

"He isn't. Why would he be?"

"He shouldn't be. Why is he upset with you then?"

"Just preoccupied," Harry said. "He befriended a geologist who hammers him daily about the folly of carving up the eroding rock of a millennial river."

"I bet Ben is sorry he ever made the gentleman's acquaintance."

Harry almost smiled.

Gina wanted to say—just like I'm sorry I ever made yours. But she didn't mean it. So she couldn't say it. She fidgeted, studying the hem of her properly long skirt. No shoes in sight this time, or swollen ankles on pavements, no blue satin ribbons, bare elbows, mouthfuls of fragrant air. "I haven't seen you in Lawrence."

"No. Is that your question? I thought my sister explained. She had to take over for me. I've gotten enormously busy here."

"So I see." She watched him standing with his hand in his pocket in the middle of the street.

"Esther is swell. I think you'll get along with her. She has a good head for business—much better than mine."

"Really? You had been doing quite well yourself. Salvo and I wanted to ask you about opening a beer garden in the back of Alessandro's. We think it would bring in even larger crowds on summer evenings, or for Saturday afternoon drinks."

"That's a good idea. An excellent idea."

"There's room in the back, but the area would need to be paved with stone, and tables and chairs would need to be bought." She broke off. "Maybe some landscaping," she added quietly. "Some flowers."

"Yes, why not? Some tulips in spring." He blinked. "Absolutely. Leave it with me. I'll talk to Billingsworth about it tomorrow. He'll increase Salvo's line of credit to cover the expense."

"Thank you."

"Of course. It'll be good for business."

"Yes." They stood. "Well, that's all I came to ask," Gina said. "I'd better head back. I don't want to miss my train. Though it's not far from here, this is much closer than Old South. The station is just up the street. Up Causeway. I passed the men fishing in Mill Creek." She paused. "Not ice fishing. Just ordinary fishing."

Ever so slightly he shifted on his foot toward her—just an inch. But Gina noticed. "Oh, by the way," she said, as if just remembering. "I almost forgot. Congratulations on your engagement." Her voice was brassy bright. "Three years in the making, huh?"

A long slow blink was Harry's only response. Now he moved a foot away.

"Your fiancée sounds like a very special girl," Gina continued. "Esther kindly directed me to the *Boston Register* announcement. She is quite the socialite, your Alice."

Quietly Harry agreed that Alice came from a good family.

"I should say. And she is very beautiful."

He squinted at her, trying to see her more clearly through his narrowed vision. "Thank you," he said.

"Is your father in business with her father? For the raw materials?"

"Sometimes."

"For example, is any of the lumber used for Salvo's restaurants from your fiancée's father?"

Harry became stuck for words. "The contract my father has is with East Timber. So, yes, I suppose so."

"Well, the quality of the wood is excellent." Gina became stuck for words.

"Gina, I deeply apologize if anything I ever did or said was misconstrued by you in any way to cause you aggravation or hardship."

"Of course you didn't. No need to apologize."

"You are a very . . ."

"Please, no need to say more."

". . . spirited and delightful young lady."

"Thank you."

"It has been a pleasure to help you and your family, and I wish you the very best. If there is anything at all I can do to help, please don't hesitate . . ."

"Thank you." Her lip trembled ever so slightly. She hoped he didn't notice.

But he did notice. Because he stepped toward her, hat in hand, and lowered his voice. "We are from different worlds, Gina!" he said in a near whisper.

"Absolutely. No need to . . . please . . ." She wouldn't and couldn't lift her eyes.

"And—I'm twenty-three! And you're—"

"Almost sixteen . . ."

"A child."

"Harry!"

She was surprised she had raised her voice, the way she was feeling—so flattened. Yet she found the strength from somewhere to stop him from speaking. She raised her palm and shook her head, took two breaths to keep the tears from her eyes and two steps back from him because sometimes you had to put up your hand against the people who had the power to wound you the most. "Most sincerely, you helped my family, my brother—you saved him." One of her hands went on her heart. "I'm always going to be grateful to you for giving him a chance to realize his dreams. I don't want to cause you a moment of trouble. With your father, or sister—or fiancée. No more words are required." She took another deepest breath. "Or desired."

"Gina . . ."

"There is nothing between you and me."

And before he had a chance to speak another stilted syllable, she swirled around and walked unhurriedly down the street and away from him.

Once, last fall, Harry had reluctantly admitted to Ben, after much prodding, that the one thing about her that seemed slightly older than her years was how she carried herself, how she walked with dignity, with understated grace. He thought that especially intensely today after he had pricked her pride and hurt her feelings, and then watched her walk away like a high society duchess. His skimmer hat still dangling from his fingertips, he shifted half a step to go after her, his heart pounding, and then looked up and from behind the second-floor window frame caught sight of Ben's stricken face.

Lifting his hat in a short salute, Harry replaced it firmly on his head, and turned toward the harbor, away from Ben, away from Gina, away from the fishermen of Mill Creek.

7

"Gina," Angela consoled her, "you think you weren't smart enough for him? That's how you know he is right—you *are* still a child. Don't you know anything? The cleverest woman is the one who makes her man seem clever. Men don't like smart women. They don't like educated women. They certainly don't wish to have them as wives."

"He does."

"Why do you think this?"

"Because the woman he asked to marry him went to Radcliffe!"

"Oh, phooey, Radcliffe." Angela couldn't be less impressed. "You say it like she received a diploma. Harvard calls Radcliffe its 'annex.' They throw them a *certificate*! A bone to placate them for not giving them a proper degree. So what? She went to a library. Read some books. Maybe someone spoke to her about the books she read."

"Ange, you're describing what an education is."

"No. An education is wisdom acquired through experience. And you have neither. For all I know neither does the lumber princess."

"Then why would he want to marry her? I know he felt something for me. I know this."

Angela sighed. "Gina, he is a Harvard graduate, and you hate school and are counting the days until you can quit. He is a wealthy Bostonian, descendant of warriors and Founding Fathers, and you're an immigrant wearing hand-me-downs. You wear the clothes his cook throws away! Just think about that for a second. Also he is nearly a geriatric and you're at the beginning of your life. Also, his fiancée is a debutante who has gone to fifty balls and who has traveled to Paris. You probably can't even find Paris on a map, darling."

"I thought you just said education is not important?"

"It's not education. It's *everything*. It's the station in life. He is Grand Central Terminal in New York. And you're Jericho, Utah."

"Utah? Do they even have train stations in Jericho?"

Angela gazed at her with affection. "My point entirely." She lay down on the bed next to her cousin and put her arm around her. "Read some books by all means. Save for a new feather hat. But, angel, if he doesn't love you because you haven't read *The Manifesto of the Communist Party*, he isn't going to love you even if you do."

"You're wrong."

"Will he fall off his horse for you like wild-eyed Tommy?"

"He'd never fall off a horse, he is too good a horseman."

"So not even you could throw him off his horse, Gia?"

"You're impossible. Have you heard a word of what Mother Grace teaches Verity and me?"

"Fortunately for me, no."

"She constantly quotes us Marcus Aurelius."

"What a helpful and historically-minded Reverend Mother she is."

"She is a humble servant of God. She tells us, *hasten thee to the goal. Lay idle hopes aside. And come to your own help, if you care at all for yourself, while still ye may.*"

"You see," said Angela, "what I take away from that is that the humble servant of God who knows about these things ordered you to lay your idle hopes aside."

"And, what I take away," said Gina resolutely, wiping her face and getting up from the bed, "is *come to your own help, while still ye may.*"

Part Three

Earth's Holocaust

Oh, she has decked his ruin with her love,
Led him in golden bands to gaudy slaughter,
And made perdition pleasing: She has left him
The blank of what he was:

John Dryden

Chapter Thirteen
MINSTREL SONGS

"THE question before us, then, is not *are* there class antagonisms. Because we know that's as old as the sea. Of *course* there are class antagonisms. The question before us is, how are they different from the Roman antagonisms, or from the Greek? How are they the same? And where will they lead us? What can we do to resolve these differences of class, this fundamental unfairness in the distribution of wealth in this country and all industrialized nations?"

Someone shouted from the back of the room interrupting his flow. "Do away with industry?"

"Okay, Mr. Smith, and thank you. Please raise your hand next time, but I appreciate your contribution. Certainly we can try to do away with industry. Do we want to go back to agrarian times? Reaping the land by the ox and plow?"

"That's not very fair to the ox," Edgar from the front piped in.

The students laughed.

"And there is a lot of antagonism in *this* class," said Murdock. "What do we do about *that*? Maybe we should start with that, then follow by dismantling industry."

Harry, Edgar and Mr. Smith leveled disapproving looks at Murdock. He was always saying provocative things to distract the class and unsettle the professor. Harry sighed. Was it time to go?

"For Thursday, please write me two thousand words comparing the serf to the modern urban man working in factories: five similarities, five differences. Write that down. I don't want you to come back with just a paragraph on one disparity."

He watched them wearily as they shuffled out, and got his lesson plan together for Economic Theory after lunch. When was spring recess? Must be right around the corner. No one wanted to be inside now and even he was looking forward to the end of term and summer. They were sailing to Europe for two months in August and September. So much to do before then. His doctoral thesis was due in three weeks. He wasn't going to enjoy the unseasonably warm weather; he was going to be in Gore from dawn till closing.

Down the hall he spotted the chair of the History and Political Science Department, Thomas Carver. Who could miss him—the man looked seven feet tall. He had been raised on a farm in Iowa, which is why he taught the Economics of Agriculture so passionately, and he rowed crew in Cornell, which made him broad-shouldered and imposing. "I can pitch hay with the best of them," Carver was fond of saying. Harry thought it was his way of intimidating assistant instructors like him.

"Professor Carver!" Harry hurried to catch up. Was it his imagination or did Carver hasten his step when he heard Harry calling? He had been trying to get an appointment with him for weeks. He wanted to teach another course in the fall—maybe Outlines of Economic History of Western Europe in the Nineteenth Century. Three courses would make a full load, and would take his status from an adjunct to an associate. He might actually make a salary then, rather than just a stipend. What they paid him now wasn't enough to pay for dinner at the Colonial Club with his friend Vanderveer.

"What is it, Harry? I have a meeting I can't be late for."

"Professor Carver, I left you a letter a week or so ago"— Harry was nearly panting, that's how quickly he gathered speed to catch up with the man—"with yet another request to add a third class to my curriculum. Have you had a chance to think about it?"

"I barely had a chance to read your note, Harry," Carver said.

"But you did read it, sir?"

"Yes, but . . . I'm late for my Methods of Social Reform. Would you like to sit in on it with me? Why don't you come? I'm discussing Communism today."

"Thank you, sir, but it's my lunch hour . . ."

"Of course. But you know, I offered you the opportunity to guest teach it with me in February and March."

"You did, sir. But I was—still am—finishing my doctorate."

"Your colleague Mr. Broun, also working on his Ph.D. by the way, took two full months to explain socialism, communism and the single tax to my students. I take one month of April to refute." Carver smiled lightly. "What's happened to Mr. Broun, do you know? I haven't seen him since April began."

"Yes, well," Harry nodded his head from side to side, "I think it's not because he doesn't wish to be refuted, sir. I'm certain he does. It's just that the, er, baseball season has started . . ."

Carver laughed. "Say no more. Let's hope I see him again before October."

"About my letter, though . . ."

"We'll sit down next month, all right, you and I, and . . . talk to my secretary. Set up a time. Right now I'm late." He sped up.

"But do you think it might be possible?"

"We'll talk next month!" Carver rushed off. Was it Harry's imagination, or was the professor avoiding answering? Had he promised the class to someone else? It was probably that Edward Gay—he was always making up to the chair with his novel ideas. He had started at the bottom two years ago, suddenly recruited a wife, produced two children, and not five minutes later became associate professor. He was probably looking at a full professorship next year.

It was so irritating. Nothing was the same in the department since Cummins left in 1902 to become a Unitarian minister. Despite Carver's assertion that he wanted to make the economics department the strongest in the nation, it had been all downhill from there. Carver was always trying to persuade the "unenlightened" as he called them. Harry suspected that Carver must have counted Harry among them.

He liked teaching, mostly. He liked being able to read the books he wanted to read and then distil the meaning of the important parts for eager Harvard undergraduates. It appealed to him purely on that level. On another level, it pleased him to know that no one in his family had ever been a professor, at Harvard no less.

But he hadn't expected the students' apathy, coupled

with their staggering arrogance. Their lack of understanding was firmly partnered with an indifference to it. He hadn't anticipated haggling with them over grades, or prepared himself for marking, term in and term out, the most inane, thoughtless, last-minute nonsense. He was teaching basic economics, the building blocks of business administration, of management skills, of politics, of law, of engineering—by God, of nearly everything! And yet many of his students understood nothing of profit, of statistics, of demand, of operating costs, of trying to organize business and economics into a coherent whole. At first he thought it was his fault. He was not good enough as a teacher, and so his students were falling behind. He stayed late at his windowless office, trying to come up with bright examples, trying to make them understand materialism, dialectical and otherwise. They would have none of it. The more he tried to explain, the more they made themselves immune to understanding. So he started performing economic experiments in class. He built a model factory in his classroom, separated his students into owners, managers and workers. He showed them how a factory controlled by the very few and labored in by the many eventually grew into disparate worlds, separated by lack of a common language. All seemed to be to no avail.

In the late afternoon, Economic Theory went no better than Outlines that morning. The freshmen were done sitting in a classroom. Spring was here, the buds were about to burst, the air was aromatic and, unusually for Boston, it had been quite warm. It would change, it always did, but while it lasted, no one wanted to be stuffed inside talking about markets and manufacturing and millionaires.

It was five o'clock when Harry left University Hall, and still light. Everyone was out and about. A glance at Appleton, a brief vivid memory of Ben sitting on the chapel steps—proximate yet far—waylaid Harry for a moment. He stopped and looked around Harvard Yard, at the crisscrossing paths, at the elms, at the patches of serene sunlight. He needed to go to Gore Hall to work, but it was so mild and pleasant, and from Harvard Square he could hear the wafting of guitar strings, accompanied by a raucous young vocal that already sounded drunk, though it was barely opening time on a Monday. Tentatively he took a step toward Mass Avenue, wondering if he should call on Vanderveer for a game of billiards at the recently built Harvard Union. But, though he wanted to talk to someone about Carver and his mysterious vacillating, he didn't want to be cooped up inside, even with good company. He decided instead to walk to the river. He had a little bit of time, he wasn't due in Brookline for dinner with Alice and her mother until eight, and a stroll down the Charles was exactly the kind of impulsive thing he said he always wanted to do but never did.

He crossed the Yard intending to exit through Johnston gate. Easier said than done. It was congested at this time of evening, emptying out onto Peabody Street, and he was delayed by a gaggle of young women, who were loud and slow-moving. As was the habit of young water birds when they banded together, when they came to an exit or entrance, instead of hurrying through it, mindful of whoever was behind them, they stopped and with increasing excitement began honking about some female fool thing or other. On this fine evening, Harry felt peevish. They were keeping him from his impulsive plan. He wanted to keep strolling, but instead was forced to stop, and worse, forced to listen. He thought that as usual they would be talking about their hair, or perhaps about ice-cream cones at last year's hugely successful World's Fair, or perhaps about the Summer

Olympics also just passed. But no, they were talking about Eugene Debs, of all things!

"He said he was for socialism because he was for humanity. Isn't that powerful?"

"Yes, yes, brilliant!"

Debs, president of the newly formed U.S. Socialist Party had recently spoken at Mass Hall. Harry was surprised that a week later, the delinquent girls were still discussing him. Had they been logjammed at Johnston gate all that time? He could not discount the possibility.

"Yes, but did you hear what *just* happened?" said a tall girl. "The Supreme Court barred the state of New York from setting the maximum number of hours one can work in a bakery!"

"And this is good?" a shorter girl asked.

"Oh, yes!" the tall one replied. "It's a leap for liberty. We work as much as we want—or as little."

Harry fought the overwhelming urge to exhale derision from his throat. *Another* anarchist, this one in his way.

"At the same time," the brunette continued, "that's not all we're trying to achieve, of course. We want to be paid more, too, for the hours we do work, be they many *or* few."

The girls clucked that yes, getting paid more was better. Because they wanted to have fun, not just work, they wanted to go dancing, get their hair done. One of them imitated a dance step right in front of him. Harry wilted. It had almost been a real discussion for a second.

"Excuse me, please," he said to them loudly, trying to push his way to the gate without accidentally touching any of them. Not one of them moved or even acknowledged that they heard him. "Pardon *me*," he said, nearly falling against the tall brunette who, while continuing to speak, gracefully moved out of his way. He glanced at her, irascibly at first—then with astonishment.

"Gina?"

She spun around to face him. "Harry—is that you? Well, hello."

"*Gina?*" said the shorter one. "You have the wrong person. That's not Gina."

"I *am*, Sophie," said the brunette. "Gina is my given name." She smiled politely at Harry. "How have you been?"

Dumbfounded, he took off his hat and held it in his unsteady hand. Now the girls and Harry were *all* blocking the way out, a yardful of disgruntled students behind them. Finally they made their way out of the wrought-iron gates and stopped against the fence on Peabody.

"I've been well," Harry said. "And you? It's been a long time." Her friends encircled them, appraising him.

"Has it?"

"Yes, five years, I think."

"Five?" she said. "It can't be."

He hoped she didn't notice his flushed skin, didn't hear his inexplicable stammer. He couldn't get his words out. Was this really Gina? He bit his lip from following up his thoughts with some inanity. "How are you?" was all he said.

She was restrained and formal, and this made it easier for him to get his composure back.

"I'm doing well, thank you."

"What are you doing on campus? And what do you mean, your name isn't Gina?"

"Gina was too ethnic," she said. "Too Italian. The American equivalent is Jane. I liked that. So when I applied to college I gave my name as Jane Attaviano." She spoke almost without a trace of accent now, just a subtle misplacement of the accent and a light appealing rolling of her vowels that made a simple "*applied to college*" sound like flowing sultry candy from her mouth.

Harry smiled. "Can't get too far from the Italian with that last name."

"I don't want to get too far from *that*," she said. "I carry my father's name proudly."

He stammered again. "You applied to Harvard?"

"Well, no." Faintly she smiled. "Harvard doesn't educate women."

"Yet!" piped in Sophie.

Now it was Harry who felt like a fool. He wished Sophie weren't standing so close, pulling all the other girls to listen in. He just wanted . . . he didn't know what he wanted. "Are you going to school?"

"Yes, I'm at Simmons College on the Fenway. Do you know it?"

"Vaguely." By which he meant not at all.

"They opened their doors to women in 1899. So I applied after I graduated."

"Good for you. Long way to commute, though."

"I don't commute, I live in the residence hall. Sophie! Wait for me—I'll be just a minute."

"How is your mother? Your brother?"

"Everyone is doing fine. You?"

Returning, Sophie tugged at her arm. "Janie, come on, we gotta go. We still have to eat before the meeting."

"Meeting?"

"Yes," Gina said. "On Mondays, the Daughters of the Revolution meet."

"To discuss . . .?"

"Tonight Mother Jones is speaking about the dangers of letting children work at the textile mills and the mutilations they suffer on the machines."

"Mother Jones?" muttered Harry. "I didn't know she was still alive."

"Tireless at seventy-five," said Gina. "Um, would you like to join us or do you have to run?"

The river forgotten, his dinner plans all dispersed in the heady breeze, Harry mumbled non-intelligibly and found himself walking down the street alongside her. Well, alongside *her* and Sophie and four other friends, who he wished would all (temporarily) vanish.

"You've gotten taller," he said, glancing at her feet to see if perhaps it was extra high heels that made her stand half a head above her compatriots. She was nearly his height. He glimpsed stylish black pumps but couldn't see the heels. He became distracted by her slim gray dress, fitted through the bodice, slightly flared in the skirt. His gaze traveled upward. Her hair was up in a loose bun, brown and wavy. Her makeup was light, but her features looked dramatic— her long eyelashes extra dark, her eyes a deep cocoa, her eyebrows theatrically arched, her teeth sparkling, and her mouth—in the curve of her lips there was no hiding the intoxicating Sicilian immigrant behind a sober Beacon Hill name like Jane. Harry found himself becoming light-headed. Long and limber, she bounced as she walked. Five years ago Harry must have overlooked the harbingers of her present height. He had been careful to overlook so much. Perhaps the length of limb had always been there. Her face and neck were smooth and tanned, her southern skin naturally darker than her pallid northern friends.

As they walked, he shuffled, trying to count his steps. Math flew out of his head. How old was she now? Twenty? Surreptitiously he glanced again at the rolling curve of her slim hips cinched under the long narrow waist. Could it be that she still didn't wear a corset? Impossible in today's day and age. All the women wore the S-shaped corsets, so popular in the Edwardian fashion. Even Esther had got into the swing of it, uncomfortably. Harry teased his sister mercilessly about never being able to sit down. But Gina remained straight and slender, except for the natural arcs and swells of her body. Disoriented, Harry looked away before he tripped and fell.

He knew the restaurants had been doing well; Billingsworth kept his banker's eye on them. A while back Harry asked Billingsworth if Gina still worked at Antonio's by the station, but Billingsworth said he hadn't seen her in years. If you want I can ask Salvo, he said, but Harry adamantly said no.

Yet here it was, trouble next to him, sashaying to Harvard Square in her smart parlor heels, trouble glittering from the rings on her fingers and the buckles in her hair. Trouble smelled good too, or maybe that was one of her friends. It was hard to tell, they all walked so close together, in a lupine pack. Harry nearly prayed it wasn't one of her friends who smelled like the beach and books and brine. He inhaled when they stopped for the light, and was simultaneously relieved and agitated to realize, no, it was her.

"I don't know if I can get used to calling you Jane," Harry said. "You might have to start calling me Harold."

She agreed gamely. "If you call me Jane, I will call you Harold."

He didn't really want her to call him Harold. Posh and proper people called him Harold, like his work colleagues. His friends and family always called him Harry. And he didn't want to start calling her Jane. She was Gina to him, though Jane somehow suited her new, taller, confident self more. Then again, she had always moved with pride and poise, even when she had just stepped off the boat.

"Harry."

"I'm sorry, what?" He had stopped listening, absorbed in his thoughts.

"How is married life? Do you have any children yet?"

"Oh, you're married?" said Sophie on Gina's right.

"Not married yet," he replied and volunteered no further.

"Five years and *still* not married?" Gina chuckled lightly.

"You sound like my father." But he said it amiably, as if being like his father was the best possible thing she could be.

"How is Ben?"

"Good." Harry rolled his eyes. "When I say good, he isn't dead yet, so that's good."

"Why would he be?"

"He's down in Panama fighting off malaria, standing all day long in five feet of foul water."

Gina clapped her hands. "That doesn't sound like much fun, but I'm so proud of him. I always think of him when I read about the plans for the canal in the paper. Sounds like they're almost ready. Did he just leave?"

"He's been down there nearly five years now."

"Five years! So he left back when—"

"Yes—just a few months after you—" He didn't finish and she didn't finish. It was best forgotten and left unmentioned. A raw sorrow still laid out on Charter Street. "We're all proud of him. He's been toiling there, building up the infrastructure in impassable mud during the monsoon season—a thankless task. He didn't think it would ever happen, the whole project has been in such a state of disarray. But Roosevelt may finally be serious about excavation. Ben is assistant engineer, second in charge only to the chief engineer, but I think he's getting a new boss—John Stevens, who was put in charge of construction by the president himself. Stevens is not even in Panama yet."

"Amazing," said Gina. "Please give Ben my regards when you write to him. And what about you? What are you . . ." but her attention drifted from Harry. Some young men were loudly calling for her from across the square near College House residence hall. Despite the saxophones and the French horns, Harry heard them vying for her attention. He had no doubt it was for *her* attention. Her girlfriends were mere collateral. The men were harmonizing in a sing-song from across the street, making complete fools of themselves. "Hey, you Gibson girl . . . look at me . . . hey hey, Gibson girl, turn your eyes to me . . ."

He thought with contempt, no serious young woman is going to fall for such tomfoolery. But she was laughing—she obviously found them amusing!

"Well, look," he said, deflated, "I've got to run."

"You're sure you don't want to come with us?"

He glanced at the wild pack across the street, cater-wauling, gesticulating to her. He looked down the street to the river, to his other obligations, none of which he could see clear to. He narrowed his eyes. "Where are you headed?"

"Quick dinner, then the amphitheater at Sever Hall. Joe Ettor is speaking after Mother Jones."

"Ah." Harry nodded approvingly. "An Industrial Workers of the World crowd."

"Yes. We're preparing for the convention in Chicago at the end of June."

"He's a good speaker, I hear."

"He's all right," said Gina. "But he's no Emma."

"Emma? You mean Goldman?"

"As if there is another. Will you come?"

He glanced peripherally at her friends, then more intently at her in the Harvard Square dusky sun. What he wanted most of all at that moment was to catch up with her for five minutes, without the boys, without the girls. "What about afterward?" he asked. He would go to the library, pretend to work, and wait.

"I've got plans after," she said. "Sorry. Maybe another time?"

"Yes, maybe." He stepped away more definitely. "It was nice to see you again. Please give my regards to your brother." He put his hat back on his head and resisted the urge to bow deeply. He bowed to her slightly.

"And my regards to your sister. Has she married?"

"Yes, yes. Married a doctor last year."

"Oh nice, a doctor. Goodbye, Harry!" She was dragged away by her friends.

I'm studying to be a doctor too, Harry wanted to yell after her, vying for her attention. Maybe not a medical doctor, but an intellectual doctor, of thoughts and letters. Would you like to know what my doctoral thesis is on, which I'm desperately endeavoring to deliver on the first of May? Would you like me to sing it for you? "The limits of ratio*nality* . . . in Bakunin's 'God and the *State*' . . . as compared with Marx's . . . *con*sciousness-altering, *e*conomic de*t*erminism as a material foun*d*ation . . . for *all* in*d*ustrialized civiLIzaaaaation!" Does this impress you? Harry watched them as the boys caught up with the girls across the square, three varsity men standing encircled by five women, their athletic non-dialectical bodies turned toward the Italian Gibson girl who stood nearly eye to eye with them. Isn't she a looker, Harry thought, turning away, walking briskly back toward Cambridge Common where Clarence was waiting with the car. No going to the river now. He needed to rush home and change or he was going to be late for dinner.

The next day he told Clarence he would drive himself to Cambridge, where he stayed all day at Gore, eking out a few minutes on his thesis, staying until five, though his classes ended on Tuesdays before lunch, and then went out into the square to look for her. He checked the bulletin notices of events at Harvard for a list of upcoming speakers. He meandered for two more fruitless hours, and finally drove home.

On Wednesday after lunch he got into the car and headed across the Charles to Simmons College on the far end of the Back Bay Fens. The Huntington Avenue Baseball Grounds were very close to here. Perhaps she was interested in baseball? The 1905 season had just started. Two years ago a former Harvard pitching coach named Cy Young won nearly half of all the games the Boston Americans played and last year pitched the first-ever perfect game. Maybe Young's prowess on the mound would impress an Italian girl. Harry had some time to think these thoughts as he walked in circles inside the small common grounds that connected the Simmons main college building and the Beatley Library. How was he going to find her? And if he did find her, how was he going to explain what he was doing in the middle of an all-women's college? Was he going to have to fake an interest in the vacuous Sophie?

Reluctantly he left. Not only did he *not* have a plan, but this was completely out of his area of expertise.

But the next day, a Thursday, he was back at Simmons. He was hesitant to walk inside the main building, because it was full of women. He decided to walk the short blocks to Brookline Avenue where the dining hall and the residence halls were located. But that part of campus was even more full of women. At least at the college the professors were male.

He inspected the girls at the dining hall serving food, and deduced none of them were her. Returning to the campus, he walked inside the main building. He explored the art gallery, the closed Office of Admissions, the conference rooms, the cafeteria. There was a community common room; she wasn't in it. There was a tea room; not there either. He ventured into the wing with the music rooms. Maybe she had started playing a musical instrument. Nothing would surprise him anymore.

When he didn't find her playing the piano, he went to the college bookstore. He saw her immediately, behind the counter, busy with a sale. Puffed up by his amazing detective work, Harry hid triumphantly in the aisles, eyeing some books, and when his hands were suitably full of diverse and acceptable works, he stepped toward the counter, as casual as could be.

"Harry." She smiled. "Hello again. What are you doing here?"

He laid his books on the counter. "I was buying tickets for the Boston Americans at the nearby Huntington Grounds and remembered I needed a few books for my dissertation. What are *you* doing here?"

"I work here." She glanced down at his choices. "What, the Crimson doesn't sell Hobbes and Burke?"

"I'm not at the Crimson now. You don't work with your brother anymore?"

"No." She began to ring up his purchases. "I help out on the weekends sometimes."

"You don't return to Lawrence often?"

Guiltily she shrugged. "Not too often, as Mimoo never fails to remind me."

"You work every day?" He was peppering her with questions. Their transaction was almost over; he had a lot to ask.

She told him she worked Tuesdays and Thursdays. He didn't take his eyes off her. She looked a little more down-to-earth this evening; rather, a little more brought down to earth by her subdued work clothes—a maroon shirt and a dark green skirt. Colors of Simmons? Still she'd have to wear a hood in order to hide her hair, her mouth . . . "So how was Joe Ettor?"

"Oh, we didn't stay for *him*," she said. "They wanted to go out walking instead." She rolled her eyes, as if she just couldn't believe it. "The boys were all done with speeches after Mother Jones. She put them off politics for good."

"Did she?" They went out walking! "I'm surprised she didn't put them off women."

Gina laughed. "Yes, she kept hammering at the men about how they needed to work more and be paid more while *we* stayed home and took care of their babies."

"The progressive varsity boys didn't like that?"

Gina took his money, making sure he put it down on the counter first so she wouldn't touch his hand. He noted that, the auspicious properness of it. It seemed so deliberate.

"They're just in it for the good time at the moment," she said, giving him back change.

"And who can blame them?" He took his books and changed the subject. "Huntington Grounds are quite special."

"Oh, I know," she said laconically.

"So you've been? You like baseball?"

She shrugged. "We can't really afford it. Sophie and I saw the opening game a few weeks ago. We stood on the street and looked over the fence. And what do you know, the police came to shoo us away. As if we're not allowed to stand on a public avenue. It's preposterous."

"I guess they didn't want you watching the game for free," said Harry.

"That's what they said. But we're on the street! Last I checked we are allowed to walk down city blocks without being harassed by the police. They told us we were loitering because we were standing in one place. Said they would arrest us if we didn't start moving. I said to them, if they didn't want us to see the game, why didn't they build the wall higher?" She laughed.

"Let's hope Charles Taylor, the owner of the Boston Americans, doesn't take your advice." He stepped closer to the counter. "Perhaps you and Sophie or any of your other friends would like to catch a game sometime?"

"Perhaps." She sounded non-committal. "You'll have to explain the rules to me first."

"All right. Now?"

She smiled as if thinking of something else.

"When are you getting off?"

"At six."

He glanced at his watch. It was five-thirty. "I'll wait," he said, moving to the edge of the counter.

She helped a few more customers, adjusting the buttons on her elaborate sleeves.

"They must pay you well at the bookstore," he said.

"Not really. I make spending money for the week; why do you say that?"

He pointed to her clothes. "Some fine thread' you're wearing today. The other day too," he said carefully. It was out of line to mention a woman's attire. She was making him forget his manners! She was making him forget a lot of things. Perhaps he could be saved by her ignorance of the inappropriateness of his observations.

"Well, thank you. But no, I get these from sewing. I make dresses for the girls in my residence and their mothers and aunts and cousins, and in return they pay me with silk and linen and combed cotton." She smiled. "Good bargain, right?"

He appraised her even more fully, if that were possible.

Velvet too, he wanted to add, noticing the soft ivory fringe on her sleeves, her neckline, her waist, the ribbons in her hair. "No one can do that at an urban college," he said. "You have to know how to sew."

"Fortunately I do. Pippa taught me well." Her smile faded. "She went back to Sicily, you know. Her father died—she wasn't in great health and wanted to stop working. She left three years ago."

"I'm sorry to hear that. Your mother liked the company."

"Yes. Makes it harder on me when I don't want to go home."

Harry was grateful a customer came up to pay and the conversation shifted. "You must be an excellent dressmaker. And there I thought all you knew was how to spin wool." It caught in his throat to mention it so casually.

"I know a little bit more than that." She smiled. "I don't spin wool anymore. Those days are behind me."

Why did that make him sentimental and foolish? "You don't dye yarn either?" He glanced at her hands, white, soft, unblemished.

"No. No touching wool anymore. I sew now."

He stood silently, trying to calm his whirr of regret and nostalgia. She was grown up. She didn't spin scarves from blueberries anymore for the grave man with the clipboard. It was the romance of it he had found so heart-stopping, the mystery of the thing he didn't understand at all. There was no way to tell her this.

"Thing is," she told him, "I have a paper due tomorrow on Edgar Allan Poe."

"I know a lot about Poe," said Harry. "He was melancholy. I'll help you write it. I'll walk you to your residence hall, if you like. Where do you live?"

"Evans. But, um, I'm not going there." She glanced at

her pocket watch. "Emma Goldman is speaking at seven o'clock."

"Where?"

"Where?" The white teeth were on full display. "Old South, of course!"

"Of course. But what about the paper on 'Annabel Lee' you simply have to deliver by tomorrow?"

"It's on 'The Tell-Tale Heart' actually." She shrugged. "Goldman can't wait. But Poe is dead. He can."

"Ah."

"Did you maybe want to . . . come?"

"To hear Emma Goldman?"

"She's riveting. Have you ever heard her speak?"

"Can't say that I have," he admitted. "But that may be deliberate. I don't think much of her politics." He didn't want to tell Gina the extent of the stinging contempt he held for the anarchists. She seemed so blithely enamored with them. For some reason, women found all that talk of liberty appealing.

"Oh no, she's splendid." Gina got her long green coat from the closet, her matching bag and said goodbye to her manager.

"Isn't Emma Goldman the one who wouldn't condemn Czolgosz for assassinating President McKinley?" Harry held her coat open for her, almost touching her as she slipped her arms inside the sleeves.

"She's the one, but she got a bad knock for that. She condemned, just—not promptly." Gina buttoned her coat and adjusted her hat. "I do have to run though."

"Did you make the coat too?"

"Of course."

Harry clicked his tongue in admiration. "Are you meeting your friends?"

"Often they come, but not always."

Now it was his turn to shrug. "Fine, let's go hear this Emma Goldman." If there was even a small possibility of her friends not coming, he would drag himself to Iceland to hear the lover of imprisoned Alexander Berkman.

They walked out to the Fenway. "We'll have to catch a trolley car," she said squinting down the avenue for one.

"How about if we get into my car instead and I'll drive us?"

"Oh!" That delighted her briefly as if she was relieved. "So you finally did get a car. Well, congratulations. Is it a Benz like you wanted?"

"Well remembered. Unfortunately no, it's an Olds Curved Dash Runabout."

"Well, still, must be convenient."

"It is. It's even better when Clarence drives me, then I don't have to worry about leaving the vehicle. But he's been busy with my father lately."

The car was a souped-up horse carriage with the fixed engine crank in the middle between the one long seat. But it had an overhead canopy and side curtains, and a mother-in-law seat in the back. "I don't have a mother-in-law," Harry clarified. "It's just what they call it."

"Oh, I know," Gina said. "So how fast can this baby smoke along?"

He laughed. "It can get up to twenty-five miles an hour. It's got exactly one cylinder and five horsepower."

"Let's see what it can do."

But once inside the car, she sat primly, her hands on her books on her lap. He tried to impress her by driving nearly 20 mph. She remained neutral.

"Your mother lets you live by yourself in a dormitory?" Harry asked.

They turned onto Commonwealth. He slowed down. He didn't want to get downtown too quickly.

"Not by myself. With three other girls. You've met them. Sophie, Julia and Miranda."

"Still."

"She wasn't happy about it, if that's what you're asking."

"I should think not. Nor your brother."

"Luckily for me, Salvo has become embroiled with so many girls at once that in between that and the restaurants, he simply doesn't have time to chaperone his twenty-year-old sister."

Things had changed in big ways and small from five years ago. She was so self-possessed, so unflappable.

"Harry?"

"Excuse me, please. What did you ask?"

"So what are you doing with yourself these days?"

"Teaching economics at Harvard and . . ." He was going to tell her about becoming a doctor. She had been so taken with Esther's choice of spouse.

"Economics, really?" she repeated. "So Emma should be fascinating for you."

"I said economics, not politics. And you're on first name basis with her?"

She chuckled. Harry was flummoxed. Now he didn't know *how* to bring up his idiotic doctorate.

She picked up one of his books off the seat. "So what's a devout Marxist like you doing reading *Reflections on the Revolution?*"

Was she teasing him? He almost drove off the road. "Hardly devout," he said slowly, trying to focus on the dark space in front of him whooshing by. "And I read Burke only so I can refute him."

"Ah. Of course."

"What about you?" He reached over to glance at her books when they stopped at a light. "Mikhail Bakunin? Really?" Harry leafed through the rest. "Chernyshevsky? Mary Wollstonecraft—of her I approve."

"Have you read her *Vindication of the Rights of Woman?*"

Honestly, Harry was going to crash into one of the brownstones on Commonwealth if she didn't stop. "I may have perused it. But why the Russian anarchists?"

"They have so much to say. Also Emma recommended them."

"I see."

"Chernyshevsky is almost deliberately abstract, but Bakunin is quite provocative, though I don't agree with many of the things he wrote and believed."

"I should hope not."

She shook her head. "He advocated collective anarchy, but I think it was just his way of using the collective as the authoritarian power he decried in world governments."

Harry muttered something unintelligible.

"He opposed Karl Marx," Gina went on. "Yet created another system of oppression. If I were braver, I'd ask Emma this question. She takes questions at the end but I never manage to speak up."

"Well, crowded meeting halls can be intimidating."

"Wait till you see how many people will be there!" She clutched her books excitedly.

"Bakunin was a peasant," said Harry. "All well and good in the Russia of the last century. But the rest of the world is industrialized. The serfs have been long freed."

"So you know a little bit about Bakunin?"

An ideal segue. But he couldn't insert his neatly fitting doctoral dissertation topic into their discussion now. Because now it seemed mean to wave the banner of his postgraduate education and his years' long expertise on Bakunin and Marx in front of her flushed and eager face. Mean and unchivalrous.

"Chernyshevsky is better, don't you think?" She went on without waiting for his answer. "Deeper philosophy."

"Son of a priest who became a radical atheist? I suppose."

"You really know your anarchists, Harry."

"What's more remarkable, Gina, is how well you know yours."

The car ride was over much too soon.

Inside the meeting hall it was noisy and crowded. "Even better attended than Ben's mother's meetings," Gina cheerfully pointed out. He felt lucky to find two seats together.

"I haven't been inside in many years," Harry said.

"Funny, because I come every week. They're always having lectures here of one kind or another."

The talk was titled "Anarchism as it Really is." He flapped the brochure shut just in case a derisive sound tripped from his tongue.

Goldman had several speakers before her, but when she finally came onstage, close to eight o'clock, she received a ten-minute standing ovation, none louder than from the young woman next to him. The adoring smile on Gina's face alternately amused and enthralled Harry. Personally he found Emma Goldman homely.

"She's not going to win any beauty pageants, is she?" he said to Gina while they were still standing and clapping.

"Really?" she said. "Then why does she have a constant parade of lovers around her?"

"I cannot account for other men's taste," said Harry. Goldman's hair was messy, her glasses obscuring, her clothes dowdy. She was short and bulky. She didn't even venture the ten steps up into the wineglass lectern, but stood instead eight inches above ground on a makeshift podium. "And she already has a lover," Harry reminded Gina. "He's in prison for murder."

"Well, she can hardly be expected to wait for him, can she? She is a sensualist."

"Emma Goldman is a *sensualist*?" Harry didn't know what he was more astonished by: that Goldman would be so defined or that the Sicilian Aphrodite next to him would so define her.

Someone yelled from far behind them. "Janie! Janie!" This was accompanied by a high-pitched whistle. They both turned around. A strapping man was waving and unsuccessfully pushing his way to their seats. Gina waved back. Harry hated him instantly. You whistled for dogs, not women. Maybe you whistled for Emma Goldman. "Tell him to stay where he is," Harry said. "There's no room for him here."

"Wait till you hear her speak," she said leaning to him. He had one breath to inhale the scent of her auburn hair, and then Emma Goldman opened her mouth.

"*This is what I believe,*" she yelled, to sudden hysterical applause. "*The anarchists are right in assuming that the absence of government will ensure the widest and greatest scope for unhampered human development, the cornerstone of true social progress and harmony!*"

Her audience clapped after every sentence. Her speech should've taken fifteen minutes; instead she was onstage for over an hour.

"*Anarchism, to the great teachers and leaders in the spiritual aspect of life, is not a dogma, not a thing that drains the blood from the heart and makes people zealots, dictators or impossible bores.*"

When they finally filtered out of the hall onto Milk Street, it was well after nine. Harry was reeling.

"So what did you think?" Gina asked.

"She is persuasive," he admitted. "She's a good public speaker."

"You mean the best public speaker in American life today?"

"I guess that's what I meant," he said, wanting to smile.

"I want to be just like her," Gina said.

Harry held his tongue. He wanted to say, please no.

"Anarchism is a releasing and liberating force because it teaches people to rely on their own possibilities, teaches them faith in liberty, and inspires men and women to strive for a state of social life where everyone shall be free and secure."

"I love what she says about women," Gina said as they walked from Milk Street to Washington. Harry couldn't remember where he had parked his car. He hadn't driven to this part of town before and he felt disoriented, remembering too late that he had plans with Alice. He glanced at his watch reluctantly. It was almost nine-thirty! He *really* needed to run. Yet he couldn't leave her in the middle of the crowded darkened street. Faneuil Hall was around the corner and drunken navy men abounded near Quincy market, the docks.

"Wait here," he said. "I'll go find the car and drive you back."

"I'll walk with you," she said. "You're going the wrong way. You left it on Tremont Street."

"There is neither freedom nor security in the world today: whether one be rich or poor, whether his station high or low, no one is secure as long as there is a single slave in the world."

"Janie! Jane!" Two young bucks, entirely different from the ones in Harvard Square, ran up to them with Sophie and Miranda in tow. "We tried to get to you," the taller of the men whined. "You didn't save us a seat like you *promised.*"

"We couldn't get four more seats," she said. "It was crowded today. Soph, Miranda, you've met Harry. Archer, Dyson, this is Harold Barrington."

"How do you do." Utterly without enthusiasm the three men shook hands. "What college do you gentlemen attend?" Harry inquired.

"The Evening Institute for Younger Men," eager, wiry Dyson said proudly. "We're in our last year."

"Congratulations," said Harry. "Isn't that being offered at the YMCA?"

"No," Archer drew out, giving him the cool once-over. "It's *affiliated* with the Y, but the Institute has its own campus, just two blocks from Simmons. And what about you?"

"Harvard, class of 1900," Harry said.

"Good on you," Archer said. "We rowed against you in crew last year. Beat the daylights out of ya." He laughed. "Didn't we, Dyse?"

Harry nodded. "It was an exhibition race for charity, as I recall? Not the Yale–Harvard Regatta."

His smile dimming considerably, Archer pointed the way down to the Commons. "Come on, Janie. I'll get us a carriage on Park Street. The round-table discussion starts soon. We host tonight. Let's hurry—I want us to have a little fun before your curfew. We have hot food. You must be starving." He waved his bear-like hand near her honey arm, and she stepped away from Harry, careless and free. "Harry, do you want to come? You'll even out our numbers."

"Oh no, no. Much as I enjoy symmetry. Maybe another time. I've got to run myself. Will you be all right getting back?"

"Worry not, my friend, we'll take care of her," said Archer.

"Goodbye!" she yelled to Harry with a jaunty wave,

already running with them to Park Street, to where he couldn't even imagine: to seedy common rooms where the round-table discussion with hot food took place until midnight . . . Is that what they called it nowadays?

"No one is safe or secure as long as he must submit to the orders, whim or will of another who has the power to punish him, to send him to prison or to take his life, to dictate the terms of his existence, from the cradle to the grave."

He found his car after wandering for half an hour, and kicked all five horsepower into high gear to Brookline; he arrived just as Alice and her mother were being served dessert.

"Darling, did you forget about us?" Alice said plaintively. "You *never* come this late."

Irma, with pursed lips, said nothing.

"I'm very sorry, darling," he said. "I was at Gore working and got so carried away that first I completely lost track of time and then I fell asleep. Right at my table over my books. Please forgive me."

"Oh, my poor darling!" she cried, jumping up to embrace him, to pat him tenderly. "You have been working yourself to a skeleton! Mother, did you hear?"

"I heard," said Irma.

"Are you hungry?"

"Famished."

"He didn't even have time to eat!" Alice rang for Sheffield.

"You must forgive *me*," Alice said with a sheepish giggle. "Because Mother and I were convinced you were playing billiards and drinking with your friend Mr. Veer."

"That would be highly unlikely," Harry said, waiting to be poured a glass of red wine, "since one, I don't know a Mr. Veer, though I am friendly with a Mr. Custis, and two,

President Eliot does not allow alcoholic beverages on his campus."

"Yes, but technically," said Irma, "aren't the billiard rooms right outside Harvard Yard?"

Harry blinked politely. "Still college property, Mrs. Porter."

"Harry, please," said Irma. "Call me Irma. There is no need for these forced formalities after all this time."

"Yes, Mrs. Porter."

"It is not only because of love of one's fellow-men—it is for their own sake that people must learn to understand the meaning and significance of Anarchism, and it will not be long before they will appreciate the great importance and beauty of its philosophy."

Friday came and went. Harry taught his two courses, graded some papers, consulted with six students, attended a faculty meeting, attempted to begin a semester plan for next year, chewed half a dozen pencils down to their stubs. At six in the evening, he got hold of himself and went to the Colonial Club. It was Friday night and he was meeting Vanderveer and C. J. Bullock there.

Usually Harry enjoyed spending a few hours in the company of his friends, even though Bullock, a decent enough chap, was another stair climber. Class of '04, he got hired by Carver last September to assist with the chair's classes and for the spring semester was already instructing two courses of his own. This, while Harry spent three years getting his masters and the last two preparing for his doctorate. It beggared belief.

Tonight he didn't care about any of it. Tonight it was *all* vanity.

Vanderveer didn't get under Harry's skin because he was associate professor in the English Department, and whether he became chair at twenty-seven, or taught four Chaucer courses and six Shakespearean seminars was all dandy with Harry.

"Harry?"

"Hmm?"

"Something must be terribly wrong," said C.J. "We've been here an hour and you haven't said one thing I wanted to punch you for."

"Give him time, C.J.," said Vanderveer. "The evening is still young."

Vanderveer was a very tall, very thin, Nordic warrior of a man, who had the deepest voice Harry had ever heard, and his bass so frightened his students that no one dared even shift in their seats in his lectures, though he regularly went seven or eight minutes over time, praising Chaucerian wit and Shakespearean sonnets.

Vanderveer was also nearly entirely apolitical, knew nothing about baseball, had an unseemly passion for tennis, entirely unmatched by his abilities, and made Harry feel completely right while everyone else was completely wrong. The Dutchman was just below Ben in Harry's hierarchy of regard for his friends.

"Mr. Veer, Mr. Bullock, gentlemen," Harry said, "I don't recall you saying anything witty or wry to warrant my rapier retorts. I'm waiting until you say something spectacularly stupid."

"Stop calling me Veer," Vanderveer said.

"Vander, don't get churlish on me. Ask the waiter for another drink. But not in Dutch, no one will understand you."

"I'm fourth-generation American, you insufferable snob," Vanderveer said, gesturing for the waiter.

"Ah, so an immigrant."

"And the name is Vanderveer."

"Don't get stroppy, Vander. Just because you can't win a single game of tennis. Try holding the racket with the flat part pointing toward the ball."

Vanderveer turned to Bullock. "C.J., I don't understand how you can have made up lesson plans for courses Harvard is not even offering."

"I'm going to speak to Professor Carver about adding them to the course selection next semester."

"Anarchism repudiates any attempt of a group of men or of any individual to arrange a life for others."

"Leave C.J. alone, Vander," said Harry. "Concentrate instead on your serve. Because you well know that concreteness of plans is a mark of every unsuccessful man."

C.J. flipped Harry the bird.

"By your own words shall thou hang thyself, Mr. Barrington," Vanderveer said with a smile, raising his glass to Harry.

"Anarchism rests on faith in humanity and its potentialities, while all other social philosophies have no faith in humanity whatsoever. The other philosophies insist that man cannot govern himself, that he must be ruled over."

The weekend was spent in a monotonous fog, in which Harry was forced, as if on a convict-gang, to grudgingly participate.

He kept repeating that he didn't fully recognize her, but that wasn't it. He didn't fully recognize himself. He didn't know who he was.

As for her, she definitely wasn't the girl who had walked away from him on Charter Street five years earlier. She had kept vestiges of herself from back then—the roll of her vowels, the swell of her lips. *Gina.* His mouth softened when he sounded out her name to himself. *Gia. G.* What's happening to me? he thought. This isn't me, not remotely like the man I am, he lamented silently, sitting outside on the lawn, waiting for the Porters to arrive on Sunday. Ellen had already joined them but fortunately Herman was showing her his cigar collection from Cuba while she was accusing him of colonialism. They were all having late brunch outside; it was such a glorious April afternoon. Harry had forgotten to ask her what she was studying. Was anarchy a major at Simmons College for women? And what good was it for women to pursue anarchism? How did this help them become wives and mothers? This was one of the reasons Harvard kept resisting conferring the Radcliffe girls with a formal degree. To what end argued President Eliot persuasively.

"Nowadays most people believe the stronger the government, the greater the success of society will be. It is the old belief in the rod. But we have emancipated ourselves from that stupidity. We have come to understand that education does not mean crippling and dwarfing the young growth. We have learned that freedom in the development of the child secures better results, both for the child and for society. Freedom for the development of the woman secures better results both for the woman and for society."

He had forgotten to ask her what she planned to do when she graduated. Was this her last year? She might have told him—but he didn't remember.

How was he going to get through today, through Monday? He was still sprawled in a daze on the lawn. He looked up and saw Herman standing in front of him.

"Son, what are you doing?"

"Reaping the fruits of idleness, Father," replied Harry, tilting his head back in the Adirondack chair.

"Get up, please, and greet our guests. Don't be impolite. The Porters have arrived. Orville is itching to talk to you."

"About what?"

"About the choice of countries for your summer trip."

"I'm going to suggest he travel to Europe with Mrs. Porter and go wherever he likes. I would never presume to tell a grown man what European country he should and should not visit."

"You will say no such thing." Herman prodded his reluctant son toward the house. "You know he just gets overly excited. He is always listing to one side or the other."

"Why can't he be even-keeled like us?" Herman and Harry began walking toward the French doors, waving to the Porters.

"Perhaps because you and I need a slight imbalance. Where's your sister—Orville, hello!"

A panting Orville shook Herman's hand. He was rounder, heavier and balder than he had been five years ago.

"*Anarchism is not a cut-and-dried theory. It is a vital spirit embracing all life. Therefore I do not address myself only to particular elements in society: I do not address myself only to the workers. I address myself to the upper classes as well, for they need enlightenment even more than the workers.*"

"Ellen, when is Ben coming back?" That was Esther. Harry blinked. Hours must have passed. Brunch had been served and cleared, the coffee was cold in Harry's cup, his lemon sherbet long melted. "Last time he wrote, he mentioned returning in May sometime. Isn't that right, Harry?"

Harry stared at his sister. Marriage didn't agree with her. She had become more gaunt, angular. The laughter lines had faded from her face. Her skirts had gotten plainer, her blouses less lacy. She wore barely any makeup.

"If you say so, Esther. Where is Elmore?"

"He is on call at the hospital today. One Sunday out of four. But do you think Ben will return early?"

"I don't know," Harry said. "Last time he wrote, he went on for nine pages about the detonations of the earth and how he had recently finally got permission from Roosevelt to build a lock-step canal instead of the proposed sea-level one. He was also recovering from yellow fever. So I don't know."

"Did he say he would try? Or how long he would stay?"

"He will probably go back soon, Esther," said Ellen. "He is needed there. I don't think he can get away for long."

"Life itself teaches the masses, and it is a strict and effective teacher. Unfortunately life does not teach those who consider themselves the socially select, the better educated, the superior. I have always held that every form of information and instruction that helps to widen the mental horizon of men and women is most useful and should be employed."

"Mr. Barrington, sir, I wanted to bring something to your attention," said Alice.

"Is it that you're not calling me Herman? Because I'm bringing that to your attention."

"Yes, sir. But this is actually about your son."

"What has he done now?"

"He is working too hard, Mr. Barrington."

"We must be speaking about a different Harry."

"I'm serious, sir."

"I won't even talk about it until you call me Herman."

"Yes, sir, Herman. But he is not eating, or taking care of himself. He is losing weight. Just look at him." They all stared at Harry sitting like a glassy apparition on the patio. "He is so anxious about this doctoral deadline that I'm beginning to suspect he may have a breakdown. And then he won't be healthy enough to travel . . . and we have such a busy summer planned."

"Ah, yes, darling," said Orville, "now that you bring it up, Harry, tell me again the order of the countries on your itinerary?"

"Daddy please, later for that. I'm trying to talk to Mr. Barr—Herman, about my concerns. And then you can talk to Harry about your concerns. But me first, Daddy, all right?"

Harry snapped out of his trance. "Orville, what are you worried about? We're going on the Orient Express, I promised you that. But not until we see Italy and Greece."

"Italy is having unrest," said Orville.

"You don't say."

"It's very tumultuous over there."

"Is it indeed?"

"There is volatility, tension. I worry that Italy won't be good for Alice."

"I'll be fine, Daddy," Alice cut in. "You're talking about a girl who stood on the wrong side of a badly barber-chaired stump after a hundred-and-fifty-foot hemlock split vertically and fell the wrong way and still managed to get out of the way."

"You knew what you were doing, princess."

"I was nine, Daddy." She patted her father. "How bad can Italy be? Besides, Harry really wants to see it."

"Do you, Harry? *Do* you really want to see it?"

"See what?" Harry said. "Um—yes, why not?"

"There's trouble there," Orville said. "There was a general strike, I read."

Harry tried to focus. "That was last year, Orville. It lasted four days."

"There hasn't been an earthquake in southern Italy for almost twelve years," Irma said suddenly. "That means they're due. They have too many volcanoes there, Harry.

One of them is bound to erupt at any moment. Like Vesuvius. I'm afraid Orville may be right on this point."

"Etna is twice as large," Harry said. "And ten times as active. Etna is the most active volcano in the world." He chuckled, oddly, and then stopped, mid-laugh. "And do you know why?" He sat up straight. "Because Zeus after his raging battle with Typhon, the monster of all monsters, he with a hundred fire-breathing serpent heads, picked up Etna and buried Typhon underneath it." He smiled, as if reminiscing. "That's why it's called the mountain of fire." He stopped and watched the puzzled faces all around him. "He is trapped under there for eternity," Harry explained, puzzled that they were puzzled. "That's why Etna is in a near constant state of activity—but don't worry. We're not going to Sicily." He tried not to sound wistful. "We'll be fine. Right Alice? Irma, you worry too much."

"Yes," said Alice. She was testy. "And about *all* the wrong things, Mother." She turned to Herman. "I wanted to ask your advice. Harry won't hear of it, but what do you think of postponing . . ."

"Postponing?" Harry exclaimed.

"Yes, darling. Your dissertation. Explain to Professor Carver how difficult it's been for you, and how you simply must have more time to finish successfully."

"Are you that far from finishing, son?" Herman asked. "I thought you were close."

"He's always in the library," said Alice. "I never see him. But it's too much to finish in three weeks."

"I'll be fine," said Harry. "I may ask for a June first extension if I feel I absolutely can't deliver. But I'm not worried."

"Also, you're thinking of going to Russia," Orville said, not willing to let it go. "And that worries me, frankly, even more than rumbly Italy. Russia is in real upheaval."

"Etna, too," Harry said quietly.

"Well, Russia just had themselves a revolution! They're fighting a debilitating war they can't win with the Japs, and some Grand Duke was just blown apart by a nail bomb . . ."

"That, ladies and gentlemen, is Anarchism. The greater the opportunities for every unit in society, the finer will be the individual and the better for society; and the more creative and constructive the life of the collectivity. That, in brief, has been the ideal to which I have devoted my life. Will it be the ideal to which you will devote yours?"

"I'm not the Tsar's uncle," said Harry, "and things have quieted down quite a bit since February."

"It's dangerous there. I recommend the Orient Express. Paris, Vienna, Bucharest, Constantinople—now that's a trip."

"That does sound wonderful, doesn't it, Harry?" Alice took his hand.

"Yes."

"Darling, do you think we'll have time for Italy, for Russia, for France, *and* for the Orient Express?"

"And Greece. Of course we'll have time. We're going for two months."

"What an adventure!"

"Alice is right, though. What about your doctorate?" Herman asked.

"I'll just have to finish, won't I?"

"But will you?"

"Yes." He tried not to sigh. He turned to Ben's mother. "Ellen, how is Josephine?" Josephine had been diagnosed with cancer last year.

"Thank you for asking, Harry. She's not well."

"I'm so sorry. I thought she was getting better?"

Ellen shook her head. "Wishful thinking on our part."

"That's terrible. Where is she now?"

"She is staying with me in Back Bay." Ellen shook her head. "I don't know how much longer we can take it. The nurse is having a terrible time with her."

"What other choice is there?"

Ellen shrugged. "No choice really. Home, or . . ." She didn't finish.

"Maybe another nurse?"

"Your sister is a grand woman," Herman said. "She's always been a shining star. Tell her that, Ellen."

"She knows, Herman, she knows how you feel. Thank you." Ellen lowered her head, as if perhaps a listing of Effie's accomplishments in life was not what Effie needed at that precise moment.

But no one knew what Effie needed. No one knew what to offer.

Suddenly the conversation lagged.

"*For in the last analysis, the grand adventure, which is liberty—the true inspiration of all idealists, poets and artists—is the only human adventure worth striving and living for.*"

Harry roused himself and looked around. His family sat around the patio table, serene yet lost in thought, attractive, sociable, mannered, familiar. Everyone was trying to figure out what to say to Ellen about the critical illness of her oldest sister—except for Harry, who was studying Alice's sweet, concerned face.

"She just needs someone kind to sit with her, Mrs. Shaw," said Alice to Ellen, patting the older woman's hand. "She just wants a little compassion."

Ellen nodded at Alice, her severe expression softening. "You're so right," she said, squeezing the young woman's extended hand. "I think that's probably all she needs. But I'm so busy. And the nurse is inadequate."

310

Harry marveled briefly at Ellen who once again managed to shut the conversation down with that last statement. Was she asking for someone else to come and sit with Effie? Was she implying that other people, present company included, were less busy than she? What to say to this?

And then his blinkless gaze traveled back to Alice, sitting by his side. She was such a wonderful girl. Reaching over, he took her hand and squeezed it. He wanted to say he did it because the scales had fallen from his eyes. But that wasn't quite it. He didn't see new things here. He saw old ordered things with a clearer eye and a cleared head. What *was* he thinking? How could he have allowed himself to stumble into such an irrational state? All the preparations for their hectic summer, their travel itinerary, his doctoral presentation—for five enraptured minutes he had become blind and lost the plot he had been so carefully forging. It was lunacy. He laughed at himself, poured some white wine for Alice, and resumed his pleasant droll conversation with her and Esther and his father, this time fully engaged, vowing to forget and then actually forgetting the yawning mutiny that ruled beyond the lush and landscaped lawns.

Chapter Fourteen
THE HIGH PRIESTESS OF ANARCHY

1

"HARRY, did you hear? Emma Goldman is starting her own magazine!"

"What, she got tired of getting arrested for reading *Lucifer the Lightbearer*?"

"Mock if you want."

"I want to mock."

"I told you she's a genius. She wants to call the new publication *Mother Jones*. What do you think of that?"

"I have no opinion. Men will never read it."

"That's where you're wrong, Harry. Everyone will read it."

"Men won't. They will think it's a publication on mothering."

"What, men don't understand metaphors? They don't

think *Atlantic Monthly* is a magazine on the ocean tides, do they?"

"I believe they do, yes."

"Oh, go ahead, poke fun."

"I'll go ahead then and poke fun."

"She is touring the country now. She's not going to be back this way until May."

"That's too bad."

"Harry!"

"Isn't there another anarchist we can go listen to? What about some of your Italian counterparts? Cafiero? Malatesta?"

"How do you know so much about Italy? Malatesta is selling ice cream in Naples. Cafiero died in an insane asylum."

"Do you think anarchy made him insane?"

She pealed with laughter. "No—a group of peasants eating black bread."

"No, I think it was anarchy. Bakunin also went mad."

"Because of strong sorrows."

"No, I think it was anarchy."

"Harry," said Herman, "Billingsworth informs me you're buying an astonishing number of books from the Simmons College bookstore."

Without a beat: "They have a large selection."

"The Crimson doesn't?"

"It's too crowded, I can't browse. What's the difference?"

"No difference. Isn't Simmons an all-women's college?"

"That's why they have so many books in stock; the women don't read."

Esther made a muffled sound over her marmalade toast, but observed him carefully.

"Don't study me, Esther," Harry said. "I'm not a textbook. You know I'm going full steam on my doctorate. I received an extension. I present in June and I have no time to waste waiting for volumes to become available at Gore Hall."

"I haven't said a word, Harry," Esther said, with Elmore by her side, who was reading the paper on Sunday morning, paying no attention to the customary squabbles between the siblings. "I'm scrutinizing you."

"Well, you keep at it," Harry said, wiping his mouth and rising from the breakfast table. "I'll be a doctor of philosophy and you'll have a degree in scrutiny."

"Why don't you have Clarence drive you anymore?" Herman persisted. "It would make things easier for you, especially when you keep getting back so late. You wouldn't have to worry about the car."

"I'm not worried about the car now, Father. I spend so many hours at the library that I don't want to tie up poor Clarence for hours just waiting for me. And if I really get tired, I can bunk with Vanderveer. He is always offering his floor to me."

"Why don't you work at home?"

"Can't concentrate," said Harry.

"Have you had a chance to speak to Carver about your next year's course load?" Herman smirked. "I should think as soon as your thesis is completed, they will make you an associate professor without much ado."

"Let's hope so," said Harry, pulling in his chair and stepping away. "Seems about time. I've been toiling as an adjunct for five years. I finally have an appointment with him next week. Now, if you'll excuse me, I'm going to drive to Cambridge and get some work done."

They were meeting in the Cambridge Commons and then walking to the library together. She had a paper due on the defiance of social conventions and the class struggle between Thomas Hardy's Jude Fawley and Sue Bridehead and he had promised to help her with it.

"On a *Sunday?*"

"Gore is open seven days a week, Esther," Harry said. "Much like a hospital. Right, Elmore?"

Elmore put down his paper and kissed Esther absentmindedly on the head. "That reminds me. I best be heading out myself. I'm on call until Monday afternoon. Harry, can you give me a ride to Mass General?"

Wincing, Harry said, "Sure, but hurry up. The library is not open all day, you know."

2

"Harry, you're a bright young man," Carver said. "I liked you very much when you took my Methods of Economic Investigation graduate course."

"Yes, you gave me an A." Harry sat in the dark paneled office across from Carver and struggled not to look at his watch. They had been talking for over twenty minutes and just got around to the purpose of his appointment. It was nearly four o'clock. Harry liked to be at the bookstore by four, so he could loiter around her for two hours before she got off work. But the meeting, which was supposed to take place in the morning, had been pushed until 3:30 and so here they were: Carver delayed and Harry in a hurry.

"Yes, you were an excellent student." Carver coughed. He had been coughing a lot the last twenty minutes. "Though slightly argumentative."

"Not true, sir." Harry smiled. "Give me one example."

"Can I narrow it to just one? Oh, you were joking. I see.

Very good. But I'll give you one anyway. It's a matter of fact not opinion that curbs on immigration will absolutely increase labor's marginal product and therefore wages, but you, though an ostensible advocate for higher wages, still managed to argue that curbs on immigration would do no such thing."

Harry paused, trying not to smile. "Okay, another example, sir."

Carver laughed. "Like I said, a fine student." His face turned serious. "But it's one thing to sit in a class, and quite another to teach it."

"Tell me about it."

"As I hope you know, the first principle of any worthy teacher, especially of a topic as complex as economics, is to make the students understand the foundations of the subject matter."

"I agree."

"Here's the rub." There was another coughing fit. This one required first a handkerchief, then a trip to the restroom. "Harry, your students are coming to me with alarming frequency, complaining that they don't understand what you're teaching them. The grades certainly bear that out."

"I find a number of them lack a desire for learning."

Carver opened a folder on his desk. "Let's see. Bullock teaches my other comp econ class and his seventy students received twelve As, thirty-seven Bs, and nineteen Cs. Four unfortunately did fail. But still, that's about the normal curve for a beginner class like his. I can show you the records, preceding even me, of the commonality of grades given to first-year students."

Harry sat. "I don't follow."

Carver opened another folder. "Here is your class. Let's take the semester ending next month. You have sixty-eight students. You have given out two As, eleven Bs, forty-four Cs, eighteen Ds, and you're failing ten."

Harry was stymied. "*I* didn't fail them, Professor. They failed themselves."

"All right. But do you see what I'm getting at?"

"Not at all."

"How do you explain the sharp discrepancy in grading between yourself and every other instructor in the department?"

"You didn't mention every instructor. You mentioned one other." Harry shrugged. "I'm a tougher grader than Bullock. He wants to be liked. I want the students to learn."

"That's admirable. But your students are *constantly* in my office complaining about your grading policies, about their grades, their term papers, their essays. They complain about the questions on your tests, about the topics for your papers. They complain about your comments to them. About your antagonistic manner in the classroom. Many of them have told me they feel you have an agenda. I hear many times a semester that you're less interested in teaching them economics than you are in foisting your set of beliefs on them. Many of them have said that you present your data in a skewed and biased way. When they ask you questions, I'm told you don't answer them or answer them incompletely or answer a question they're not asking, or resort to ad hominem attacks in order to embarrass them into staying quiet next time."

Harry sat stunned. "Professor, why have you not brought up any of this before?"

"Oh, Harry, but I have. We sat down with you last August before the new year began and I asked you to reconsider your methods. Do you remember?"

"Vaguely."

"And the year before that. The year before that you were coming out of your masters dissertation and were very green. I attributed some of these problems to a lack of experience. But it's been three years now. Something tells me this is how things are going to continue with you."

Harry pondered. "Perhaps I should grade on a curve."

Carver shook his head. "It's not about that. I see you're not denying what the students are saying."

"I'm not going to defend myself against a couple of disgruntled freshmen."

Carver looked inside Harry's folder. "I received fifty-seven complaints about you this semester alone. That's from two of your courses. *Fifty-seven*. Do you know how many complaints Bullock received? Three. That's total for the year."

"I told you, he sucks up to the kids. What's to complain about? He gives them all As! I wouldn't complain either."

"Your A students also complain."

Harry became quieter. He began to understand Carver's continued avoidance of him, his silence on Harry's requests for an added class, his discomfort at being approached by Harry in the staffroom.

"We need to resolve this before you take on another class in the fall," Carver said. "We need to approach this in a different way."

"What way?"

"Have you considered English?" asked Carver. "Professor Kittredge is a fine chair, and a good friend. I can speak to him and see if there are adjunct courses available."

"In *English*?"

"Yes. They read a book. You talk about it. You give them a test. Maybe ask them to write an essay. Talk to your friend Mr. Custis about it. He is an excellent instructor of English."

"You think I'd do better in English?" Harry shook his

head. "Professor Carver, I'm about to present for a doctorate in *economics*. Why would a Ph.D. in economics suddenly get transferred to teach English?"

"English may be a better fit for you. I think there is either something about economics you don't understand or something about teaching you don't understand. I sincerely hope it is the former, not the latter."

"I understand both quite well."

"All right. In any case, I'm afraid your methods are causing unnecessary conflict in my department."

Harry shifted tensely in his chair. "Can I get three courses to teach in English so I can get a full salary?"

Carver stared at him in amazement. "Harry, I have to persuade Kittredge to let you teach even one. You'll have to show him you can do it, and that you can follow his departmental requirements."

"I've been teaching here for five years! C.J.—Professor Bullock has been on a full-time salary his only year here. And he doesn't have a doctorate. How long before I can teach a full load?"

"You're putting the cart before the horse, I'm afraid."

"I need a job, Professor," said Harry. "I need a real income. I can't just be coming to your classroom, refuting your refutations about communism."

Carver smirked. "Come now, Harold Barrington. Pick a mansion to live in. This is not your dinner."

Harry got up. "That's where you're wrong, Professor. It *is* my dinner. My dinner and my life."

"I have been asking you for two years to teach a curriculum based on our department's criteria, and you have refused. This tells me you are not interested in a salaried position."

"I have absolutely adhered to the prepared curriculum."

"Really? You've taught your students about prices and

319

markets? The role of profits and losses, big business and government, productivity and pay, controlled labor markets? You've taught them time and risk, investment and specula-tion, national output, money and the banking system, government finance, international transfers of wealth? I think the only thing you may have taught them is myths about markets, and non-economic values."

Harry took a step away. "I'm not a performing monkey," he said. It was 4:30.

Carver stood up. "You're supposed to be a teacher of economics. I've heard you recently praising Emma Goldman's speeches at the faculty lounge. Personally, I wonder if that outrageous anarchist with the silver tongue has seduced you, made you daft in the head."

That's when Harry walked out. Carver was right. But it wasn't Emma Goldman.

3

To plumb the Marianic depths of just how far he had fallen, in May he allowed himself to go with her to one of those round-table discussions he'd been hearing so much about, at which a group of derelicts she called her friends, mostly male, sat in a small community common room, indeed around a circular table, smoking, drinking, and trying to sound like Eugene Debs, a gifted orator, which these louts weren't. Gina wore her hair loose, barely up, and a red silk blouse with a beautifully fitted camel-colored skirt. She perched on the edge of her chair, which happened to be next to his, long legs crossed, smoked, and though she was turned halfway to him, listened embracingly to her friends' anarchic inanities. When she laughed, her large hoop gold earrings shimmered and shook and more strands of her hair curled down around her neck. Harry hadn't wanted to go. But what did his desire have to do with it? *He eats not, drinks not, sleeps not, has no use of anything. Take all,* he thought, *the world's not worth my care.*

Her friends—Sophie, Miranda, Julia—they were just pencil etchings. She was oil on canvas. She was Michelangelo's sculpture, they mere drawings in an anonymous notebook.

"All this fine talk about doing what you want," Harry said to Dyson, the shortest and most insufferable of her friends after they'd had too many beers. They had no wine for Harry, or whiskey, so he remained stone sober and humorless. He would not drink beer with the hoi polloi. "But what happens if we're all anarchists?"

"The world is a free and fantastic place." Dyson slapped his best friend Archer on the back, as if he had just scored one. Archer, in his pristine and starched suit and tie was sitting on the other side of Gina, insinuating himself into her line of sight. Harry was wrong. Archer was the most insufferable of Gina's friends.

"Everyone doing what they want? Taking what they want?"

"People will police themselves. But they'll be free to do it."

"And if they don't police themselves?"

"Then they'll be shunned."

"Shunned?"

"Ostracized."

"Yes, thank you. I know what 'shunned' means. So each little community of anarchists will police themselves?"

"Exactly right, my good friend."

Harry wanted to tell the intolerable fool not to call him "friend". Only one person was allowed to call him "good friend" and he was still in Panama, much to Esther's dismay. "So, pretty much like local government now?"

"Not government. Local."

"Right. Local government. And what happens when your local anarchist goes twenty miles south and robs the fruit-stand in Danbury? Who's going to police him?"

"It'll all work out," cut in Archer, the whistling pursuer. "No one will be robbing anyone."

"In dreams it works out," Harry said. "On the pages of Rousseau and Hobbes, it works out. In smoky beer halls it works out. We've got seventy-five million people in this country. That's a boatload of people to be beating their own drum, doing what they want."

"Everyone will be free and happy," said Archer, getting another beer and pouring off a little into Gina's glass, which further aggravated Harry.

"You're talking about a political movement!" said Harry. "Not a day at the park." Like the Sundays at Cambridge Common he spent with her, Thomas Hardy and his repressions be damned.

"Bakunin is right," said Archer. "And you're wrong."

"I haven't told you what I think," Harry said. "How can I already be wrong?"

Dyson drunkenly picked up the thread. "Bakunin told Marx plain and simple that Marx's plan would make serfs of the very men Marx purports to free."

It pained Harry to ignore him, so familiar was he with the unresolved bitter conflict between Marx and Bakunin, unresolved because neither man's plan had yet to be applied to a place or location or country. "Anarchy means you live without rules," Harry said, desperately regretting having long ago chosen this particular topic for his doctoral thesis. It was beneath him to prepare to argue his sophisticated complex case in the storied halls of Harvard and simultaneously be dragged into a brawl with such boors.

"That's right. You live free."

"Can a hundred million people live without rules?" asked Harry.

"Can the state make infants out of men and then expect them to contribute to the social order?"

"Answer me."

"You answer *me*." Dyson banged his glass of beer on the table for emphasis.

"You can't make a civil society . . ."

"Who said anything about society? We don't want you trespassing on our unfettered development as human beings."

"Someone is bound to trespass on somebody's unfettered development, surely?"

"Yes, but your way lies tyranny," Archer piped in. "You've got built into your social order the force of one group of men upon another."

"And women," Gina said.

Archer and Dyson waved her off condescendingly. She wasn't Emma Goldman, or Mother Jones. They could do that. But Harry didn't wave her off and he also would not argue with her. If she declared tonight she wanted everybody's right to beautiful and radiant things, he would have agreed with her with his whole heart.

"Do you know the difference between real and pretend rights?" Harry asked Archer and, receiving no answer, continued. "Do you accept that there might be a conflict between claims of freedom and claims of order?"

"No, I don't accept it," retorted Archer.

Gina smiled like a cat. "Ah, Harry," she said. "Haven't we become quite the Burkian?"

He almost couldn't continue. Gina not only knew who Edmund Burke was but was teasing him about it! "Hardly. I'm merely presenting a dialogue to arrive at the truth. Free men accept the natural limitation on some of their rights to organize a government for the good of the people," Harry said. "To represent the will of the people. Men *and* women." He almost smiled at her, but didn't want vile Archer to see an intimate interaction between them.

"Not me," said Archer. "I don't accept it."

"Not me," said Dyson with a burp. "I don't accept it either."

"See, here's the difference between you and us," said Archer, chugging down his beer like a farmer. "This is where you and I are dialectically opposed. You keep talking about *society*, and we are talking about *individuals*."

"Yes, your plan is to abolish all government."

"And your plan is coercion! Benevolent, malevolent, who cares, coercion is what you preach!"

"Look," said Harry, "I believe we should have a different kind of government than what we have now. God knows there's room for improvement. What's *your* grand plan?"

"Any imposed rule weakens man because it takes choice away from him."

"And woman," added Gina.

"I know what you're doing," said Archer to Harry. "You mock everything that's fatal to your philosophy."

"You flatter yourself, Archer. Yours is not a philosophy but a dim song in the field flung far."

"Janie! Do you see how he mocks you?" Archer exclaimed. "*Our* philosophy, and I include my friend Jane here, is that any attempt for man to rule another man is wrong."

"Yes." Harry nodded. "In a nutshell that *is* your absurd philosophy."

"My way, we are free and happy. Your way makes slaves out of men. Your Marxist creed will make chain gangs out of free men, and *I'm* absurd?"

"Not just absurd but dead wrong! Have you not been paying attention? Men are desperate to reorganize themselves into a new order!"

"Not me. Not Jane."

Harry took a breath. "Why can't you understand that liberation of the individual is not possible until the masses are freed first? But how can you be free when you have to mark your time at the factory you work in? You work the hours *they* state, you collect the wage *they* give you. What rights do you have? Where is this freedom you keep bleating about?"

Archer shrugged. "OK, so in your land of unicorns the factory will be owned by the state. Everything else will remain exactly the same."

"By the same you mean better."

"Christ, you are naïve! It'll be a thousand times worse. At least right now the jerk that pays my wage at the sugar plant is not pretending he is paying me peanuts for my own good."

"The socialists will not pay you peanuts. They will pay you a good and decent wage."

"Keep dreaming."

"What is it about work that's so distasteful to the anarchists?"

"We happen to believe," Archer said with grandiose pomposity, "that four to five hours of work a day is plenty. *More* than enough. We're not interested in the left-wing proletarians telling us otherwise. Right, Janie?"

Diplomatically Gina said nothing.

"You want everyone to be free from oppression," Harry asked, "or just you?"

"We'll start with me. After that I don't care."

"I didn't think so. But for change, there must be action. That's the loudest support of your own heady principles."

"Inaction is also action!"

Harry laughed incredulously. "Forget about the socialists. You're not going to make it five minutes in the *capitalist* world."

"Exactly. Because you want to force me to do what *you* want to do. Under you and your ilk, dictatorship *of* the proletariat will swiftly become dictatorship *over* the proletariat, won't it?" Archer now laughed at Harry.

"You're a fool," Harry said, standing up, and putting on his fine tailored wool coat. "Do you even know what the word 'proletariat' means? It means 'worker.' Your anarchist hero Bakunin writes about the *working* man. Not a dolt like you. You don't believe in revolution. You believe in evolution."

"That's quite a trick," Gina said, after they had parked and he was walking her very slowly back to her dorm. "In five minutes to alienate all of my friends by pronouncing them idiots."

"It was more like thirty minutes."

"They're not fools, Harry. They're my friends."

He struggled not to snort. "What happened to Verity? She was nice."

"She is married and lives in Boston. She doesn't go to these meetings anymore."

"Sensible girl."

"For marriage or for her political apathy?"

Sideways he glanced at her. "Both," he said. "I thought she was going to become a nun?"

"She joined the Sacred Heart Sodality, but then fell in love in a boat on the Merrimack."

He wanted to ask her to go in a boat with him on the Charles. On Sundays in the summertime they rented boats at the Harvard dock and a flotilla of them meandered through the wide harbors. He bit his lip not to ask. "Oh, too bad about her," Harry said. "She was so righteously political."

"She was never serious," Gina said.

"Funny. Ben's mother Ellen thought she was more political than you."

"Goes to show you must never judge a woman by appearances," said Gina. "Verity is having her second baby. How bourgeois is that?"

"Terribly." Harry smiled. "What, Emma Goldman doesn't believe in children?"

"Of course she doesn't," said Gina. "She says children are the antithesis of liberty."

"Well," said Harry, "I happen to agree with her there, I think it's best she doesn't reproduce."

"Harry!" They walked in silence for a few moments.

He wanted to offer her his arm, but it wasn't raining, or snowing, or slippery out. Treacherous, yes.

"I don't think you'll be able to come visit with my friends anymore," she said.

"Is Archer really your friend?" He couldn't hide his animosity toward the hulking brute.

"He's not so bad," she said, gently knocking into him.

"No?" Harry shrugged. "Well, none of my business."

"What, you think he likes me . . .?" Gina smiled. "No young woman is going to hate a man for being a little bit in love with her."

"Not even when he is so blatant about it?"

And she, breaking all rules of acceptable behavior, without being asked took Harry's arm. "Especially not then."

It was dark as he walked with her. He couldn't have walked any slower.

"Do you have a little story to tell me?" she asked.

"What kind of story? Something clever? Or something funny?"

"Why not both?" She squeezed his arm.

"A visiting instructor was interviewed by the president for a position in the economics department. He had been an esteemed professor in Wisconsin, I think, I can't remember. And the president says to him, Professor so and so, we are very impressed with your work. However there are stories concerning your relations with women, and I must assure you that such relations would not be tolerated at this university. And the professor replies, Mr. President, after having been introduced to the wives of the members of the economic faculty, I can assure you, you need have no misgivings."

She laughed throatily, echoing her delight into the elms. "Are you making that up?"

"Why would I make something like this up?"

"I don't know—how attractive are the wives of the economics professors?"

"I've never noticed, so how attractive can they be?"

He always found it wrenching to leave her at the door. The light was on over the small porch of her residence hall. They routinely bucked up against the curfew. Today, they stood together maybe three minutes before Gladys, the residence manager, poked her nosy head out the front door and in her patronizing voice said, "Miss Attaviano. Curfew."

Harry wanted to touch her, oh the desperation of his ostentatious desire.

And as always, the more intensely he felt their imminent separation, the further he stepped away. "Goodnight," he said, with his hat in his hand.

"Goodnight. Thank you for taking me home."

"Of course." He chewed his lip in agony. "Gia?" She was

outrageously beautiful standing under the streetlamps. Harry couldn't be far enough away.

"Yes, Harry?"

"Your Emma Goldman is giving a speech in Portsmouth in two weeks." He stepped a little closer. At that moment the front door of the hall opened again.

"Miss Attaviano," the sonorous voice streamed.

"Yes, Gladys, one minute, please." They stopped speaking until the RA reluctantly closed the door. "Where is that?"

"New Hampshire. Right on the border."

"That's far."

"We can take my little clipper. Spend the day. It's on a Saturday."

She too chewed her lip, not answering him. Behind her the door opened. "Miss Attaviano . . ."

"One minute, Gladys!"

The door slammed disapprovingly.

"Well?" he said. "What do you say?"

"Hmm," she said. "What is her topic?"

"What is her *topic*?" That one Harry did not expect. "Puritanism and free love."

Gina laughed. "OK, I'll go to that one. She is quite lively on the subject."

"It's good that I didn't say industrial trade relations."

"Oh Harry."

He carried her "Oh Harry" with him all the way home into the deep night. He was no longer steering his own ship. What did he want? He didn't know. He wouldn't allow himself to think past a brief, blissful, luminescent moment, flying with her like Icarus too close to the sun.

Chapter Fifteen
ON THEIR KNEES BY THE SEA

"*M*ARRIAGE *and love have nothing in common. They are as far apart as the poles. They are antagonistic to each other. Now it may be that some marriages are based on love. There may be cases where there is love in marriage but I say love continues in spite of marriage, not because of it. Marriage is a failure that only the very stupid will deny.*"

It was standing room only. Harry leaned to a rapt Gina and whispered, "Just think, we almost missed this."

"Shh."

"*From infancy the average girl is told that marriage is her ultimate goal. Like a mute beast fattened for slaughter, she is prepared for that.*"

"Gina, I think she just called you a mute beast."

"Shh!"

"*This creature enters into life-long relations with a man only to find herself shocked, repelled, outraged beyond measure! There is a criminal ignorance in matters of sex that is somehow extolled as a great virtue! It's deplorable!"*

Harry watched Gina's face, which she tried to make inscrutable. "Harry," she whispered, "Emma is front and center, not to your right, where I am."

"I can't watch that homely woman talk about love."

"But you can watch me listen to her?"

He didn't say a word.

Gina turned her gaze to the stage. "I don't think it's love she's talking about. Now shh."

"You were talking and I'm supposed to shh?"

"The moral lesson instilled into a young girl is not whether a man has aroused her love, but rather it is, 'How Much?' Can a man make a living? Can he support a wife? From the outset her dreams are not of moonlight and kisses, of laughter and tears . . ."

"Dreams of tears?" said Harry.

"Shh!"

"Instead she dreams of shopping tours and bargain counters."

"I'm beginning to be sorry I brought you," said Harry.

"No, no, she's wonderful, are you listening?"

"I don't have much choice," he said. "I'm not Louis."

"Who's Louis? Shh!"

"As to marriage being a protection of the woman, the very idea is so revolting, such an outrage, such an insult on life! It reminds me of that other paternal arrangement—capitalism. It robs man of his birthright, stunts his growth, keeps him in poverty and dependence. Both are a travesty on human character!"

"She is making me want to defend capitalism," Harry whispered. "When is the free love bit coming? I'm getting tired of standing."

"Love is the strongest and deepest element in all life! The

harbinger of hope, of ecstasy, the defier of all laws, of all conventions. Man has conquered nations, but all his armies could not conquer love. Man has subdued bodies, chained the spirit but he has been utterly helpless before love. High on a throne, yet he will remain poor and desolate if love passes him by. Love, ladies and gentlemen, has the power to make out of a beggar a king."

"She's finally making a little sense," whispered Harry, leaning closer.

For another hour, maybe three, Emma Goldman railed against the early feminists who were shackled by Puritanism. She was funny, bitter, loud—tremendous. If it hadn't been for the folly of anarchy, Harry would've worn a Goldman pin on his lapel. He had to admit her libertarian principles were at the very least entertaining to listen to.

She talked about freedom for all women, freedom from marriage and children, the right to love whoever the woman chose and whenever; she yelled in protest about secret abortions and the denial of contraception, shouted about the Puritans making single women nuns or sluts, as if there was no in between. Playing to the grim Portsmouth Puritan crowd without humor or imagination, her impassioned speech fell on deaf and disapproving ears. Harry was neither, but he was keenly aware of the laughter and the applause coming from the animated and rejoicing woman to his right. Gina smelled so good, and her radiant face was aglow with the revolution.

After the meeting, they stood around in a crowded, smoke-filled room, while nearby was the beach, sand, ocean water—and privacy! Oh anarchy!

Impatiently Harry rocks from foot to foot. Gina won't stop talking politics to people she has just met—current events, Boston finances, new developments, possible wars. When did she get so fiery?

He catches her scent again. Her hair twists in the salt air and his heart with it. He wants there to be heat—why can't today be the kind of day they've been having recently, full of glorious warmth? Yet now when he craves the sun, it's overcast and chilly. The ocean breeze is cool through the finally opened doors, and she is breathtaking, like an open furnace, and the wind from the sea has taken his sails up and away. She doesn't want to leave the post-lecture party—they are offering wine and cheese and canapés. She is dressed better than anyone else there. Harry has noticed that the anarchists are not particularly well put together—but she stands out in tailored velvet and smelling of vetiver. Is he light-headed because he hasn't eaten and has had too much wine? He asks her to come for a walk on the beach. She glances outside where there is no burning fire and no red wine and says it looks cold. He gives her his jacket, and finally she leaves with him, but on the beach her hat blows off her head, and he goes chasing it and she laughs. While he is running down the dancing hat, she takes off her shoes and waltzes by herself on the sand.

He comes back to her. Twirling on the sand, she quotes Emma Goldman to him in a song. *"If I can't dance, I don't want to be in your revolution."* He steps up. Come on, Gia, he says, be in my revolution.

She is barefoot on the sand. Where are her stockings? She hasn't taken them off; they're not lying in a heap nearby. When his open palm goes around her waist, he can't feel her corset, he feels velvet and under it the curve of her natural waist and lower back. Suddenly he has three left feet and, usually such a capable dancer, can't move backward or forward. She steps on his awkward toes a few times, laughs, and they trip and fall to their knees on the sand.

What's gotten into you, Harry, she says.

I can't imagine, he says, his eyes roaming wildly over her flushed and eager face. Both his hands are entwining the narrow space from which her hips begin.

It's late afternoon on the wide Hampton beach; it's gray and foggy when he kisses her. He's never kissed Sicilian lips before, only Bostonian. There is a boiling ocean of contrast between the two. Boston girls were born and raised on soil that was frozen from October to April and breathed through perfectly colored mouths that took in chill winds and fog from the stormy harbor. But his Sicilian queen has roamed the Mediterranean meadows and her abundant lips breathed in fearsome fire from Typhonic volcanoes.

He kisses her as if they are alone at night—as if she is already his. His arms wrap around her back and press her to him. They become suspended, he floats like a phantom around her in the moist air. He won't let her go, he can't.

Harry, she whispers into his mouth.

Let's go, he breathes out, right *now*, let's go.

Yes! Let's go swimming, she says, still in his arms, pulling slightly away to look at him. I haven't been in the ocean in . . . she trails off. Harry, I've *never* been in the ocean.

It's not that he doesn't want to give her the ocean—he wants to give her everything—he'd like to be there for her first swim in the Atlantic, but how should he *politely* explain to her that now is not the time?

We didn't bring any swimming clothes, he mutters lamely, tilted on his axis, unable to tear himself away from her Belpasso lips. His holds her face in his hands. She is like grains of sand already slipping through his fingers.

Come on, we're alone on the beach, she says, still on her knees. Who in their right mind would be out here in the cold to see us?

Cold? Inside he is combusting—at any moment, lava is going to pour forth from him.

To entice him, as if he *needed* enticing, seducing, mesmerizing, she opens her radical blouse, unhooks her revolutionary undergarments, and reveals her proletarian body to him. Reveals her neck, her high young breasts, the promise of her bare stomach—jumps up and runs into the water, like a Modigliani nude. He follows faithfully, his empty arms stretching out to her. The icy rolling waves knock her down, he retrieves her, but she is thrilled to have been tossed and squeals with the joy of it, and in the foamy water throws her arms around his neck, presses her naked breasts, her cold dark nipples against his bare chest and kisses him like madness all salty and wet and whispers, Harry, do you have any idea how long I've dreamed of this? He is so weakened he is afraid he'll pass out. A wave comes, knocks them both over, and spares him the indignity. All good sense abandons him, all hope, all reason. This way ruin lies and desire to trump all sanity. Step right up, like a carnival wheel on Revere Beach, and ride that tiger.

She remains in the water longer than his reverie lasts. He has no plan, he has not thought this through, he only knows what *must* happen next, what is the absolute imperative. How he gets there is immaterial.

Not even the dunes separating them from the distant boardwalk, from the civilized houses, will help them. Harry, she whispers, we're in a public place . . . oh *now*, she whispers. She says this because she finally realizes the looming peril to herself on the sand in the open air under the sky. Yet what Harry sees is an empty beach and a bare, gleaming goddess in broad daylight under his fevered hands.

Harry, God, wait, Harry!

You flaunt the blaze of yourself in front of me and then you say wait Harry? Harry can't wait.

In damp clothes haphazardly thrown on their bodies and sand grinding in their shoes and hair, they detach themselves however briefly and stagger out onto the boardwalk almost like any other cultured couple enjoying an afternoon saunter before dinner. Instead of drinks or dinner, he finds them the poshest guesthouse, and she says, no, that is too expensive, and he says, if I could, I would buy you a Medici palace. The Seagate Mews overlooks the sand and the water where he kissed her. Much later from their balcony, they search for the spot on the sand where they had lain.

The proprietor tells them dinner is promptly at seven. Harry asks the woman if they could take dinner up in their room. Is there wine? Is there a bath? Is there wood for the fire? The dinner request, though unorthodox, is reluctantly complied with. Ah, so you're newlyweds? the dour woman says to them, writing something down in her daybook.

He twitches, paling, not answering, while she giggles, blushing, and answering, yes, how did you guess?

It's Saturday evening and not even dark out yet, the dinner has not been brought, nor the wine, and their bodies are peppered with sand. They descend onto the rug on the wood floor because he doesn't want to get the crisp white sheets all gritty. He is thinking ahead. He is on his knees because he is about to worship her, but stops himself because she needs to be on the altar of the raised bed. He gets water and a sponge from the basin and washes the sand from her feet and her fine ankles. You want me to touch your ankle, Gia, he whispers, in memory of the distant quarry, both his hands gripping her ankles. I'll know if it's swollen, broken . . .

Yes, touch me, Harry . . . nothing is broken.

You want me to wait for you, Gia?

No, carry me, put your hands on me, put your mouth on me, he is already over her, trembling as she trembles, shuddering as she shudders. He is on his knees and she is his bride on the crisp white linen.

Have you got nothing to say? He whispers, knowing he himself is without words. He cannot believe what has happened, what is happening.

What took you so long.

So long? He runs his fingers down the length of her naked body. We barely just met. He heaves himself over her and kisses the underside of her breasts. He puts her nipples into his mouth to hear her moan, and closes his eyes, his mouth pressing into her heart.

We met six years ago, she whispers.

That doesn't count.

Doesn't it?

Does it?

He glances up to gape at her, but his vision is blurred and he feels unsteady like a man who just learned to walk, to breathe, to see—a man who's come out of a coma and is weak in his whole being.

Why didn't you come to me back then? she whispers almost in a cry. Didn't you know how much I wanted you?

Tell me how much you want me now.

She doesn't tell him. She climbs over him and shows him.

I didn't come to you then, he says when he can speak again, because I didn't want to lose my life.

Oh, you know Salvo is all talk.

That's not what he means, but he doesn't explain. As if he can.

Besides you know how my friend Ben felt about you, feels

about you still for all I know, though we never talk of it. There was nothing I could do.

But you wanted to.

I wouldn't let myself even want to. He takes her hands, caresses them and kisses her fingers.

But you wanted to.

I admit to nothing. He kisses her palms. These hands had made him something long ago that he treasures more than any other possession he has. He won't even wear it, because he's afraid the scarlet threads will unravel. He keeps it wrapped in tissue, in a box in his room, and only takes it out when he wants to remember what can't be remembered. Someday he might tell her how he adored the roughened hands that could make something so beautiful. She won't understand because what he values she throws away. *Where your treasure is, there your heart will be also*, he whispers, and she applauds him for quoting Jesus. He didn't know he was.

Dov'è il tuo tesoro, sarà anche il tuo cuore, she murmurs in Italian, an aphrodisiac even stronger than anarchy.

Still astride him, she rubs her salty perspiring body over him, she caresses him with herself from his feet to his open and famished mouth.

I've lost the power of misery, he whispers to her. I'm parched into silence. I've lost the power of thought.

The moon is still full. We have time. We have nothing but time. She says this and then the sun rises over the ocean. Just like that, the night that had no end ends.

But if it wasn't for your friend or your life or me so young, what then?

You mean if all circumstances were completely different? And if you weren't so beautiful and Italian, if your breasts weren't lush and your hips didn't sway into my heart . . .

Is that where my hips sway? Your heart?

She paralyzes him with love. He wants to ask if he is her first, but the truth of it is, he feels like she is his. He can't believe the bounty that life has blessed him with for one briefest night.

He is helpless. He doesn't know what to do.

That boy who follows you around, Archer, what do you plan to do with him?

I'm not with Archer. I'm with you.

Tonight, yes. What about when I leave you?

Don't leave me.

Eventually I have to go.

Don't go. She lowers her face into his neck, her cocoa hair falling onto his chest. Now released from its refined shackles, the soft, messy curls tumble down her shoulders, onto his chest and stomach and face. His hands are in it. He's never seen hair like this before, so long, so wavy, so exotic. He's never seen anything like her before.

There is a fireplace in the room. He throws kindling on it, a log, keeps it going through the cold morning. He pulls the thick eiderdown onto the floor and lays her down on it, covering her with himself to keep her warm while she scorches him with her body.

Sunday morning becomes Sunday afternoon.

I am bone of your bones, she whispers to him, I am flesh of your flesh.

At his distant house, a universe away, down the coast, his family is gathering for Sunday lunch. Orville and Irma are bringing Orville's brother, invalided after a logging accident. Ellen said she might bring her sister Effie who is feeling a little better.

Harry has to go home. That's what he tells Gina, still naked, still in bed. Sunday lunch when everyone's gathering is sacrosanct. She is puzzled. He can't say, if I don't show up, they'll know something is wrong. I won't be able to explain. I've never not been there. He can't tell Gina about the Porters of Boston.

They dragged their drained, reluctant bodies out. The day was gray, and the ocean waves broke downcast over the sand. It threatened rain.

"Whenever momentous things happen," she said, "the day is always like this. It's never a sunny day with the horizons clear in every direction. When I came to America through Boston Harbor, it was like this—and now today."

"That's a small sample," he said, putting on his tie. "Only two." He wished he could speak more plainly to her. He had wanted to talk to her during the night, but no speech had been possible. Speech was a controlled thing. Talk was what you did on the green lawn at the Barrington homestead. Talk was not possible with the windows open and the blue moon shining and her moans muffling into his naked collarbone.

They had a little balcony, all white, where they stepped out into the cold covered by a large woolen blanket, to get some fresh air because they were burning up and couldn't breathe. He wanted to ask her things then, he wanted concrete answers to his vague questions, he wanted affirmation of the undeniable; in the end he stayed mute because that's what was possible. He wanted to tell her he hadn't read enough poetry about love to understand what was happening to him.

But it wasn't just about love. It was a shifting of the sands under his feet. It was a crumbling of the concrete on which he had built his life.

He had to stop the car somewhere around Newburyport, where the Merrimack River emptied out. He took her hands in his. "I don't want to go home," he said, lowering his entire face into the palms on her lap.

"I know," she said, stroking his head, bending over to kiss him. "Nor do I. My place is with you."

"You think so?"

"I've always thought so."

"What about the vultures that surround you?"

"I don't like that image," she said. "I know you're trying to insult *them*, but in the process you're insulting me. What do vultures surround? Carrion."

He was shamed by an immigrant for whom English was a second language.

"You are right. I'm sorry." He wanted to ask her if what he had suspected was true. Did she remember her girlish crush on him when she first came to Boston? He was afraid to ask; he wanted the illusion to continue.

She had said something to him in the night—or was it a dream, a fervent prayer? He thought he heard her say, "In the beginning there was you. It's all there is." He didn't ask her. What if he misheard, and she was forced to lie, to please him?

He had wanted to ask her if she had had other boyfriends. She seemed so self-assured. Is that what he was, a boyfriend? And Archer too? Though she had cried with him last night, he didn't think it was from discomfort. If he weren't a man, he would've cried.

Is there anything you want to tell me? he had said.

Is there anything you want to tell *me*?

He paused, observing her scrutinizing him, her chocolate eyes open, focused, her mouth slightly parted, barely breathing, trying to catch his next words, as if waiting for him to say what couldn't be said, tell her of things that couldn't be told. He said nothing. It would've ruined everything, and he wanted only to be ruined.

I love it when you press my face between your breasts, he whispered instead, willingly lost in the moment of other inexpressible things. I love your long legs. He showed her why. Because she wrapped them around him, pressing him to herself, like a bow on a gift, you're mine, her legs murmured, smooth, silken, tanned. I've tied you up with a ribbon inside myself, only I can unwrap you, her bare clutching legs murmured, and I won't unwrap you until I say you can go. Not yet. Not ever.

Chapter Sixteen
VIOLET CATASTROPHE

1

HE waited for her at Evans with an exorbitant bouquet of roses from six until eight-thirty when she finally showed up on Archer's arm, laughing delicately at something he said. Harry had no plan to deal with Archer. His stinging rebuke to Gina came in the form of his throwing the ocean of flowers at her feet.

She was the one who came to visit him at the economics faculty lounge—not even that day but the following, an eternity away from his hurt and his flowers.

"Don't be upset with me, Harry," she said. "I don't know your intentions."

"I thought I made them clear in Portsmouth," he said, leading her down the stairs and outside. Awkwardly they stood in front of the white colonial building on the green lawn, while down the road the horses and the trolley cars clomped by.

"*Did* you?" she said, and he didn't know what she meant and didn't press to find out.

"Is Archer competing for your affections?" he asked, afraid to look her in the eye lest she see his enslavement there.

"Is that what you're doing, competing?"

"You tell me."

"I'm just hedging my bets," Gina said. "After you're done with me and have moved on your merry way, I don't want to be left holding only your bouquet of roses."

"Who said I'm moving on?"

"Aren't you?"

Not that night—unless you called the Ambassador suite at the opulent Hotel Vendome moving on.

Archer was still hanging around her at the bookstore, near the counter, near the register. He wasn't buying, he was loitering. The presence of the malevolent interloper grated on Harry, and this was also something he wasn't familiar with, the feeling of acute hostility like a poisonous worm inside him. He wished for Archer to be struck down with malaria. Was dengue fever something Ben could bring with him in a bottle when he came back?

"You have to tell me what you want," Harry said.

"Why don't you tell me what *you* want?"

"I think it's obvious." It was all he could do, not to fall on his knees every time he saw her.

"Isn't it obvious with me?"

"I don't know. I don't have a panting farmer hanging around me when you come to see me."

"You just hide them better."

He didn't know what to say to that, so he said nothing.

Where are you going to take me today? she asked, when it was May, then June, warm and hotter, when the coats came off her shoulders, and flowers and feathers went in her hair. Her dresses got lighter, and her sleeves got shorter, and now when they strolled from Simmons across the Fenway and down to the Charles, where they sauntered like lovers down the secluded promenade, he could watch her wrists in public, adorned with silver bracelets. He wanted to buy her gold bracelets and diamond rings and kiss the hands and wrists that wore them just as he kissed her feet and ankles. He brought her gifts in small red velvet boxes, and then would find Archer staring during an anarcho-syndicalist symposium; when she applauded, Harry's 18-karat gold bracelets jangled on her elongated elegant wrists and Archer gaped at them.

Harry wanted to challenge the man to a duel and kill him. He wanted Gina to tell him never to come near her again. He took her in his car up to Revere where they ate in a tiny secluded dining room and then retired upstairs to the bed and breakfast, which he rented by the week though he could only bring her there a few afternoons, and on Saturday nights.

His father said nothing, but in his peripheral vision Harry had begun to notice a certain reticence in Herman on Sunday afternoons, a certain incommodious reluctance to tease. It almost seemed as if the more abandon in Harry's secret life, the more restraint in his father. Harry was not one to initiate conflict; he was content as long as his father said nothing.

And Herman said nothing.

Harry remained preoccupied with trying to figure out how, if not to kill Archer, at least to move him permanently out of the picture.

"What do I have to do to stop him from coming to see you?" Harry asked her one late Wednesday afternoon deep in bed. Soon he had to be going; in another world he had his customary dinner plans with Irma and Alice, but in this world the windows opened onto a small private garden, and the air smelled of the nearby sea. Harry was suspended, imprisoned. Plum Island was a ferry ride away. Perhaps they could take the ferry there. There could be a storm, and they would be trapped with no way back to the mainland. He spent an inordinate amount of time dreaming of an enforced imprisonment, with no way back, no route of escape and no chance of anyone finding them. Why was that so enormously appealing?

"Do you not know?" she said.

"I really don't."

"Why do we come all the way to Revere?"

"It's not far. I thought you'd like the drive." He pulsed the tips of his fingers against her moist mouth. He couldn't stop touching her. "Do you know what a *violet catastrophe* is?" His lips found her clavicles, his hands turned her over, his mouth traced the nape of her neck, the blades of her shoulders, the small of her back.

"No. But sometimes I think I might like to stay in Boston again."

"But not right now . . ."

"No." A small anguished breath. "Not right now."

The next week they went back to the Vendome in Boston. Harry registered himself under a pen name, as if he were a writer, and paid for the night by cash like a thief. He had told Billingsworth he was buying gifts for his friends, and wanted easy access to plenty of money. This is what he said. But he craved the intimacy of the anonymous white room in a tiny town with the floor-to-ceiling windows and ocean light to illuminate her.

I *need* to stay here overnight with you again, he whispered to her. It was a Monday.

Last time, I got into so much trouble. I have one more year left of school. I don't want to be kicked out.

Of course not.

Tell me what a *violet catastrophe* is, she murmured. It sounds frightening.

In classical physics it's when an idealized physical body will emit radiation with infinite power.

She moaned.

They were fused into one another, in a time crucible.

They went to Revere in the afternoons she didn't work and he didn't teach. Sometimes when they wanted a gulp of salt air, they went out for short walks to the pier, or to the antique shops on Main Street. She liked so many things; she displayed infectious girlish delight in the simplest of pleasures. And also in the most complicated.

He wanted to give her one of everything. He told her that once, whispered it to her in a flame, and she laughed and said, like what, a child?

He pulled away. "You want me to be the father of your child?"

I'm just teasing you.

He wanted to buy her one of everything.

You can't buy me that antique table, Harry. I have nowhere to put it. I'm not allowed to have my own furniture at Evans.

He bought it for her anyway. She took it home for her mother.

So now my gifts of passion go to Mimoo?

He bought her a bench she had sat on for a single moment and said was nice. He bought her hats and lady purses, silk gloves and diamond necklaces.

And yet, despite the ritual adoration in Revere, every Monday and Wednesday, unfailingly, Archer was at the bookstore come six o'clock when Gina finished work.

One particular Thursday, Archer asked her to go with him to see Eugene Debs speak.

"I'd love to," she said (and this after an unbridled rainy Wednesday afternoon they had barely lived through together!), "but he's been sold out for weeks."

Archer waved a set of tickets in front of her with a self-satisfied grin. She clapped, Harry's bracelets jangling. "How exciting!" she said, and turned to Harry. "You want to come too? Debs is amazing. He's going to be president of the United States someday, just wait and see."

"Um, I only have two tickets, Jane," said Archer. "One for you, one for me."

"Oh, that's fine," Harry said. "I wouldn't be able to come anyway to hear his fine eloquence."

To her credit, Jane looked disappointed.

"And the reason I can't come," he continued, "is because Ben's Aunt Effie is very sick. Remember her, Gina? Josephine Shaw Lowell. She's been unconscious the last few days. We're afraid she's close to the end. I was thinking of going to visit her."

Gina's demeanor changed. "I didn't know she was sick," she said, coming around the counter. "Of course I remember her. She is such a fine lady. What happened?"

When she heard that Effie was in Back Bay and the nurses were hopeless, she said, "Harry, I know someone who can help her. We should go tonight. Especially if we want Rose to make a house call."

"Go where? And who is Rose?" *Did* they want Rose to make a house call?

Gina told Archer she would not be going with him to

see Debs, much to Archer's annoyance and Harry's satisfaction. He was using Ben's critically ill aunt as bait. Was that truly wicked, or just a little bit so? Well, why not? Damnable Archer was trying to use the oratorically excellent Eugene Debs as bait.

"Where are we headed?" They were on their way to his Runabout.

"Concord."

That's another thing he had that the athletic clown didn't have. A Runabout. And his father had already ordered for him the coveted American Mercedes, the first Benz to be built directly in the States—

"My friend Rose," said Gina, "helps people like your aunt."

"And how do you know a Rose from Concord?"

"I worked for her for three summers, as part of the Sacred Heart Sodality. She opened several homes for the terminally sick, and the girls from St. Mary's took turns going to Concord to help her. I still take a train out there every once in a while if I have the time. Not often enough. She is always short-staffed."

"Oh." Harry fell quiet. "Is Rose a Catholic?"

"I believe she is. Does it matter?"

"I don't know. Ben's aunt isn't."

"Rose wasn't once either."

"What was she before?"

"A Unitarian, I think. A Puritan?" Gina smiled. "She converted with her husband a few years ago, and when he died, she became a nun."

"Her husband put her off men for life?"

"Maybe he was irreplaceable."

Harry wouldn't entertain such a thought. "I don't know about this, Gia," he said.

"What are you worried about? Either Josephine believes or not. The rest is irrelevant."

"Right, that's what I mean. I have a feeling she might not believe."

They were nearly in Concord when they had this conversation.

"Look, Rose is a Dominican nun and she helps sick people," Gina said. "She helps them because of her faith. Who do you think helps sick people? Nonbelievers?"

"Sometimes, yes."

"Okay. Either Effie wants help or she doesn't. Rose will visit. Effie will decide."

They drove in silence for a few minutes. Gina studied the map. It was still light out, dusky. But then Harry had to know. "How does your Emma Goldman square with Jesus?"

Gina looked up from her map and eyed him warily. "I spend no time squaring that circle," she said. "Emma is Emma. And Jesus is Jesus."

"But you idolize her."

"I think she is an incredible woman, yes. I think Effie is an incredible woman. But wait till you meet Rose. So what? I don't have to agree with everything. I can pick and choose."

"Pick and choose anarchy?"

"Why not." She turned to the side. "Emma talks only about the life of man on *earth*, how best to achieve his fullest potential."

"She is aggressively atheist."

Gina shrugged. "I ignore that part. I leave to Emma the things that are Emma's."

"Is that a quote from something?" he asked, and that's when she turned back to him.

"Harry," she said, "for all your elite education, you sure

350

do have holes in the things you know. Have you never read the New Testament?"

"Why, have you?"

"Oh, Harry."

What did *that* mean, Oh Harry? In Concord, when they stopped at a train crossing, he took her hand, kissed it, turned it over, kissed the inside of her wrist, left his lips on her, closed his eyes, inhaled her. The car ride was both too short and too long. It was too much of one thing and not enough of another.

"You're just upset because of Archer," she said.

"If you know that, why do you keep upsetting me?"

"What am I supposed to say to him? He doesn't know about you and me."

"So tell him."

"What do I say?"

Harry was silent.

"That's what I thought." She pulled her hand away from him. "Train's passed," she said, turning her head to look out of the car.

She directed him to Lexington Road. They drove by a Ridge House guesthouse, which Harry made note of, just in case, before stopping at a yellow-washed, gabled Victorian with three pink chimneys, a covered wraparound porch and a rambling fence around the overgrown property. The plaque by the gate instead of a house number read simply "The Wayside."

Harry parked the car and stared at the plaque for a moment . . .

"The Wayside?" He turned to Gina. "The Alcott sisters' home?"

She pointed down the road to the nearby brown house. "That's theirs now."

"So who lives here?"

"Rose."

"Isn't this where Nathaniel Hawthorne lived?"

"Not for many years. Harriett Stone lives here now. She's known as Margaret Sidney, the children's book author."

"I thought you said Rose lives here?"

"Harriett lets her stay here when Rose is in the Boston area. She spends a lot of her time in New York—"

"Wait, this isn't—" Harry broke off. "Rose *Hawthorne*?"

Gina nodded.

"Nathaniel Hawthorne's daughter?"

She nodded again. "His youngest."

"She is a Dominican nun?"

"Yes, it was quite a big controversy when she and her husband publicly converted."

"For the love of God, Gina!"

If Harry was flummoxed in the car, he became completely tongue-tied when they were let into a neat, dimly lit house, where a smiling, bright-faced woman in nun's vestments and black habit rushed out into the entry hall and hugged Gina like she was her prodigal daughter.

"Rose, this is Harry," Gina said, pulling him forward.

He muttered something about very much enjoying her father's seminal works—none of which he could name at this crucial moment, of course. He thought Rose's eyes were too sharp, too smart to be a nun. She seemed to understand too much of the secular world.

"Thank you," she said, eyeing him, rolling the rosary beads between her fingers. "So *you're* Harry."

He gaped at Gina, who turned her back to him, and whispered a quiet explanation to the nun.

The Scarlet Letter, that was one. *The Blithedale Romance* and *The House of the Seven Gables* two others . . . Damn the brain. What did she mean, So *you're* Harry?

Rose was a small woman, and after looking up and listening to his tall, lithe lover, all the while patting Gina's face and arms, Rose came over to Harry. They were still standing in the vestibule. "My father wrote many wonderful things, didn't he?" she said. "I wish he were alive to write more. I was thirteen when he died."

"I lost my mother when I was thirteen," said Harry.

She studied him intently as if they shared a vital bond. "That's a lot of pain for a boy to carry, losing his mother."

"Yes."

She made the sign of the cross on him. "Shall we go visit dear Josephine, her whole life a servant of God and man?" She put on her cloak and bonnet and took with her a small Bible lying on a shelf by the mirror. "But please don't drive too fast," she said. "I'm not used to these horseless carriages. Everybody keeps telling me they're the future. I prefer a bicycle."

"I should think it would take a few hours to get by bicycle from Wayside to Water Street in New York," said Harry.

Rose laughed. "He's funny, Gina," she said. "Very good." As if it were Gina's doing that he was funny!

In the car, Rose climbed into the passenger seat, while Gina tried to arrange herself in the mother-in-law seat which faced outwards to the road and was nothing but a tiny saddle. She had to fold her gazelle limbs in and was virtually crouching.

Harry took one look at her and gave her his hand. "Come," he said, pulling her up. "You can squeeze in with Rose and me in the front." Was he being chivalrous, or was he just afraid of sitting by himself with Nathaniel's daughter? What if she spotted holes in him too with her keen Hawthorne eye?

Concord was less than twenty miles from Boston. On the way, Rose told stories of Josephine's tireless work for the women of New York for the last twenty years. Her National Consumers League had made the workplace a much safer place to be for men and women. "She is the main reason there are no sweatshops in New York anymore," Rose said. "The women live longer, work fewer hours, get more pay for the hours they work." She also created the House of Refuge for Women, Rose said, which gave young wayward girls some useful skills and got them off the streets. Harry wanted to see his friend Ben, yell to him, Benjamin, do you hear this, Nathaniel's daughter loves your Aunt Effie.

He asked her how she knew so much about Josephine.

"I live in New York for much of the year," Rose said. "And you can't live in New York and not know about Josephine Lowell. But tell me about yourself, Harry. Gina tells me you're a professor of economics?"

When did Gina tell Rose this, Harry wondered, glancing at an impassive and composed Gina sitting between them. "Adjunct professor," he corrected her. He didn't want to lie to a nun, of all people.

"And you're completing your doctorate this year?"

"Slowly, but yes," he said, as if in a confessional. He hoped they would get to Back Bay sooner rather than later. He didn't want to hazard what else he would have to divulge to the nun if she asked.

"Gina tells me you're quite progressive in your politics."

What did that mean? "I suppose so," he drew out. "But only if it's good to be progressive in your politics."

Rose laughed gently. "I believe very much what my father believed on this issue," she said, "that no matter how lofty our objectives, the only true reformation should begin and end with the human heart. Without the slow progress of

354

conscience on that score, all our other projects will be doomed to fail."

"I agree with you wholeheartedly," Harry said.

"Do you?"

"Why, yes. In my dissertation, I extrapolate at length about this very thing." He took a breath as he drove carefully, not to jostle the divine sister. "Form follows function. Content follows form. But form lags for a while behind its content. So first our external conditions must change. And then our ideas, habits, customs and beliefs will change accordingly."

Rose looked at him bemused. Glancing sideways at Gina, she said, "Hmm. That's actually the opposite of what my father meant."

Harry frowned. His hands tightened on the wheel. He wasn't going to argue with a nun, but he was convinced they had been talking about the same thing.

"What I think is," Rose said, "that the passionate improver of mankind through the false means of external conditions will more often than not turn out to be the destroyer of souls."

"Oh, look," Harry said. "Here we are. Clarendon Street. Why don't I let you off on Commonwealth, while I go find a space to park?"

They waited for him on the cool and darkened street.

Once inside the house, Harry wanted Gina to wait in the hallway, but didn't know how to say that to her. He said, "Let Rose go in by herself. We'll wait here."

"Don't be silly, child," Rose said, beckoning them both. "Come. Do God's work and sit by the sick."

On the first floor of Ellen's narrow corner brownstone, Josephine lay in the parlor room in a makeshift hospital bed. No more Anti-Imperialist or the New York Consumer League. In her own refuge for women, Josephine, reduced and diminished, half a Josephine, looked like she was sleeping. Rose went up to her, whispered, prayed, said *Josephine . . .* and the sick woman opened her eyes. She was too weak to sit up and greet her distinguished visitor whom she recognized immediately; nor did Rose desire it. Josephine's eyes traveled around the room. Imperceptibly, Harry stepped slightly in front of Gina as if to shield her from view. Josephine's gaze stopped on Harry, traveled from him to the groomed Italian woman standing next to him, and darkened.

"Harry, is that you?" she said, attempting to sit up and failing. "You naughty boy. You haven't visited me in over a month, and now you come unannounced and bring guests? Rose Hawthorne of all people? How are you, Sister Alphonsa? I'm happy and yet desperately unhappy to see you at my side."

Rose took Josephine's hands into her own. The nurse standing nearby made a throaty sound, and pointed, she thought surreptitiously, to the plastic gloves that covered her hands to the elbows. Rose's expression hardening, she caressed Josephine's arms up and down with her bare hands, and said to the nurse, "Can you please go make us a spot of tea? With honey and lemon. And for your future information, cancer patients are not contagious. Not the least bit so. You may remove your gloves with impunity."

Josephine watched Rose with respectful bemusement. "How can you be sure?"

"Eight years of experience."

"Next you'll say lepers are not contagious."

"Oh no, they are, quite," Rose said calmly. "We still don't wear gloves when we minister to them." She perched on Josephine's bed, not letting go of her hands. Harry and Gina continued to stand at the foot of the bed. Josephine continued to eye Gina, much the way Rose had just eyed the fastidious nurse. Cold seeped into her ailing gaze, a judgment. This didn't go unnoticed, not by Harry, not by Gina—and not by Rose, who, kneading her rosaries, opened the Bible and said, "Gina is the reason I'm here. She asked me to come, to pray with you. Shall we pray?"

Josephine closed her eyes.

For ten or fifteen minutes, Rose's lips moved loudly, inaudibly, in a tidal cadence. No one else spoke. Josephine lay without reaction.

"Effie," said Rose, "how old are you, dear one?"

"Sixty-one."

"So young. I am fifty-four. I thought you were a New Yorker. Why are you here?"

Josephine opened her eyes, stared accusingly at Harry, then at Rose. "Why are *you* here?"

"To help you."

"But I am not impoverished."

"No. You are rich with love. Look at Harry who's known you for fifteen years. Look at Gina Attaviano, who has met you once and yet went in the night to Concord to bring me here for you. You should go home, Josephine. Go home to New York. Your mother awaits you. Your other loving sisters. We'll transport you. You need the rest of your family with you now. And they need you."

Josephine shook her head.

"I know you don't want to burden them. But you must go home to your daughter. Carlotta knows you're a good woman. Now show her what a strong woman you still are."

"I do not feel strong. Not particularly good."

"You are both. I can arrange for you to be transported back."

"No, I can't move from this bed."

"You can," said Rose. "I've seen a lot of sick people. It's not yet your time."

Josephine looked at quiet, kind Rose, with her serene voice, and hope mixed with something else flickered in her eyes. "You know my daughter is not in New York," Josephine said, nodding toward Harry. "She is here in Boston. As is my sister, Ellen. As will be her son, Ben, who is, as we speak, on his way home from Panama. We are all here for this boy's imminent wedding."

Harry's stomach dropped out from under him like he was falling. He held his breath and said nothing and looked at no one.

Rose turned her steady gaze on Harry, and on motionless Gina by his side, who was clutching the footpost of the bed. "The wedding is not until July, I believe," Rose said slowly, turning her gaze back to Josephine. "Your illness has imposed limitations on you that make you struggle. One nurse is not enough, I can see that by her exhausted demeanor. The last thing you need right now is conflict. You should be with the sisters who can care for you around the clock. Why don't you come stay at our home in Concord? Carlotta can take you there."

"I thought you ran the Rose Hawthorne Home for Impoverished Women?"

"It's called Rose's Home," corrected Rose. "For the sickest of the sick and the poorest of the poor." Rose stood from the bed. "You want to be loved? That's where you go."

The drive back was silent. "Josephine is a remarkable woman," Rose said to Harry. "You must forgive her."

"Nothing to forgive," said Harry. He wanted to say that if only he were a woman, and incurable, he might like to go to Rose's Home where he might be loved. He felt precious little of it in his car at that moment. Gina had not uttered a word.

"Harry," said Rose, when they were almost at Wayside, "have you had the opportunity to read my father's stories, either 'Earth's Holocaust' or *The Marble Faun*?"

"I haven't had that opportunity, I'm afraid."

"In *The Marble Faun* he writes that sin, for all its consequences, may be enlightening. Because although it burns, it wakens."

"Well, here we are," Harry said, pulling up to the darkened gate and pulling on the brake. He thought a moment and then turned the ignition off. "Let me walk you inside."

"One can pretend sin is a theological sham," Rose said to him, as she hopped out of the Curved Dash, "but only at one's own peril. Goodnight, Harry. Gina can walk me inside. Come with me, Gina."

Harry got out of the car, helped the women out, though one of them was an icy woman and did not take his proffered hand. He closed the gate behind them, taking care to close it quietly, not slam it, climbed behind the steering wheel and waited. For one second, maybe as many as ten, he contemplated turning the crank and driving away. It was a moment that would remain with him for many years to come.

2

Gina got back in the car, and he could almost hear her wondering if she should climb into the child's seat in the rear so that she wouldn't have to sit next to him. But she stayed put. So did he.

"Well, are you going to get going or not?" she said. "I've got early classes tomorrow. It's nearly 10:30 already."

He sighed. "That's all you have to say to me?"

"There is more to say?"

He turned the crank, drove down the block, but didn't get far before she spoke.

"Were you *ever* going to tell me?"

And he told her the truth. "No."

"You were going to just get married and say nothing?"

"I didn't know what to say."

"So your plan was to say *nothing*?"

He said nothing.

"Rose is right, sin burns, yet wakens," Gina said. "How fallen do you have to be, Harry Barrington, to live like this and yet shamelessly demand from me every day why Archer, my good and faithful friend, keeps coming by?"

Harry allowed himself a pretend casual shrug. "I feel what I feel," he said. "That I can't help."

"You know what you *can* help, though?" she snapped. "How you act. How you carry yourself. What you show to the world."

"I didn't know what to do. This caught me by surprise." You caught me by surprise.

"*What* caught you by surprise, Harry?"

"I'm sorry you had to find out like this."

Now she laughed, falsely hearty. "For *that* you're sorry? Harry," she said, and he could only guess at the expression in her eyes since he couldn't face her. "Just so you know, you were the *only* one who was surprised by tonight. I've known all along."

He shook his head in disbelief.

"Oh yes. Since before you ran into me at Harvard. I read all about your impending nuptials in the newspaper announcement last March. I knew about it. Sophie too. Miranda and Julia. Rose—yes, even she. My mother knew about it. Angela. Salvo knew about it. You don't want to know what he had to say when he found out *whom* you were marrying. *Everyone* knew, Harry," she said. "The only one who seemed *not* to know about it was you. Are you surprised you're getting married? Has it sprung on you like a leak?"

They sat. He reached out to take her hand, and she yanked her whole body away from him, nearly falling out.

He caught her by her upper arm, brought her to him, held her. "I have no life," Harry said. "Don't turn away from me. Don't pull away. You know, you *know* I can't take one breath in a day that doesn't have you in it."

"Don't try to win me over now. What's the point?"

"Don't be flippant with me, Gina. You flung yourself into my heart, poured yourself into me like magma, don't pretend what I'm saying is false. You *know* that my first thought and last thought and every thought in between is you."

"I asked you to stop. This isn't helping."

"You're right, you will be the ruin of me."

"I don't want you . . ."

"Don't speak."

"Harry, you're getting *married*!" Gina cried, with shaking hands, trembling lips, a quavering voice. She lunged at him, flung her arms at him. "In three weeks you're going to marry another woman! You're going to marry Alice!" She put her face into her hands and sobbed.

"Gina," he whispered to her on the dark street, under the lamps all burned down, on an avenue so quiet they were the only two people awake. "I cannot marry Alice."

"And yet . . ."

"I can't *not* marry Alice." He groaned, doubling over the steering wheel.

She groaned too. They sat apart, speechless in their misery.

361

He began to speak, but she shook her head vehemently to cut him off.

"I just want one day of strength," he said. So I can know what to do.

"Who's going to give it to you, Harry?"

"You."

"You're wrong. You can't ask your lover to be your judge. I'm not the one to give you strength. You don't give me strength. You make me weak. You haven't prayed a day in your life, have you?"

"When my mother died was the last time."

"What did you pray for?"

"That it wasn't so."

"Well, you might need a little of that praying spirit now," she said. "Because this is so."

"Gia, *please*."

"You want me to give you strength? All right," she said, folding her arms over her heart. "Here it is. Drive me home. Let me off at the Fenway, say goodbye, go home to Barrington. Don't look back. Never even think back. Blow me a kiss as you leave. That's how you do it."

"You know that's impossible."

She expressed her doubt in an anguished cry. "You are Harold *Barrington*! That's the truth of who you are. And I'm Gina Attaviano from Belpasso. That's who I am. My father the barber scolded me to remember where I came from. So I give you a little bit of his wisdom. Remember where you came from, Harold."

"Did you not hear when I said to you that you have left me for a blank?"

"You're afraid of me," she said suddenly. "You're about to marry another woman, you're five minutes from walking down the aisle with her and you are too afraid to tell me!

You're afraid of your father. Harry, you've spent your life being afraid. God help you. Don't choose, don't even *think* about it. I'm telling you what to do. Go do what you were born to do. Go do what you were meant to."

"You don't mean it."

"With all my heart," said Gina. "Don't fracture yourself for me. You aren't mercury." She didn't bother to wipe her face. "You can't form back into a whole. Your fragmented self won't put itself back together." But she was crying desperately.

"You want me to marry someone else?" he yelled.

"Yes!"

"You mean that?"

"Yes," she said, weeping into her sleeve, her shoulders heaving. "Because my love is greater than my selfishness. You can't be divided. You have to remain whole. That is my commandment. *That* is what Rose Hawthorne was counseling you."

"What do *you* want?"

"I want you to marry Alice," she said, not looking at him. "You can't humiliate her three weeks before the wedding. She doesn't deserve it."

"You're mad, you've gone mad. You think *this* is the sin? What about living a life that's a fraud from morning until night? That's not a venal sin? Corruption, deceit, pretense, hypocrisy, what do you think all that is?"

"Better than what you're contemplating," she said. "I see through the glass darkly to the other side."

"You don't love me," Harry declared. "No woman who loved a man could say this."

"You're right," she said, shaking. "*Io non ti amo.*"

Stunned, he sat and watched her turn away from him, her face covered.

Grabbing her arms, he squeezed them, shook her wrists, shook her, took her wet face into his hands. "It's too late for this grievous wrong," he said, pressing her to him. "You knew what you were doing, like gunpowder setting yourself off inside my heart, you knew it when you danced naked into my revolution. Well, this is what revolution looks like, Gina. It's violent. It destroys things in its path. It eats its own children. It makes the same mistakes as the generation before it. It wastes, and profligates and breaks apart the things that were whole. *That* is what a revolution is. That is what revolutionaries do. After you've taken my whole heart, you can't tell me this isn't what you want. You can't unstorm the Bastille. You can't uncross the Rubicon, you can't disarm the Colonials. This is your path to freedom. Me. Now get up and walk it."

"No," she said, barely audible from weakness.

"Walk it," he said, pressing his fingertips into her shoulder blades, "or throw yourself from the fucking bridge."

"I will not prove my love for you with false choices or false miracles," she whispered.

"You just told me you didn't love me," he said. "You told me you want me to marry someone else."

He released her then, let her go.

"Is this what you meant," she whispered, "when you called it '*violent*' catastrophe?"

He sat there mute. "That's not what I called it," he said at last. But that's what it was.

"I am yours, through and through." She was barely audible through her swollen mouth. "I always was. You never asked me, because you didn't want to know, but know this—everything in my American life I did for you. Everything. If you only knew a quarter of the truth."

She curled herself into a ball, her back to him. He drove

her home, and when they stopped in front of the gate to the residence halls, nearly closed for midnight curfew, she didn't speak, just stumbled out of his car and staggered onward.

He tipped his hat as he watched her go, blowing her a kiss, wishing for the high bridge himself, for instant oblivion.

Chapter Seventeen
THE MARBLE FAUN

1

"Darling, I picked out two hymns, but I thought you could select a couple yourself and we'd narrow it to your favorite and my favorite?"

"What hymns?" They were standing inside the Algonquin Club ballroom looking at the arrangements of tables. Rather, Alice was looking. Harry was there in body only.

"Yes. I don't know what your favorites are."

He pretended to think. "How about 'Are You Washed in the Blood'?"

She pretended to be aghast. "Harry! You're joking, right?"

"Why?" he said with a straight face.

"For our *wedding*?"

"Oh." He thought. "How about 'Till the Storm Passes By'?"

She gave him a quizzical look.

"'In the Hour of Trial'?"

"If you're not going to be serious . . ."

"I gave you three suggestions and you don't like any of them."

"I picked 'The Voice that Breathed over Eden' and 'Oh Perfect Love.'" She took his hand.

He forced his mouth into a smile. "See how easy that was? We'll go with your choices then."

A beaming Alice moved on to the guest list. "The District Attorney, the Honorable Mr. Pritchard, should sit at the table close to us in the center, don't you agree?"

"Who? Oh. I suppose."

"And you said earlier you might have found two extra ushers?"

"I said that?"

"Yes. Remember I told you I have twelve bridesmaids, but you have only ten ushers?"

He tried to remember. "I told you, you had to cut two of your maids loose. Ten is tops, Alice. No more will fit in the church."

"They stand behind us." She giggled. "Silly. We can fit fifty."

"Heaven forfend."

"I can't cut two of my friends. They'll be very upset."

"And I can't, as a last-minute invitation, suddenly ask two men to attend a wedding. Everyone else was invited eighteen months ago." He lowered his head in shame.

She sighed. "I know, darling. We've been planning this a long time. We're almost home."

"Tell two of the ones you like least," he said, "that you'll buy them a new dress as recompense. And they'll still be invited to the reception."

"I don't know. I'll see." She chewed her lip. "Did you remember to order your gifts for the ushers?"

Now it was his turn to chew his lip. "No."

"Harry! You're running out of time. Do you know what you're going to get them?"

"No."

"Oh my goodness."

"What? I suppose you already have the bridesmaids' gifts?"

"The gifts for the rehearsal *and* the wedding. Of course. Weeks ago. My maid of honor Belinda gets a pearl brooch. Very fancy. How about a humidor?"

"For Belinda?"

"For your ushers, silly boy."

"What's a humidor?"

"Harry! What are you going to get for Ben?"

"A mosquito net?"

They stood as if at an impasse in the middle of the vast room with floor-to-ceiling windows.

"I thought we could sit under a shower cascade of white and crimson roses?" Alice said, pointing. "Wouldn't that be lovely? Over our bridal table?"

"Yes, if you like."

She squeezed his hand. "Did you get me something beautiful?"

"Did I get *you* something beautiful?" he repeated. "Like what?"

She tutted. "You are such a joker," she said. "Maybe you should try for a career at a carnival instead of a college. Have you decided where Ben and Mr. Veer should take you for your bachelor evening?"

"When Ben gets here, he can decide. Or the Dutchman will choose, but Ben won't like it."

"Oh no, Harry, I *really* hope you're joking this time. You

know you had to reserve a place weeks ago. Ben couldn't do that from Panama. You're joking, right?"

"Of course, dear." He walked around the tables, in a haze.

"We will have a Viennese dessert hour at midnight," Alice cooed. "The chef will make Bananas Foster on the spot. Ben will be pleased."

"Why would Ben care?"

"Um—because of the *bananas*?"

"Oh."

"Harry, what's wrong with you today?"

"Today? Nothing." A grimace contorted his lips. "So much to think about. Why Viennese hour? Don't we have a bridal cake ten feet high?"

"Because it's beautiful at midnight to have a buffet of sweets with the violin quartet serenading us." Lightly she grazed his cheek. "Don't worry, darling," she murmured. "Oh, and about the flowers . . . I thought of having not just ferns and palms at the church, but also Japanese maples and Himalayan blackberries, tied with ivory satin ribbons, and then to cap it off, lilies of the field!—to symbolize our humility," she explained. "And white sweet peas. Sarah said sweet peas smell terrific—the Book of Life began with the man and woman in the garden full of flowers . . ."

"And ended with the Revelations," Harry said blackly.

"What?" Alice frowned. "Oh, before I forget, please don't forget to invite George Lyman to your bachelor evening. Because my friend Clara is hoping he will get the hint and follow suit, right after us. Oh, darling, I don't know what I'm more excited about, the wedding itself or our two-month-long wedding trip to Europe." She lowered her voice and looked around before she proceeded. "Or perhaps just the wedding night?"

Harry, who was touching the white linens on the tables,

stared grimly at her. "Hold on about the wedding night a moment," he said, also lowering his voice. "We are having a wedding to which five hundred people, including the Governor of Massachusetts, are coming, and you stand here and talk about humility? Perhaps the lesson of the lilies is lost on you, Alice."

Color drained from her cheeks as she searched his closed and cold face. "The Archbishop of Boston is going to marry us," she said in a tremulous voice. "You think that's too much?"

2

Harry was rushing, late for an appointment and then the train to Chicago, when Louis knocked on his door.

"I can't right now, Louis. Whatever it is, it's going to have to wait." He still didn't have his tie on or his belt. He was taking a surreptitious bag with him, and didn't want Louis to see it. He pushed it with his foot behind him and stepped forward toward the open door.

"All right, sir. But you have a visitor downstairs."

"I don't have time for a visitor, Louis. I just told you. I am egregiously late. Who is it?"

Louis's eyes were twinkling. Harry bolted past his semi-retired butler and took the stairs three at a time.

In the parlor room, Ben waited.

Harry must have looked shocked to find Ben at his house. Even as they hugged, Ben laughed. "Harry, why are you looking at me as if you've seen a ghost? I'm Ben. Benjamin Shaw. Remember? Your best friend."

"How could I forget?"

"Also your best man. You remember that part too?"

"Also hard to forget." Like the assembly line full of robots that Henry Ford was foolishly trying to string together, Harry repeated key sounds to try to pretend there was logic in his speech pattern, all to cover his terrible confusion.

"Why do you look as if I've drained your blood? Where's your sister? Is she happy I'm back?"

"Happier than she has any right to be."

"We should all go have lunch. I'm starved."

"Ben, I . . . I'm so sorry. We have so much to catch up on . . ."

"I'll say." Ben was thinner, tremendously tanned. His drawn face was now framed by a trimmed and neat beard. He still looked happy, but older too, and hardened, like he had gained wisdom through experience.

"You don't look as if you've had malaria."

"That's because you didn't see me when I had malaria. Though I will admit, I looked better than you do right now."

"How are you feeling?"

"I'm not contagious, if that's what you mean. Esther!" Ben called happily up the stairs.

"She's not here. She had to . . ." Harry looked around in desperation. His sister could save him. "Esther!"

"She is not here, sir," Louis said. "She went to town to buy a new purse for the wedding."

"Esther needs a *purse* for the wedding?" said Ben. "I find this peculiar."

"Many things are strange, you're right." Harry cracked his knuckles tensely. "But Ben, right now I've got an appointment that I simply can't skip. I never would've made it had I known you were coming."

"Old friend, what do you mean? You *knew* I was coming. I sent you a telegram, telling you I'd be arriving on the 25th of June. Which is today. And you sent me one back saying you would meet me at the Freedom Docks. Do you remember?"

Harry did not remember. He didn't want to admit to Ben that upon receiving his telegram, he promptly sent Clarence to compose a reply. Clarence did as he was told, but the downside of delegating this sort of thing meant that Harry had no knowledge of what he had agreed to.

Right now he was painfully aware of the date. And of the train bound for Chicago in two short hours.

"Have you ever known me to pay attention to dates, times?" Harry smiled, pacing like a restless stallion about to be let loose in the wild. "Please have lunch with my sister. You'll make her day. She's been waiting and waiting."

"No, she hasn't." Ben laughed. "Why do you always make up stories?"

"I'll be back in a while, and then we'll catch up good and proper. Are you staying with your mother?"

"My mother is living with another man."

"Doesn't answer my question, but yes. She is seeing Tobias. I met him a few weeks ago. Quite argumentative."

"For you to say that, he must be unbearable."

"Quite."

"She's living with him in the upstairs room, and down-stairs, my poor Aunt Effie has taken over the entire floor."

Harry's gaze clouded. Not noticing, Ben proceeded. "There is no room for me. Mother tells me I can sleep on the floor of their bedroom. I told her I had yellow fever and was terribly contagious. I was hoping you'd let me bunk here. Can Louis help?"

"We'd love to have you. Esther will be delighted. Louis will fix you up, talk to him. But loudly. Now . . . I must run. Forgive me?"

"Don't think twice about it. How is teaching?"

372

"Great!"

"How is Alice?"

"Excellent."

"Esther? Still married to that medical moron?"

"The head of surgical obstetrics who is upstairs putting on his socks and listening to your every word? Yes."

"How little I care for his title or his presence." Ben grinned. "Though I wish he weren't here. I don't want to hear him taking me to the woodshed about Panama and the mosquito hunters."

"Don't worry, he won't. He's never here."

At that moment, Esther walked in through the front door carrying five large bags. Harry groaned with naked frustration.

"Ben!" She dropped all the bags onto the hall floor.

"Esther!" He opened his arms.

They embraced like old friends. Esther patted Ben's back gently, and held on to him, for an extra moment or two. They kissed on both cheeks, stood and grinned at each other. Harry tiptoed past them on his way upstairs.

"You've gotten quite thin," Ben said. "Is it because you've stopped eating bananas?"

"That must be it. And you've gotten very tanned. I barely recognize you."

"I have no choice, standing all day long in mud under the sun."

She still held his hands. "I'm so happy you're back. Are you hungry?"

"I haven't eaten properly since the day I left." He smiled to let her know it was only partly true. She smiled back to let him know she knew. Food problems for the Panama Canal workers were legendary.

"Come with me, Benjamin. I'll have Bernard make us some lunch."

In his coat and hat, Harry, with a bag in hand, was squeezing past them in the hall.

"Esther, you look rather splendid," Ben was saying. "Like aristocracy. Marriage agrees with you."

"Does it? But you look so thin, Ben. It must be terrible down there. Why do you insist—"

"Esther, the man is starving," Harry called to her from the door. "Stop nattering and feed him."

Absent-mindedly Esther glanced at her brother. "Where are you off to again?"

"To see a man about a horse." He tipped his hat. "See you two later."

"Your friend just came five thousand miles!" She turned to Ben. "He is never home anymore. And I mean *never*."

"Harry," Ben called after him, "you'll be back for dinner? We have many things to discuss . . ."

Harry did not answer. He was afraid it was going to rain in Chicago, and had brought down a raincoat, carelessly throwing it over the umbrella stand, where it still draped, waiting for him. He was also out of words. He bolted out the door, in his best suit and shiniest shoes.

"Why are you taking a raincoat?" Esther called after him. "It's a beautiful day."

"Is it a beautiful day everywhere?" Harry called back, running down the steps to the street.

3

Esther wanted to sit in the formal dining room, just the two of them, but Ben insisted on the casual family dining area overlooking the back garden. Louis served them cold shrimp salad, asparagus with Hollandaise, mustard chicken, white wine, bread, butter, and a plum tart for dessert. Ben barely spoke for the first ten minutes, eating voraciously while Esther watched him.

"I'm sorry I missed your wedding," Ben said. He swallowed his food, and smiled. "Perhaps if you would've made me best man, I would've come, like now."

"I don't know what I was thinking," said Esther, waving off Louis and herself pouring Ben more wine and serving him more shrimp salad. "It was fine. It wasn't the ostentatious pageant you're about to witness."

"Did you go on a wedding trip too?"

"We did, but only to New Hampshire. Elmore had to be back for work. We had two weeks."

Ben shook his head. "Well, your brother, as always, couldn't have picked a worse time to get hitched, let me tell you. Our entire Panama operation is hanging by the bitterest thread, *and* I just found out my boss and staunchest ally, chief engineer John Wallace has handed his resignation to Roosevelt—while I was en route. What a nightmare."

"Resignation! Oh, no. Why?"

"I keep writing to you why. The whole thing is a complete shambles, that's why. It's barely held together with spit on paper. Everybody is always sick, there is no good food, sanitation is non-existent and the trains run on broken rails. Now that we're actually down there . . ." Ben looked skeptical. "And if I feel this way, me, the biggest proponent of the Panama experiment—I'm telling you, Est, the Americans are going to have another civil war over this, and this one is going to be worse than the last one. It's a good thing Elmore isn't here."

"Tell me about it."

"I know I'm going to catch hell for it from him."

"But Ben, you didn't have that many illusions, did you?"

said Esther. "All you did was study this for the Isthmian Commission before you went. You knew the terrain wasn't going to welcome your little digging experiment."

"Did I know about the mountains, and the lakes? Did I know about the river that needs to be crossed fourteen times if we're to build a sea-level canal? I think that's why my dear friend finally has had it. Roosevelt was demanding results—let the dirt fly and all." Ben scoffed. "Let the dirt fly indeed. We're digging, digging, and we know the railroad is too old to sustain the millions of pounds of excavated spoils, and the river keeps flooding, and the mountains keep sliding into the ditches we've just dug . . . Wallace finally threw up his hands."

"Have *you*?" Esther said quietly.

"What?" Ben blinked with exasperation. "Not yet. But only because I'm like my mother—a stubborn mule. I'm going to lose my job. You'll see."

She hid her excitement. "Because you came here for Harry?"

"No. Because I'm one of the few who is telling the president we can't build a sea-level canal."

"What?" Esther sat puzzled. "What other kind is there? A flying canal?"

"You're funny."

"You're the only one who thinks so."

"That's why they're bringing in John Stevens. He's a civilian, not Army Corps like we really need, but he cut his teeth on the Great Northern Railroad, he knows what he's doing. He says we can't build a sea-level canal either." Ben rolled his eyes and laughed lightly. "Poor Stevens hasn't even arrived yet, and is already having a fist-fight via telegrams with Congress, with the Army Corps and with the president himself about the best way to build the canal.

376

Mr. President prefers detonations through shale. It yields visible though impermanent results."

"When do you think you'll know if you lost your job?"

"But Stevens asked him," Ben continued, "do you want to build the canal in ten years or fifty? Because *that's* what's at stake. Do you want to spend two hundred million dollars or four billion? Because that's what's also at stake." Ben shrugged. "I give poor Stevens a year, two at most."

"Ben," she was concentrating, "what are you talking about? How can you build a canal that's not sea-level?"

"You're absolutely right." Ben spaced his hands on the table, three feet apart, palms down. "But what do you do when the left side"—he raised his left hand eight inches off the table—"is that much higher than the right side?"

"Sea-level is not *level?*"

"Correct. The Pacific has more salt. So it's less dense. It has stronger currents. So it's higher on that end and lower on the Atlantic side. The canal would have to be built much wider than we're planning, to accommodate the changes in the water flow. But there are mountains and a lake in our way."

"Ben . . . it sounds insurmountable," said Esther. "You know, I'm sure the Army Corps will transfer you back. There is so much you can do around here."

In a familial amused gesture, Ben patted Esther's constricted fist. "Est, you want me to leave too? Stevens will have no one left to help him. I'm the guy on the ground, the guy who's been there from the starting gun of American involvement. I can't quit now. Not when doom and failure are so close. Who will they blame when it all turns to dross?" He squeezed her fist. "Tell me about Harry. How has he been?"

"Good," Esther said. "Except . . . well, listen, it's hard to judge a man by the last two months of his life before a wedding. You know Harry. He has to think about everything for five years before he undertakes a project. He's like your Panama."

"What, he thinks the marriage is happening too fast? Too spur of the moment?"

"I don't know what he thinks. Probably he'd prefer to have finished with his doctorate."

"I thought he *was*! His deadline was in May, wasn't it?"

"He missed it," Esther said. "And asked for a July extension. But now it hangs over him. He's been working too hard and just seems . . . distracted by the details, what can I say?"

"So where was he running off to?"

"Who knows? He's been doing that a lot. Shopping for gifts? Last-minute things?"

"I've never known Harry to buy anything for anyone," Ben said. "Louis buys."

"Louis has not been buying," said Esther.

They had finished eating, and were sitting at the table at right angles to each other, their conversation waning. Ben said he was getting tired and perhaps if Louis made up a bed for him, he could have a nap before Harry returned.

Esther rang for Louis. "I'm happy to see you, Ben," she said. "Harry's really missed you."

"Yes, so much so that he bolts the day I arrive and even worse, makes friends with a Dutchman."

"Yes, well." Esther pursed her lips. "Vanderveer Custis is an acquired taste. I hope you will enjoy his company."

"Acquired taste like Elmore?" Ben said, lowering his voice.

"You don't have to whisper, Ben," said Esther. "Elmore is at the hospital."

"Oh, good." They both laughed. "You've been married now, what, two years?"

"Almost."

"Are you and Elmore planning to start a family?" Ben smiled. "I would like to become Uncle Ben to a little Esther."

"What about to a little Elmore?" said Esther.

"That would be quite insufferable," Ben said.

Esther smiled at first and then, very carefully, she shrugged. Her shoulders sank inward almost imperceptibly were it not for her words underlining her body language. "Man proposes, but God disposes," she said. "We haven't been blessed yet with a family. Though let's make a pact: when you become Uncle Ben, you'll have to move back home."

He took her hand. "Our pledge is iron-clad," he said. "I'll get sacked long before that. When I make my report to the president advising our solution to the sea-level canal, he'll come to Panama and detonate me himself."

Esther couldn't hide her delight with him. "What is your solution? Paving the canal with bananas?"

"Close. Building three concrete dams through which the ships are raised"—he smiled broadly—"and then lowered."

"Like a river dam? Ben, that's cracked. You can't do it."

"We'll see about that."

Louis entered the room, received his instructions, and promptly left to prepare Ben's quarters. "Will your father allow me to invite Mr. Vanderveer Custis for dinner tonight?" Ben asked. "He and I should go over our plans for the bachelor evening. Harry won't mind if we discuss it in front of him?"

"I think it would greatly amuse him," said Esther. "I'll see if we can contact Mr. Custis through the English Department. Go rest, Ben, please. Harry will be back in an hour or two."

4

"I never cease to marvel at the beauty of this church," said Irma as they stood in the entrance to the enormous St. Paul's Episcopal Church in Brookline and admired the pews and the altar. "Look at the opal glass windows, the stained glass stations of the cross. It's stunning." She glanced lovingly at her tense and distant daughter. "And you in white silk with a tulle veil, and a bow of white taffeta, holding a spray of crimson roses, why the whole thing will be like a painting!"

"Mother, could you please not change the subject? I've just told you, we have a serious problem." Alice clicked her heels in unison with her tongue as she walked down the center aisle counting the pews. "Harry has to see this, Mother. I need to bring him here immediately."

"There is nothing *to* do," said Irma, her consoling hand out. "Don't be upset. We'll fit everybody in as best we—"

"I don't know *how* we're going to do it!" Alice interrupted. "We have seating for five hundred and seven hundred are coming!"

"Alice, dear, you're getting yourself in a lather over nothing. They'll wait in the narthex. We'll open the doors."

"Mother!"

"What do you propose? We can't change the venue of the church at this late date. Everyone is coming here."

Alice folded her arms, and paced up and down the aisle. "Maybe we can remove some of the ferns, here and there, and take out these giant planters of lilies," she said. "Harry was right. They're completely unnecessary."

"The flowers are what people will remember."

"Well, perhaps we should have only invited the flowers," retorted Alice. "Because the entire church will be turned into an arboretum and there is *nowhere* for human beings to sit."

"Five hundred human beings will sit."

"If we throw away fifteen rows of flowers, we can fit another hundred."

"We can't throw away the flowers, child!"

"Oh, please. Of course we can. Let's put the flowers in the Algonquin. And in our house. We have seventy-five people coming for the wedding breakfast. Let's positively suffocate them with flowers. We'll give planters away as gifts."

"Darling . . . the church must be decorated with flowers," Irma Porter exclaimed. "It's not a wedding without the flowers. This is *your* Garden of Eden, darling."

"I'll be holding a bouquet, Mother," Alice said in a no-nonsense voice. "So will my bridesmaids. And let's give Harry an extra large boutonniere made from some of the flowers that are taking up all this precious room. Let's go and talk to the priest about it. Oh!" she lamented. "I wish Harry could help me. He'd know what to do."

The mother and daughter proceeded to the rectory.

"I haven't seen him around this whole week," said Irma. "Where has he been? He didn't even come for Wednesday dinner as usual."

"I know," said Alice. "To be frank, I haven't seen him either. Or heard from him. I think he is trying to finish his doctoral thesis before our wedding trip."

"I thought he was presenting that a few weeks ago?"

"He was, but he couldn't finish. He said he had too much on his mind—because of the wedding. He can hardly be doing doctoral work when we are soon sailing to Europe." Her whole face flushed with anticipation. "I wish we didn't have to come back so soon. Two months is not long enough, don't you think? We'll barely be able to spend two weeks in Italy."

"It'll be wonderful just as it is," said Irma. "The less time in Italy, the better."

"Oh, Mummy." Alice took her mother's hand while they waited for the priest. She tutted, suddenly remembering something else. "The string quartet maestro asked me if I wanted to keep them for the Viennese hour at midnight. But we'll already have a symphony band playing. I don't know if the quartet might not be nicer, though, at that hour of night."

"Ask Harry about that. Don't make this decision on your own."

"I tried, Mother! Yesterday Belinda, Alyssa, Clara and I all called on him in the late afternoon."

"And?"

"He wasn't home! Esther and Ben were there and Esther said he was out. But she said it oddly. I asked if I should wait. She thought about it for ten minutes and then said, I don't think so. Not no. But I don't think so."

"So what did you do?"

"We waited a little bit. They were quite hospitable and funny. Mr. Barrington came home, and we had a wonderful evening. He is such a nice man."

"Yes." Irma's face was expressionless.

"At dinner Ben entertained my friends and Esther by making everybody laugh. Then he and Elmore got into a tremendous fiery discussion about Panama to the delight of all, especially Mr. Barrington. Elmore called Ben a ditch-digger. Ben called Elmore a mosquito-hunter! We didn't leave until nine in the evening."

"What—and Harry didn't show up all that time?"

There was just the slightest pause.

"No."

"And no one spoke of it?"

"Not a word! As if he didn't live at the house. No one even mentioned his name."

"So what did you talk about at dinner? Besides Panama."

"The wedding of course! We've been talking about nothing else for two years."

"The wedding without mentioning Harry? That's quite a feat."

"Well, we mentioned him in his role as the bridegroom. As in, how much of the bridegroom's tuxedo and morning coat should be white? Should his waistcoat also be white? Could Ben make sure Harry's patent leather shoes are shined the night before? Has he picked up his silk black hat? And what does the bridegroom think of the 'Strains of Lohengrin Wedding March' instead of Mendelssohn's?"

"All without mentioning Harry's name?"

"Yes! And no one said, oh, look at the time, I wonder where Harry is. Mr. Barrington regaled us with stories about the people who were traveling from all corners of the globe to see his son get married. Colonel MacKenzie, Mr. Barrington's personal friend is arriving all the way from California. And Judge Blackhouse, who apparently never goes to these things, is an honored guest. So is Supreme Court Justice Wendell Holmes. Mother, he asked me to play something on their piano. He said Esther hadn't played in a long time. It was a little out of tune, their Kimball, but I played 'Consolations,' and made only one tiny mistake. When I finished and turned around, Esther had tears in her eyes. Even Mr. Barrington looked a little misty." She straightened her spine. "Well, why not? It's a beautiful piece, Mother. So that helped pass the time. At one point, Rosa had to step outside for something and when she returned through the front door, Esther and Ben jumped nearly to the ceiling. When they saw it was just the housemaid, they sat back down like someone dropped potato sacks on their heads."

Irma was pensive. "Were they waiting for Harry?"

"I don't know. I found the whole thing unnerving. And as you see, without him we don't have answers to a dozen questions."

"Well, of course. You're having to make all the decisions."

"Yes!" Alice said, overburdened. "But he told me last week that he thought loin of pork *and* lobster Newburg was too much, and didn't go together. Yet he didn't come up with anything else. I told him, propose something else. You know what he suggested? Lasagna!"

Mother and daughter made an exasperated interlocution. "He will never stop with his jokes, will he?" said Irma. "Not even at a time like this."

"I know, Mother, I know. The other week we were going over the colors of the flowers and he asked why the roses had to be crimson. I told him, Harry, because of Harvard, remember? And he said, yes, but in a tone that made me uncertain he actually did remember. So, as a joke, I asked him if he'd prefer pinks and yellow organdies instead? And he said, why not?"

Irma steadied her anxious daughter. "Don't worry, darling. It's good he is letting you decide. Believe me, you need that in a marriage. You want him to be malleable, to do the important things how *you* like, not as he likes."

Alice agreed half-heartedly. "At least he's bought me a wedding present—finally. God, I thought he'd *never* get it done."

"How wonderful! How do you know this?"

"Because I couldn't take the suspense anymore. You know how I hate surprises. And to be perfectly honest," she said sheepishly, "I was a tiny bit afraid he'd forgotten. So I asked

Billingsworth. I begged him to divulge. And he told me that Harry had apparently bought an *exquisite* gold and diamond watch *and* a diamond necklace!"

The mother and daughter couldn't speak for a moment, in their excitement. "So when he finally takes the leap, he really goes overboard," said Irma.

"Doesn't he just, Mother! Oh, I really wish he could help me decide on these flowers."

Irma took her daughter by the hand and led her back inside the church hall. "We'll tell the priest we want to bring in more pews, darling, and remove the flowers as you suggested. I fully believe, the more people in the holy place to witness your triumph the better."

"I couldn't agree more." She kissed her mother in gratitude. "Oh!" Alice exclaimed. "What a brilliant spectacle it will be!"

5

In Chicago they stayed at the Palmer House on Monroe Street. The convention was for three days in the middle of the week, and they had bought tickets well in advance. Two hundred anarchists, socialists, radical trade unionists, opponents of the American Federation of Labor and Harry and Gina gathered in Chicago for one of the seminal events in the history of the trade union movement—the foundation of IWW, the Industrial Workers of the World—though Harry and Gina never left their hotel, barely left their hotel bed.

The Palmer House, destroyed in the Great Chicago Fire mere days after it opened in 1871 had been restored to its original opulence. Everything in that hotel from the lobby upwards was rebuilt on the grandest of scales. Harry told

Gina the hotel was the outcry of romance in the fight against the drudgery of daily life. "So we can forget our life for just a few minutes, and rejoice here as if there is nothing else."

"But Harry," said Gina, in his arms, "there *is* nothing else."

"There isn't much," he said, locked inside himself in a compartment that was becoming smaller and smaller. The lobbies had to get grander to obviate the airless quarters inside him, like steerage berths on a sinking ship. The guesthouses just weren't doing it any more.

It rained for three days in Chicago while the collectivist anarchists butted heads with the insurrectionary anarchists, and the anarcho-communists dueled with the anarcho-syndicalists. "Direct action" man Big Bill Haywood made an uneasy alliance with "ballot box" guy Eugene Debs while radical Lucy Parsons bitterly and publicly fought with revolutionary Tom Haggerton. Meanwhile Harry and Gina spent the rainy days allied in bed, smelted together, caught in their own insurrectionist downpour and venturing to the door to pick up the room service and the newspaper to read all about it. Italy, Iberia, Innsbruck were dots on the maps of their bodies that they kept connecting, drawing over with the piercing needs of their protracted couplings.

"Gia, do you care if I'm rich or poor?"

"Makes no difference to me."

"But all things being equal . . ."

"I'd like to wear a white hat and live in a house with two staircases."

"So you do mind. But what if I have nothing?"

"You have everything. It's I who've got nothing. Except you."

"What if there is nothing else but me?"

"That's all I want. It's all I ever wanted."

She wasn't answering his questions even though she was pretending to. She was giving him what she thought he wanted.

"Your father, was he poor?"

"Yes. But we always had enough. No more, no less."

"But what about his violins?"

"He built them only for America. We never touched the violin money."

"Until you buried him with it."

"But what a funeral he had. We carried him through the streets of Belpasso and the procession after him, three hundred people, all wept. The bells rang for him in ten churches."

"He was an amazing man by the sound of it."

"Yes, and careful with his money." She kissed Harry's neck, nuzzling him. "My father was a great proponent of having only one of what you needed. He wasn't concerned about having two combs, two belts, two handkerchiefs when only one would do. He had one pair of scissors for twenty years."

"I have never met a man like that. I wish I could have known him."

"Me too. But I learned from him, my darling. I'll be careful with our money. You'll see."

"I don't want children, Gina."

"Lord, of course not. Children? Nor me. Progressive women don't have children nowadays. It's just not done. You know what Emma says about children: they're soul-destroying."

"I'm serious."

"I'm more serious."

"Other people's children are nearly intolerable."

"Why qualify intolerable?"

"Quite right. But also I know women who suddenly mold their whole being around the new life that is forming."

"That would not be me, darling. I'm here to change the world."

"Children can't be the reason for your whole existence!"

"I couldn't agree more."

"Nor should they be."

"Harry, we are speaking the same language."

He saw her then, really saw her, her open Italian face, the shining black-brown eyes, the ready smile. "But you said you love me," he said.

"You are what I love most in life."

"If it weren't for me, would you *want* to have children?"

"Never," she said, adamant and fierce. "I didn't come to America to tie myself to babies. I'm my father's daughter. I have a lot to prove." Gina smiled. "We're too young. We will never be young like this. I want to have just us, Harry. I want to get my degree, I want to work, to travel. Do you know I've never been anywhere but Lawrence and Boston?" She giggled. "And Italy, of course. But there is so much I haven't seen. So much I haven't done. I want it all." She held his hand, lying happily in his arms. "I want it all with you."

He was pensive, pondering. "But Gia," he said with puzzlement. "What if *I* wanted children?"

"But you just said you didn't."

"But say I did. What if I told you I wanted children?"

She drew rings on his chest with her graceful fingers. "I would want what you want," she said at last. "That's the truth. Left to my own desires, I wouldn't have children. But if that's what *you* wanted, then I'd want to make you happy. *Perché ti amo.*" She stared at him in the big bed in Chicago

388

while down the street the anarcho-syndicalists were drumming out their historical grievances, making speeches, rousing crowds. "*Il mio cuore*," she said, "isn't that what love is? Trying to make happy the ones you love?"

"I don't know what it is," said Harry. "I suppose we're about to find out."

Chapter Eighteen
EARTH'S HOLOCAUST

1

THE train returned them to Boston late on Friday night, and after dropping her off at Evans Hall, Harry took a carriage and appeared at his own house in Barrington, stealthy like a thief. Everyone was sleeping except Louis, who was sitting in the drawing room, napping in a chair by the extinguished fire.

"Louis, what are you doing? Why are you up?"

"I was not up," Louis said, slowly rising, "until you woke me. Are you hungry? Do you want me to prepare a plate for you?"

Harry was famished. Louis knew this. He walked with the butler down to the basement where the kitchen was and sat at the cook's wooden table, while Louis set out the utensils and brought the plate of food he had left all prepared and covered.

Harry tore into the cold meat, some potato salad and bread. Louis stood by the door, waiting for Harry to finish.

"Are they angry?"

"I don't know what you mean, sir. Why would they be angry?"

"Are they upset with me?"

"Why would they be upset?"

"Are you playing games with me?"

"No, sir."

Harry put his plate in the sink and was about to go upstairs.

"May I just mention, sir, this is not the suit you left here in, five days ago."

Harry was wearing a much less smart suit, now wrinkled, a traveling suit.

"You're observant, Louis."

"I know your clothes, sir. I know your best attire when I see it."

There was no bow tie, no crisp white shirt with gold cufflinks, no polished patent shoes. "Yes, this definitely isn't it. Well, goodnight."

"Yes, goodnight, Master Harry."

The next morning he was awakened by shouting from downstairs.

"Louis, go get him immediately! What time did he come back? I told you to wake us as soon as he walked through the door, why didn't you do so? Louis, where did he say he was? What do you mean you didn't ask? Go wake him, right now!"

Harry spared Louis by coming downstairs. "Esther," he said sleepily. "Why are you shouting?"

"Harry!" Esther was red in the face. "Where on *earth* have you been? You ran out on Monday saying you'd be back in a little while." She hadn't even dressed, or done her hair. That was so unlike Esther. She looked pale and disheveled.

"I'm back now," Harry said calmly.

"Five days, Harry! That's not back in a little while! That's vanishing!"

Harry's father was in the family dining room, in his usual spot, drinking his tea by the picture window, silently.

"Where did you go? We were worried sick."

"To Chicago. Why were you worried? I'm a grown man."

"You went to Chicago." Esther repeated it dully. "Why?"

"For the IWW convention."

"For the *what?*"

Herman stood up from the table, from his empty cup. "Esther, enough. Harry, why don't you come into my office? Esther, dear, please get dressed. Ben is bound to be downstairs any moment. You don't want him to see you in your housecoat."

In Herman's study, father and son sat across from each other, separated by a giant wooden desk, not speaking. Harry's hands were on his lap. Herman's were on his desk. He was studying his hands, not his son. He looked through some papers, putting on his glasses to do so, then took the glasses off again and finally stared at Harry. "Billingsworth has been reporting to me some unusual spending patterns from you in the last few months," Herman said. "There have been odd expenditures here and there." Herman shrugged. "As you told your sister, you're a grown man, and it was none of my business. I thought soon enough you would have to answer to a number of new people. I didn't want to burden you with a pointless interrogation."

"Unlike now?"

"But with this latest," Herman calmly continued, "you're making it my business, unfortunately. Do you want to tell me what's going on?"

"Not really," said Harry.

"Why did you go to Chicago?"

"I don't know if you've read about it in the papers . . ."

"Please don't tell me you went to Chicago for the socialist conference."

"Industrial Workers of the World—but yes."

"Is that why you've been going to Portsmouth? And Newburyport? And Revere? Is that why I've been getting invoices from the Vendome? I'm surprised you've heard of the Vendome, much less been frequenting it."

Harry and Herman sat still. Time passed in ticking silence before Harry spoke. The study was quiet like a tomb, no sounds from the outside, no windows open, no creaking— just two beating hearts with a desk between them, a life, a past, a life past.

"I'm sorry, Father." Harry took a deep breath. "There is no good way to say it, no good way to tell you. But . . ." He broke off, collected himself again. Then exhaled and raised his eyes. "I don't want to marry Alice."

Herman was unmoved. "Is that what Chicago was? Cold feet? It's a little late for that, don't you think?"

"Is it?" Harry said quietly.

"The wedding is the weekend after next."

Harry sat motionless.

"Son, you've had eight years to vacillate." Herman was measured. "You're scared. That's understandable. I was terrified before I married your mother." They both lowered their gazes. They had never spoken of how that turned out.

393

"I'm not scared, Dad."

"Then what is it?"

Harry's mouth twisted. "I just don't want to marry her."

Herman nodded shortly, matter-of-factly. "You're scared."

"No. I just . . . I can't *marry* someone I don't love."

"Nonsense. Of course you can. And how could you stop loving someone *before* marriage?"

"What do you mean?" Harry frowned. "Better than after. Truth is, I never loved her."

Herman shook his head. "I don't believe you."

"I don't know how else to say it."

"Why would you agree to marry her?"

Why? Because it was the right thing to do? Because we were a good match? Because it's what everyone expected of me? Because our fathers have been in business together for fifteen years?

Harry said none of these things. He suspected his father knew most of the reasons.

Herman made a pacifying paternal gesture. "Son, maybe it's better that way. I loved your mother when I married her, and look." They stared into their separate spaces when Herman spoke those words. "You think your sister loves the dolt of a man she is with?"

"The dolt you foisted on her?"

Herman waved off the comment. "They're also a good match."

Harry didn't want to tell his father that had circumstances been different and Ben hadn't run off to Panama leaving his sister desolate, Esther would have never agreed to wed Doctor Good Match.

"You should have thought of all this before today."

"I'm not thinking of this today. You're asking me. I'm telling you."

Herman pondered, then shrugged philosophically. "Well, nothing to be done about it now."

Harry stood up. "Here's the thing, though," he said. "We have to fix it—"

"There is no fixing it."

"All right, but come a week from next Saturday, I cannot stand before the altar of God next to Alice. So I need to figure out what to do."

"If we're going to do that, figure things out, I mean, why did you get up right now as if you're ready to leave?"

Harry sat back down.

"Harold," Herman said in an even, no-argument voice. "I realize you're having a crisis, and I don't mean to"—he took out and stared at his pocket watch, then out of the window, at his son—"make light of your concerns. Certainly I don't have to remind you that seven hundred people are coming from all over this country and a number of others to share in your celebration."

"You don't have to remind me."

"Many of them are already here."

"How could I not be conscious of this," Harry muttered.

"What? Oh, yes. Conscious indeed," Herman said pointedly. "Josephine is surprisingly clear-headed for someone who is at death's door."

"How—how do you know?"

"I went to visit her."

Harry stammered. "When?"

"Two days ago."

"Why?"

"I went to visit her," Herman replied, "because she is sick and needed company. But also, we were very concerned about you, I don't have to tell you that either. You must have known what your infantile disappearance would do to your family, to Alice, to Ben. I went to see her because I thought she might know where you were."

"But she didn't."

"No. That part she did not know."

Father and son said nothing. Harry felt Herman's eyes on him but he'd be damned if he would meet his father's gaze.

"Your wedding, which we have been planning for two years, is the event of the summer, of the year—hell, of the decade," Herman said, gliding over fragile yet clear-headed Josephine like he was on ice skates, even though what was unsaid was like a glacier beneath his blades. "The wedding dress hand-made in Paris, the Grand Ballroom at the Algonquin, where dukes and princes marry, the field of exotic flowers, the first-class rooms for the attending guests, which, in case you forgot, include the Mayor of Boston, the President of Harvard, the Governor of Massachusetts, a Supreme Court Justice of the United States, several old and infirm authors, several critically ill friends of our family, and the Secretary of Defense!"

"I didn't forget," Harry said quietly. "I know all this. I'm very . . ."

"The details have all been taken care of," Herman interrupted. "Only one thing is left. And that is for you to walk down the aisle and wait for your bride." His voice thundered. "You *know* we cannot cancel it. This isn't a tawdry scandal, Harry, this is your life." He folded his papers as if the conversation was done.

But Harry knew it wasn't done by a long way. "I'm sorry, Father." He kneaded his hands. "Truly I am."

"Sorry for what?"

"Father, I can't m—"

"Harry, I have been more than patient with you, more

than. But in one minute I'm going to lose my temper. I called you in here not to argue as usual, but to talk some sense into you."

"It's too late for that, I'm afraid."

They stared at each other. After a long moment, a muscle moved on Herman's face. "Who is she?"

Harry said nothing.

"What? The cat got your tongue? Tell me. Shout it from the rooftops. If it's love, don't keep it a secret. Who is the girl?"

"You don't know her."

"I hope I do not. But who is the girl who brought Rose Hawthorne to Effie? Is she also a nun?"

"Father, please."

"Ah yes. I shouldn't think so. Harry, we might have to adjourn this meeting. You need time to think, and frankly I need time to calm down." He looked remarkably composed when he spoke.

Harry shook his head. "I've been doing nothing *but* thinking . . ."

"No, you've been doing other things." Herman raised his palm. "Harry, forgive me for stating the starkly obvious, but if you commit yourself to this plan of action, it won't be just me you will show contempt for. The humiliation will not be just mine and Esther's and yours. What about Alice? You might not love her, but why do you despise her and want to hurt her? She has been nothing but good to you. Her parents have treated you with kindness, like a member of their own family. Have you no regard for your friend Ben, who had to get special dispensation to take a month off work, just as crucial construction is getting underway on the canal and there are a number of personnel changes right above him? His job is in jeopardy because he took

397

time off to stand by your side. His time, his effort, Alice's wasted years, can't be just another black joke to you. I refuse to believe you can be that cold-blooded."

"I will make it right with Ben." Harry had to force these words out. He didn't know how he was going to do that.

"What about making it right with Alice?"

Harry shook his head.

"What about making it right with me?"

Harry shook his head.

"This isn't just your life that's going to be affected . . ."

"That's just it, Father. For everyone else, it's a five-minute gossip." He saw his father's face. "All right, maybe an hour's worth of idle talk."

Herman stood up. "Don't degrade me by reducing my reputation that I've spent a lifetime building to nothing more than a byline. Don't insult me. I've asked you to go and think about it. Are you refusing to do even that?"

Harry just shook his head.

"This has gone beyond the pale," said Herman. "This is no small rebellion or feisty upheaval. If you continue on this path, you will ensure shame for our entire family, for my brother and his children, for your sister, her husband— it will be a stain on our good name. Everyone who has been associated with you or with me will be tainted by this. This will destroy my relationship with Orville. You *know* there is nothing that will make it right."

"Father, it'll blow over. You'll see."

Herman continued to stand, looking at his son with an expression that could best be described as disgust. "You are doing this deliberately. I refuse to interpret it any other way. This is a malicious act on your part, knowing how many people you are going to damage, how many personal relationships, how many business dealings, how many friendships you're throwing away. This is an act of dismal disloyalty to your family."

Harry said nothing.

And then Herman's voice got lower and colder. "There are things you obviously don't understand. But since you insist that you're an adult, I'm not going to insult you by treating you like a child and explaining to you the simple things that every adult would know when finding himself in this situation. What I'm going to insist you do is leave my study and take stock of your life, of your future, of the duties before you. Come back to me tomorrow morning."

"Father, do you know what adults do?" Harry said, lifting his head. "They make their own choices."

"You understand nothing. This is not what adults do. Who ever told you this? Adults do two things—they work, and they face down their obligations. That's all. But yours is the common curse of mankind—ignorance and folly."

"I am neither."

"You are both."

"This marriage is not just about how I feel about Alice. It never was. I knew that. I accepted it. But I didn't care about it before."

"A week before your wedding is when you started to care?"

"Yes."

"And that doesn't seem malicious to you?"

"You can't choose who you fall in love with, Father," said Harry. "Or when."

Herman was utterly unpersuaded. "You can absolutely choose what you do about it."

Harry stayed silent.

Herman tried again. "You say you fell in love," he said,

"but you won't tell me who it is. You say you fell in love, but you've barely had enough time to take the girl out for a stroll down the Charles, much less to have a proper courtship. What do her parents say about this?"

"I don't know."

"Splendid. So you haven't discussed this with her family either. This affair is so serious that in the five minutes you've been dragging her to Seaside Cottage, you've managed to dishonor her too, taking no heed of her reputation such as it is—for she only *might* know, but I know *you* know that no self-respecting woman of any kind, of any stature, high or low, gives herself so freely to a man. Well done, Harold Barrington, my son. Well done!"

"Don't talk about her like that."

"What kind of family would let you take their daughter to hotels and guesthouses all over New England? Where is her chaperone, her own sense of *any* decency!"

"Father!"

"Don't *they* keep watch over their own daughter?"

"I won't listen to this anymore."

"Only to the sound of your own voice, eh?"

The fire of Harry's interior monologue must have been evident by the chill on his face. "I don't wish to discuss my personal life with you," said Harry. "I have no intention of submitting a list of her credentials for your approval."

"Does she have that long a list?"

Harry blinked. "This is not your little construction project in North End."

"No?"

Harry trembled. "No. You have no earthly idea, *none*, what I feel about her."

"Of course I don't! Why would I? How could I?" Herman was bitterly loud. "No one else but you has *ever* been in love! Why, they created the word just for you and your consort."

"Father!"

"And you can't have been feeling this deep and abiding love for long, Harry. The first bill from a bed and breakfast, or at least what I *hope* was a bed and breakfast, didn't arrive at my desk until late May."

"Oh, yes, how could I forget? Daddy still pays the bills for his grown son."

"And how has Daddy ever prevented his son from acquiring the responsibility to try to pay his own bills?"

"I *know* responsibility."

"Abandoning your bride a week before your wedding day after an eight-year courtship meets the strict moral code you've set up for yourself?"

"Father, I *won't* talk about this . . ."

"You will talk about this as long as you need to, to see the light."

"That will never happen."

"Ah!"

Both men fell mute with the strain of keeping close to the chest all the things they wanted to say and couldn't. "Look," Harry began, softening his voice, trying to sound more appeasing. "I'm *sorry*. All I can do is apologize."

"Bullshit. That's *not* all you can do."

"I will make this up to you, Father. I promise. I will—"

"Harold, if you go through with this," said Herman, "there will be nothing you could ever do to make it up to me. Nothing. I will not recover from your betrayal, from your act of vengeance, from your assault against me. Believe me when I tell you this. Know this to be true."

Harry stopped talking, and just sat and stared at his father. Herman squeezed his hands painfully together. "Son, please! Just think about what you're contemplating. We're a *week* away!"

"I know. I can only . . ."

"I asked you to think about it."

"I have."

"What, in the last five minutes?"

"I can't marry Alice, Father. The rest is immaterial. What more is there to think about?"

"Why haven't you talked to Ben about this?"

Harry became lost for words. He couldn't talk to Ben about this, and he couldn't tell his father why he couldn't talk to Ben about this.

"This isn't about Ben."

"It's not about Ben, it's not about me. Then what is it about?"

"God! How long must we keep at it?"

"Until you see reason."

"I saw reason. I saw it just in time."

"Harry, if you *insist* on having your own way in this, I must tell you—"

Harry stood from his chair. "Before you say another word, Father, let me stop *you*, please, so you don't waste your time trying to persuade me by all the considerable means at your disposal to force me to do the impossible."

"How can it be impossible?" Herman yelled. He actually yelled. "It wasn't impossible two weeks ago, it's not impossible now. Remember my law: Do the thing, and you shall have the power. But they who do *not* the thing, have *not* the power."

"I know your law well," said Harry. "And you're half-right, sir—it wasn't impossible two weeks ago. But," he added, "it is impossible now."

"Nothing is impossible."

"Oh, this truly is." Harry stood cold and composed. "And I mean this in the full Holmesian meaning of the word. Impossible, as in it cannot happen as planned, no matter what we say in this room."

"That's melodramatic and absurd—"

"And the reason for that," Harry continued calmly, "is because I married Jane Attaviano last Monday before we went to Chicago."

There was only a gasping, as Herman Barrington lowered himself into his chair. The grandfather clock ticked behind Harry. Everything else was ominously still—no noise, no wringing of hands, no gnashing of teeth. They weren't women, they were men. They were Barringtons. And when faced with shocking news, they turned to stone, and were silent like memories. In the room, the silence was broken only by the rustling of the paper under Herman's fingers.

"This is Salvatore's sister?" he said. "The Attaviano immigrant?" Herman said *immigrant*, but he might as well have said *simian*, that was the uncomprehending and disgusted tone he used.

Harry said nothing.

Herman finally got up, tall and proud behind his sixteenth-century solid walnut desk. "You have *greatly* disappointed me," he said to Harry. "There is really nothing more to say. And yet—this terrible, life-destroying choice was worth making."

"Life-creating," said Harry. "And yes. What does that tell you, Father? All these things laid out before me like bars in a prison, and yet I still chose her."

"It tells me you are a foolish, underdeveloped man. This is deeply unworthy of you. And yet somehow *you* feel elevated by the degradation. You've always struggled with

403

your duties as an eighth-generation Barrington, as a *Mayflower* descendant. You've always been impulsive, despite your paralyzing indecisiveness, and will do any stupid thing to satisfy what you perceive is your only real desire. You are not practical. You are unattractively selfish. You don't care about the people who love you, who you're supposed to love. You don't give a damn about your friends, you care not a whit about your family. These things should scream out to your chanty bride like a Hydra-headed clarion call. Yet somehow I don't think she sees this."

"You'd be right. And stop insulting her."

"Oh, you've already taken care of that. Why would you marry so precipitously? Have you abased her further, if such a thing is even possible, by making her with child?"

"No," said Harry. "I married her to take away *your* power to sway me with money." He stood straight, stood firm. "To take away your power to persuade me with inextricable obligations to your crown. To take away my own weakness at being threatened. I didn't want you to diminish yourself by blackmailing me into a loveless marriage for the good of all, and I certainly didn't want to lose respect for myself by being persuaded by your high-society, first Boston, arguments. I didn't want to *tell* you that I loved her and wanted to marry her. You would not have believed me. I had to ask myself if I was prepared to give up everything: my position and my purse. To convince you of the sincerity of my emotions, I am prepared to give up everything. I didn't want your counter-arguments to show me all I would have lost. I didn't want the balance of what is right for me to be decided by the strings, financial and otherwise, you hold over my head. By marrying her I removed your ability to control me, and my temptation not to lose what I want most." With satisfaction he folded his arms across his chest.

"Now our discussion, by necessity, can only be about the future."

Herman walked around his desk, past his son, and flung open his study door. "Your curse is folly and ignorance coupled with wanton pride, and never has that been more on display than this morning." He was ice cold. "Don't you understand anything? There will *be* no discussion. Because now there is no future. Leave my office, Harry."

"Why? Because unless you threaten me with destitution, you can't speak to me about things that matter most?"

"You don't know a blessed thing about what matters most." Herman no longer looked at his son. "Leave my house," he repeated. "And never set foot in it again."

2

It took Herman a full ten minutes after Harry walked out to collect himself to face Esther and Ben, who were anxiously waiting—obviously (by their tense demeanor) having heard snippets from the raised voices in his study.

Herman, impeccably dressed for the day, walked into the dining room and stood before his daughter and Ben. "I'm going to the bank," he said in a low flat voice. "I have some business to attend to. Esther, can I count on you to get in touch with Alice? Sooner rather than later, I would think. The poor girl is going to be devastated either way, but let's not compound her shame by not letting her in on the hoax perpetrated upon her."

"What are you talking about, Father?"

"Oh, have you not heard? We were loud enough. The wedding is off, I'm afraid," Herman said in his precise baritone. He stood straight, his gray eyes resolute and

405

inscrutable, betraying no emotion. "Your brother has decided that he would prefer not to marry Alice." Herman said it dispassionately but sharply, leaving his daughter and Ben to think about the word choice rather than the content.

"Oh my God," said Ben.

"What do you mean?" said a confounded Esther. "Harry has to pick up his wedding suit before five o'clock this evening."

"You'll need to call Stan and cancel that. Pay him, of course. Apologize for the discourtesy." He looked at Ben. "Benjamin," he added, "I'm sorry you had to travel all this way, but you know your Aunt Josephine is quite poorly. I saw her a few days ago and she barely recognized me. And I'm certain that your mother, who hasn't seen you in years, will be delighted to spend some time with you. I can write a letter to John Stevens on your behalf, if you wish. I know him a little from my railroad days with Flagler. So please— don't think of this as a wasted journey. Think of it as a family gain—for you. Go take Esther to the horse races, Ben. Elmore is always at the hospital. She'll appreciate the company. Right, darling?"

"Father . . ."

"Esther, the less said about this the better. I would prefer we did not talk about it at all. Soon I will have to insist on it, once the commotion has died down."

"What do you *mean*, he is not getting married?" Esther repeated.

"No," said Herman. "That is not at all what I said. Review my words."

Ben and Esther stared at each other dumbly.

"I said he is not going to marry *Alice*."

"You mean . . . he wants to marry someone *else*?" said Ben.

"Children, it's best you don't delve into this too deeply," said Herman. "I assure you, in it you'll find nothing but heartache. Just leave it be."

"Father, wait, please!" Esther jumped up, then became more dignified.

"It's no use," Herman said, "you trying to be a lady at a time like this. The most crass of all things has happened. And that's not even the worst of it. This is the time to let yourself go, Esther . . . We won't, of course. Because that's not who we are. I will add only one more thing, in case it's not clear—your brother is not to come back to this house. He is to be turned away at the door. I am never in, you are not receiving, the kitchen is not available, nor Louis, nor Clarence, nor Bernard, nor Rosa. From now on, you and I, Esther, will operate as if I don't have a son and you don't have a brother. He has turned his back on his family. Reluctantly but resolutely we will react accordingly. We will reciprocate in kind."

"Father . . ."

"Please call on Alice this afternoon. Promise me? Go with Ben. She'll need you both. And Ben, you might want to see your Aunt Effie sooner rather than later." Herman raised his eyebrows a little. "While she is still a quarter lucid. She knows some things she might be able to impart to you."

And then Herman put on his tall hat, took a little bow and left the breakfast room, speaking quietly to Louis and Clarence in the hallway, before he walked out the door.

A stunned Ben turned to a numb Esther.

"You know one reason why we can't build a sea-level canal?" he said. "Because it requires us to excavate one billion cubic yards of earth and sediment to reach sea-level all the way at the Continental Divide. And even if we do this, because of the monsoon season, six months out of the year, despite our continued detonations, the Chagres River becomes a muddy, raging torrent and ruins all our plans. And yet," Ben added, "it seems like a carriage ride in the sunny Common compared to what's happening here. Next time I will know better than to ever complain."

"That's it? That's all you have to say?"

"Rain, beloved Zeus," Ben said, raising his palms to the ceiling. "Rain on the cornfields and the plains of Attica."

3

Herman was still at his offices on Kenmore Avenue, just off Barrington's Main Street, past the white steeple church and the fine hotel restaurant. He was in the presence of Billingsworth and three of his lawyers when Orville bounded in, demanding to be seen. He had been panting in the carriage all the way from Brookline and he was severely out of breath now.

Herman slowly dismissed Billingsworth and the lawyers.

"Why would you allow this?" Orville bellowed to Herman, before the doors were fully closed and the lawyers left.

"Thank you, gentlemen," Herman called after them. "We'll finish up tomorrow morning. Shall we say 8:30?" From behind his desk he raised his eyes to Orville—round, perspiring in the early July heat with anger and his exertions. "I didn't allow this, my friend," he said. "This is not *my* doing."

"This *is* your doing!" Orville yelled. "This is the son you raised! How far is that apple falling from the tree?"

"I know you're upset, but do not speak to me that way."

"You expect me to speak politely at a time like this?" He was hyperventilating.

"Please calm down, Orville. You're going to give yourself an infarction."

"I wish I could be struck dead! Do you have any idea what my daughter is going through . . ." He couldn't finish. Getting up, Herman came around the desk to comfort him. But Orville recoiled, teary with hatred. "You raised him to do *exactly* what he wanted. You gave him options, you gave him freedom, you said his freedom to make the right choices was more important to you than anything!"

"I never said this, I never taught him this," said Herman. "You *know* that my whole life I have battled with him to teach him just the opposite. To teach him to balance with dignity on the tightrope between what was expected of him, what was absolutely required of him, and what he wanted. You know better than anyone, because we have talked about it enough times, that I tried to persuade him to see the third as a natural extension of the second and first."

"Oh and a fine job you did with your boy, Herman," spat Orville. "Do you remember what I said to you when you simply shrugged after learning he was going to teach for no money? I said to you then, pretending it's okay is going to hurt him in the end. It's going to make him think no matter what he does, it's going to be fine by you."

"I wanted him to get the rebellion out of his system," said Herman, "so that when he married your daughter, he could walk through that narrow gate proud."

"As I was saying"—Orville was choking on his words—"*your* decisions have made this debacle possible. Have you thought about my daughter? Have you thought about her even for a second? She waited for your disgraceful son for eight years! Now what does she do?"

"Alice is a lovely girl," Herman said. "She is going to be the talk of the town."

"For all the wrong reasons! What man is going to want her, knowing she was ditched at the altar days before the wedding?"

Herman paused to think. "I tell you what," he said. "Send out cancellation notices. Write that it was Alice who has decided to postpone the wedding indefinitely. Let this be *her* decision."

Orville's bluster subsided slightly, but not his anger. "You will pay for those cancellations."

"I have no doubt this is going to cost me plenty," Herman said. "But it's not about money, is it?"

"Why did he do it anyway? He is such a coward, your son. Nothing military about him, is there? Wouldn't even tell my daughter in person! Sent his sister!"

"No. Yes. I agree." Herman opened his weary hands.

"I feel sorry for you," Orville said. "I always envied you, having a son, *and* a daughter. I wished I could have had more children with Irma. But now I see—better to get it right once than to have many and raise them like you raised yours."

Herman had had enough abuse for one day. "Yes, my old and about to be former friend, but you might want to ask yourself," he said, "how you managed to raise a daughter that even a vulgar son like mine could cast aside."

Red in the face and wheezing, Orville swore. "This is the *end* of our partnership."

"More's the pity for you," said Herman. "Lots of trees grow in New England." He turned to the window to signal the meeting was over, the rancor, the relationship, everything.

"You always said expect nothing and you won't be disappointed," Orville said before he left. "How did that work out?"

"I don't know," replied Herman, staring at the dogwoods and the sugar maples. "That advice was for other people, not me. I expected everything, and yet look what I got. Still nothing."

4

She was waiting for him at Simmons. They went out onto the Fenway, holding hands while they strolled like lovers, kissing under the elms.

She asked for details and wouldn't rest until he had told her every nuance, reported every inflected syllable.

"Let's go see your father together," she said. "I will make it right. I will explain to him. I will say we love each other."

"You are crazy."

"We can't let him be upset, Harry. Let's go talk to him. I know parents. They get angry for a little while, for a day or two. But then . . ."

"Let's give him a day or two," said Harry. "A week if he needs it."

She didn't know what to do about Alice. She had counseled him to go and speak to her directly, though she knew how difficult that would have been. But she believed Harry owed Alice at least that much.

"What's the *most* I owe her?" He refused to do it, despite Gina's remorseful repentant pleading.

"Gina," Harry said, "I know what you're trying to do. You want their approval for what we've done. But we're never going to get it."

"Sure we will."

"Never. Do you think your family is going to make peace with us?"

She looked at him as if they spoke a different language. "Of course," she said. "They don't have a choice. They're my family."

"Hmm."

She told him not to worry, appearing wholly optimistic. Families sometimes reacted strongly at first, she assured him. Sometimes even overreacted.

He was skeptical.

"They *will* accept you, Harry, they will grow to love you. You're family now. That's stronger than anything."

"Are you sure about that?" Harry said. "We haven't been to see them. We didn't tell your mother we got married before a justice of the peace, not in a church. Your mother is going to be all right with that?"

Gina pulled up her shoulders as she pressed herself against his arm. They had left the Fenway behind and come out to the Charles, ambling lazily down the embankment. "She will be fine." She paused. "Eventually."

"What about when we tell them we aren't going to have any children?"

"This is what a modern marriage looks like," Gina said. "I will explain to them. They wanted me to be an American lady? Here I am."

Harry remained unconvinced.

Gina said she was certain that when Salvo and Mimoo learned that she had married Harry, and was now going to be a Harvard professor's wife and live in Cambridge while he became a doctor and taught economics and she finished her degree, they would feel that in leaving Italy Alessandro's dreams for his two remaining children had been fully realized. One was a successful restaurant owner, the other a professor's wife with her own degree. "That's such a fine thing to be." Gina was delighted and cheerful. It was warm, it was summer, she was a newlywed, her soul was filled with bliss, she told him.

"The only dark spot on it is for Alice," she said.

But even the prickling guilt of that couldn't keep her sad for long. She couldn't wait to get back home, to tell her mother, her brother, Angela, Verity, Mother Grace, all her friends at the mission the wonderful news; she wanted to celebrate with her family, and then, "in due time," to celebrate with his. She told him she had come from a long tradition of extravagant weddings, revelries that went on for days, food to feed half a county, drink to quench the thirst of the same.

Harry, exhausted, worn out by the disorder of the day, looked at her askance as she talked of dancing and feasts.

"That is not *our* tradition," he told her.

"I know that's not true. I read the details about your wedding in the *Observer*. Five hundred guests, Harry?"

"Seven hundred." Harry couldn't make her understand, nor did he want to. He wanted to be wrong, and found her infectious joy charming and more attractive than his own sour pessimism.

He told her they would wait and see. He smiled to let her believe she would be right and not he.

"In the meantime, we have to go eat and sleep somewhere," he said. "Where to now, my darling bride?"

They hadn't expected the harsh strength of his father's reaction; they hadn't planned for such a contingency.

She said, let's go back to the Vendome. We love it so. But he had taken out cash for Chicago and it was almost gone. He didn't want to spend the last of it on a lavish hotel. There would be time for that. But now wasn't the time.

"Can we stay with your friend Vanderveer?" she said. "I'm dying to meet him. He sounds positively heavenly."

Harry didn't deny Vanderveer's sublime gifts, but didn't think the Beck Hall residence assistants would look too kindly on a married couple staying in Vanderveer's triple suite.

It was dark by the time they finally made their way on foot to North Street station. And because they had nowhere else to go, and were tired and hungry, they went to the only place they knew for sure would take them.

They went to Lawrence.

A week went by. Then two. Then a month. In August the letters started coming.

> To Harry Barrington
> Dear Harry,
> Father has asked me to write to you again to let you know that since you haven't come to collect your personal things, they have been packed up by Louis and placed in crates. We are awaiting your instructions as to their disposition.
> This is all I can say. Except . . . Ben did not lose his job—despite your best efforts. Even in this you couldn't succeed.
> Yours truly,
> Esther

> To Harry Barrington
> Dear Harry,
> A man has only one thing to barter with and that is his good name. You were my friend, and I had the highest regard for you. I know that you have been calling on me, and I wanted to write to you to make my feelings clear. When I heard about what you did, it made me sick, I wanted to go and Daniel Boone it. I didn't know you were a double-crossing snake. Goat shepherds behave more honorably than you. A man can

be brilliant yet an imbecile about getting along with others. That is you. You relate poorly to people and the secret of a good life is fairly simple: because of this, you will always have a conflict-ridden life instead of a pleasant one, and if success comes to you at all, it will come at a heavy price. Please stop calling on me. I have no interest in seeing you or being introduced to your bride. C.J. Bullock signs on in sentiment to this letter.

Yours truly,
Professor Vanderveer Custis IV

To Harold Barrington
Dear Harry,

Thank you for coming in a few weeks ago and speaking to me and to the Chair of the English Department, Professor Kittredge.

We have reviewed your record and after careful consideration we regret to inform you that we cannot offer you a teaching position in either department at this time.

It is of great concern to us that for reasons you did not elaborate on, you have decided to abandon your promising doctoral dissertation. I would have been glad to give you more time, if needed, you were so close to the end. It is unfortunate and inexplicable.

However, in light of what you and I talked about in April, and given the problems we discussed with the form and content of your teaching methods, it seems best that you find yourself another line of work. Professor Kittredge and I have no doubt that you will be successful in your chosen endeavor, and we wish you best of luck and every success in the future.

Yours truly,
Thomas Carver, Chairman of the Political Science Department

To Salvatore Attaviano

Dear Mr. Attaviano,

This is to advise you that you are currently in default of your uncollateralized loan agreement dated March 15, 1900, which expressly stated you could not be more than thirty days late with any payment. In carefully reviewing your payment record, it has come to the attention of this bank that you were sixty days delinquent in December of 1902, and another thirty days in December 1904, and sixty days in June of this year, 1905. You have failed to repay the bank the interest and penalties inherent in your late payments. As you are now in default, you have thirty days in which to secure a new collateralized loan and convert your existing mortgage with us into a new account with another bank. Alternatively of course, you are welcome to pay off your loan in full.

Please give this matter your full attention, as in ninety days, legal proceedings for the recovery of the debt will commence against you. As we also hold the mortgage paper on your two restaurants, please be advised that we will apply any accrued value in your properties to satisfy the unsecured debt you have with us before we authorize the transfer of your debt instrument to another lienholder.

Yours sincerely,

Gordon Billingsworth

To Harold Barrington

Dear Harold,

I was hoping that good old-fashioned pride would stop you from making a scene such as I overheard yesterday afternoon, but you never seem to subvert my expectations, no matter how low they are. Perhaps this is what you're learning from the Italians, how to behave in public.

Clearly our conversation back in July has flown into one of

your ears and out the other, so let me reiterate some of the highlights of the last morning we spent together, so that we can avoid this unseemly contact in the future. I'm going to have to insist on the last part.

Esther had sent you a note about your personal belongings some weeks back. Though we had packed them up for you, you chose not to come for them; hence they've all been donated to charity.

I am somewhat though not extremely surprised you stopped working on your doctorate when you were so close to completion. You've again left me in the awkward position of trying to explain your inexcusable actions to the Dean of Students and the Department Chair. I cited temporary insanity; it seemed as fine a reason as any.

Regarding your brother-in-law, whose plight is clearly what brought you to my house in such a fit of ill-temper: five years ago I gave him preferential rates and preferential treatment because of you. I loaned him an exorbitant amount of money to help you. I didn't hold him in any regard whatever, then or now, but as you can imagine, now I have no interest in supporting either you or your new family. I have no interest in continuing any business relationship with him or you. As you have exercised your prerogatives, I have exercised mine. You said to me you didn't care about anything peripheral. I will choose to take you at your word.

I overheard you shouting something about trusts. I don't know what you mean. My half of the family business was yours and your sister's, the family money was yours and your sister's. There was never a need for a trust from me—you simply had access to everything, at all times. That was your life.

Now you have access to nothing, at all times. That is also your life.

417

You have shown me by your black contempt for the fruits of my profound labors that you do not consider being my son as carrying with it any sort of obligations whatsoever. As your mentor Eugene Debs says, "Every capitalist is your enemy." This is plainly what I am to you.

Demands are so always so disempowering, Harold, because they require someone else to respond.

Empower yourself. If you or your brethren would like a loan, I suggest you go to a bank and apply for one, like everyone else. You want money? Get yourself a job, like everyone else. But my doors are closed to you. Permanently.

Very truly,

Herman Barrington

5

She is putting fresh flowers in all the vases while he watches her. She arranges them all, going from room to room, even placing some in the porch to welcome visitors. The sun is shining on Summer Street, and he sits at the small table trying to figure out what to do with his day. Everyone else is working, and they are alone. He wants to go to the library, but she wants to go horseback riding, and then she wants to rent a boat and go for an afternoon ride down the Merrimack and afterward she wants to go up north before it gets too cold, maybe to Maine; she's heard there are some beautiful islands off the coast where they could maybe rent a room and catch some lobster, and pick berries, and get marooned by a storm that would close the ferry service. She giggles as she imagines this out loud, musing half in English, half in Italian, stepping away from the vases with the blue and yellow lupines, cocking her head this way and

418

that, to appraise the arrangement better. She squints, she smiles.

Now that they're married, she leaves her hair down when it's just the two of them, and strolls around the house in a sheer day-dress that leaves nothing to the imagination and makes it difficult for him to string coherent thoughts together. To watch her like this is to believe in all the miracles of the universe. To touch her is to believe in God. She doesn't seem worried about anything. Though perhaps if she knew about the peril to Salvo's business, a letter Harry instantly intercepted and hid, trying to decide what to do—and if she knew about the letter from Harvard and, most important, the letter from his father, which stated that despite his new bride's fetching cheeriness and divine disposition, there would be no trips to remote and blissful isles because there was no more money, perhaps if she knew about these things, she too might sit like a gray cloud at the table, hiding missives in her fists; she might even stop arranging the flowers. In *paradiso*, she says, there are always fresh flowers, because they represent all the beauty of temporal life—gorgeous, yet fleeting.

Are we in paradise?

Of course, *mio amante*, she sings to him.

When she is not decorating the gates of Eden with flowers, she is packing to move to Cambridge before the new semester starts. Expelled from one place, from another. Where is left for them?

He loves to watch her, even when he has too many things to say, like now. She chatters about things he can't explain away, and she in her sheer dresses and glowing skin and coffee tresses is the epitome of hope and joy, feelings he has had a dearth of, and barely knew he had a dearth of until he met her. He doesn't know how to tell her about anything. He doesn't want to upset her for even a moment. She hums so sweetly about the possibilities of youth.

Finally she notices how long he has been sitting there watching her. She walks up to him at the table and kneels on the floor between his legs, to be closer to him.

"Why do you worry so much, my husband?" she says, looking up at him. "Why can't you believe, like me, that it's all going to work out? How can it not? We were *meant* to be together, Harry, you know that. We are fated, you and I."

"*You* are fate," he says, bending down to kiss her upturned mouth, her sweet lips. She always smells of vanilla and mint leaves. She smells and tastes like no one else. "You are the Moirae, weaving and spinning the cloth that is my life." Caressing her face, he thinks a moment. He doesn't want to admit to her that he remains troubled by the introduction into Rose Hawthorne's world, by the things the nun has said to him.

"What if your Rose is right?" he asks, gazing at her, his palms leaning on her shoulders. "There's been a conflagration, Gia. So many things have gone into the bonfire, just as Rose's father wrote. Many of the things you say you deeply want."

Gina shakes her head. "I have the one true thing I want. He is sitting at my table like a sad fish, looking all glum."

"I've thrown it all into the fire," Harry says. "All the bottles and the war chests and the books and the spirits. I've kept one item that you once gave me, one scarlet thing, and one small note my mother left behind for me, also a scarlet thing. But that is all."

"Are friends and death in the blaze too? Trees and the ocean and mornings?"

He nods. "Everything."

She shakes her head. "You didn't hear Rose correctly, and you haven't read her father's story. That's not the meaning of it. In 'Earth's Holocaust,' it's actually the opposite."

"Perhaps I should read it then, before I draw analogies," he mutters.

"If you burn the earth itself to a cinder," she says, "none of it matters, because you haven't burned down the only thing of consequence."

"Which is?"

"Your human heart," says Gina, squeezing him, kissing his hands. "And you know what's in mine?"

He knows. But she tells him anyway. *"When I am dead and opened,"* she whispers, *"you shall find Harry lying in my heart."*

But Harry is not being truthful with Gina. He *has* read Hawthorne's indelicate story. And it is she who has misunderstood it, not he. For, without also burning down the human heart in the apocalypse, Hawthorne wrote, *forth from it will reissue all the shapes of wrong and misery.*

"There will be days and summers with you like this," she exclaims. "We are so blessed. And it will only get better."

Harry nods, smiles, but doesn't speak.

O, take my word for it, it will be the old world yet!